Chapter on Love

Chapter
on Love

TRANSLATED BY

Erika Mihálycsa

Contra Mundum Press   New York · London · Melbourne

Library of Congress Cataloguing-in-Publication Data

Szentkuthy, Miklós, 1908–1988

[Fejezet a szerelemről. English.]

Chapter On Love / Miklós Szentkuthy; translated from the original Hungarian by Erika Mihálycsa

—1st Contra Mundum Press Edition
406 pp., 6×9 in.

ISBN 9781940625409

   I. Szentkuthy, Miklós.
  II. Title.
 III. Mihálycsa, Erika.
 IV. Translator.

2020930203

Table of Contents

Chapter on Love

Women that are things against my fate...

(Th. Randolph, 1638)

I. The Mayor

1.

They had started building the cathedral so close to the near-vertical mountain slope that during construction the girlish counter-gothic of the branches, leaves, and foliage arced inside the white gothic ribs. The town lay among short, cozily, sweetly bloated tree crowns: five rabbits squatting in a pentacle around a cabbage stalk would offer such a view of their ovoid spines. The sole exception was Monte Solario, which could be called neither a mountain nor a hill: it was a solitary, rusty stage, on whose upper fringe shrubs and trees suddenly erupted, dipping their wild long hair in the wind. At the bottom of the wall the cathedral in progress resembled a skeleton propped up by the side of an ostrich-feather fan of the latest fashion. Monte Solario was the enemy of time and of the passage of the parts of the day: in the morning, when the surrounding meadows had already melted in the sun like the host in a devout mouth, this shaggy scenery still retained the dawn, laying its quadrangular shadow (at the moment, one single square cut out of a chessboard) across the whitely chirping town like an envious mask. The skylarks were swirling in the dawn light like the shower of gold over Danae's Eros-harbors, but the envious mountain slammed a black mask on Danae, in vain the skylark-shower sizzled, drizzled above her. Likewise, in the evenings, the mountain carved the town out of the dusk concert flooding the horizon: the forests were already crumbling in the yellowish evening mist, like Pythia's sobriety above the divine fumes; silence was setting in the shape of violet butterflies on one swing-grass meadow after another, all the rivers were embalming their bodies with sweet death — yet the town still preserved the day; although its environs were more lit by the whimsical glass blooms of sunset, and the town was blacker than the mountain's shadow, the town was the day, and around it, the landscape was the silent swoon. It was now midnight, but the Nessus-shade tailored to the town's slender body had not yet disappeared completely; the hills around it swelled up from the garish moonlight like veils from the wind or the womb of mythical virgins from unheard-of birds, but the town itself was untouched in the moon-deluge. The moon soaked everything: it stood among the woods, towers, barriers, stars, sleeping birds and kiss-mowing bats like foam in the hair undone by a shower — if by accident it ended up in the tidal path of some selfish, childish star, it was absorbed in it as a weary kiss is absorbed in a wider embrace.

That morning the town's most illustrious son, the pope, died. In the wee hours when the lean hands, asleep in the clock face's white lap, are still trying to convince that it is night, and only the trembling of the horizon (no light yet, just the inner trembling of darkness — the way the skin of sleeping animals sometimes twitches) signals the coming of a new day, a knight stopped at the town hall's entrance. On the empty square, man and horse felt uneasy. Tubs lay scattered in disarray by the well, the funereal urns of yesterday, and the rusty vertebrae of the well's chain thrust upwards like the skeleton of the long-disclosed gossip of women now fast asleep. Startled, the horse gave a loud, whooping neigh.

The mayor was still up. They said he spent half an hour each with his frolicking guests, then in the council chamber, and so it went from ten in the evening until four or five in the morning. When the clock struck the hour in the gloomy council chamber, he carefully folded his documents, took his candle, and stumbled all alone along the moldy conservatory of stairs and secret passageways into his own quarters, drank and sang, then when the clock struck there too, he groped his way back to the town councilors, now green in the face with the effort of staying awake.

On only one occasion was he late, having dropped his candle. When the messenger arrived, he was with the councilors. One of them was just venting his incredulity that the mayor returned home every time he left them: they were convinced that every half hour he visited another mistress, that he had vowed to cuckold five husbands or deceive five fathers in one night.

That he had cavorted with his guests during those half hours was no more true than it was that he had visited one lady after another. Whenever he left the council chamber, he had three errands: first — to console his ailing wife; to aid the handmaid with the poultices; to check what medication she should take; second — to make the envoy of Pistoia fall head over heels for his daughter and son: the three of them were sitting in a *studiolo*, rather drunk, the boy with a notebook and a long plume, the girl with whimsically unbuttoned, semi-undone clothes. She had a peculiar technique (no doubt extremely useful in politics) of unbuttoning something after almost every glass the Pistoiese drank, freeing pronouncedly large buttons from pronouncedly large buttonholes distributed in pronouncedly important places, or of unthreading broad, spectacularly colored ribbons from dramatically trimmed holes, and in the wake of these unbuttonings and unthreadings, strikingly white patches of skin, or strikingly inner-looking inner silks of lingerie, gushed forth, all that without the girl becoming in point of fact any more naked or "relaxed." This female was all openings, hanging ribbons, ripened buttons turning loose from their holes, lace-foam and shoulder-exhuming, exhibiting all the symptoms of depravity — and yet she was properly, moreover: modestly dressed. That diplomatic dress created by the father was soon to become famous in all of Italy. One could hardly imagine a gentler, more childish scene than the two siblings with the half-drunk envoy. The sister is all pseudo-nakedness: with rapture she abandons herself to the pleasures of imagined real nakedness and demi-monde manners;

her pseudo-coquetry drives her to wild hyper-coquetry — whereas the brother, with a sizable spectacle, keeps jotting down on the spot, with his caricature-size plume, under the very nose of the inane Pistoiese, the deceitfully learnt secrets. This was the mayor's second errand: to check on his two children in the playroom of diplomacy, to read from the notebook the news they twisted out of the envoy, and to put them to immediate use in the council.

The third errand took him to another sickbed, this time of a former mistress. Perhaps it was the most important of all, although the mistress in question was quite insignificant as compared to his wife and children. Still, such a visit is worth looking into, because in her house there was *silence*, so there he could pore for the lengthiest time over this or that unsettling element of his life.

2.

On one such occasion the mayor was sitting in the antechamber with his long, thick walking stick, in his tall, beribboned, and buckled silk hat. The chair he took at the insistence of the housemaid was very small, its legs shaky, so sitting on it was more tiresome than standing. The mayor enjoyed great respect in the coquette's house, at least he was much curtsied and groveled to, which made him feel with particular intensity what a caricature he was on the premises: he knew all too well that the ceremonial respect paid to his standing made sense only when he was exercising his rank and profession, in his office — the deep curtsying and greetings, the titles luxuriating in yellow bunches, and the deceitful invocations seemed to him farcical tricks in his own home, let alone here. His apparel was also carnivalesque, the ill-matched rags of an old, amateurish Pierrot: half affected mask, half affected sincerity, striving at secretiveness, while at the same time showing off his standing.

What was the main source of comedy or tragedy here? Every-thing, we might say: his clothes, his office, his desired-undesiring desire, the huge walking stick, this awful and barren reed-tower of luxury and terror, his age, the day's age, the late afternoon, the fact of waiting. To be waiting for a woman: can there be anything more laughable, more murderous to desire? There are only two things that are real: to be relentlessly acting, moving, working, lying for the woman, and when the leaf of the last lie had burnt out to the edge, to be with her straightaway, to possess her. But waiting? In those moments of waiting that interposed themselves between desire and consummation, resembling neither, one real-izes how little desire is a thought oriented toward a *purpose*: how much it lacks in elements of reason and will — that desire is nothing else but fantastic anticipation, the barren mythology of possessing the woman, in which we do not want, do not seek, do not look for the woman, because there is no need at all for that looking-for, since the woman is already present in desire, albeit in an exaggeratedly colorful fantasy-world driven to a paroxysm of excitement, but nevertheless already present — only the waiting embosses it on our consciousness that that presence is not yet the real, but only the anticipated one, and when that awareness should prod us to start wanting, looking for, calling, and order-ing the woman around, we feel little inclination to do so: the love instinct is so realist, it shows such a deathly unhedging lucidity & undeceivability, that it knows this primitive alternative alone: woman is either here or is not here — and if now (during the water-air-colored interregnum of waiting) she is not here, then woman is the everlasting Not-here herself, the Olympian demon of negativity, the everlasting No, absence inescapable in the world. That is why one cannot "wait for" a woman, and generally for anything, that's why longing (which is already a concrete form of possession, even if only in fantasy) and waiting (which is simply a pause in being, cannot be oriented toward anything, because its essence is precisely the radical disconnectedness from any cause or purpose) are mutually exclusive: this is why the mayor, too, had felt his present role in the antechamber to be a folly, quite extraordinarily laughable. To be waiting: now, now you should be purpose-made, O woman, and yet this will quite obviously never succeed! Can something beautiful, something pleasing, be "purpose"? No, no, and yet again no. The beautiful always exists *now* — beauty is a thing inseparable from the present, from the *hic*-most *hic* and the *nunc*-most *nunc* — it is always being embroidered on the inside of the instant's dark curtain with its luxuriating *praesens*-inflorescences, *praesens*-shadows, with the not-to-be-temporalized richness of its now-now-now perfume; woman, and all beauty, is always the becoming-more-existent of an already existing state, the ripening and blossoming of the now into all-too-now — it is never something-yet-to-come, something to succeed. The "future," the "tomorrow," the "will your lordship kindly return in half an hour" can be legal protocols, maneuvers, now and again history or drama, but never: beauty, woman, bliss.

What cut-and-dry schemata, what lackluster, distorted formulae the black vegetation of desire and the proximate reality of the actual woman were for the mayor: the morning desire, when with unexpected clarity, in the nakedness of possibility, the woman came to his mind: he didn't touch, didn't see her eyes, mouth, the self-sabotaging ring of her hips, but only thought of them as mathematical signs of possibility; and that is verily the most inflammable oil of love, the precision not of reality, but of possibility. But where was that pathos now, when every second they might let him in to her? Fulfillment? What an empty word.

3.

The setting sun shone in through the half-open window: the
landscape was already in a profound torpor; the waters, houses,
hills were dark green: warm, mute, and full of sleep-swamped
loathing. Above them, the sun was radiating red, aslant, haughty, vociferating its gibberish, its rays short like sunflower petals:
what does this dark, provokingly and musically tragic late afternoon want from him, poor mayor, who had forgotten to align his
desires, born in the morning bed, with the advancing hours, to
mold them into morning, noon, afternoon, sunset desires, and
now felt at this idyllically dark and ghostly "late" hour (it's much
later in the afternoon than in the evening) as though he were
still in his nightshirt: waiting had rendered all his desires past,
old-fashioned, strangely inelegant.

Because the mayor's life was decidedly not easy: with strange
and obdurate simultaneity he strove to turn his love into poetry
and elegance, lyric and cosmetics, death and mannerism. Something unspeakably difficult: his very looks testified to the difficulty and striving. His silk hat was the geometric god of ceremoniousness, rank, gentility; his lace cuff was the embodiment
of irony toward all eros-dispossessedness and eros-crucifixion;
his awkwardly vertical walking stick, held out as far as possible
before him, was ceremoniousness, posturing, and etiquette self-
imposed to the point of sadism: in sharp contrast to those, the
shrunken, pale cheeks, the greenish fate-hollows under his eyes,
his trembling hands, his shoes' upward-curling toes (as though
he never dared touch the soil, the steady ground of life, just as he
shrunk from hot or too cold water) all spoke of the consuming
world of poetry, of metaphors, of beauty.

Where was the morning pathos? How clumsy to have misunderstood desire and conformed to it, coming here! He felt a
slight nausea at the odor of his wife's powder and perfume, which
he always applied abundantly before visiting his mistress, for fear

his wife would discern on him the latter's ointments; there would be no time to cover himself properly in that servant's mask on his return home. It was the drag of fidelity and infidelity: the perfume of his wife brought home to his mind, as though it were not perfume but the organic-most vapor, fume of Catholic morality — yet at the same time that home was unreal; uncreditable; a lie. What if the mayor died here, in the coquette's waiting- or consulting-room? His corpse would be like a nauseating flower, the smoking lily of fidelity: when they unbuttoned the shirt above his heart and peeled the silk stockings from his knees, his wife's perfume would puff forth in ever-renewed clouds of unprecedented strength — what used to be the discrete accessory of his home, a trembling, matronly, melancholy nuance, would on this dead, aged body be an ostentatious, foolish, and whorish bluff, a nearly blasphemous degree of hypocrisy. Isn't that the most beautiful symbol of my fidelity: to die in a coquette's waiting-room, but almost intoxicating everybody with my wife's cosmetics? My wife had never been vain; perfume was on her body like the distracted replay of the last chord of bathing, a farewell rather than a hail to her body — she had certain gestures which gave that odor a touch of askesis, of the balm destined for the corpse, of the resentment-fuelled withering addressed to the husband, a defiant, stylized autumn; and now that melancholy odor, psychologized back and forth with matronly restrictedness, suddenly becomes pungent, a signboard, a buffoonish gesture, under which her husband lies, stiffened into eternal infidelity.

What is my faith? This perfume-hypocrisy and perfume-sincerity: my wife, like the crucifix, cardinal, or abstract point of reference, compared to which everything else is a lie; as compared to which nothing can ever be what it is; the flowers', seas', stars' hot need for sincerity appears all distorted, travestied, diseased and crippled — I couldn't furrow my nose into the snake-Gorgon-like, earthworm-writhing petals of a single chrysanthemum, knowing all too well that whoever has a wife cannot really smell a flower, because that odor kills God, woman, child, and those beings thrust out from my life like thorns on a leafless, flowerless stalk — I could not dance to the call of one single star spurting forth from beneath the dark blue shirt like the sky's nipple, because I know that he whose legs have once started that Artemis-cold star-jig will never return home; for that reason I baptized the chrysanthemum a "beautiful flower," planted it in my garden, and kept telling my acquaintances in an artificial tone, "It smells nice, doesn't it?" — that's why I only dared look askance at the stars, those large, solitary, fraying-edged buds, and waited for my wife to say distractedly — while waiting for the carriage at the gate —, "Look, what a beautiful star!" to which I answered with a scared "Yes."

I have lied to you, my wife, about the flowers and, what is even more sinful, I have made the flowers lie. But at the same time I have been faithful to you, as one cannot but be true to the crucifix and to abstract points of reference: I liked it that you made me and the whole of nature a lie, knowing and consequently intuiting that that lie is the essence of the world, the divine-most marrow of young branches, the stone of cherries, the gaping, glacier-green navel of love. Because I was born to be every moment a defender of faith and a heretic, an inquisitor and the anarchist of the goldfish dancing in the vases, of women toppled into bed, of tousled, undulated nights. And much as I hated you for making it impossible for me to become the utterly free martyr of chrysanthemums and stars, I adored you, because in that way I indeed sensed the whorish nature of chrysanthemums and stars, because I saw that whatever I considered divine was also sophistry, and what I considered real was also hypocrisy. And now as I sit here, perfumed to death with your "spousely" odor, have I perhaps not found the ultimate symbol of my fate: I am hypocriticking with your odor, but it is so strong that me into yours it kills, your odor is a masquerade on me: a grotesque nose or *wurstchen-lips*, a carnival drag, but also the deathly degree of your reality, my cloud-coffin, my grateful and humble incense offering to you.

4.

O, let me enjoy to the fullest all the tragic beauty and burlesqueness of my position and, since love turned out to be my destiny-most destiny, let me live to the fullest what is so typical of love in the life of men and women: what they coin their obscene jokes, puns, pornographic images from, and from which they draw most of their arguments and potions for death, for the overlong, myriad-colored mosaic-like neuroses, blasphemies, despairs. I am not long for this world, I am old and sick, so I can afford the luxury to single out an hour of the late afternoon and decree it to be of symbolic value, the hour when I feel my amorous infelicity to be at the same time a joke and a tragedy, the most exquisite ethical metaphor and fishwives' silliest gossip: I long for both perspectives, because the whole of mankind longs for them; I reach up with ten fingers among the leaves, almost oily now with the sunset, into the landscape, which is the first and last form of beauty, into the inhuman metaphor of destiny, into the soul-less, redemptive world of sunbeams, fish, flower-silhouettes, but with these same fingers I long to put the crimson of the most laughable parody, the lowly grimace of all mockery, on myself; I want to see myself and all love as joke, filth, a pagliaccio's hokey-pokey.

Who can decide which? Who can decide, what was in fact the birth of Venus? Did the sea toss ashore the corpse of a filthy sea-dog, or did the divinity indeed become a woman on a shell's cloven fringe? We would need to daub both those awful hypotheses on the wall of the coquette's salon: the dumb corpse, and the redeeming, morphinizing-into-nature feminine apparition.

Is there any more beautiful expression of the *landscapality* of love than a female face immersed in deathly silence? Is there a better expression of the *burlesqueness* of love than scandal — for instance, that I am discovered in this salon?

The lukewarm air, like body and spirit in the dying, started decomposing into coagulated warmth-blots and cold breeze-ribbons, as if the whole world were now falling apart to illustrate with histrionic brutality the theologians' eternal discourse: "What is made of parts will perish, only the One will be preserved forever." The huge sun now spurted directly into the room, all sharp, murderous redness, and yet ineffably diaphanous, quiet and transient; the salon took on the bloody judge's robe of some unknown charge, indeed of a sentence, but at the same time intensifying the room's quiet, its being-beyond-life and beyond-partisanship, its quiet scent of moral insanity, its feminine decadence *&* academic whorehouse-nature — like the face of a slightly feverish man falling quietly asleep: flushed, but smoothed out; more inflamed and bolder, but at the same time more dreamlike and inert.

The nuance! Doesn't it also belong to that forcedly symbolic amorous afternoon? Isn't it the crown witness of love's vain trial? The nuance of sunlight between riotous redness and sweet narcotic, the nuance of the soul, the nuance of time — the evasion of impressions, the paradox of feelings, the spring-wreath of hypotheses, the endlessness of self-analysis? That, that too I will have to have daubed here — the old mayor thought, who in his lordly absent-mindedness was starting to take the brothel for a museum —, the goddess of nuance and the goddess of the simplest instinct (is there such a thing?). Don't we sometimes feel that love is nothing more than one single tremor of a sole nerve-end of pleasure, and fail to see anything else there with the best intentions? And don't we at other times feel that love is the most complex of complexities, the pandemonium of logical and natural self-contradiction, the demented tapestry of psychology and theology?

5.

This, for instance, is such a typical "love"-whatsit: the wild-dull red "nuance" on the armchairs, vases, and on the weary stone, lacking-in-sunlight-appetite, of my fever-withered ring. And yet there hangs under my clothes, deaf and dull, the organ: the one-and-only industrial instrument, the democratic-minded foe of nuance, the purple-nosed demagogue of Shakespeare's plays. Let both run their course: let love be today a million poetic sophisms, logical shadow-puppetry, and let it equally be urination's foul-smelling little brother.

And you, setting sun, watch over this dual play: because inescapably you are a part of it. You are the other end of love, whose one end is within us: in the shape of psychology, in the misshapen larvae of crooked, twisting anthropomorphisms. And the other end is you: the star, the farthest inhuman substance, so alien, so selfish, so nihilistically a flower, that everybody worships you as a god. There is something hymnic in my old invocations, which in my present position is rather poor style, I'm afraid, but exactly what is needed: primal, deathly, *non-plus-ultra* poor style. That is the true face of Eros: murderous pastiche, the carnivalesque burial of "taste."

On the armchair's velvet upholstery (this abundance of velvet in the coquette's room spells out old hags, *bel-esprits*, moss, cold flourish, artificial pleasure) the late sunlight became almost mauve, as if all the violets had turned into magic mist, into air: I can see not a single violet, there is nothing visible or tangible, but their scent's dew-iced and opiate-dreamy tide becomes all the more overwhelming, and my "violet-disposition" (what passions you harbor, old bucko!) all the more pervasive: the unexpected skin-pleasure of my fingers as they touch one another, withdrawn from the glove's insides, in my lungs the air's blossoming-into-flower and strangulation-into-buds in the two great half-acts of breathing, my body's prolonged, swaying, towing ashore and

anchoring in the slackish port of my shirt and stockings — all
of this is some kind of violet-consciousness originating in the
mauve that lurks in the sunrays — all those little neuroses that
we hesitate to call metaphors of the nervous body, or logical
feeler-tests, those tiny sensitivizations, decorative psychological
images and style-affectations: they are all part and parcel of love.

6.

O, Sun: shall I cite the broad-berthed stanzas of your legends, or
shall I rather apply myself to your small psychological influences;
O, Love: shall I drag forth drab, brutal female shapes, Danae-beds
dished up in the street, or shall I diligently weave the human lace
of your psychologies? Enough, enough of both. Enough of this
tableau: of the birth of Venus — of the sea splashed and foamed-
all-over with gold, swinging huge wave-roses, wave-chains and
wave-vases, wave-lamps glowing with the sea's Neptunian indis-
cretion, and wave-vines between the twin pillars of night and
sunset — now the waves seem to besiege the horizon's Euclidean dam, they hurl themselves on its geometrical edge like supple
green panthers on their prey, they twist themselves around it as
a python enamored of a tiny hummingbird twists itself around a
palm tree, they cut into it like a sparkling knife, melt it, lick it as
the male tongue licks the half-open female lips — in one moment
it indeed seems as though the horizon were falling apart like an
orange with loosened sections, in the next moment it again appears sharp, like the white border ribbon, suggestive of hips, of
Plato's idea-world; and beyond all that raving there you are: red,
myth-drunken, myth-snobbish, and myth-martyr Sun (I know
that I am sitting in a slightly passé salon in a silk hat, with my
freshly ironed gloves smoothed out on my knees, but in love there
is and shall be no separate bourgeois salon and separate myth
of poet-beasts, there shall be no separate Venus and separate

space-filling *petite femme*): the waves thrash upon one another like black hawks or gigantic, steel-green leaves, the feathers are flying and the forest-smell is evaporating in plaited threads — it's impossible to tell if the cause of your stupor and your reddening is that sea in labor, that sea combing its hair, or if the sunset color is the dropping banner of your foreignness, of your anti-human-ism and anti-sea-ism. And next to you is night: the wave, the peel of whose silky back has mirrored your late purple, suddenly slips off your optical foot-stool, to drop into the blue chalice of the approaching night — snakes can perhaps flash with such deathly and barren flirtatiousness from a red leaf to a blue flower in the jungle —, on foam-baroque oxygen's toupee all your apocalyptic crimson glitters still (O Pindaros! ... my silk hat), but in the fo-cal point of glass breasts, night's wondrous blue already started thickening. It is on that sea, in that hour, that Venus was and is being born, forever: night-blue, sea-mourning, sun-blood — that is your staffage.

It is to you that I pay homage, in my meticulously polished shoes that the skivvy had such a hard time shining: because nei-ther of us can stoop anymore with our rheumatic lumbagos, to help her get at it more easily I, with great difficulty, placed my foot on a kitchen stool, but couldn't keep erect and, thrown off balance, I tumbled against the wall: it is to you I pay homage with this slender green flask in which the dubious, foolish acids of the potion against venereal diseases glow — the apothecary pours it in those thread-thin glass tubes purposely, so it is easier to wear: it is to you I pay homage with those whitish pills in the snuffbag where they play hide-and-seek like tiny bird eggs in a too thickly padded nest — an excellent medicine against the conception of children: it is to you I pay homage with these documents that are the symbols of my lie — at home they believe I left for the town council: it is to you that I pay homage with those dried, chamo-mile-scented leaves that I start chewing in the darkness of nuptial chambers, for they stop the vehement urge to defecate that as a rule follows my amorous gymnastics: my whole ramshackle, repulsive chemist's store, my low-caliber, demeaning lies, my imbecilely ornate, stiff apparel: they all pay homage to that Venus born of storms, Sun, night — Venus is one, love is one: even in the troubadours' stage-perfect kisses there stinks my mean chemist's store, there rattle my gaudy phials, over-commented with dog-eared paper slips; and it radiates in my rheumatism, in my calculated crippled embraces, in my nuptials shrunken to amateurish chemistry, it wreaks havoc, uncompromisable and young, the one and only troubadour to the one and only Venus.

Who dare draw a line between Brueghel's sorry dens and Adonis' sun-anointed body, between Danae's shower of gold & the thick sweat drizzling down on my mistresses?

That is not the contrast between beauty and ugliness, between the myth of the "Eros-fit" and the revenge-realism of those slowly drowning in impotence — that is perhaps the wrestling of God and the devil: of an utterly hysterical, unearthly lunatic fakir-idealism and an utterly infernal, suicidal resignation, a rolling in the impossible, into the limits, into the nasty absurdity of all love.

Be then born, Venus, in spite of everything, be born here, whoop your evening song above the antique filigree clavi-cembalo, let the waves thrash their fins above the loose-legged whorehouse chairs like dying sharks, let the sea's salty and Venus' Olympian odor be mixed here and now with the odor of my stale-going medicine — from now on I will cease to pay such pedantic heed to love.

7.

How beautiful you are, nascent Venus: the waves are in awe of you — when your yellow knee first surfaces from under the falling eyelids of two waves, like the embodiment of the vision of love, like the sea, the world's first-ever "gaze": then the waves suddenly roll back on themselves, the way in which stiff folios take up the form of their case the moment they are released by the hand, rustling into a ring — they even withdraw their voice with a ululation: all of a sudden everything is heard in reverse — they deliberately bleach their color, their cowardice drills strange, whistling whirlpools, in other places flat surfaces appear as dim, unmirroring mirrors — perhaps the murmuring waves had cascaded apart before the Jews as they now do before your knees.

Your knees! Of course you have to start from your knees, not from your breasts, your portrait, or your ankles: your ankles are beauty, your lap death, your portrait human, your breasts a landscape — yet you are love, that is, the hardness of the kneebone and the knee's shapelessness, semi-roundness, semi-cubism, an animal knot, wreck, white patch of skin, and crippled-evenin-sanity, inhuman, naked, senseless: *eros*. You are born from the sea, but the sea repudiates you: perfumed, banished embryo in that giant, puritanical womb of Aeschylian boorishness. Even the fish flee from you. When night's near-blue darkness illuminates far ahead (a color with extreme color-ambition and with more luminosity, even if dark, than colorless brightness) the waves smoothed into awe, one can see in long white lines, like a threadless, slender row of pearls or petals blown in the wind, the Venus-eluding, fleeing fish — that crowd of fish and snakes running away from you in a straight line almost reminds one of a constantly intensifying scream. Above you large birds swing like flying waves rolling over your body: they are not gulls, bohemian initials of the sunrise at sea, but ravens that believe that the sea has thrown up a white-anointed corpse, the relic of some shipwreck, perhaps Helen murdered by the Greeks, that signboard of the brothel of Troy. The shell on which you traveled from the depths to the surface has also left you. Its bluish rim has submerged in the dark like a second dream into the first one:

who cares about you, who summoned you, goddess, whose birth is accompanied by the shadows of death's birds? The Sun cannot set or rise to a new life — it is almost paralyzed in its large poppy-mask: one moment it is loud musical compassion, the next a speechless executioner. In that moment the ships fall into confusion on every sea — the seamen are pulling with ghostly anxiety at the pallid bareness of the veils —, in the ports the tide swelling in disjointed time rubs in the boats among the houses — everybody is scared and cursing, and not even you, Venus, know what to check first: if you have smeared enough paint on your lips, or if you still have the obulus for Charon that a loitering mortician put into your mouth after your death.

8.

And how boring in you that death-sex duality, how unbearably flat your paradox has now become to me — even more unbearable than your vulgar simplicity: were you flower and nothing but flower, or death and nothing but death, I could take that simple-minded homogeneity better — but that mythic mingling of life and *nihil*, of peasant antics and Hades-mourning that appeals to poets, philosophers, founders of religion and the slightly refined: that trick (for it is one!) is what I can least suffer in you, Venus. Your "refinery," that internal contradiction, that provocative, flashing "eternal dilemma" of yours: that is your most vulgar adornment. Now, when you appear in the shape of a corpse on the sea's million-winged, roaring catafalque: your corpse-ness is just a cosmetic maneuver — the priests and poets who with "profound" insight sense death in your kiss and infernal venom in your womb's secret flower, don't feel real death but only a decorative, aestheticist cardboard death that has nothing to do with real death — which is not the opposite of kiss and of your womb's torchlike, flaring-up fecundity: for that death (your present death-mask included) is simply identical to life, with kiss — *merely* a linguistic device, a technique of phrasing for a more emphatic expression of life's lifelikeness. So many painters painted Aphrodite on one wall of the salon, and Thanatos on the opposite: were they opposites? No. Did those painters have an inkling of death, real death, when they were speaking about and daubing how, in love's embrace, the ovary thirsting for the seed of the grave gapes open? No. There was æsthetic in it, "tragedy": and tragedy is nothing other than the ballroom mask of death, its etiquette, substitution, euphemism.

Now, as I am sitting here, in a brothel's shabby "parlor" (in such a place, "parley" takes on an eerily parodic sense): once again, and perhaps for the last time, you, Venus, appear to me like beauty and like death, although I won't let you get at me as æsthetic and as "death" (the two are the same thing). Yes, you are beauty, yes, you are death: but such beauty is unknown, mysterious, unavailable with the worthless instruments of art and with the doltishly self-deluding ones of intuition — it cannot be trusted to the conceited tracks of symbols, or to the impotence of metaphors: perhaps it is simply life's most basic stimulus, the vibration, the divine radiation that on the blind and mute mirror of non-being made the first crease, the first barely noticeable, but infinitely significant wave (sex-appeal understood simply as *to-be-appeal*) — and yes, you are death: prosaic, repulsive non-being, base-beyond-all-realist-and-verist-guttersnipe, stupid, senseless, nauseatingly misshapen death. Your real rouge and grave-hole lie beyond the dualism of the phrase "rouge and grave-hole." And now you can go on boasting about your would-be-death for all I care.

9.

At long last some skivvy-like creature came out to the mayor and told him that soon he could go in — the woman was indisposed, and feeling particularly sick at the moment, but she would be fine in a few minutes. The high-born guest should definitely not leave. The mayor, however, was of the opinion that he should leave — there is not much to do with a sick coquette. He didn't opine so from the merciless point of view of the lecher, but on the contrary, from that of the moralist: bodily suffering is so sacrosanct that his presence could only profane it: an occasion might be created for some unbearable tragicomedy, or for some sentimentalism unworthy of suffering — what is more, even for some rough blackmail. In the next instant the woman herself cried out from her room in a screeching voice, "Don't go, don't go!" The skivvy asked him drowsily if in the meantime he would like to have another woman, not in a separate room, but here in the parlor. Then, when the mayor turned down that offer with some awkward and unself-conscious gesture, she said curtly: "Tip." The mayor rummaged in his pockets, dug up a yellow coin, and tossed it to her.

What is more repulsive in love: money, or psychology? When everything is about the tip, or when everything is about ethics? Which is the greater lie: pudenda exchanged for currency, or pudenda exchanged for spirit?

The thought that the coquette was sick filled him with peculiar anxiety and bitterness, because his wife also happened to be sick: she had asked him not to go to the council but he, pale servant of conscientiousness, went all the same. And now he finds sickness even here. Can the one without body also get sick? His wife didn't provoke in him the slightest bodily pleasure, but even so, and perhaps precisely because of this, she was a bodily reality, whereas the women in the brothel who only featured with their bodies remained forever schemes, mere abstractions — can such formulae ever be sick? All of a sudden he somehow found the fact of sickness repulsive: at home his wife, himself, or his son were sick — but here there was no living, real, bodily person whom sickness could beset, the brothel's inhabitants were not human beings, so if sickness made an appearance here, it was not somebody who was sick, but "sickness" being present without its human pendant. When the woman cried out to him through the door, "Don't go," it was not a woman but sickness calling. So, dehumanized, sickness seemed vulgar and dumb: sickness requires intelligence, which of course here was entirely absent. Sickness will cast a stupid person into unfathomable depths of stupidity — that sent a shudder down the mayor's spine.

How ridiculous he looked between two sick women — his wife's illness turned into morals, every cough, vomit, or sweated-through poultice of hers was the rash of life's inextinguishably ethical nature (an ethics independent of good or evil, obscure and indefinable, but still sorely present), whereas that woman of the brothel was but sickness as nature's bogus error, without any moral or bodily meaning, physical evil for its own sake.

On the one hand, there was a world of difference between his wife's and his mistress' sickness — the former representative of inhuman moral(s), the latter, of inhuman error; on the other hand there were many awkwardly outward similarities: medicine in identical-looking flasks from the same pharmacist on the skivvy's tray, the same shade of silence, the same sounds of vigil, worrying, indifference — why did he come here? For denying his wife's sickness, or revisiting it? That newly-learnt sickness humiliated his wife in thought, something she on no account deserved, but his wife's sickness rendered the coquette's ailment elevated, distinguished, tragic, something the latter could by no means claim a right to. All in all, how basely, weedily selfish was his role, of performing psychological color-blending, play analysis (is there any other?) on two women's suffering.

10.

He picked up the silver coin that he had dropped on the carpet when he gave the tip. That small movement bathed him in two worlds: first in the late sun's unexpectedly hot, red-purple sheaf (actually golden), then in his own countenance, for the silver coin lay before the shadow-veiled mirror. Whenever he bowed down, blood rushed to his head, he felt his whole body, his innards and slowly paralyzing limbs, becoming one vast black collar tightening around his neck, pressing into his head, and growing the foliage of transitory death's thick toupee on his brow — his whole body (not his blood) was thickly flowing into his skull. That triggered a strange mood in him: he felt death's precise fingerprint in it, something that scared him, but at the same time he was aware of its voluptuous distance from death, and knew that it was something so momentary, mechanical, and derived from natural causes, that it could have nothing to do with death — he was even glad that he would get used to the idea of death in its idyllic form: that very "O, this is not yet death" would become his death-style proper, or death-habit, so to say; at such moments he could feel all his bodily functions in his head: he could feel his stomach, heart, and footsoles like his nose or eyes — they were no longer "shading" his consciousness in the shape of moods, but bumping into his blood-swamped brain with sculptural, solid surliness, and that condensed humanity filled him with satyric humor, nauseating self-complacency. When he reached for a fallen spoon, napkin, or for a document blown off the table to give a hand to a woman or clerk, they could see a new man rising.

In its swoon-like unconsciousness the head, filled with blood to bursting point, suddenly became hyper-sensitive to ephemeral traces of smell, color, or heat: inner darkness and stifling pressure, while dumbing him down, apparently blunting him into an object, liberated him in the next moment: he was swimming, hovering in the infinite bounty of ephemera and nuances; he felt that he was at the same time a pig bloated tenfold and a decadent poet composed solely of nerve junctions — even now, as he reached for the coin that had rolled under the mirror, he felt all the paralysis and swollenness of a stroke, but the warmth of the sun on his aged skin, the late color of time on his hesitant, wing-like, fluttering eyelids, opened a free butterfly existence for him: on top of his diabetic, arteriosclerotic, dense organism, this butterfly-like mood of freedom appeared like an unexpectedly vivid, slender flower on the end of a hideous, swollen cactus.

He had heard that extraordinarily sensitive people, the familiars of soul-perfumes and mimosa-poetry, are all nerves, their bodies porous, a mosaic threatening to fall apart any minute, whose splinters are only kept together by capillaries that look like a leaf's veins: the whole person is nothing but one transparent, yet densely woven net or sieve, through which life's phenomena can flow unhindered, touching now one thread of the net, now another. He knew that if ever there was a man who could claim no such comb-body, it was he: even when he wasn't forte-d by the piano pedal of brain hemorrhage, he knew his body to be an impenetrable, componentless dough, incapable of any sensitivity. And now he realized that he had been wrong throughout — moreover, he couldn't even imagine how anyone could be eminently irritable by physical, natural stimuli if their body was not so swollen and homogeneous: when he felt all his blood pressing directly on his skin, he found its nerve-less, psyche-less "animal" stiffness to be incapable of any mimicry, its stroke-tension to be much more sensitive to the impossibly fine shades of heat and (through his eyelids) of color.

That is wholly natural: real "sensitivity" is not a matter of nerves but, on the contrary, of "chemical stains." He couldn't have given an exact definition of where he saw the physiological essence of "chemical stains" in the body, as opposed to nerves — perhaps he had always seen in nerve-sensitivity something

altogether human, almost rational, whereas in chemical sensitivity he saw a sensitivity free from any human relation, the "senseless," impossible-to-psychologize and impossible-to-symbolize
alteration of certain chemical compounds under certain chemical
conditions. The best example is to think of the skin (and what
else do humans have in the end?) — there are nerve-skins and
chemical skins, or in other words, mimicry-skins and landscape
skins: compared to the latter's unbound sensitivity, the former
can hardly be called "sensitive."

The mimicry-skin is capable of accompanying any, ever-so-
slight psychic experience with tiny shifts of wrinkles: it is liable
to quivering, permanent proliferation, all in all, to the boundless
spatialization of *plastic* shades. Primarily, it follows one's "inner"
life with a fast-paced, elastic change of its forms, and only to a
very small extent with an alteration of *colors*. The main characteristic of such skins is an abundance of small wrinkles and an even
color, preserved under however extreme climatic changes — as a
rule it sits loosely on the face.

The chemical skin (and such was the mayor's skin, especially
during the swollenness of bowing down) is, in contrast, thick,
non-malleable — its muscles don't in the least follow the owner's
will or psychic life: it is not felt to be skin but armor, an accursed
mask independent of its owner, who is incapable of smiling or
moping with such skin; on it, in place of a smile, a paranoia-gri-
mace, in place of crying, a wound-torso appears — but under the
impact of whatever slight heat, light, or touch, it reacts with the
full range of its external and internal components: from the comb
it gets white blisters, from daffodils, tiny bluish blackheads, from
the sun, moldy-looking rashes, from the briefest sleep, waxen
pallor, from a fleeting sexual arousal, scarlet stains, from washing, peeling-off rags, from the lack of washing, greenish-brown
strips. Those are not "psychic" matters and not metaphors: they
are made possible precisely because, strictly speaking, the psyche,

consciousness, doesn't go skin-deep; the skin is all alone, left to itself, indifferent to human life, playing out its chemical spectacles for their own sake. And that latter is the real "sensitivity": "real" in the sense that with it, one can learn, perceive a lot more from the external world than with the mimicry-skin.

Those two skins correspond to two human types, and what is more, to two types of culture: to the culture whose keyword is "nerve" and its central rite, psychoanalysis, and to human-less culture whose keyword is "chemistry," and whose central occurrences are the most basic exchanges of substances, electrons, valences. The most characteristic gesture of the nerve-skin owners is startled "shuddering," their sound the "whine" — but that "sensitivity" can hardly mean much for the intellect: the jar on the nerves, skin-shock, are barren things that don't transmit anything about the world. The subject of the chemical skin doesn't whine, is by and large no princess on the pea — phenomena do not touch it as the point of a needle touches a membrane, or a key touches a thin chord, but rather, as water touches the rag, ink the blotting-paper, smell the air. That is why the expression "chemical stain" came into his mind: there is in that pre-stroke sensitivity something primarily not punctiform or linear, something counter-ornamental — always a cloud, diffuse, but more concrete, singular and precise at the same time.

Consequently, the mayor saw clearly the mood style of his old age with its small acts of promiscuity, about to be abandoned — old age also meant a swollen body & sensitivities beyond the human: his body had grown heavy, his belly had become rather too much of a belly, his rheumatism-banded knee the utmost of a knee; his body didn't wither, didn't decay, but on the contrary: ripened into a fruit, became a selfish and unavoidable, lascivious mass (perhaps a stroke is more of a birth than being propelled out of the womb), the positive-ad-nauseam drag of "masculinity" — but out of that rude example of masculinity, precisely due to its "rudeness," an unsuspected richness blossomed from the chemical capacities of perceiving the outside world; when his body had paralyzed into itself (became a "wreck"), it became the purest and most tireless mirror (for the skin is a mirror) of the reality (for him certainly) never available to knowledge. That is how he awaited, again, the bed: as if he were going to a drugstore, and listening to Orpheus's unintelligibly-real melodies.

11.

The bed? If he remembered well (a long time had passed since he was here last), the coquette's chamber had no bed but a divan, or more precisely, a large area in one corner of the room covered in pillows and bedspreads and not delimited in any way from the rest of the room. As if the eternal difference between divan and bed were proclaiming the eternal difference of mistress and wife: the divan is always ready in a minute, is not linked to a separate sleeping-place — the divan is free, simple, unlimited, and mundane. In the mayor's mind few things were as different as bed and divan. First of all, the bed always meant the dry opposition, beyond the realm of colors, of black and white; in the darkness of the night, some greyish-white stain, like the withered petals of a flower sunk into a well. The bed is something mystical, something legal, something deathlike: approaching it is always ceremonious, reserved, portentous. We approach it for sleep, for nuptials, or for illness — are there any more awkwardly pathetic things than those, the three figurative versions of the ancient theme of death? By the bedside, stripping is always ghostly — ghostly if, in shedding our daytime clothes, we cover our body in the superstitious shroud of our nightshirt, and ghostly even if we consciously choose to be naked. The bed's canopy columns, curtains, bedspreads reminiscent of the grave or of a half-open envelope, slow down the pace of the stripping, thwart it into sanctimoniousness.

The bed swallows us like some Moloch or a whirlpool: it is not we who strip by its side but the bed that pulls off our clothes with its magnetic eyes; it is not we who get into it but the bed that catches us as the candlelight catches a moth. The bed does not, cannot belong to life: lying down in the bed is getting to a nunnery, renunciation, detachment from everything. There is something nauseatingly tragic in its clumsy anthropoid proportions: the pillow for the head, the spread for the body's skin (here these two are the "hat" and "clothes") — what a simplification, what a distortion comfort is. Because the bed is comfortable. One can move at ease in it, the mattresses, pillows, bedspreads are so obedient, so subserviently malleable. But who has never felt that that comfort and freedom is the relaxation of death, of utter annihilation?

In contrast, the divan is not the organ of such liturgical peculiarity, house rules, matrimonial rights, night measured out in hours, and of stylized death, but the eternal *à propos*, the thoughtful minimum necessary for lying down; in fact it is merely the handle of horizontality. It always merges easily into the day, its limbs are not permeated by the clock-strikes of a long night or by the overlong months of some sickness: the divan always means minutes, blossoming ephemerality, the little time-melismata stuck distractedly into the day's buoyant, airy praesens. The divan is the mistress' indispensable ground, her vase: that is where she feels truly at ease. The divan's appearance changes little in the course of its service — the bed always ages like a human being. Is there a more awkward sight than a freshly made bed? Is there a more awkward sight than a slept-in bed in the morning? The divan doesn't know such distinctions. Bed sheets! Fresh bed sheets! However fresh they are, I still have the feeling that the bed got dissected and its white innards are laid out to me, like the dismembered infants' limbs at the fabled mythological banquet. During the day, the bed is somehow bearable — on its spread bloom a couple of fairyland birds, watched over by the family's dragon coat-of-arms, but in the evening, it is dissected — whatever is beautiful on it is taken off, laid elsewhere, offering only its turned-out, cold entrails. How can it inspire people to rest that something alarmingly, clinically anatomical is exposed to their gaze? And if in the evening the image of the bed, "made" (sadistically vivisected), is so depressing and numbing, in the morning it is no less piteous: all crumples, hollows, stains, shiftings-apart, smell. Can that indeed be the symbol of rest, of restedness with humans? Jacob's body could be no more broken and torn after his wrestling with the angel than such a human bed after someone has taken a "sweet nap" in it. How many rags, how many wrinkles, how much agony-yellow and agony-sour there is in such a bedroom! Is that indeed the mandatory milieu of health, that legality, the wife's prescribed stage?

The divan is not such a blindly humanized object: it has no mask during the day and no anatomy in the evening — it has no old age, no psychologized-to-death mimicry in the morning like the bed: the divan remains largely unchanged, it is "just a place" as compared to the chosen places. The bed is on the one hand something far too legal, article-like, and on the other hand something far too vital (that is, too closely related to death and reproduction): the divan, the mistress' flying throne, does not serve the law and does not serve life. The real mistress is no instinctual being and no lustful being: she is equally alien to all kind of morality and to all characteristically biological gestures: stormy feelings, perversities, leaden faithfulness.

In a man's life it is always the wife (the bed) that is the biological, and the mistress (the divan) that is the more abstract matter. The mistress cannot be but abstract, since her principal trait is that she is always *going to be* — in opposition to the wife, who always *is*. The mistress is eternal seduction, sex appeal incarnate, which on such occasions is a hundred times more valuable to the man than his wife's (as the case may be) concrete and extraordinary beauty. The divan is the well-tuned and dedicated instrument of that fictitious "going to be," of this abstract "appeal": the eternal "eventually," the symbol of the "perhaps now," "maybe here" unfolding, scintillating through the day, the transient vessel of dressed-up and never-quite-getting-undressed people.

How different are bed and divan under the aspect of luxury and ornament: even the most ornate divan and the most ornate bed can never meet for as much as a moment, not even on the shared plane of decoration. The ornate bed is always something robust, static, traditional: if it's a cage, ornament makes it more cage-like; if a medieval romantic well, ornament makes it more bottomless. In the gravity field of the bed the airiest ornamental figures suddenly acquire leaden weight: so does the rainbow become a pillory and the rejuvenated feathers of phoenix birds, hailstones. It is the exact opposite with the divan: there, luxury is always ethereal, fleeting, dressing gown-like (for the lesson, compare a silk dressing gown to a man's nightshirt), daytime, fanciful. Because only the day breeds phantasms, only mundaneness leaves room for hallucinations and Euripidean "eidolon"-Helens: night is vital and legal, that is, fixed and unalterable to the highest degree. Between an ornate bed and an ornate divan, a first essential difference is, that in the case of the bed, one can always sense the bed separately, to which decoration was added as an afterthought, while in the case of the divan, the ornament is the divan itself: in a room with a divan we feel that there can be no more beautiful spatial ornament than a place for lying down, that life's greatest luxury is horizontality: *"Oh fleur d'espace: coucher avec ..."*

What was his life if not a ceaseless vigil between bed and divan? He could have looked for other symbols, equally expressive as bed and divan, but those happened to come to his mind first while waiting. Perhaps "symbol" is not the right word because, after all, the slimy, patterned reptile scale on the snake's spine is no snake symbol, just as neither its antlers nor its forest are a stag "symbol." Wife and mistress are no less different than stag and snake: it is not two women of the same type in two different social positions, but two creatures belonging to utterly different species — one can't even call both women. The one has grown into the divan, is identical to it — and of the other, the bed is not a chance location, but her body, essence, organ, or symptom. As you like.

That is the way it goes with the other "symbols" too: they are *not* symbols. The two kinds of redness for instance: the redness of the divan-woman is rouge, eye shadow, blush — that of the bed-woman is blood, that is, the chosen fluid of life and morals. The mistress doesn't have blood, merely make-up: the ancient organ of mask, lying, ephemerality, exaggeration, play, decoration, hypothesis. The wife has no make-up ever, only blood: the ancient organ of self-sacrifice, death, child, fight, sincerity, horror, truth, sickness. The gesture of the mistress applying rouge and the blood-drawing suicidal gesture of the abandoned wife are not symbolic but organic movements: how much the shape of the blunt rouge stick (a mixture of chalk, seal wax, and broken twig), its ingredients (brittle and sticky, waxen-melting and clay-stiff), the trace of its trajectory on the mouth, its rhythm, interruptions, self-correction, self-assured arc and cautious groping, mean the whole mistress, everything that the *maitresse* is. And next to her, the suffering wife's blood pouring on the bed: as the divan's space-frivolity had already included the rouge's eternal flight (the most classical act of that certain "going to be" and "appeal"), so in the crumpled bed sheets' human tornness and sweat there had already been included all the defiance of the gushing blood, all its muddy drowsiness, its morals distorted into intrigue-mongering, all its maternity-residues, all its biological selfishness. The trajectories of the rouge running emptily on the mouth and of blood streaming, gurgling in the folds of pillows, are equally eternal:

not in their metaphysical but in their geometric concreteness —
there is in the mouth's arc *qua* arc some inexhaustible undulation,
soaring and descent, momentum and withering, which refuses
to be completed, being so much the divine breathing, pulse of
divine symmetry — and in the blood gushing from the wound
we find the boundlessness, the tragic insatiability of all spring-
wells of every life shapelessly and abundantly pouring forth:
the death- and life-muses entangled into one another in blood
cannot be stopped — there is no limit to amorphousness: it is
the divine breathing and pulse of divine nonsense. A pair of lips
arching into proportion-refinery — is that what "remains" of the
one? (What a curious instinct or convention, to use the word
"remain" when talking about the increase, and not the diminish-
ing, of something!) And the other: an unstoppable, blind biological stream? Such questions are important, what is more, defining
here and now, in the coquette's antechamber: for, after all, he is an
old man who would like to find out before his death what, in the
deepest roots of his roots, "wife" and "mistress" had been. And
why he had needed both equally, why choosing between them
had been impossible.

Divan-bed, rouge-blood: what else? Perhaps mirror and
night: the mistress always sees herself in the mirror, is always
doubly with herself — the wife is always in the night, can't see
herself, is always by herself without herself — is the mistress one
more and the wife, one less, if they are one? In that very moment too he was standing before a mirror (when he picked up
the coin) and for a moment felt dizzy from the reflections of all
the mirrors he had ever seen at his lady friend's: for a moment
his whole life became identical to the frantic yes-ing of the Mirror, as though he had never encountered any other phenomenon
that bestowed happiness. A huge mirror in a huge room in which
a female head, proffered up in one sole reflection, is surrounded
by blind-bright space — ornate Venetian mirror where the flow-

ers glowing in from the outside and the female hair form one single light-tiara, rolling glass-tow; a palm-slender, ribbon-like mirror by a pool, steamed over by the water's lukewarm vapor and signaling only one or two stretching blots of the toweling, nude body; a little pocket-mirror which only illuminates a tooth, a rash, a mislaid hair, while the face remains a shapeless stage setting; jocose altar-mirror, triptychs and glass pergolas in which daylight stands white and scintillating, geometrical and pseudo-virginal, like ice-cold water in sunlit glasses: all that is but disappointment, illusion, chaos, logic — glass walls drifting apart in candlelight, moonlit *"nosce te ipsum"* settings, the missal stand-like tin boards of proletarian rooms, the spheric and icosahedron mirrors of alchemists and doctors: all that is the mistress' realm, all that is the mistress. Always twice and always less-than-once: and as a result of that doubling, always lighter, more worthless, nothing-er. The mistress: perspective without human presence. The mistress is an optical flowering, as opposed to the biological flowering of other species: view without plasticity, color without life's thick-set chemistry, movement without strength. And when, following those mirror-visions, he had trans-imagined the wife's self-cancelling ethos-night, he asked himself again, like one who didn't get one step further in his insatiable investigations:

12.

What was that, what were they in his life, those two worlds, the world of the wife and the world of the mistresses? Were they opposites — were they women? How did those worlds begin, live, end? For it was certain that now it was over — love's arching bridge had crossed over to the last pillar: the river quietly reflects the image, wearing the shade like a chastity belt or funeral diadem: the bridge is ready. Indeed, his whole life appeared to him not as "life" but as bridge — a haughty, fountain-like arched water-jet whose cool and prickly pellet-dew he felt splashing on his skin, whose shadow, moving like a snake's tongue, taking small bites of the night, he could sense on his way, on his plate, and on his office desk: the women were compasses, waving in vain in the direction of strange poles — those had shaped his life the way it had been: them he had to thank for all his thoughts and gestures, and yet, those women had somehow never been — his love life had been no life, least of all *his* life.

The wife's world began with a flower: with a solitary, huge calla in a squeezed-in, overcrowded garden — that garden was perhaps smaller than a room, but rich and inwardly unlimited (after all, it is not the infinite horizons that give one an overwhelming experience of the greatness of space, but the very inward-placed "inwardness," the landscapes with a very umbilical-whirlpoolish center) like a jungle — some indefinite hybrid between an aquarium and a dream, a womb and a jewelry casket. Here he once waited for the young lady of the house: rain, about to abate, was rattling down on the glass roof like transparent metal blood, gaudy sunlight was already pressing down in the grooves, but inside everything was brown, mossy-smelling, and nauseatingly warm. He didn't know what he found more pleasant — being in oak parks diluted with vast lawn-trays, or in that stifling, root-psychologizing lair. The calla stood alone, quite high on an artificial little mound: the sheer fact that it didn't grow on the ground, from the height of his feet, but in line with his hips, was strange — if one sees a flower at this height, it is usually not growing from the ground but bathing in a vase like a bored Leda.

With that flower, the wife began: it was a mysteriously singular and superb flower — with one sole petal and one stamen. Is that the expression of the indissolubility of wedlock, of destiny's sore unambiguousness, the emblem of monastic life — or is it the expression of murderous perversion lurking in nature, of shameless "frivolity," of hysteria ceaselessly striving toward the very essence of essentials? She is my wife: this sentence, resolution, or completion in effect independent from him, hovered at all times on his lips like a hesitant silk-worm on a half-gnawed mulberry leaf.

Simplicity! Is simplicity simple? Does that one petal not achieve to be simple, one-petaled rather than three- or five-petaled, and thus "complicated," along the most artificial, affected, what is more: *crippled* lines? What is that flower: Eros or counter-Eros? There are people who, sickened by the sloppy sweat odor of kisses and embraces, take refuge in flowers: from the uncontrollable saliva dripping from a kiss, to dew; from perfume, to smell; from the bed's corkscrew-like, copulation-kneaded darkness to the roots' earthly darkness, from the self-lacerating frankness of desire to the flower-cups' senseless openness: could they be right? Is the calla's dew, smell, root-Styx and openness really the pure "idea" of what in love can only feature as pathology or caricature? Or is flower, on the contrary, the parody, and love, the pure realization? There is an absolute relation between the two, not only in the broad community of colorful vitality, but also in the minutest, microscopic details.

And up to the point when the girl's family put to him the question, when the wedding should take place, in fact little more happened than the vision of that lone flower in the botanical trinity of mysterious conservatory-life, ice-cold morality, and *recherché* lies. What on earth did the calla's silken-snowy, broad collar, its orange-gold pineapple-mosaicked, quivering giant stamen have to do with the scene that played in the small corner-room between him and his bride's mourning family?

13.

It was late afternoon. He was vexed: that very morning he learnt that the mayor had chosen him as his secretary. The mayor had received him in his office before a vast mural depicting an extraordinarily important town council meeting: a splendid garden of colorful clothes, somber clouds, hovering feathers, and shiny weapons. Public life! Will it be as festive, as carnivalesque, as much a lust-concert as this painting, or as festive and responsible ad nauseam as the mayor's manners foreshadowed? Everything the mayor ever spoke about was, how every stroke of the pen can be fateful, how wars depend on every word uttered, how every promise tied you to the Vatican like an underworld umbilical chord: the public person's life is nothing but prudence, diplomacy, hypocrisy, and blind self-sacrifice. The poor boy was trembling like a dog dissected alive. How could you possibly reconcile so many things: the most resolute heroism and the most histrionic hypocrisy, the fatalistic sticking to your promises and eternal trickery? Which will it be, then? Instinct? Intuition? Nose? Now he almost burst out laughing when he thought about these qualities: he felt so annihilated, so completely paralyzed and dumb as if his whole bodily existence had been nothing but a continuous stammering, begun before the beginning of time and going on endlessly. What, then, about that jolly, parakeety, splendid image? There everything was so buoyant, so ballet-heroic and flower-like as though history were a germination and flowering of human seeds as whimsically spontaneous as it is of plant seeds. Whom should he believe: the decoration, or this deathly responsibility-masquerade? Which of his life's primal wells should he let loose in his political career: suicidal ethical instinct, or suicidal comedy instinct? What will he turn into, a civil servant or a buffoon?

Everybody around him would go on to become a politician the way poets become poets: they would compose aphorisms about Turkish battleships, chime rhymes on pope and emperor, heap metaphor upon metaphor on reckless viscountly marriages and pseudo-excommunications; while history would foam around him "en fleur," he would keep promises, watch over the authenticity of seals, stick to contracts. Even though the mayor didn't in the least resemble the painting's primal colorfulness, behind his official sanctimony he could nevertheless perceive a certain anarchy, a certain vegetally luxuriating moral insanity, Antichrist-freedom. He felt that public life bore the same emotional paradoxes as love: the eternal panorama of faith and faithlessness. Where are those delicate, evanescent borderlines where political honorableness & this unmistakable stink of primordial amorality meet?

A huge crucifix stood on the table; from one of its arms hung the mayor's white glove, like Christ's torn robes. He didn't for a moment feel it to be an empty formality beside the mayor's flabby frame: for there was certainly hidden, leaden suffering in his male lard and reasoning — the Antichrist was howlingly Christ-like. But the hanging glove, this tiny blasphemy, was also symptomatologically creditable: from behind the Christ-like eternal despondency and vanquishedness, irony radiated like a goldfish flashing from a pitch-black Japanese lacquer pool. All extremely unsettling, of course. Now and again servants and masters came in, some through a massive wooden door that was larger than the castle gates and thicker than a house-wall (all the more wonderful for closing so silently), others through some allegedly secret flush door. Sometimes they brought documents, at other times utterly feminine objects, pearls, flowers. In the two doors all love's alternatives were enclosed: what was essential, sincerity or secrecy, and was secrecy not merely would-be secrecy? Do diplomacy's many veils and its sexual-looking discretion indeed keep secrets quiet, or do they amount to nothing more than the artificial living-through of mankind's ceaseless need of secrets — that is, of its utter lack of secrets? Or is secret in fact the real thing, and sincerity the posturing? Which one should he believe:

the wooden door or the little flush door? Mystification, mystification, he kept repeating to himself, while a houseboy led him to the stairs. But this "mystification" upset him; he could no longer recognize himself on the street; he was a changed man: if the mayor's office and manners had such an organic power, then calling it either humbug or value is mere wordplay. Awfully *intensive*: is there in fact any other sensible adjective for the matters of life?

14.

Such thoughts were in his mind while he walked toward his fiancée's house to report his first visit to the mayor. As soon as he left behind the large bronze gate that in the sunshine appeared like a hedge trimmed after the French fashion, with its light-green rusts and molds and with the half-opening, half-blunted buds of its armored knobs, he met a group of lancers. First he took them for watchmen on their round; their weapons calmly pointed at the sky, like reeds sticking out of a forsaken lake's surface — those few metallic threads, terror's strings tuned with the sharpest of ears, made him forget the whole town: everything vanished, the bridges that almost rowed and sailed along with the ships, the sweetly throbbing pulse of the surrounding hills, the people's and church-towers' ring-fingers — those slowly quivering lances proceeding in parallel movement were as alone in the blue sky as the odd blade of grass grown too tall, when you lie in the grass looking up at the sky. Order cut off from everything: God, the life of cities, order which only exists for itself, with a million sensitive nerve-endings, entirely blind. Only when they got closer did he see that they were leading a man in shackles, in whom he recognized the town's fanatic insurgent, the unshaven, filthy Giampione, who according to some was trying to win over the town's down-and-outs to the side of the Duke of Urbino, and according to others was an idealistic religious reformer.

Whether henchman or founder of a religion, he fundamentally differed from the mayor of the bulky desk, sigil-keyboards, and the uncannily objective gloves.

This, too, is "history" — the young man slogging toward his fiancée said to himself — and I don't know which lies closer to my heart: diplomacy or revolution, the etiquette of law, or the shapeless howl of suffering? Public life: that was the only ideal his father had inculcated in him, and he now felt it to be nothing but a dreadful lie, which did not mean of course that the mayor with his demonically calculating diplomacy were a "liar," or the arrested anarchist were merely "posturing" — no: the mayor and the heretic (if he was really one) were both sincere, straightforward characters — lying was not the moral flaw of individuals but quite simply, a tragic and inescapable trait of existence, of all action, all moving out of passivity: everything was different from what it would have been worth being. If there is to be a dialogue between the mayor and the heretic, will it not be meaningless from the get-go? Which of the two loves the people truly: the virtuoso of legal acts, or this cellar-prophet? The young man's head was swirling, burning — he had been launched on a career and had no inkling what to do.

His soul was chock-full of the infinitesimal differentiations of legal manuals, the enticing tapestry of game rules and gospel ethics, which brought his nuance-perverted rationalism to an almost raving ecstasy: he was a born mathematician for whom politics meant Euclidean tournaments — but his soul was also chock-full of the fantastic portraits of the slums' down-and-outs, the Bruegelesque extras, the gnomes, whores, lepers, beggars, and women caught in labor in staircases, the disfigured dead of battlefields; it was chock-full of the hospitals' perfume blended of Christ, alchemy, and sadism; he was a born folk tribune for whom politics meant eternal sexual-theological intercourse with all forms of suffering. Luckily for him, this inner struggle between the diplomat and the rebel, the rationalist and the mystic, which would likely mark his life, was for the time being very far from any decisive situation: for to play it for him now were strangers, separate characters he had nothing to do with after all.

15.

The street exhaled the odor of fresh cherries, which only the humid smell of shady walls surpassed in pleasantness: benumbed, he could dip his spirit into it all, the sweet impressions of the senses, which are such a far cry from the fictions of public life. Odors vanish, the occasional vista of a house, flower, or woman is wiped out in an instant — and yet, what an extraordinary power, in this "evanescent perfume" bemoaned for the millionth time, of the irrefutable worthiness of faith, of almost-material eternity, in contrast to the dialogue between the mayor ratiocinating, and the heretic gesticulating, for the common good! With infinite gratitude he burrowed into the calm veil of "frivolous" impressions: he let his entire soul adhere to the stirring, reminiscent of a sleeping bird's body, of a minute-hand, to the dull thudding of a street vendor's rolling melons, to the hawsers' putrid whiskers that a wave's touch would now comb straight and now undulate and scatter in a thousand directions, depending upon whether they were hanging in the air, pulled down into a vertical whorl by the water's weight, or ended up beneath a tiny surf; he entrusted his soul to the mess of the houses, to the quietly exciting fact that streets were not built in a straight line and the houses were not built at the same time and in the same color, but whimsically, as if they were not the result of human will but had been tossed ashore by the sea or wind, like broken shells or fallen leaves. Before him, the town was napping in the peaceful hues of chaos and idyll: when he looked at a fisherman smoking his pipe or a fishwife playing cards, he couldn't imagine why anything like "public life," anything like politics, should exist at all, whether of the mayor or the founder of a religion, for everything was idyllic; when his eyes scanned the biological hodgepodge of the houses, he felt there was no need for politics at all, for there was no "polis" whatsoever, only the beyond-the-human free play of chemical substances, the chaos of flowers, fumes, deathless arch-rags.

How many worlds, and none of them knew of the others, although each wanted to influence the others; how many separate worlds that are so essentially foreign that they should obviously not as much as know of one another: the fight between the mayor and the anarchist; the fishermen smoking their pipes and playing cards; the arch-seaweeds in the depths of diluvial oceans; his own analytical and imaginary invalid body and soul; his bride's family dead-set on marriage: are these really together in the world? Do they not absolutely repel one another? And yet they keep crossbreeding, mainly because humans are so naïve and insensible (they have no impressions, only thoughts) that they enforce such crossbreedings: of arch-seaweeds with marriage, polisless fishwives with politics. When will they ever cease their senseless disharmonies? Or is this what makes life, that these mutually repelling worlds have to be mixed, whether we want to or not? Might the contrast of these worlds not be a real antagonism — are they perhaps not worlds at all, but merely perceived as worlds by a nervous young man's musical soul, so that he would hear music, harmonies and dissonances, where there is no music of any kind? In this absent-minded eunuch mood he arrived at his fiancée's house.

16.

They received him in a disused bedroom. Their sight made his head swirl: all were in mourning — women in long veils, men with ceremoniously vacuous smiles, an unctuous, mundane bishop with two mud-green-faced friars, a tertiary priest with a doorknob-yellow skull and a Roman nose, keening women in all kinds of folksy lace headgears sucking on candies, and at the door in black, a group of mercenaries. Burial residues, apparently. The keening women were probably still waiting for tips, the friars (the company's naïve bear cubs) were about to start bawling some valedictory prayer, the bishop wanted to convey, through a half-gnawed sandwich, some shapely and chic consolation to the family who were listening with dumb shivers — what was he doing here? why did they let him in? whose is the death, where is the corpse, among the loitering soldiers, simoniac viveurs, holy friars, tear-dropping machines, beastly blind blood-relations and mute flowers?

His fiancée didn't feature much in his consciousness, being in fact merely a dissonant little symbol, the mis-struck chord of these two tones, two worlds: the biological riddle of the greenhouse calla and the mourning family's darkness. Without considering his two impressions "true," he dimly felt that all he could have to do with women in life would be to compile small variations from botanical & climacteric motifs (the word "climacterium" came to mind, because he felt this burial to be no "event," but the family's physiological history). Girls! Do girls exist? Supposedly they do, since he himself was "courting" (?) one; what is more, he had even heard people say that he had a "bride" — but the word and fact of "girl" and "beautiful girl" were for him at most social formulae, polite turns-of-phrase, the kind of euphemism behind which they hide the flower's secret and aging women's pathological degree of reality. His "courtship" had been an acquaintance with aging: in the girl's house he always found old people who harbored some utterly unearthly, fictitious image of "man," who always had to be martyr and merchant, ward and murderer. For this reason he didn't feel a "man," not even when alone with her: from the paintings on the walls, from the armchairs' lace spreads, from the honey-molten afternoon lights through the half-lowered sail-colored curtains there poured forth, equally and ceaselessly, this utterly doltish fiction of manhood to which every clock hand and teacup expected him to conform. The only way of escape was in utterly primitive and soulless (if such is possible) sensuous play — although taking full bodily advantage of the girl seemed no less fictive and grotesque than the "ideal" about which the mothers caught in the vortex of their barrenness used to daydream.

Calla, old-age hysteria, mechanical sensuousness: there were no other elements to his "love" — and so it went for years. It was the same today, when with surprise he heard a houseboy announce that he was expected in a room he had not yet seen. Handing over his hat and cloak he felt it in his body how, in a matter of minutes, he was metamorphosing from a living human being into an algebraic sign of bridegroom prepared for the senile: in no other house in the world would he be expected to give up so wholly on life, the outer world, that is, on all the colorful uncertainties, and to only open his mouth when he could say something positive. This "positivity" (the pampered ghost of those divorced from reality, of melancholy, of old fogeys) scared him now more than ever, for his soul had never been so "decent folk"-loathingly wavering and problematic as after his visit to the mayor. They are going to interrogate him. What should he answer? He asked the houseboy if there were special guests in the house, and learned that they were funeral guests — his bride's brother-in-law had died. This of course meant that the widow, the unknown sister, was here.

17.

The sister: for years she had lived far away, in a different city, & now that her husband was dead, she returned to her mother. He had not seen her yet. He had two decisive impressions connected to her: her handwriting, and a painting that for weeks he had believed to depict her, when it turned out that in fact the model was no relative at all, but some Venetian painter's mistress. The painting hung in a completely dark salon like a little velvety orange blot inside a huge, blue-blind pansy. His relation with this painting and this salon was the sole thing remotely reminiscent of love, if indeed the word love has any logical contours, including a balance between a certain primitive physiological selfishness and a certain poetic nostalgia. The salon's Byzantine darkness, the portrait's golden luminosity, the awareness that this room had been the study of his fiancée's deceased father, the happy freedom that the presence of an unknown woman, the presence of distance meant in the somber house: all this, he thought, might resemble other people's love. He lingered here whenever he could. This sister would some day become his mistress — he lived this daydream for about three weeks. This was the time when the thought of marrying his bride didn't horrify him, when he wanted to become a member of the family, kept repeating aloud the word "bride," which to him had a lyrical, touch-me-not-yellow sound and feel, like early morning incest.

In his mind he could never separate the idea of the family from that of incest, and for him to have social intercourse with the wife's sibling meant incest. "Family" for him meant these two end-poles alone: either the petit-bourgeois idyll, some sort of protestant-puritanical respectability, a trade association for daily sloppiness — or a biological group whose members jollily mix their blood and seeds to the point of exhausting mathematical variations and combinations. The "sister's" likeness meant the latter: all of a sudden the bride's body became valuable, because connected by blood to the sister's body. Curiously, but also naturally, during these three weeks he didn't feel the slightest desire for the kind of clockwork-carnal taking advantage of his bride, which had taken up the better part of his afternoons for two years: the bride's body in and of itself was such a tiny atom in the family's body that it could on no account constitute a sensuous stimulus, could not mean body. The bride was mere spume, sun-spark on the broad, spiritual, poetic body-wave, Venus-tide, which the unknown sister's portrait had opened to his eyes, and which also included the mother, beautified, embodied, together with her despondent grey-haired siblings.

The young man, disgusted as a rule by the very word relative, all of a sudden started looking for yet more relatives, for girls, matrons, little boys, and the defunct, so that he could finally feel "*one* body" between his fingers — the sole, ghostly nude of *one* family. Incest spiritualizes. The portrait bore a likeness to the bride's face: how wonderful that what in his bride's skin had long bored his fingers existed once more as the unknown — and this delighted him not out of selfishness, but out of rectitude, a goodness toward his bride: he didn't have to lie to her that she was beautiful, for indeed — through the unknown sister's portrait — he found her beautiful. Besides, one couldn't tell if he worshipped the portrait-sister because of her younger sister, or if he worshipped the latter on account of the older sister? The fine chemistry of known and unknown: one of the most important parts of love. The portrait was a secret that inebriated with the scent of the known; the bride was boredom from which glowed, enclosed like a flower, an unknown possibility, like a white mask from behind evergreen leaves. He lived simultaneously in an aquarium and on Plautus' stage: the two lookalike sisters brought the mysterious monotony of heredity, of thousand-year-old inertia to his mind, behind the two faces all of a sudden he felt a thousand faces forgotten-into-the-world with the self-same imperviousness: the two portraits were dulled into the sleepy rhythm of nature, annihilated into trite herrings. But this nihil was sweet, pathetic, & redemptive. On other occasions, however, his mind wandered to the comedies of mistaken identities — to the pleasure of mixing-up, the eternal excitement of quid pro quo. How entirely grand!

But what now? He was here. The age-old reaction, "run away from reality," would be of little use. Hey, presto then, up to the old bedroom. The sister's husband is dead: this belittled "the family" & much belittled the sister's erotic chance. Before facing reality, he wanted to take one more look at her pseudo-portrait: to see it for the last time the way he had seen it so far, perhaps a bit for conspiring against reality, perhaps to promise that he would live for the image ever after, and for this reason tear the image to pieces: he, the boy, with his own hands, lest reality, the living woman, destroy the portrait with the usual reality-posturing. Let reality come second after his hands! He asked the houseboy to point him in the direction of the old bedroom, for he would go there later alone: first he would like to pass by the "dark" salon for a book he had forgotten.

The sister's handwriting and portrait had always been opposites, so much so that he had never asked his bride if the portrait indeed resembled her older sister. He found out only by accident that it didn't depict the sister. What was curious, or natural, was that this awareness hardly changed his relation to the painting: for him it remained the sister. Because for him "the sister" was some kind of biological abstraction — his soul and body were in acute need of some sister-like entity, an any-sister. When he reached the salon he found he could no longer establish any relation with the picture: by all appearances, reality got there first while he lagged behind — the simple, empty awareness that the sister was already in the house annihilated the picture: this was a proper in effigie execution. All he could see was the sister's handwriting: her whole body, character, voice, was identical to her crow-feet alphabet, even her hidden-most joints were Ks, Rs, Fs. Who are *you* then, Venetian model? A countess, courtesan, æsthetic space-filler, or the myth of a life? Come, join me *against* the family!

18.

The painting managed to combine, with particular skillfulness, a kind of numbing, warm harmony with a constitutionally alien, distorting, tragic and grotesque style. The gaze merged into that melodic, golden "distance" that only painters can render: this distance is infinite, like a god's undisturbed sleep; it has no purpose, no limits, and yet, despite its shapeless, eternal spatiality, it is idyllic, closed, like a lamp-shaped, lamp-glowing womb — young children imagine the immaculate conception like this: the infant Jesus hovers together with an idyllic park inside a golden, rainbowy soap bubble beneath the Virgin's bowing, quietly leaf-shooting breasts. The portrait's eyes looked into this essentially *painted* distance, that combined boundlessness and womb-enclosedness, having seamlessly adapted to the dual nature of space: the gaze was hesitant, splenetic, and vacuous, the affected piano-pianissimo pitch of vertigo, but at the same time it caressed every single object in the background and of the invisible but requested foreground, holding on to them, empathizing with pulleys, clouds, tackle. And curiously, all this psychic easement, dissolving, sorrowful softness emanated from an angular, gothically broken and twisted body: the brooding woman's half-nude posture outdid the German peasants' wooden crucifixes in its Art Nouveau-ish appearance. But one merely acknowledged this fact to oneself — the unwitting, inert expressionism of clumsiness didn't thwart melancholia's softly meandering lines in moving from the image to the spectators' ingle-like eyes, on the contrary: it heightened them, unmistakably recalling such moments and positions of amorous embrace where both bodies are twisted and deformed to the utmost gothic extent, while the souls and lips, eyes and fingertips, exhale the most idyllic, most pampering goodness. The half-nude was surrounded by that certain background-landscape which, in the onlooker, forever erases the contrast of dream and realism, kitsch and "Pan revelations," stylization and

narrow-mindedness, convention & heavenly excitement — this
is simply beauty, composed of its eternal elements: nature, shady
melancholia, truth, habit, pure sensation.

19.

For the young man the greatest significance of his acquaintance
with his bride's family was the fact that it banished any fleeting
impression devoid of practical use, most decisively, into the characteristically "male" world of sins and perversions. It never ceased
to surprise him, this sensitivity on the family's part with which
they intimated beforehand, from his gesture or breathing, whether the next sentence was going to be "sensible" or impressionistic,
and if the latter, they either gestured at him to stop before he
could utter it, or tried to wring out, with painful obdurateness,
the "sense." The first time he felt this strikingly was when, at the
beginning of their acquaintance, he praised the girl's clothes: he
spoke about her lovely red blouse, red gloves, crimson shoes, in
a tone of enthusiasm that was particularly repellent to the family — one that renders the superlative degree of delight in the
object beheld by miming the spectator's impotence and utter defeat when faced with the wondrous phenomenon. "After such a
red shoe-toe nothing remains to be seen," this was what his voice
conveyed. But the ones impatiently waiting for the tirade's end
asked nervously: "What then?" He wondered at this and, voice
grown husky, could only answer: "That is all I wanted to say."

From this moment he withdrew into his cocoon and didn't
talk about his impressions. The family had educated him well:
they managed to stifle all his impressions into the world of sin.
Because the young man was first and foremost a mime, a copycat:
if he had spent two years planning the killing of his enemy and
finally found him alone eating soup, instead of stabbing him in
the back, he would at once start imitating soup-eating with his

rapier, sharpened for two years, attentively observing the spoon's sinking into the soup, its rise and journey to the mouth. And so it was with these old folks: he immediately imagined himself in the place of their grey blindness to impressions, & treated every object and fleeting color with this mime-like mimicry-blindness. In his perception the most abrupt duality was born: to see something meant henceforward to twitch into *en garde* at the first sensory stimulus, uttering with every inch of his body: "I don't see you," and store away the sight's violent optical self-offering, which went on nevertheless, in another constitutionally alien plane: into a definitely non-subconscious but rather, absolutely core-conscious layer, where the shades of an impression were barely more than known, but where no sentimental consequences were given space. The "no!" and some unfeeling sensorial "objectivity": into those two worlds the prospective relatives restricted his impressions. Now when for the last time he was looking symbolically at the sister's portrait, he set free the feeling-train of his impressions: how strong, foliage-, and silk-like, how "sinful" they were!

Sin, sin, sin: when, what did he in fact feel to be sin? This distracted question had no ethical stakes (nor could it, being so clearly subjective and æsthetic), and that was precisely the reason why it preoccupied him. There and then, in front of the picture, he answered his own question squarely and concisely: "sin" always meant something very logical and very sentimental — for him those were the sin-moods. Very *logical*: to this category belonged his amorous sins, his smaller or bigger so-called perversions. All "perverse" actions (so he believed) boiled down to somebody doing on certain occasions, with certain organs of theirs (since we must needs speak of these organs), what can be done with them, following the most natural *logical* deductions: they don't do what they theoretically should learn to do (that is, normal sexual intercourse), but what they readily imagine, with the help of primitive logic, to be the most simply and practically doable. In such situations the organ always features like a *logical* premise, not a natural tool. Homosexuality is, for instance (to take only one of the otherwise not too many variants), simpler, more primitive, more *logical* than its normal counterpart — if one is ceaselessly thinking of his organ, then the first step is its quantitative enhancement, its mathematical multiplication: and this is a *logical* reflex procedure. (It would be preposterous to take the stressing of perversity's rudimentary, logical, barbarian-rational character for its apology: these "perverse" skills were so insignificant in the young man that it wouldn't even occur to him to worry about their attack, much less their defense.) Besides being a product of *logical*, not sensuous instinct, perversity is naively "practical," meaning that someone treats their sexual instincts and organs decisively non-sexually, just like the other objects of practical life: flowers, threads, pen, brush. There are obvious consequences of the well-known fact that for us, in the beginning (which coincides with the end) sexual life means an unknown *object* in our body, rather than the intimation of some unknown relation in our soul: and we certainly do not start from taking unknown objects to women, but investigate them in our own rudimentary laboratory "experiments." In addition to primitive *logic*, primitive *experimentation*. With some this goes smoothly throughout a lifetime, with others it gets enveloped in processes of conscience and blunt sin-perfume, due to the circumstances of their lives: this last one was the case of the future mayor.

But he felt the same sin-mood when he was very *sentimental*: when he felt the yellowness of a flower with all his nerve-fringes and wisdom teeth to be yellow, if he unexpectedly glimpsed again his memories whizzing in the direction of evening's cool pier, if he saw a grievance of his to be highly motivated, feeling its cause like a glistening mirror: on such occasions the emotion simply amounted to suicide, with the defiant morphing into yellow, memory, cause: with the total annihilation of humanity and individuality.

The portrait of the pseudo-sister kindled such sin-moods in him: a blue mountain as it melts, like sugar, between a cloud's lips, a paper-thin cypress that cannot make up its mind whether to definitely trade in its crown for its shadow; a lake reflected wanly, with "the realism of non-attention," which in its melancholy hide mirrors the mill's blades, blossoming into flowers of gravity, as a fainted or dying man's glassed eyeballs, impervious to the world, reflect a tassel of a pillow or a leftover cobweb on the ceiling — with the impotent acuity of unwillingness-to-look-evermore.

Minutiae! *This*, then, is forbidden to me; this is what I'm excluded from. How interesting: the mothers of girls as a rule loathe young men for their gambling, drinking, boisterous lies, for being vain and idle — that is, for having all too concrete and gross defects of character; me they loathe because I see almost microscopic details, atoms on, in, objects. The young man was no poet or painter, no artist of any kind; he was not absent-minded, nor a daydreamer by temperament; he dressed to perfection, fenced decently, his manners were dryly mundane; his only suspicious traits were these small observations: he would say of a pair of shoes not that it was durable or too wide or too tight, but that it was like a red wild flower — and of a red wild flower, not how long it would last and whether the gardener would know how to handle it, but that it was "red" (for this is indeed a microscopic, hidden trait of a red flower: surprising as it may seem, this was his only sincere experience in his conversations with his fellow human beings).

Of course, the elders' nose was not deceived: they smelled out unmistakably that *this* was the true enemy of women, the "harmful" male: not the Don Juans, not the bohemian artists, but these nuance-spotters. For they will be forever unable to see a girl as one concrete, ethical human being: the girl will always be a mere nuance, sex-shot, fabric pattern. For the Don Juans, the woman is at least a *human being* as long as they care about her — but for such a man, she's merely a cluster of optical stimuli.

20.

He shut the door behind himself and went up the stairs. After getting a view of the company of mourners, he stopped by the giant curtain that hid the tiny antique bed (for ten-centimeter damsels, one thousand centimeters of virginity: was the bed curtain an illustration of this feat of maternal fashion design?) and by the sister's clothes of mourning. She held her hat, although she had obviously been there for some time already — this gesture at once made her obnoxious in his eyes. She was very pale; her hair was pressed into shapely waves, but while such artificial waves hover above certain faces like the dizzying wreaths of play, here they merely laid bare the crippled nature of artifice — never had waves been so un-waving as on this head. They were like a lightning-fast violin passage rendered with the stuttering skills of an apprentice violinist: even if mathematically every tone may be pitch-perfect, the whole is no more than a Bruegeliad. In truth they were "wave"-shaped waves. The hair sat on her like a wig that might fall off at any moment: there was no trace of psychology in its color or texture — and yet where should a widow be wearing her soul if not on her permed head? Not by any chance in her "interior," or "heart"?

Under her low, empty brow and her long, arched eyebrows two huge eyes hovered. Sentimental, passionately deep mirrors, which were at first sight nevertheless gaudy denials of "nuance," of the millstones, cypresses, blue mountain cliffs. Where did this duality come from: the alternating voices of poeticism, or violin-spheres on the one hand, and of inquisitorial limitedness and aridity on the other? The cause must be some banal physical trait, for instance, the fact that what on others as a rule measures two millimeters, here is one millimeter, or the other way round; the sheer fact of their excessive bigness explains this duality. They were sad eyes, but even this sadness gave the impression of clumsy defiance and girlish ignorance. One couldn't explain these eyes by labeling them histrionic, mask-like: the entire woman was infinitely removed from any kind of posturing. Were they insulated eyes? Did they sit among the face's lime crystals like a chord complicatedly mixed into an exquisite harmony, surrounded by a thousand cacophonous noises? Did the reflection of the skull-face's wry Puritanism fall on whatever was poetry in their color and size? An eerie, mystical burning glowed darkly in those foliage-density gathering eyes, lake and ostinato-topaz, without wood or coal, oil or oxygen: and yet it burned on. Perhaps it was precisely this physical excess of beauty that rendered them prosaic: they were overmuch an *object*, just as the waves in her hair were too much lexicon waves. If one imagines an eye separated from the face, on one's palm, it will inevitably appear hideous — all of a sudden, pupil and its colored ring lose their dimensions, becoming meaningless mathematical locations on a white sphere. When he imagined the sister's eyes afloat in a bottle of formaldehyde, he found those eyes beautiful even *there*: they had shades even without the shades cast by the lid; even there, the vitreous body's jelly was psychic foliage-density. Was it the poetry of inexpressiveness at its highest degree, or the deadly barrenness of absolute psychic shining? In nature's experimental garden those eyes were like certain over-refined fruits — grapes: and every single grape on the bunch is huge, falling on the others in wondrously swollen and slender ovals, like the fog-hormones of Io-seeking Zeus; their color is gold and pallor, spring-green and autumn-velvet — but their taste is nil or sour, their seeds large and spiky, their peel thick, unchewable and bitter; the most refined is here *at once* monstrous and ideal. Those eyes were like that, it seems — some kind of inner lie, pathology of perfection. But their pathology was no Basedow-like swollenness: even in their huge proportions they were soft, pastel-like, free of plasticism. This woman had perhaps never yet *looked* with these eyes: was their "soul"-permeatedness not in fact a soul-lessness?

"Absolute" mirror: if a flower falls into the eye, she will not "see" it, but the flower chemically transforms, re-colors, reshapes the eyes' substance, and in this way the eyes' wondrous richness is this chemical anarchy — the vegetal, mushroom-like proliferation of millions of lights and forms on the iris and the pupil-ring — because they couldn't penetrate as deep as her consciousness, they shot roots and a million parasite branches and leaves, *outside*: on the eye's body itself. This would be a particularly interesting version of blindness: absolute *seeing* and never looking, which transforms the eyeball chemically, botanically, as a thousand kinds of seed transform a miraculous soil. These eyes resembled, to the point of identity, the mother's eyes, yet there this poetry of barrenness was not felt in the least. One moment he delighted in seeing the mother's lucidity replicated in a young woman's body, beautified, made acceptable by this young femininity — the next moment he felt that there could be nothing drearier than this impotence to experience, emanating from such a young woman.

He looked at the people sitting in the room again and again. "They're all dead." And then said, with an almost religious greed: this is good, this is the way it has to be, it couldn't have happened otherwise with me. "Come, join me against the family," that is what he said to the portrait — but why? Why *against*? The world of "nuances" (water-mill! mountain cliffs! cypresses!) and the world of woman-shaped death are far too large realities to be drawn into the ridiculous comings-and-goings of enmity, of pro and con. Strangely, his two thoughts, that attacking the sister's death-eyes would be ridiculous, and on the other hand, that some day he would kill this woman and the deed would be the only achievement of his marriage, this murder would be his wife's money, clothes, nudity, and offspring: those two thoughts occurred to him at the same time, without disturbing one another in the least. He almost saw the sister dead, as a stairway railing's last baluster on the verge of the night, and explained to her in haste: "I didn't hate you, I didn't, not for one moment!" Hatred, murder, is triggered by speech, by action: if only this face could go on hovering silently forever, it could not be hated — a *phenomenon* cannot but be beautiful. But it will most definitely *speak* — one could tell by her posture that it will do nothing but speak, that she will consciously go to great lengths to avoid the possibility of being "phenomenon."

21.

When he stepped in front of the sister, he hastened to express his sympathies for her bereavement. "Thank you," she said in a voice that was the perfect continuation of her whole appearance: one couldn't tell if it strove to be a recherché salon-glacial voice that hides all feelings, or if, on the contrary, it was sincere feeling that distorted it, making it sound so arid, reminiscent of the dull thumping of wooden statues. "So you will excuse me if I go down right now to talk with the gardener about the wreaths," she said, turning to her mother. Then all of a sudden, to the young man: "We have heard that you are now the mayor's secretary." "Yes indeed, where have you heard it from? I thought I would, I could be the first to tell the news, because I'm coming from him." "O, we have our own secret spies, we knew it before you did." "I'm in a dangerous situation, I had better watch out." "Indeed you had better," the sister said in her clay-like, stocky voice, which was made all the stranger by the fact that not the slightest shade of humor could be detected in it. She said each word with pains-taking stress — one could tell that speech was a logical burden to her, that she took words seriously, as she did the money that she was incapable of playing with. "By the way, when are you planning the wedding?" the bishop standing about in his funeral finery asked all of a sudden. (The keening women were still in the room.)

He looked at his fiancée: she was sitting on the edge of the bed with drooping shoulders and hanging head, like a scolded child. The large white curtains fell in broad clouds, shells and petals, making it impossible not to think of Jupiter approaching Io. Is this then the foreplay of the nuptials; is this how marriage begins? How scrawny and meaningless she is! The oft-mentioned "virginity" was like some old piece of furniture, or a clock ticking away perpetually under a bell jar: wonderful and boring, valuable and ridiculous, an antiquarian item in which only weak-chested pedants and seventyish snobs can find some interest. The word "marriage" and its reality became for him forever identical with the setting of this scene: the bishop, attempting in vain to tuck his tulle handkerchief into his shirtsleeve, because the black coat-of-arms was embroidered on it in such a hard thread that the fabric wouldn't fold (black seal on a dandelion puff-head!), the keening women's purple nose and bony hands, as they keep sniffing left, right, and center, like beagles after the servants had torn the game from their jaws; the grumpy soldiers in their black robes tossed to the side; a couple of dawdling old baronets as they dangle their stiffly held out fingers, because they got muddy and wet at the grave; a girl's bed made of creaking wood, not slept in for years, with bed-laces ironed and starched into awkward angles; giant alcove-curtain, meaninglessly vegetating above the crippled bed-casket; a shrunken little man on the edge of the bed, as he blinks fearfully in his direction and in the direction of the burial's impassive administrators.

What kind of body could the sister's have been? How much would that certain jus primæ noctis been only a *jus* in her life, how fully was she a codex- and canon-woman, far removed from pleasure and even farther from tragedy? There is nothing more frightening than such a puppet of matrimonial rights in place of the woman — even now she was the schemata of "the latest dispositions regarding the widow," of "inheritance," not a human being.

And precisely because of this she had an overwhelming erotic aura: this was her chastity in widowhood, her Lesbos-ostentation in her abstract state: her body radiated unself-consciousness to such extent, it was so clear from her voice and gestures that her flesh-substance had never been used as flesh-substance, that this emanated a beastly spiciness. On her lips one could read: "the wife kisses the husband," on her hands one could read: "the mother defends her child," in her eyes one could read: "the sister watches over her younger brother, so he doesn't fall into the hands of depraved women": and these principles and articles forever insulated her from kiss, child, body, her clothes of mourning highlighting this insulation in the clearest possible terms.

The prospective relatives who continued discussing the date of his marriage were an unspeakably *cowardly* bunch: one could see that they had no inkling of life & reality, and that everything was the result of their trembling fearfulness — the bride was cowardly like a punished child made to stand in the corner, the sister was cowardly like a magistrate who attempts to ward off a rampant revolution with obsolete articles of law, the mother was cowardly like a demented suicidal bird who in her frenzy flung herself on a spearhead. And while he himself was cowardly, how different his cowardice was from theirs! And yet the cowards in black held him firmly in their grasp. "When are you going to take your vows?" The vow: what is that? Some official custom, contract, signature, like the ones filled in by vendors for their transactions. The vow? Calling God as witness? God: where are you — who are you, to be dragged into this company's puny machinations? God: this is the grand mania of saints, the dreadful ascetic logic of ermine-wrapped priests, loneliness' most mordant liquor, the sum total of male secrets and male Art Nouveau. To these people? To take the vow? To recite in public? To call You, Lord, as witness, here? Clad in too tight clothes in which one sweats profusely? To smell nauseating incense from the altar?

What for — who has willed it? He could not suffer this preposterous mingling of bureaucracy and rabid theology that the word "vow" embodied. And all of a sudden he realized how infinitely he hated this sister. He felt hatred under his chin like a glass cube: the cube was transparent like air, was like nothingness baked in a mold: the cube was sharp and precise, it was what it was: hard, unbreakable, heavy: nuptial-kiss on gravity's leaden lips. The amateurs loitering about would call hatred a whirling ocean, or gushing lava, but they didn't cover his case — his hatred was not a passion, not an "emotion," and not a "principle," but some mathematical intentionality of his whole young life, an abstract line. I will live in this dual world forever: to be inebriated by the beauty of my enemies, to look at my murderers as one looks at a flower, to listen to their curses as one would listen to a clavicembalo sonata: oblivious to the fact that they are humans, moral beings, and to sense them only as stains of color, musical conceits, and delight in them. And then again to suddenly obey the glass-cube's punctual power, which had also been present in me throughout, distant and foreign, invisibly balancing the sweet frivolity of dehumanizing impressionism.

That's why I have to be in the town-hall among state-bells and state-candles, state-whores and state-heroes, state-mimes and state-animals, so that my dual perception of man may flower to its fullest: my precise hatred and imprecise love. In how many ways I have imagined, in the course of a few brief moments, the sister in this sad bedroom: I saw her in bed, with a deathly pallor on her face, in her nightshirt peeling off her shoulders like sunburnt skin, as she gazes at the small phial of poison with which I would take her life — death, now, will for the first time release her body from her body: her breasts swing in death's monsoon like a yellow daffodil that opened today, these two fairy glands are all cool gold, all snaky-shell-like petals — and the frightened sister is scared not of death but of her beauty, of her nipples' charging, bell-ringing rose-ness, that stings her more than the snakes' bites stung Cleopatra: mother and doctors see on her body the grey creepers and Cyrillic puzzlegrass-growth of death, but she knows that death is a secondary matter, something she knows, something she had been at one with since childhood — what is killing her is her own beauty weighing her down because of the green poison. O, some day you must expiate for having appeared before me in the funeral staffage! You will become a Baccha, my mistress, my murderer. Some day I will stand before my judges because of you, between the giant, senseless balance's two scales, I, the exact pointer: in one scale the judges, the law with its "truths" incommunicable to humans — in the other, you, the woman, the female mask with its million-color nihilism incommunicable to humans. A destiny I need to assume — the calla down in the greenhouse, the illuminated initial of my love-litany, is grand and beautiful, but its end is yet more important and beautiful: the Parcæ, the marriage, the vow, the murder.

Looking at his bride, she asked, "When are you going to take the vow?" Startled, the fright-sparrow perching on the bed's edge looked at the mother. The mother said nothing, only watched the bishop's mouth for what he would say next. Power of the cowardly: the bishop was like a conductor or an alchemist, who shapes the voices and substances of fear into classic forms: from the bride's playroom shivering, the mother's spleen reminiscent of infinite marshlands, he fashioned one date: "Next Sunday." "All right," he wanted to say, but his throat gave no sound. Dark fell.

22.

Wherefore the mountains, clouds, flowers? When all there is is human beings? Never had he felt more their only-human nature as in these days: never had landscapes and time been murdered

with such resoluteness as the mourning family did in this moment. There was no escape, everything was *human* here, he had
to adapt, re-orchestrate his whole life to humans. Was it possible
in such a short time? Slowly the bridges' shadows lay down on
the rivers, as if they had poured out like resin from the pillars:
what did it mean for him now, starting from the knowledge of
his wedding date — what does it mean, counted in "humans"?
Where can he find a dictionary, a conversion device for it? What
will become of us, my bride? While you were perching on the bed
and I watched you with eyes hollowed by melancholia, a bitter
version of annunciation came to my mind. You the Mary, I the
messenger angel: above us, destiny, the Moon, or a gospel, falling
star or redemption — in any case, something very black and divine. Around us, the trees in spring: there is no more mysterious
light-canon in the world than the lightest-green buds and the
Moon taken together. The buds are already half-open, quivering
with a hum between the point's needle-minimum and the foliage's rose-flames — the twigs are being strung away from them,
and against them, cobweb-like, but never with them. The clouds
are gliding upwards in dizzying diagonals, like incense smoke on
a rail, their edge silvery from death's toga praetexta, their insides
all rust-bubbles — and above them all, the Moon, surrounded by
a few stars: its halo is like the white organza collar of certain evening gowns that flow in spirals and paragraph lines down wom-
en's arms, breasts, sometimes down to their ankles — diaphanous and mist-like, sharp and diffuse, erotic and Artemisian. The
stars are lonesome, forsaken soprano-splinters, aquarelle-buttons
not yet touched by the wet brush that is preparing to daub the
Moon on the firmament of the Annunciation. This spring night
is ours, my bride: with its quivering trees, skirt-breezes falling on
the stairs. You are sitting by your bed, praying. To your left is the
bed, on the right the large, man-size stone amphora, perhaps you
inherited it from the Danaids. Are human beings human if there
is no Danaid-fountain by their bed?

The bed is a cassette of *small* desires, the border, the strait-laced nest, the amateur coffin; the vase speaks of and to boundless desires — it is the bottomless vortex of life's most ancient nostalgias, of perversities and exacting theologies, of true death, true Summa, true kiss. And you, too, bride-Madonna, are reading your petal-paged prayer book between those two? Your hair falls on the pages, among the lines of the letters springing from hair to linden-fruit and from linden-fruit to hair — what prevails in the end: the texts' ancient stiffness, or the snaking tide of your soul piled up in your hair?

Is it not the same if I feel us to be Madonna and messenger-angel, or Eve and serpent? Both tell the same story: a woman is torn from the humanistic idyll of habit, and wrung to become the tragic puppet of God's selfish destiny. Poor woman: your first suitor in Paradise was the devil, the second suitor in the manger was God — are not all brides compelled to suffer these two biblical courtships and this infernal-heavenly sposalizio? We suffer it: I am Satan and messenger-angel, you are Eve and Madonna. This is marital eros: not sex, not beauty, but the erstwhile goal in Paradise: "knowledge, knowledge," and the erstwhile goal in the manger: "suffering for the world, for the creature." Don't you feel, my bride, that now, merely by knowing our wedding date, we are already omniscient and omnidolent? The impressions, beautiful pictures, and fleshy-leaved neuroses have all wilted off me — I don't see the world: I know it. And it is you I thank for this, Parcæ.

23.

The sister said that she would like to say a few words to me in the chapel. What strange places they choose nowadays — first the old bedroom, this snuffbox-shaped showcase of virginity, and now the chapel! I followed her happily, eager to see what she would be like on her own — the moment she got up I was heart struck. My love was kindled by the way she got up: while sitting, she was so much a statue, so much an impersonal thing belonging to the sepulchral family unit, that the sheer fact of becoming a singular person turned into an amorous intercourse, the simple rising from the chair, into a stripping. I knew that she was about to deliver some moral lesson, and I could feel beforehand that my promises to be eternally faithful to my wife would turn out so sloppy that she would perhaps suffer me taking her hand or sitting with my body pressed to her. Besides, some childish and therefore lifelong snobbery had prodded me to court the sister, the family's metronome. What if I declared my love to her there in the chapel, or even underway? And even if the houseboys were to kick me out through the servants' door, wouldn't this one kiss, however unsuccessful, however much a false tone, be much more comforting for my whole life, than my marriage with her sister? What is "the true one," I asked myself: woman as tragedy, like the ancient Eve-Madonna nonsense — or woman as a momentary sensuous mania, one sole bodily climax? Never have I seen these so sharply before as now — never have I understood so clearly that I wanted both: from the wife, the moral of destiny, from the mistress, the body's positive comedy.

But the moment when I glimpsed the woman rising from her seat, wasn't I merely manipulated by ambition — didn't I solely and exclusively fall in love with the "dame" in her, weren't the concepts of kiss, body, mistress only my snobbery's ha'penny masks? Or was my old impressionism triumphing against all odds: was I admiring the rise of female body X, the emergence of legs instead of a trunk — did this make me forget everything? Her gait very nearly drove me mad: swishing of skirts, tipping of shoes, the forever-active springs of some matronly-obstinate goal in her pace, the variation of leg-shape and skirt-cloud, the over-affirmation of the denied widow-body precisely by denial, the senselessness of marriage, and within me, the smarminess of the feeling of making part of the family (and its haughtiness vis-à-vis the houseboys), mixed with the vivid consciousness of the depraved lover, of love's anarchist: this was more than enough to inebriate me.

The chapel was small, a peculiar mixture of a basilica-model and a salon. How strange the lights falling among such arches: greenish-yellow sunrays, as though penetrating through yellow spring tree-crowns, goldfish-ponds and green soap-bubbles, the whole thing a dissolving mist — and yet molded into the church's strict forms: to the edges of columns, barrel-vaulted windows, compass-dogmatic archivolts. This is the essence of the church: light's unmistakable Whistler-taste, and the strict technical-designed form of the same light.

We sat down in a stall far from the altar. "I know that you see in the fact that I called you to the chapel something far-fetched and melodramatic, but it isn't. With us the chapel is not only the place of liturgy but also of conversation." "I am happy that you called me here, and you are mistaken to believe that I am an enemy of melodrama. I have to confess that I consider you to be its enemy, so much that this very word you uttered, 'conversation,' came as a great surprise. I felt you to be so much a giver of orders to hold conversation naïve, the dolts' luxury." "I would like to know indeed why you imagine me so? Did my sister depict me as such a selfish tyrant, or is your own fancy so spiteful to believe me so, after barely a quarter of an hour's acquaintanceship?"

"Please forgive me. I am a peculiar, or perhaps all too normal blend of observation of detail and hallucination, therefore of razor-sharp knowledge and absolutely mendacious mis-imagination of people. It would be out of place to gloss my character here at length — all I ask from you is that, until you get to know me more closely (which is, after all, perhaps no aspiration of yours, but will happen in time, willy-nilly), you trust me: I am doing my best to be good and just. I like puzzling words, bluffing in words and deeds, I see plenty of ghosts, I harbor a good few superstitions, poses, even a couple of illnesses, but even behind these scenes I am: I, and there you can breathe (to pull some rhetorical weight) the strictest atmosphere of 'moral seriousness.'" "Are you entirely sure of that? What if that moral atmosphere is but stage perfume?" "You know too well that I am incapable of refuting this hands-down. I leave the matter to you." "Do you love my sister?" — she asked all of a sudden.

Never has the word "love" been threaded among so many contradictory associations since it came to be used in Europe — everything I have felt around this word since I set foot in the old bedroom leapt into one sole paradox and vanishing point here, below the chapel window. This woman doesn't know what love is: she is oblivious of it to such an absolute extent that one imagines oneself in a geological era when the only beings to populate this planet were sexless plants: some fantastically large and bountiful flora, whose luxuriating vegetative image, however, lacks the remotest touch of attraction, of cohabitation: garish colors that lack the illusion of kiss, inescapable for us. Absolute freedom, but also absolute asceticism; boundless frivolity, but also boundless blindness. This woman is *free*, freer than I or anybody from her environment, but in this dizzying, horizon-less liberation she is all alone, like a glass thread in outer space. For her, love is not only the *illness* of free human beings, of sister-children, of men, of intrigue-mongers, an illness one must take into account: it isn't something to heal, eradicate, but to put down in one's accountancy book as "human calculus." In her whole behavior there was something of the terrain between the blasé nurse and the venal advocate. For her, love meant (of course all this is merely a phonetical deduction, not a deduction from her character) the man's bourgeois self-sacrifice: not heroic, but quotidian — she imagined that the world was made up exclusively of actions ("all the rest is that whatchyacallit psychology"), and those must all be oriented toward his wife — she knew actions to be so utterly actions that she didn't know they had motifs, that while being done, the action develops its own selfish, self-serving atmosphere, it generates a wealth of associations independent of its purpose — moreover, standing in sharp contrast to it: in her adherence to the principle, "*everything* for the wife," she wasn't in fact imagining anything grand, but simply a "pro" prefix to money, politics, literature. She was visibly at her very best when she inquired after somebody else's love for somebody else — for her this "objectivity" meant love's authentic color: love's essence was that it was the business of *others*.

But one can't utter the word "love" unharmed: however much it was an objective calculus for this woman, the word love bore, inseparably sedimented in it, the biological recklessness of yesteryear's lovers, today's flowers, and tomorrow's ocean fish, the eternal mess of poetry, inebriation, tragedy. That unwitting summoning of spirits did not escape the sister: it would be far-fetched to state that as much as a fleeting nostalgia for that love of others crossed her mind, but on her face you could see the shadow of ignorance, of clumsy modesty briefly acquiescing. She was afraid that if now I was going to make declarations about my love for her sister, that declaration would be worse than unfaithfulness: in its poetic width the undeniable anarchy of Eros would be made manifest. I wanted to scare her.

When we were sitting on the bench facing each other: I felt that for me this was the last permitted erotic sensation. If I am to be fully pedantic, not even that, but I was not quite married yet, and I was saying good-bye: not to sensuous pleasures, sentimental confessions, but simply to the perspective from which I was looking at her in this moment — merely an independent theme in the air, which I could have no moral relation with.

When I made up my mind to speak about my faithfulness to my future wife, I wanted to be sincere: in the presence of the sister I felt the influence of *theme*-girls hovering in the air so strongly that in my panic I wanted to cling with all my strength to faithfulness, to asceticism. Yes, I will be faithful: fantastically, wildly, saintly faithful, precisely because I am so bottomlessly unfaithful by nature. In love there is no other choice, no more intelligent alternative than faithfulness' asceticism-blindness, or the anarchy of impressionism: here in the chapel the two were side by side. Both are horrid, I want neither: neither marriage's *only*-moral tension paralyzing trees, lakes, gods and parents, nor the ceaselessly on-varying beauty, psychological nuance-nausea of the thousand-and-one lovers, their bodily suicide at the end of the syllogism of pleasure.

What will love remain for me, if here I say my final good-bye both to the meaninglessness of sensuality and to the meaninglessness of faithfulness? Can one ever break down love into compromise-ethics and beastliness, absolute Christianity and absolute naturalness? Will the compromise not fail forever, just as the lonely careering of extremes must fail — of the self-denying man, as well as of the delirium-driven or prosaic Don Juan of free love? When, who have wrecked love so definitely? How can people marry without going mad? How can they go to confession and take communion one day, then go to nuptials the next — how is it possible that some are not turned into a St. Aloysius Gonzaga by the host's heaven-taste, and some others, into brothel-automatons by the wedding's Lethe-taste? How can they bear the paradox of "legalized pleasure"? Why am I getting married? In order to have in front of me all the time, in the shape of allegorical statues, the Christian diptych of moral and nihilism, of the allowed and the forbidden woman? I was profoundly sorry for myself: sorry for my nicely polished black shoes, the large golden buckles, the frill with the slender monogram (in elongated, thin letters, as though reflected along a metal railing), my white gloves, elastic stockings, the new silk hat I was grabbing convulsively: what is the use of all this now? All this civilization, comb, powder

— when I'm such a mess inside? People will notice nothing: they chant their litanies in front of Christ's bleeding effigy, then go about their dinner, look at the play of light dancing on a stained glass window, and still manage to bear their own faces in their mirrors; they get up from their nuptial beds & afterwards go on believing in political ideals; they marry, and afterwards they are happy: how is it possible? How can somebody have one impression and after that, *another* one: this is the mystery of mysteries.

What howling heterogeneities are piercing my tympanum here in the chapel: the sister's figure, the thought of the bride, Christ's crucifix-body hanging like a fish on a hook, the glittering light-life of glass windows, the landscape's self-servingness utterly free from humans, the chapel as part of the family villa and as God-enclosing shell, as an architect's design and as our comfortable nest, I as a "man" starting out on the road of life, and the same I as my father's & mother's backward-looking biological reflex: all these mutually exclusive intentions and objects have surrounded me in their independent, watertight forms, and it was impossible to establish a hierarchy among them.

24.

I started into the ceremonious promise of faithfulness: "Yes, I love my bride above everything else." That was my first-ever sincere declaration of love, sincere to its last atom. The sister was a Baccha and a Gorgon at the same time — who could escape it, if the complicated and diffuse mosaic-light and mosaic-shade dismembered their face to scales? "I love her above all else": whom? what? her? The impression-rag that our knees got pressed to one another on the bench, or rather, the pathetic folly that one should be made happy by such collision of knees? Do I love everything? With some amor fati vacuous to the point of humbug? Myself? My parents? The God dangling on the hook of destiny above the altar? Or do I love, with half-ascetic, half-decadent melancholia, the fundamental fact of the world that our vast love-capacity is ludicrously disproportionate when compared to the available lovables, tiny to the point of invisibility? Do I enjoy the unbearableness of opposition between the sister and the Christ-mask, my bride and my mother, myself and everything? O, dear sister, you blind and prosaic widow — why don't you pull my head into your lap to solve my sufferings with the one possible resolution: by uniting the instant, sensuous chord, and assumed doubt? If I laid my head in your lap now, it would be immaterial if I hate or desire you forever, whether you are beautiful like the trace of sea spumes running up the vertical rock-face, or hideous like a drowned abortion — if I am to marry or become a Thebes hermit: I could feel that an instant exists now, that the nerves of our body rustle together like the feathers of two sleeping birds in the wind, that we must dip our lives into the boundlessness of I-ignorance, like barren buckets into a barren well. But such things never happen; they are the privilege and curse of the mad.

"Yes, I love my bride, I love her. Don't expect me to utter the phrase, I will be faithful to her until death us doth part — this sentence only makes sense in front of the altar, in the God-shade of our vows like holy frenzy. When people say it for bourgeois poetry or legal pedantry, it becomes laughable." The sister gave a startled hiss: "So faithfulness for you is just..." "Forgive my interrupting you. The moment I uttered this I felt you were going to misunderstand me. It is not that I don't feel or don't want faithfulness, and only suffer it as a religious duty and assumed torture: on the contrary, my feeling and need for faithfulness is so great that the only expression worthy of it is the religious one." "Now you are only twisting your words because of me." "Sincerity is made difficult, darned difficult for me if you continue looking at me with the eyes of a judge, of the inquisitor living in a sea of doubt. Would it be better if I said only trite phrases?"

"Don't you see that you take our whole conversation wrong, entirely frivolously? Is your only concern here and now, to express yourself individually — and your only preoccupation, to use this or that phrase instead of this or that word? This is not about trite and individual speech, but about simple facts: about your feelings, about my sister's future happiness." (Why do I mess with these women at all, at all, why don't I stand up and go out to the meadows, to my mother's house, or back to the mayor? What need is there for this? Why don't I kill this woman right away? Why does destiny force me into this lousy swing: either kiss or poison? O, to write a comedy. *The Parcæ's Baboon*: let them laugh their fill.)

"I love her," I said. And afterwards started into something that I knew would lead to scandal: into the description of the unfinished Madonna that I saw the day before in G's studio. Why did I do this? Can one do anything else? If I look into myself, I feel that I am lying about my faithfulness to my bride, that I am lying about the love I feel for the sister — but if I were to say it aloud with so-called "sincerity," I would feel that I am lying even more patently, for I adore my bride with self-effacing pathos, and I hate the sister. I hate her: is it true? Is it not merely that one utters a small slur, then with the automatism of fantasy, stylizes to the slur the insulted body, so that one ends up killing this fictitious body: but the whole is only the dream-play of fantasy, a moment's reflex-twitch, which has nothing in common with reality: the comically-overblown lust to kill, the self-annihilating amorous desire remain forever internal, their clarity, greatness, constancy, causal logic, "irresistibility" account precisely for their nothingness, for their impracticability — such things are equally remote from moral reliability and reality. I realized in despair that I have only "great" feelings: that is, that I have *nothing*, that I am excluded from the world. The only justification of my feelings is, to wreck my life: eternal guarantees of eternal hesitancy.

"Yesterday I saw a picture of the Madonna, it depicts the Annunciation. On the left side of the painting there are a bunch of Japanese quinces with zigzagging twigs breaking into abrupt angles — some of the flowers look like chance red brush traces, others are the faithful replicas of flowers observed with a magnifying glass. Behind them, a greenish-grey wall, its upper edges sharp, as though taken from a geometry textbook, its lower stretches blurred, as though they were a rag fraying into uneven vertical threads, or the dense foliage of a weeping willow. Rain falls: the odd Japanese quince flower is like a bubble rushing skyward among the rain-needles, the other is crushed on the branch or on the ground like a dead bird. Below, in indefinite space-proportion with the flowers and with the larger than rain wall, the Virgin Mary is sitting, drenched, pressed to the ground, almost drowning in the shower. The pigeon of the Holy Ghost is tumbling in the air with wings turned inside out, torn apart: the messenger angel sits with his back turned to the Virgin, fighting the greedy spumes on the stairs of an overflowing pool, not as much as throwing a glance at the sobbing Madonna. Look, somehow this is the symbol of all love, or more broadly, of all ecstasy." "Enough of this, I am going now." With that the sister left me all alone in the church. "She is right, she is right," I whispered with quite unusually strong conviction.

25.

And yet they did give me the girl, the wedding did take place in due course, a hundred people fell ill with indigestion, a hundred got stone drunk, and on the bier of frolicking animals, the "happy" parents shivered: my pale mother, who just lost her son, my pale father, a pale sister, pale old folks — frightened, doubtful, disgusted and full of hatred. In my mother's wedding pallor I finally found the one god I could worship: love's self-consuming absolute degree, that is beyond all human and heavenly concepts. The color of the fiddlers' yellow violins filled my eyes — during the whole banquet I barely had a bite, I only drank and stared at the violins with drunken eyes: the serpentine groove of their f-holes, the strings' resiny hail-spraying on the wood, the big black keys on the violin's neck, one embellished, fret-sawed-flourished hunch of bridges — all the inane, foul music had been for me the underwater swarming of these f-eyed, key-toothed, yellow wave-hipped animals. I forgot everything, for the time the violins filled in the landscape for me: that was the wedding. Sometimes I would only see the spring yellow of a bunch of E-strings, ten to twenty sharp, radiating wires, like sunrays emerging from behind a cloud in a primitive sun-shape — around me everything was a buzzing, leaf-flavored, sharp-lined dawn luminosity. At other times I would only see the violin bodies floundering in darkness, like the warships of Salamis at sea: each one a boat with two gaping holes on the side, as they fall into a wave-vale, like an ovary into the bee-cupped flower; at other times they leap high up, up among the chandelier's nervously, sweatingly blooming candles — there was something wavelike precisely in their undulation *not* reminiscent of a geometric wave-shape, as their wood, stiff, stretched between the shoulder and a wrist, and their movement swung on the bending knees' and the forward-tilted backs' remoter swing. Then came the bows' season of hallucinations, of these strange instruments, between fluttering white peacock-feathers and rapier-points flying to their destination with deathly precision: how white they were, how extremely they tilted to the left or right, like the hysterical scales of some demented balance; and in the end the sounds, too, made an appearance, although not in their musical quality, but only in their barbarian string and noise quality, enhancing the overtones whose growth covered the violins, splaying all across them like thousand-leaved parasites, brimming like the beer-foam over a drunk glass' rims: it was after this two-hour-long violin-shower that I spotted my mother's corpse-white face for the first time.

By that time my father had already left — being seriously ill, he only attended for a few minutes, and was taken back to bed. I decided to go to him without telling anyone, so I shouldn't let anyone talk me out of this visit. Here I could not speak with my mother and, besides, I would have nothing to tell her. I left the room; in the corridor two servants were propping up a stone drunk wedding guest who had atrociously dirtied himself. Disinterested, I asked them who he was and where they were taking him. One of the servants was himself slightly tipsy and with a grin pointed at the bedroom destined for us. I rushed across the little hothouse, up the winding stairs, and entered the room. The sight of the lovely bed utterly paralyzed me: hung with sharply, metallically silvery curtains and veils, among whose folds here and there a pale white lantern or a moon-yellow spring twig was hung — the whole thing was regular-shaped like a crystal, scented like a downward-turned flower-cup, and whimsical like an octopus in nature's drawing-book: the final classicism and vacillating hypothesis of all beauty. This had been built for my wife: somehow it was so unexpected, a sexual metaphor so impossible to connect to their mole-prose, that for a moment I came to believe that I am a poor judge of character, a foolish pessimist who had so far invariably misunderstood the most poetic people, with an utterly psychological obtuseness. Muses, yes, and not Parcæ: everything is in order, and I am unspeakably happy. I pulled aside some twelve veils, all of a different fabric. A couple of the twigs fell on my head, the parchment-paper of a few lanterns knocked against the lace with lisping ts-s: at this point I saw that the sheet was all puked over with that characteristically human-innards-colored, brick-red liquid, the stench of which almost made me faint. "How good that this filth is here! This is the truth — and can one desire a more sublime dowry or wedding present?" Something cracked under my heels: it was a poem, quite obscene, written in underworld cant, about the carnal pleasures of the bridal night. I read the script, of a pornographic range unknown even to me, with well-nigh religious rapture — again I felt that it had to be so, that everything was true as it was. I stuffed the script into my pocket, in my thoughts patted the shoulder of the drunk about to be kicked out, and started to my mother's house.

26.

My father was being stripped by two servants when I entered his bedroom. It had dark blue wallpaper, and the armchair and bed-curtains were also navy blue. How frighteningly different this bed was from the bridal bed — perhaps they differed from each other like beauty from truth in the head of a naïve Plato exegete. I got a bit dizzy, something that with me didn't mean that the objects started swirling around me, but that I saw all the objects as if lifted into me: my eyes suddenly became level with people's foot-soles, with bed-legs, the roots of thin, sky-scraping cypresses, all this accompanied by a peculiar sharpness, the entirely unexpected perfection of the precision of contours: it was my utter clear-sightedness, the total absence of dimness to signal that I was close to fainting. I felt the same now about this huge bed, whose massive black columns towered in front of me with the palm-darkness of a nighttime oasis: the huge tiger-paws it rested on were about the height of my brow, I had to bear them like Atlas bearing the globe — every single object clear like a sun-lit Gothic stained-glass image: how can such petal-thin drawings have such weight, clasping me by the throat, that I can hardly breathe? What is amiss with these beds: the bridal bed, the father's bed, the bed of labor? I saw my wedding-bed: it was a phantasmagoria, an ante-diluvial sponge-fiction, dazzling hypothesis, the etiquette of impossibility, its algebra. And this, in contrast:

the myth of reality, the Doric stage of all conceivable tragedies, the Hercules-mummy of sickness, the one and only architecture I could freely believe in, without being hindered by doubt. Perhaps that was what made me dizzy, not the violins or the wine: here I wasn't constrained to be incredulous, here I could be a nervous impressionist or erudite relativist at ease, here no difference existed between natural instinct and artificial morality — the bed was here, was truly like this, could be no other way, and I could have only one relation to it: that of all-annihilating faith. And of course it was so all-powerful that I no longer felt it to be faith at all.

How could I characterize my "religion" in my mother and father? I have to start with the word "religion," the only sincere one: as a young child I used to confess little else to the priests but that I loved my parents dearer than God, that I kept telling an ivory statuette of Jesus from my father's bedroom to serve my father faithfully, that I used to hold secret liturgies to my father's hands, my mother's bun. How many times I ambled out from the confessional's grids and knee-tormenting steps with blasphemous musings, obstinately and cowardly repeating to myself: I don't want God, I don't want a confessioner, tiger-lily, Florence, I don't even want myself as long as I have my parents. I looked wryly at all the ardors of strangers that were not directed toward their parents: everything that was not parents struck me as naïve, parodic, vulgar. How could I possibly have ended up among women and in marriage? My mother meant love in the world: that perpetually sealed miracle that the relationship between two people is — my mother was the eternal measure of the "other" person's role in life (of course there was never anything to measure). My father, on the other hand, meant the biological identity of child and parent, the tragic mania of perpetual father-mimicry: I felt myself in my father, the body's solitude, the murderous asceticism of eternal unique-past. One is tempted to take it for granted that in life the mother means the biological principle, and the father, the objectivated relationship of affect, extended to two persons, but it was the other way round: I took all my thoughts, taste, manners, textile-sensitivity and hereticism from my father, and was enough of an intellectual and moralist to regard *those* things as biological, instead of the distorted monogram of the navel-chord on my belly. My mother was the eternal "milieu": the love that surrounds, the love that is theater stage, frame, clothes, that is, everything that is not-I, but the surrounding world — so she ended up eroticizing the entire objective world: trees, books, gods, time — the "other" (be it a person or an object) always meant some version of love. In contrast to her, my father did definitely not stand for the external milieu, but my inside, axis, the statue and string of my destiny, that maddening compassion that egoists as a rule feel toward themselves, the mystical ecstasy found not in merging into God but in merging into I-loneliness: the everlasting melancholia over the unsolvable mystery of the "I"; the shivering around the body, the profile, my sins, the hazard of ambitions, the dull inebriation from the irrationality of "personality." My mother's every gesture, glance, Madonna-rhythm made me believe that the entire surrounding world wanted to establish a love relationship with me: that the rivers flow toward me, that I am the bridges' last, blessed pillar, that my thick hair is a nest for the birds, that my black-rimmed stoned ring finger is the sun-dial's minute hand: I was always flooded by the world as a wound is flooded with blood — but when I thought about my father, I felt the solitariness of man, the foolish nothingness of the entire world around the grotesque reed that is "man," and at such times I felt a desperate love for the "impossibility of love."

Definitions, metaphors, botched-up myths are all useless when set against their reality: there is no way to express the absolute sense of reality that only the parents can mean; for myself, the sole necessity — outwards, for others, the classical nihil.

27.

When the two houseboys peeled off the clothes from my father's sick body, the image was like a Descent from the Cross: descent on the dark blue sea bottom, next to a clock with old-fashioned glass bell, where the place of the wood of the cross' raw objectivity is taken by the canopy bed's bulging columns. How is it possible that my father is suffering? To heal him — that didn't cross my mind: suicide was the sole possibility. In my thinking of extremes there was no trace of adolescent sentimentalism: my father was reality, the reality of my own existence, and that can hardly be distinguished from the thought of death. His favorite objects & all kinds of clothes lay scattered in the frightening hierarchy of intimacy: propped up against the cabinet, the walking-stick, on the cabinet's marble sheet, the silk hat and white gloves — and they hovered between him (that is, me) and the outer world: on the wrinkles of the freshly ironed gloves the barren dialogue of the self with the outer world showed especially clearly. The leather looked freshly washed, stiff, a formula — and at the same time, utterly crumpled, shelled; obviously in time he had "*hardly* used" them, but had worn them *out*, "consumed" them in intensity. Who triumphed: the nervous, trembling hand, or the white starch? Neither — they never as much as met. And the walking-stick with its glossy black stalk and silver knob, what did it mean most: the walk up the palace stairs, in conformity with etiquette, or the convulsive holding-on of a fist, the weakness, inner fever, the prop's eternal sincerity? How provocative, how rapier-like and woundingly mundane its slenderness, how knotty, senescent, feeble-pulsed and corpse-like its knob! And there were the cast-off clothes that no longer displayed any ambiguity or outward-turning mask: the vest, tie, the day shirt, the stockings — that is, one's *true* corpse, in contrast to the body, the way in which our body's true companions are the clothes of women, not their body. You dear shirt: with your snowy lace and large pool of sweat, how you extinguished my wife, myself, everything. Why did you allow me "deeds" — who needs life-story, ethics, event? I have never felt a profounder pathos than the categorical anti-Eros swelling down my throat like a giant tide; it is irrelevant that this anti-Eros is merely a mutation of true eros — at that moment I considered and interpreted it as being anti-love, that's how I arrived at my conclusions. Psychological revelations bore me to high heaven, generally I'm bored by everything that can be reduced to the childish scheme, "all his life he had believed this thing to be x, whereas in reality it was y."

My relationship to my father was rendered especially tragic by the fact that he had remained a child all his life, he utterly lacked all practical sense, only his richness and title allowed him to feature as a statesman: he lacked the gift for paradox, sophistry, logical sadism that suffused my self-ego — his entire life, body, breathing and gaze were inexpressibly the absurd, of which he had never as much as dreamt (although who could tell?); he had always considered himself the most rule-abiding, most respectable of human beings, who on principle loathed all forms of eccentricity. I keenly felt my inferiority to him — the pettiness of *intellectual* paradox, as compared to the sublime of the paradox dwelling in digestion, the movements of the hand, the growth of the hair; I clearly knew that this or that anarchic thought of mine was nothing more than the father's gesture exchanged into the beggar's currency of language or logic — for instance, the movement with which he sank the sugar into his coffee, or with which he wiped the cross before kissing it: when I off-handedly told him those thoughts, he was mortified at seeing that I was so different from him.

They never educated me, simply because there had never been an "I"; I have always been my father & mother. I have no existence, and here by my father's bedside, one or two hours after my wedding, I was taking the vow to my father in orphic rapture

(that was my wedding): that I don't need, and don't even want,
to "exist." I can have only one task in life: to press into the world,
by diplomacy and clumsy prophecy, by murders and troubadour-
rhymes, with religious bigotry and relentless mathematics, my
father's anatomy, to drag his body around among the people:
my entire life will be, can be nothing else but a frenzied procession, bearing my father's sacred body on my shoulder, carrying
it around in Venice on a gondola, stuck into the bridges' engage-
ment rings like a pale finger, taking it around above cannon fire
in my battles against emperor or pope like a flower on a Ghibelline or Guelf coat-of-arms; that I shall deposit it on the pillows
of nuptial beds like a corpse to frighten girls, this wedding-gift
redolent of the grave; that I shall carry it to churches like a relic
covered in wonder-resin, a provoking god flung like a glove (how
yellow!) into the slowly clotting waters of prayer; I shall carry it
to inquisitorial torture chambers and brothels, to honeycombs,
forests, hospitals, circuses. I will do so because I recoil from rhetoric, and there is no-one who is simpler than you, father.

Although my love for you has estranged me from Christ, your
suffering has nevertheless been Christ-like: you made me feel the
eternal "Christology" and the eternal nihilism of suffering, its
blind biological irrationality. If I wanted to recur to symbols (so
unworthy of you), I could start right away — in the world there is
more allegory than reality, the amount of allegory far exceeds that
of reality: even now, on your cabinet, the Pietà stands in front of
the punctually ticking French clock — on the Madonna's knees
with high spume-arching abdomen, with feet dangling down to
the left and twisted head falling even lower down to the right,
like the Christian bridge of bodily misery, the Jewish rainbow of
all unsolved pathologies: here love and suffering were restricted
to one sole figure, to one man, men had other men kill a man for
man — the love that willed this murder is a human sickness that
attacks only man, and is the precondition or product of the body,

of personality, of moral transformed into logic. Sharp individuality, sharp logic: that was the message of the statue's Gothic folly.

But there was more to the room: the room was blue, dark, warm, dizzying with the hybridized odors of medicine, into which the bed's colossal tassels hung like blossoming bells. These things had precious little of the personal, logical, or Christian about them; they were the seducing breath of nature, of eternal "what, for God's sake, is this, and wherefore?" — of the whole material existence; the inebriation, the eros as the perfume of every object: the narcosis of the paleolithic, backward-rooting family. Can there be a greater contrast than the one between Golgotha's raw suffering-nudity and the cotton-wool idyll of childhood homeliness? My father's bedroom now merged these two for me: I knew that there is nothing else in the world but universal darkness, which was disrupted along a single line by my father's yellow body of woes, and I knew that the entire world is, in spite of all: love; that drawer-handles, piano keys, figures in the carpet and half-stale medicine all go on withering and ripening from the same, lurking-bursting ecstasy. It was also clear that my relationship to women and to my wife could not feature at either end of the alternative: neither at "the one-and-only father's suffering-loneliness," nor at the orphic love-throbbing of all atoms.

28

When the servants left and the candles burnt on mutely on the right-hand bedstand (never before had I experienced such flame-muteness: every single candle was an enigma of deafness), we felt that we would hardly talk. I knew well that I didn't want this marriage to happen. I knew well that he didn't want this marriage to happen. It nevertheless came to pass due to some ridiculous treason which didn't matter in the least: we are both selfish enough to go on adoring one another, whoever happens to be around.

To adore one another? Can we — is it worth? What could we do for one another? Either succumb to our emotions in solitude, letting the world's most electric, colorful flower bloom in the sterile night of loneliness, or, instead of this meaninglessly isolated flower, "act": when giving, helping each other, sacrificing ourselves for the other we distort our formless love to the point of parody and render love ridiculous to ourselves, even triggering feelings of confusion, fatigue, unbearable unease in the other. So what can life's primordial pathos and mania achieve: neither lonely ecstasy nor ecstasy converted into action can satisfy the one who loves, or the subject of this love. Is love then the instinct of rabid realism, or of "fait accompli"-faced nothingness? I keep repeating to myself with sadistic perspicuity that I need no wife, nuptial bed, or other Tanagra trinket when I can have my father's "love-elephant": but isn't barrenness grafted onto this idolatrous vow as much as it is grafted onto trite sex-gibberish? Isn't the father and mother more completely annihilated than the woman?

The parents' essence is their bodies, their material being-in-this-world: it is them we saw first — they became the world once and for all. Mountains, fires, waters, clouds, the world's fabled components and "primordial" elements: what a far cry from being components, let alone "primordial" elements for us. They are but naïve, hypothetical aquarelles when set against the parent's body — the father's nose, the mother's lap, the father's voice, the mother's shadow: those are the primordial elements; those silhouettes, chance happenings, momentary perspectives of the parents, on which "portæ inferi non prævalebunt."[1] And now, when I see my father sick, I feel the full horror of the fact that death here truly means complete annihilation, for it is reality itself, the reality-denominator and reality-inductor of the whole world, which ceases to exist. When she appeared, when she was in the most white-hot focal point of worship, woman had never been a body of such primordial-element value: when she appeared in our lives, we had already seen theater coulisses and lies, we already knew that there is a so-called "world" outside, apart from the parents, which is nothing but marketplace buffoonery, and out-of-tune competition to the sacred, more-lasting-than-bronze ortho-doxy of the children's room. It is from this "pseudo" background that woman comes forth, and she cannot force our incredulity into faith. In fact, in relation to the parents, the word "faith" is utterly wrong and superfluously psychologizing, as is the word "doubt" in relation to women: the parent simply *is*, the woman simply *isn't*. The parents are to their deaths with absolutely equal intensity, for the gradually estranged child just as much as for the eternal worshippers — even he who never cared a continental about his mother or father knows that they represent something absolute in the world, moreover, that only they can stand for the dictionary meaning of the word "absolute." Woman doesn't live to her dying day in this white-hot or cold prestige of reality: she dies soon after the end of life in two, grows cold, simply because it was *her* we wanted as a woman, as an individual — while we didn't want the parents: them we saw first and they meant reality, the not-I. What a fundamental distinction: my father I saw when I hadn't seen anything else yet, so I learned that reality, an outer world exists. Woman? Her I sought with a special instinct, I have always positively felt that she is a part of reality who interests a mapped-off, isolated part of my body; what binds me to her is emotion, need. And despite this yawning, unsurpassable diffe-rence, how close the two kinds of love really are. To my father I am bound by savage feeling because originally, at the onset of my idol-liaison, *no* feeling featured, I was not driven to him by the limited selection of special instinct; but woman cannot ever have credit because I want her; she was born dead, because life-instinct perpetually affirms her. When a woman dies physically, it is only a psychological nuance, lyrical teint that my soul loses or gains; her death doesn't touch on the issues of "being or non-being," for we can only perceive women in line with the extravagantly idealist recipe of a Berkeley: as enticing hallucinations. But if a father dies bodily, everything, the whole of reality falls apart. This is a true reality-allure in parents, this razor-sharp "to be absolutely," and after death, this equally sharp, inorganic "absolutely-not-to-be"; utterly real reality cannot be adorned with the fioriture of doubt, it cannot be mitigated, made labile: they either are or are not, and have no transitional forms (those being the realm of affairs with women). The body of the woman of whom I first, foremost, and hindmost desire the body is not significant — the father and mother, to whom I am bound by no sensuality at all, who as "flesh" are nil for me, count first and foremost as bodies, for those bodies of theirs are the "world," "existing reality," once and for all time.

How interesting this twofold exigency for a body — as sensual gratification and as passive reality! How awkward it is for the grown-up child to see this duality: the father's body, which is reality incarnate, and nevertheless mortal, and the world's mountain-, water-, and air-body, which for him can be at most pseudo-reality, a Luciferian theater setting — but which will nevertheless outlive the father, is perhaps even everlasting! I experienced such torment of impotence by his sickbed that I could have killed someone. Who can bear it, who can will it, that my father should perish? And if he must perish, why don't I sit near him to pant in his ear in one breath, that there is nothing else in the whole world for me but him, that he is the daybreak and I, the evening, that he is the tree and I, its shadow, that he is the question and I, the answer, he is the one semicircle and I the other, he is the lock and I am the key: in other words, that it is an utterly limited system, excluding everything on earth, of which we two are the sole components, our concrete bodily reality, in whose closed electric circuit nobody can interfere, neither God, nor nature, thought, or time.

And all this in vain, for love is powerless — love cannot ease pain, it cannot defeat death. Then what's the use of it? Is it merely destiny playing its tricks on us? That bodily love shall cool in time is not a pity; it can always be rekindled with someone else, and even in its fulfillments it is perpetually a death metaphor: but the love of the parent is not melancholy, it has no act of fulfillment, therefore no perfume of death either; woman is like liquid oozing from a broken vase, while the father is like water splashed on the cobblestones by a cruel servant. If life so wills that my father, this tragic-frothed well of love, should dry up and crumble, then I cannot be bound by any kind of moral in this life: then here the highest principle is so immoral that I am free — free to open seals, blather out secrets, slaughter mercenary armies without cause or aim, make a mockery of faiths: all these are but a trifle as compared to the depravity of the life-cause.

How can we, children, bear the frightful significance of those moments when the parents are still here, living? I'm driven to say that blessed are the children who die before their progenitors: but can it be a blessing to see their contorted faces, in direr agony than ourselves? Come then, love and reality, my life's two black peacocks, who seem meek fowls when you approach facing me, but when you turn one step away and I look in your direction, you immediately spread your giant fans, your pitch-black, haughty, prudish, murderous feathers. Love? mere rose-shaped vanity. Reality? innocent victim of forever-imminent death. Is this why people live? But it's impossible — impossible that anyone could live for such.

Life runs on two planes: one is of pure existence, preserving and continuing existence — the other is the deathly chaos and power of *fake* life-contents, purposes and meanings of life that are the former's products: as if the whole grand biological energy-pageant, nature's ontology-hysteria had no other aim but to produce the greatest possible quantity of *counter*-life, be-side-life, outside-nature: feelings, instincts, tools, which, albeit having no power to realize death definitely and universally, continue showing to the end of time the panorama of Non-Being, Not-Worth, Absolute Lie, leaving us no respite.

Here we are, the two of us, my father and I: is there anything greater, more intensive, than our relation beyond relation? And this will come to nothing, entirely naught, when neither he nor I will be alive anymore. And since this is the way it has to be, why am I not in love with time, the future of mankind, and other such abstraction-fetishes tailored to cretins? The race, the grand-child, the other, the future: in reality all that interests no-one — although that is the only thing that interests "life"; how is it possible that the universal foundational law of life, and the in-dividual laws of the individuals who are the repositories of that law, should clash so evidently? There are no greater imaginable enemies than the power that makes my heart beat ("life") on the one hand, and I myself on the other hand — my individual im-pressions, intentions, habits, thoughts, relationships. Who is the real one here? Is there a real one? Are these indeed two different things? Could it be possible that this whole life process along time's generous riverbed is a thoroughly primitive and, from time's perspective, homogeneous process — but its single cross-sections are nevertheless infinitely complicated, self-serving, oblivious of universal process and purpose? Could this not be the logically well-nigh mutually exclusive relationship between "life" and "humans"?

Whoever has loved truly could not help but be struck by this question *&* all its forking paradoxes at the second, nay, the very first kiss. Does "life" *originally* want its most alive parts, humans, to be at the same time also the most counter-to-life on life's re-volving stage — or is it an unforeseen error, and the individual souls, loves, of humans are nothing but diseases previously not reckoned with, that "annoy" the universal life-process? And what is almost identical to the former issue: can the question of the relation between existence and the human being, amorphous biological flux and the shaped human individual isolated into nuances, be resolved from nature itself, within nature, or is theological admixture necessary? And the next question: is it indeed necessary to "grasp"? Is the instinct of the will to grasp not a passing disease of the human organism? Is there any justified question, at all? And yet, who could decide whether this or that question is merely a nerve disorder, or logically justified?

29.

After such a "perpetuum mobile" sweep of questions, and especially after the complete denial of women formulated before the father, he felt a mad desire to be near a woman; of course the word "desire" is merely a distant approximation of what the young man experienced. As the Antichrist to come will be nothing else but the most positive, affirmative definition of Christ, so this "woman equals naught" idea delineated, with the most fastidious plasticism, the bodily portrait of a woman: of one particular woman, whom he immediately pictured. He decided to pay her a visit that very night: because the woman was known to be a "great coquette," he didn't feel that tinge of immorality that would have assailed him, had he visited one of his mistresses instead. Some women tended to awaken his primordial, tormenting moral insanity, while others, his equally primordial, tormenting moral sanity: in the shape of passionate pangs of conscience setting in motion sizable primum malum allegories. He was just as extreme in his morals as in his other affairs: sometimes the world's filthiest and most decorative sin would appear to him as mere "impression," the half-mathematical, half-sensorial, empty constellation of colors, sounds, structural tricks, beyond the realm of logic & ethics — perhaps what the English call "pattern." At other times the most innocent thought or perception (for instance, the absolutely comfortable — for such a thing exists! — position of the pillow under the head; the degree of coldness of a glass of water) seemed to him a direct, tactile impression of Satan, of infinite evil. This female portrait that now came to mind was such a "pattern" in its absolute independence from morality — an independence which, needless to say, only a moral person would enjoy in such concrete form.

If he wanted to characterize that woman quite schematically, then he would have had to sketch on his logical, geometrical, or pictorial blackboard some kind of ideal compound of a bowstring's vibrating-taut linearity and the eternal budding, from spheres into spheres, of clouds, whipped cream, and soap bubbles. Slender skyward radiation with a geyser's fan-spread, cool, pearl-bubbling nature-gothic — and horizontal leaves, fallen blossoms on a lake surface, powdery mushroom umbrellas came together in her figure. This sweetly struggling and almost tragically reconciled duality was felt in all her movements, even if she stood still or slept, shriveled up on a sofa. The reason for this was the encounter between an extraordinarily sharp skeleton, all abrupt angularities and protrusions of joints, and an extraordinarily indolent, muscle-less, almost muddily splaying flesh-system: all bones, without appearing thin, and all undulating flesh, without for a moment inviting the fruit-metaphors one is in the habit of hanging around the "mature" woman's neck. Her shins were a perfect image of this bone-severity and flesh-abandon: big ankle-bone, shooting abrupt petals of shadow beneath; very slender ankle; thick shin-bone, from which flesh fluttered into space like thick and soft steppe-grass combed into the wind. Try as she may to cast it into geometrical vase and fish molds with colored and net stockings, her flesh obstinately recalled rolling,

half-solidified foam: one can see such forms on waterfalls in
winter — all spumes, pearls, ovals, and snakes, but the whole is
stiffened, even though thaw, fresh water oozing onto it, and the
ceaseless opalescent sport of sun and shadow make it perhaps
even more complicatedly alive and unsettling than if it were cascading freely. Such dogmatic knotting of bones and that utterly
muscle-less silk-rag tumbling of flesh struck one as peculiarly
childish: although her whole personality shone its black light-
beams from the midst of the great experience-calyx of astuteness
and passion, the body was provocatively pubertal, with all puberty's awkward zigzags and sensual daydreaming. How characteristic the relationship of the knee and the hanging flesh-sail that
followed: the knee was an Indian mace pilfered from some children's book, with the bleeding edges and angles of the tiger-head,
but the flesh running up to the hips was like a velvet rug hung
from a parapet, a neglected flag, or sail. This flesh-sail was entirely the handmaid of gravity and of armchairs: when she stood,
it trickled along the bones, padding them with a poultice, as the
slender, legal article-snaking leaves, hardly distinguishable from
the stem, wrap themselves around the stem on certain tall plants;
when she sat, it splayed to the left *&* right of the knee like some
translucent, curtain-membrane fin that rests on rockface, while
the water stirs it to and fro; when she lay down, it got crumpled
like her skirt or blouse. The most characteristic feature of this
muscle-less flesh, bare skin padded out with elastic mash, was
its *clothing*-nature: it settled into the different postures of the
flesh as a bell-voiced skirt or butterfly-nerved cloak. Following
some of her movements you could almost see how this wealth of
stalactites and stalagmites is rearranged in the new distribution
of bones and armrests, how it seeks ever anew the lowest points;
like a fawning creeper, with its brownish flowers it wrapped
itself around the gothic branches. If one touched it, one could
simultaneously feel the deathly skeleton's requiem-keyboard *&*

the eternal biological fermentation, born of water and longing to return to water: just as one could feel in women's light summer handbags the thin silk's humming naught and inside, the clattering hardness of powder and make-up boxes.

Her hips were preposterously narrow, like the point between the ends of an hourglass — therefore it drew attention to the bodies spiraling off upwards and downwards: upwards those spirals were divided into the two small breasts' focal points, whereas downwards, into the wide geometries of two bubbles. Although the bubble beneath was large like certain solitary, sharply delineated clouds on certain spring skies, and the two small globes upwards were merely fleeting anatomical trills, one felt these two forms, of such different sizes, to be no less symmetrical than an hourglass' identical cones. Around the hips the antithesis of bone and foam, string and guilder rose was pushed ad absurdum into the antithesis of naught (for the hips' narrowness was indeed the Delphic nil) and eternal onward-sporulation. What was the bubble beneath (coming into view especially when she sat on the low clavicembalo stool) if not a giant underwater jellyfish: rag, glass, geometrical ideal, deranged hormone, and the pattern of primeval beings' primitive reproduction. Everybody who looked at her perceived those hips as the gradually tightened loop on a cord, which from infinitely narrow strings suddenly becomes a knot with no volume whatsoever: and the bubble underneath, to be the first, temporary state of the division into grapes, a springboard of fissiparous generation.

The bubble underneath, hips and breasts: in fact, three phases of an incredibly dense spiraling line imagined to be alive — the bubbles were the outermost, nearly-dissolving, haircut-fringe rings; the hips were the spiral's core, starting-point (that is, only an abstract place), while the breasts would be placed between this abstract point and the ultimate circling-off in all directions: half, a statue of center-point sensuality (through their nipples), and half, the model of sensuality with a suggestion of trickling off to the four cardinal directions, through their absorption into the boyish chest. Big breasts don't give such sense of duality between point and mist, blood-buttoned origo and the monotonous concentricity of infinite circles: here, however, revolving became visible — the breasts were like a ceaselessly turning bull's-eye behind a faintly lit silk lampshade. At those blessed indeterminacies, where the mammae turn into breastbone, tide into ebb, one felt the same thing as on the edge of turning wheels: the physical, algebraic measure of speed, the palpable bravura of tempo, but also the shapelessness of the wheel's margin — red, blue, yellow are all dulled down to ashen grey, ornaments all sink into one single arc-line: these girlish breasts were fireworks, trembling candle-flames crying out like snake-tongue, and at the same time candle snuffers, shady cones, furrily benumbed, rounded silence. Despite all their nuance-meagreness (they sat on the chest like unexpectedly modulating D-major sharps in a sonata fragment: the work in its entirety is "boy," only this or that transitional tonality is "girl") they were also not exempt from the muscle-less rhythm of her other flesh, and so were able to stumble from their Platonic discretion to forthright Polynesian barbarism, taking on the disguise of a chipped wineskin, lead weight put in a stocking, knocked-off bowling pins. Sometimes the two breasts hung from her neck like two jewels, pearls, or silk scarves, pinned-on big green leaves with an odd, scrawny, brick-colored little flower in their center: while with some of her gestures the breasts merged organically into the body, to the extent of no longer seeming outward but rather, inward forms (glands ripened to feverishness, lightly swollen membrane-wigs) — with other movements, they almost tore off from the body, rolling to and fro in her blouse without leash or stalk, like lemon seeds fallen into the tea that one tries in vain to fish out with a teaspoon. One could hardly imagine anything more beautiful than this incessant play between the regularity of electric wave-rings and the drunken squandering-away of billiard balls.

Her gait guaranteed enticing syncopation: her legs were not set beautifully or in a chic manner, but rather, slightly inwards, using for foot soles all surface that could, with the authority of medicine, be declared sole; quite independently of this, she trod with highly stylized, childish ballerina-imitating suppleness — the soles slapped hard on the floor, the blunt columns of the heels turned with difficulty, creaking (like a slowed-down rattle); yet this shapeless rattle radiated a strange, half-hearted grace, amateurish and therefore angelic histrionics. What can an excessively greedy, babyishly clapping, pilfered-from-Frescobaldi sense of rhythm achieve, if its instrument is: bamboo bones and algae flesh? Her only body part exempt from the fundamental scheme were her hands. Here it was not effects of modulation, those were unified and individual, absolutely related to the body in their movement, while in their anatomy utterly alien to it. The wrists' closing jewel related to the hips' narrowness as the *agrément de la même pièce* in old music to the main theme: nothingness' elegance with two oriental ornaments — the bone's grave, fatal carbuncle, and the aorta's live-green pearl. But this naught-frill was not followed by such characteristic forms as the breasts or bubbles. Shapeless fingers a bit on the thick side — glass-holding, man-caressing, or keyboard-searching movement went through them as a hailstorm with nut-size ice goes through the thick-stemmed, languid vegetables, hitting them from the right, cutting into them from the left: in aiming, chasing, and, above all, *mis*-handling. No movement of her hand was identical to itself, the outlines of the intention stood apart from the contour of the fingers, like the engineers' straightened, vertical, punctual design of the Tower of Pisa behind the leaning real-life one. In those hands there was some kind of workmen's positivism, rawer sensuality (different from the partly mathematical, partly floral erotics of the whole nude), which could be well observed at her meals: in her drinking water, biting into bread, in her words squeezed through the food; some not feminine but rather, fogey-like gourmandizing, which of course went together swimmingly with the whole body, like a bitter-astringent scent, "souvenir de village." Thus her hands were a curious hybrid between salon, farmstead, willpower, and inertia. For the essence of the whole woman was condensed in her childish stubbornness, in her obdurate clinging-on: hence the hysterical shapelessness and precision of her purposeful movements. Those "non-refined" hands related to the fastidiousness of the compass and tweezers as crab claws: they were not precise but frantically tenacious, which compensated for everything. Because whatever they grasped, they would grasp thoroughly, and for good, and for this very reason, she had "clumsy" movements: she would hold a glass at the most impossible place, a man's head in the most inhuman manner, a piano key in the most flower-shredding style, with a predator's blind rapaciousness: in other words, hands which live ceaselessly in the trance of possession, so characteristic of the children's room. — And her face? the hair, eyes, mouth? There the physical and botanical pattern no longer holds, there the "human" begins, and the young man was overcome by some kind of demonic pudicity, rebellious piety, as he touched on this concept.

"Let's go to her." He kissed his father's hand, harrowed his brow, eyelids, and cheeks with the Pietà statue's indisputable thorns of sadness, and slipped out through a flush door.

30.

There were two places in the town that could be called, with entirely misleading exaggeration, but nevertheless with some truth, "brothels." Truth, because what ruled in those places was money and utter lawlessness, and untruthfully, because both "houses" (yet another sinful imprecision — in fact neither resembled a "house") were so antique, so full of superstitious, mythical etiquette (however ridiculous that word looks in the present connection), of historical memories, liturgy, so shot through with complications of feminine hierarchy, that the ghostly homogeneity for which such places are sought out turned quite complicated, akin to entrance examinations to masonic lodges, Buddhist sects, or amateur medical academies. The essential difference between the two houses, however, was not in their diverging traditions, but in their geographical location: one of them was deep inside the earth, in an age-old house's cellars, the other outside the town, in a place completely (*completely*) grown over with flowers and brambles — the one was love as eternal night, the other, love as perpetual flowering. The woman who came to his mind earlier and whom he now wanted to visit lived in the "night."

On this symbolic-true wedding night (is it not *truthful* that, if he had spent one half of it with the father, crumpled in sickness' shell, he should spend the other half in a brothel?) he was in such a mood that he found it infinitely important, characteristic, and satisfying down to the smallest detail, that the love-den should be black: midnight, underground, moleish, mystical. Why *must* at least one of the brothels be so netherworldly? Because throughout his life the most important component of love had been its secrecy, the furtiveness, the black mask: sometimes light silk mask (small fibs), at other times bleeding self-distortions, like in the mourners of ancient funerals (his lifelong, eternal lies made to God).

Pudicity is a secret, an eternal grabbing for cover, for blackness: how many times we ratiocinate through and through whether this pudicity is merely a social convention or, on the contrary, a primordial instinct, without ever being able to come to terms with it (probably because the question is put erroneously from the start). How often we dream the utopias of complete erotic freedom, in which not the slightest trace of freedom is possible, for in love we are *not-free*, and this almost biological bondage (our pudicity has thoroughly changed the tonality even of our most liberal bacchanals with their "paradisiac," "golden-age," "Atlantis" coitus-street-organs). In vain all Renaissance haughtiness, in vain we set up gigantic Venus statues in our squeezed-in staircases, in vain we hung transparent golden veils on dancers and had impudic bodily parts graven into the gemstones of seal rings: pudicity rests with us, the momentary fever-ritual of blushing is well alive and kicking, like an inextinguishable epidemic — a whole gamut of things are "not free." Perhaps we are doomed to continue asking to the end of time whether it is not free due to ethics, biology, irrationality, or business — who could tell if at the onset of pudicity's world-historical career stands nature, money, or some arbitrary god? And it is salutary to be so, this ambiguity is the sweet tragedy of pudicity: this is its thousandfold more-than-obvious refutability, this is its glaring, mad asceticism and its no less glaring commercial profit from the trade in boys and girls. How barren is all historical "criticism" here (it is always barren, of course, when faced with historical givens): how naïve it would be to laugh at a salon or family where man and woman could only ever converse, up to the wedding night, in the presence of a stranger, a "garde," and exclusively about the most trivial things, not even touching on the theme of love: if the man starts talking about the meeting of flowers and sunlight, the "garde" starts fanning herself more rapidly, signaling that this is already forbidden territory; who could be so limited as to thunder and spit fire against such an arrangement in the name of "nature" (*who's who,* since we are at it), pronouncing it a derailment? For isn't it the very essence of love, of sex, that we don't know what to do with it, while having to do it all the time: if we don't, we starve to death, but we have no inkling in what form to have it, we don't even know if it has any specific form. Can anyone whole-heartedly say that being enclosed among "gardes" is an "error" and total, so-called animal freedom is "right"? Does there exist, can there exist right and wrong with such an absolutely positive and absolutely shapeless instinct: isn't that question rather like asking, what is the right, the true form of water — a lake or a glass, a waterfall or a vase? Pudicity has always been a *fact* of life: sometimes raving horror at one's own body, sometimes salon posturing, sometimes religious mania, sometimes annoying neurosis — but it has been there all the time.

And here, with pudicity, lie begins, perhaps the most important part of love: perhaps its root, perhaps its fruit, perhaps the cause, perhaps the purpose of its existence, but in any case its essential organ. The thick or trimmed bushes of genitalia can be a protective mask or provocative blazon: they can be the ancient lie, or ancient sincerity, of "bios" — the social continuation of this zoological symptom is quite obviously only the ancient lie — and all love must always lie, the most nauseatingly legal just as much as the most monotonously unlawful — both have to hang on themselves kreutzer or millions-worth of fake beards.

Love starts with the denial of love — sometimes even to ourselves, but certainly to our fellow humans. Later on, with some routine, we can even make a comic cult of sincerity, confessing every single flaring-up and flirt — but this is always "sincerity," not love, so it doesn't count. Let this, always already blurred, unlocalizable "beginning" in our life (for all appoint and stylize, retroactively, their "first-ever" erotic stirring) be an actress' face in the children's theater, a statue in front of our aunt's fireplace-mirror, or a possibility of onanizing discovered quite by chance: in each case we kept it quiet after coming to know it. First and foremost, we kept it quiet, lips sealed and teeth pressed tight, before our parents, like one who really has no inkling of pleasure. Why do we keep it secret? Is it because it is so horribly simple, or so horribly complex? Onanism is simple: and in its very simplicity it resembles murder, for instance, which our judges would often punish with death. Pleasure's "simplicity," howling obviousness, its always ubiquitous handiness by default tempts one to secrecy, to covering it up with a lie. When he first discovers pleasure, the child is like a layman who has found large gold lumps in a mining engineer's bedroom, whereas the engineer would dig tunnels through the earth, based on the most complicated maps, to get a few grams of gold: thus in despair, the layman keeps the ridiculously "simple" method secret — i.e., that you only need to lift the gold from the room's floor. The whole of life, all work, physical and spiritual, is awfully long and ramified: in contrast to them, pleasure is a sudden cross-cut, shortening, aerial line, like a mathematician's "elegant" solution that cancels the intervening steps. Often this is what triggers, compulsively, the instinct of lying: the unexpected, excessive simplicity of the ways of sex.

At other times, on the contrary, it is the indefatigable and unanalyzable complexity, like in the example above, that he experienced in his early childhood: a small nude statue in front of the mirror. There was a peculiar contrast between the facing, real breasts and the dimly hovering back, only known from the mirror. Here the thing's "sex" nature was lent by the interrogations of an infantile logic, of reality and mirror reflection, recto and verso, then of the "back seen from the front" and "front seen from the back": in general, the excitement over the almost untraceable *complexity*. Later, as an adult, whenever he drank strong but sweet wine, he was reminded of that statue, for if he swallowed a draught, he would feel at once the serene golden luminosity of sugar on his palate, and the darkness of heat, of alcohol in his chest — in his child's eye, the statue's real breasts and reflected back were in some such relation: the one a sweetness, the other, a numbing of the limbs. Can one share these analytical derailments? No. One can only deny them, lie about them.

Thus, the murderous *simplicity* of one organ or another and the unfathomable *complexity* of one state of mind or another, are equally the school of lying: and can we ever produce anything else in Venus' gardens than such excessively simple mechanisms and such excessively complicated psychologies — in other words, can we produce anything else but lies? Lies which never end: the world will always be full of religions, statues, theaters, music-hall songs that will all speak about love, make an attempt at love — and the selfsame world will of course be full of people who feel compelled to live their meekest love metaphors and their wildest love scenes behind shutters falling with a loud clatter, in soundless nights, eerie dens, hidden magic altars, blackmail-prone rendezvous places. Whence this parallel, often unintelligible, in the life of mankind, between the eternal ostentation and eternal hiding of love? In the theater girls and boys watch together the inexhaustible bodily and psychic variations of love, yet from the moment they leave the theater, even the most innocent things are forbidden. Or is our world's incessant speaking about little else than love not the evidence of the drowning into subjective secrets, of all love? For *many* people, love is a free theme, a free ambition — for few people, especially two, it instantly becomes the impenetrable wire fence of taboos. The young man could only see it so: everything spoke about love, but he was never allowed to utter a single word about his love. What young boy would this duality not have intrigued?

So it was fitting that one of the pleasure-dens should be in a cellar: the barren well of denial. Will we go on to die like this? On the summit or in the depths of a bleeding, tormenting pagoda of lies? Deceiving, leaving in error all mothers and fathers, wives, mistresses, friends? Couldn't it be possible to summon them and confide that we have lied to them all, every moment of our lives? For in vain we keep repeating to ourselves that lying is no sin, & not a subjective trait of the psyche, but the ontological backbone of love (maybe of existence itself): still, it is wrong, a ballast, exhausting and mean, and if you manage to get rid of it, you instantly feel better. It is loathsome to pour medicine into the wife's spoon with the hand that has combed the mistress' hair a short while ago; it is loathsome to answer the mistress' reproachful question, "you are now thinking of your ailing wife," with "No, not at all!" — tiresome & disillusioning. But it is inevitably so, because childhood already started off with secrecy, for each and every person is forced to inhabit the untrustworthy night of subjectivity, and that night cannot be but anarchic, inhuman, amorphous.

People have no idea to what extent they have turned love into a *logical* procedure, although it is made up of only two concrete parts: the fictitious formalism of coitus, and the capriciously to-and-froing reality-moments of uncontrollable impressionist moods. But because they have insisted on turning love into logic, they forced everybody into relentless lying. Such a characteristic love-turned-into-logic is the love associated with monogamy and terribly long time-spans. As we said before, to attack the institutions (to use a word too boring even to pronounce) born of the misprision and total distortion of love, would be stark raving lunacy — yet it is a fact that such "turning into logic" is the best way of educating into mendaciousness. It is a fact that, while one feels attracted to one particular woman, another woman, or several for that matter, may appear every bit as attractive — whereas it is "logical" that, where one woman is found attractive, the other is not: what is meant here by "logical" is of course not something "correctly deduced," but always something modeled on an abstract imagining. How many times have we all cried out in despair: "I want nothing else but the etiquette of coitus I was educated into, & the individual reality of the atmosphere emanating from this or that female portrait" — while the women and the odd emerging god speak about fidelity, children, kharis, salvation through one another, and self-sacrifice: when I never want any of those. Why don't we teach these arrogant women and dilettante gods once and for all what, in love, are essentials & logical nonsense? Why do we take on the exhausting, murderous lies of marriage, martyrdom, children's crying, for the sake of the ignorami?

The young man was well aware that the absolute revolt against all moral (not some "revolution," "free thinking," or anything of the kind, but the plenitude of internal *sadness*, and impotence — that is, far removed from deeds and principles) is only a hair's breadth away from absolute moral: there is an indestructible instinct in man, which is incapable of believing that the world is essentially, roots-and-purpose, evil — if love has to be drowned in lies, misery, and nonsense, then it is obvious that the meaning of life lies elsewhere; then happiness must be quantité négligeable. Only utterly "meaningless" suffering is able to give man the illusion of "meaningfulness"; only in this can we intimate somebody, some entirely foreign objectivity and intention, independent of our will. When Christ cries out, "My Lord, why have you forsaken me?" — in this absolute melancholia, or downright doubt, he stood closest to God: there is a form of desperate atheism which is so profoundly theistic as to bounce and dance inside the deity, in its very heart, as the grape-trampling slave romps in the red grape juice. If there is *only* darkness, if there is no hope for light, then it becomes certain that some light must exist somewhere.

The closer he got to the cellar-house, the more intrusively the dwellers in eternal darkness invaded his imagination: poor Enzia, who gave birth to her illegitimate child in secret — when everybody in the kitchen was fast asleep, she got up, stumbled down the stairs with mouth gagged so she wouldn't cry out in pain to go out into the woods, but she got sick while still in the town and was found by watchmen on their night round who could hardly help her at the beginning because their heavy armor and gigantic halberds were in the way; they wanted to call a midwife, but Enzia wanted no one: she was maddened by shame when the half-drunk landsknechts unlaced her blouse & tugged at her skirt; soot from the torches trickled on her skin in hot drops, and she retched at the stale beer that they forced into her mouth: isn't all love like this, the young man thought — yelping in the night? Going into labor among horses & sour dung, then tossing the child into the water under the bridge and watching its white head turn round and round the pillar like a mad little moth in the scent of a big flower-cup? There are quiet secrets, and there are such bloody, harrowing ones: "mysterium militans" — when love needs to be kept secret with knife and snare, so that nobody sees it.

What about young prince Pietro? The pale, tittering dance-partner of princesses at court balls, tired worshipper in the chapel, on whose tongue God's body settled like a falling chestnut leaf on the garden pond: at night (this eternal *night!*) he lay, pierced through and through and wrapped up, in the court alchemist's laboratory (greenhouse, operating theater, and gold-manufacturing kip at once), to have some Spanish venereal disease driven out of his murky blood. The exotic greenhouse flowers received from women still clang to his black clothes, but his knees and wrists were covered in steaming, fetid ointments, hideous, burning bandages. This suffering, these nights of bleeding, couldn't be told to anyone: in the morning, hey-presto, one merrily blew the hunting horn, blew his whole life into the day — why indeed?

Why indeed do the poor skivvy Enzia and the sick prince Pietro pop up here? Why does one need here naively chosen "symbolic cases"? Is he himself not hiding — from his father, from his wife? Does everybody always fabricate love so utterly alone, so entirely for themselves?

Through the gate he got into the hall, into love's most magical twilight — through a narrow window on the left moonlight oozed in, and through a distant glass door lamplight stole into the deserted room: intimacy and ghostliness, perversity and sloppy tranquility at once him assailed. At last he was completely hidden, behind him he felt the thick iron door, heard the clicking of the lock: imagining the lock and key, the alcohol of being "inside" literally inebriated him — he saw the complicated mechanism, clips, well-oiled small wheels, tiny, nervous articulations, and saw-edged bands in rhythmic, spider-like movement, which made it impossible for anybody to steal in and unmask him: he was protected and free, and the two feelings were sensibly, sharply battling inside him. Protected: he could lie down, sleep, read in silence, enjoy the sweet harmony of quiet, rest, mothering caress, could forget everything in the softness of the underground idyll. Free: at once and mechanically some preposterous sin came into his mind, the breaching of some absurd prohibition, sin itself, paradisiacally absolute blasphemy.

What is the true inspiration of darkness: quiet sleep, or satanic sin? Innocence's passive closing of eyes, or raving exploitation of the body? Who knows? He couldn't decide, but he felt all the more the necessity of such a cellar den: his whole life was becoming more and more truthful through darkness.

Truthful! Isn't it interesting that, although darkness is the realm of the mask, of the lie or of pudicity, of sacred and vile hypocrisy — yet the same darkness is also the milieu of *reality*: of life and of divine truth, as seen by biologists and Byzantine mystics. Of life: this is the underground darkness of roots, the womb night of the blooming embryo, the indestructible blindness of inner organs. Of divine truth: of the god of theological negativities. God is so infinite that it is impossible to grasp, comprehend, measure him, he is annihilatingly, nihilistically existing and powerful. Deus nox. In this cellar traversed by dark corridors and barely lighted spiral staircases he didn't know what he felt more intensely — darkness as the lie of charlatans, or darkness as the sacred element of life and truth.

This then was one of the houses: where love was ontology gone wild, or nihil gone wild (do those two in their logical, that is, absurd wholeness not mean, in every religion, existential philosophy, and daily life, ultimately — the same thing?), where love, due to the manicheistic setting of darkness, became a moral issue, the very image of the individual person's eternal compulsion to lie, to betray.

31.

But there was another house full of flowers, the house of sporules, plasma, living metaphors, unknown vegetation blazons, where if it was dark it was not night's heavy, indigestible prison & mash, but only a playful figure for the former, its copy made of more feminine material, which related to true darkness as a tiny glass amulet relates to the gigantic, grim Egyptian deity it depicts. But why speak of darkness here at all, where it is such a secondary matter? Here was unchecked, uncontrollable vegetation: neither garden nor jungle, neither house, nor botanical experiment — although from case to case here one thing appeared like a house, & there that thing appeared like a garden, the whole remained an unnamable chaos.

Vegetation, the flower, is the ancient, privileged realm and metaphor of love, & the young man had often wondered whether this was justified. According to the midnight-filled bordello, love is morality; according to the vegetating bordello, it is flower: starting from these symbols that suggest themselves (one might say, "existential monograms"), it is worth asking the question, which one is stronger, how they play their role in the "impossibilizing" of human beings? Or could love's being-eternal-inner-lie and its eternally-internal life affirmation (its "biological truth") really be one and the same thing? Although he constantly refrained from such questions, in them lay the sole meaning of his life.

He knew very well that great intellects have only two domains where they can live their capacities to the full: one is the simple, Dodonean world of "ultimate questions," where "yes" is "no" and "no" is "yes," where everything is fissured into two in irreconcilable self-contradiction, and where all paradoxes are smoothed back into nihilistic unequivocalness — whereas the other is a functioning that is set in patent contrast to the former, i.e., surface analysis that is microscopic to infinity, the perfect surface-descriptions, "demented" copies made with the help of human sensibility and logical onward-atomizing.

For instance, faced with the flowery house's flowers, there are only two possibilities for the brain: either to put the question, "what is flower?" and to conclude that biology and arbitrariness, æsthetics and truth, sexuality and mathematics are identical and thus any distinction between them is entirely superfluous (as we have remarked in general earlier) — or to set out and describe the flowers one by one, with an unsurpassably minute technique of surface analysis.

There is no connection whatsoever between thinking that dissolves into infinite in-distinction ("life is death, death is life," etc.) and infinitely surface-analytical thinking: one cannot develop from the one into the other, modulate to and fro on the fairy-tale toy bridge of induction and deduction.

The sole memory that rested for his entire life from this wealth of flowers was a white anemone — if it was an anemone indeed. "If indeed": is there anything more condemnable for a learned botanist than to not know the name, however keenly aware that "the name is insubstantial"? But doesn't it already imply some surplus knowledge, advantage, and enrichment concerning the "anemone," the uncertainty whether it is indeed an anemone?

Isn't this doubt — which from one angle is uncertainty of vision — one of the most precisely emplotting perspectives? We consider the name of every object and person important, but the flower is a peculiar realm of the *name*, with an entirely maniacal intensity: it is here that the problems and bliss, all intellectual barrenness and poetic power of the salvation of naming become truly manifest.

What is there in the name of flowers? Different languages: first and foremost Latin and Greek, often the two together, preserving, so to say, almost all of language's fundamental profile, for instance the intellectual precision of Latin and the vital precision of Greek, in this or that syllable's magical-narrow ring-mounting. There is hardly anything more alive than a flower — and yet it gets the dead words of the "dead" languages. Who wins, who loses from this bargain? Is the petal rendered mummy-like by the Greek sarcophagus-definition, or does the odd Latin grammatical model-word shoot splashing sprouts thanks to its flower-host? For just as it is every bit true that between a flower and its name infinite empty space, the healthy span of irrationality spreads, it is no less true that between a flower and its name a close blood circulation is in flux, the first feeds the second, the second presupposes the first: in line with the changing relationship between one twin and the other, the foetus and its mother, the parasite and its exploited host.

What is enclosed in these words of "dead" languages? Now a metaphor, now a geometrical definition, now a proper name, which is alternately that of an ancient god and of a bespectacled botanist. The things that end up juxtaposed in compound names! Orpheus *&* Schwandtnerburgel, or "dawn rainbow" and "trifid stigma." Don't these flower-names thus encompass the *whole* of human language, both the quotidian and the artistic, and what is more, not only language, but all the tragedy, comedy, perhaps even a few triumphs, of human knowledge? For what is "knowledge" if not a mixture of metaphors and definitions — provided that there is any difference between the two? "Dawn rainbow": why do I pronounce this a "poetic," illusion-making simile? "Pentagon": why do I pronounce this an accurate description? "Pentagon," too, is something fictitious, every bit as analogical, arbitrary, and not derived from inside the flower, as "dawn rainbow." Then how nicely close the hair-splitting pedants get to the frivolous gods of the grand gestures — Linné to Apollo, Schwandtnerburgel to Orpheus! What stands before us in flower-names is the sudden reconciliation of myth and myopic cataloguing.

Impressions are everything but obedient; they are unruly & scatter-brained: so this anemone growing by (or in? above?) a brothel didn't merge with the figure of one of the courtesans in the future mayor's mind, but with that of his mother. The anemone reminded him of his mother, and his mother, of the anemone. Even though his mother was definitely not flower-bodied, white and thin, but stocky and heavy. Yet in her gaze, in her simple advice, her half-ecstatic, half-prosaic consolations, in the divine proportion of love's poetry & realism, there was such a portrait-like, precise anemone-semblance that it was impossible not to observe: the truly magnificent mothers may be fat, splaying like raw dough puffed-up with ten portions of yeast, or the fast expanding, proliferating fungi, but even so, only in the puritanical slenderness, lucid chic, and commonsense coquettishness of the anemone can we find their true effigy.

How simple and yet how ostentatiously whimsical the five petals' number five and their disposition, just like the mother's loving gaze and blessing: pure poetry, pure madness. Without resorting in the least to sterile numerology, one could go to any lengths pondering, analytically unraveling, and mutely shivering at the nature of petals disposed in a pentagon: does the fifth petal disturb the four, or seal them into more definite four-ness? When they start withering, with what *ethical* bounty they open up their petals: in their touch-of-concavity, in their wrinkles, fadings, there is such discretion, so much "meremost," and at the same time so much definite and unequivocal wanting-one-sole-thing; in their veins, life's vegetative chaos shines through — in their bending to and fro, the ghostly "humanism" of moral over-coming vegetation asserts itself proudly: if life's greatest dilemma, between ancient phallic chaos and legally codified ethical norms, stands together, it is in a mother's love, and in no flower are the terrible alternatives of life and moral expressed so simply as in an anemone. There every characteristically genital trait is balanced by a no less characteristically ethical trait: the near-pubic fuzziness of the stems by the wholly personal, humble shade of whiteness, the crumplings, embrace-serpents of the petal bands, by the hygiene, clear-sightedness, host-like etherealness of symmetry.

32.

This is how the mayor remembered his marriage, women, in this manner, verifying that experience which hardly needs verification, that the *milieu* is all: all that there ever is, is milieu, the whole of life is milieu — human-, life-, death-, time-annihilating, eternal milieu. Darkness, too, was milieu, as was the anemone island, and this alone meant anything: the somewhere, the being-somewhere, the place. This he now experienced at its most fateful in front of the mirror, in the coquette's antechamber.

Milieu: that it is *here*, not there — this is the greatest secret; the complete merger of the opposition between hazard *&* predestination, or perhaps rather, the sharpener of these oppositions. *Here*: in a room, with this shade of smell, nuance of lighting, that can be felt only here-and-now, with the mirrors piano-pedaled into dimness: here and not on the seashore (although he could have been there as well), and not in the lugubrious salon of the archbishop of Toledo (although he could have been there as well!); not feeling that utterly different amalgam of experience, memories, and designs, essentially foreign from today's state of mind, that the seashore's divine emptiness, absolute-naught hollow booming (it is not infinity!) would awaken in him (although he might as well feel that!): gulls, blue, salt, naught, India, Nereids — those don't as much as come to his mind *here* (they did come to mind!); not feeling the tragic, kitschy concentration of moral, sin, pomp-frenzy, ornate askesis, etiquette, monarch-idol and Malaga wine, which the Toledo salon exhales (he did feel it!) — people have no inkling to what infinite degree the world is made up exclusively of coulisses: drama, never human beings. Is it worth believing in a situation when it is glaringly obvious that if one escaped in that instant, in another place that particular thing would not interest him in the least, moreover: it would instantly become meaningless.

He felt himself so profoundly under the influence of this milieu that he called for the maid and told her that he cannot wait any longer, but would return in half an hour. He hurled himself into the other milieu, the street, then another, the lurking, underground corridors, and yet another, his council chamber. We are actors: transparent, un-individualized, mathematical glass puppets, meltable, bendable, hardly "somethings" on whom now and again masks like "quiet salon," "midnight street," "buzzing council chamber" are put — in the end, our whole *psychology* is such a landscape-mask rammed onto us, in which we impotently perform our pageants. Refreshed and muscular with sadness, he took his seat again among the councilors.

33.

At that moment the messenger entered: the pope was dead. As though the candles had decayed into decrepitude in an instant, they started coughing & sizzling and spread a nauseating smell

CHAPTER ON LOVE · I · THE MAYOR

of wax & grease, like the poorhouse sick when the nun, instead of wiping their feverish, sweaty backs, hastens to the chapel for an extra prayer. So the pope is dead? Frightened, they stared into the darkness outside: for the very first time they noticed that immediately above the rooftops comes the sky, with its swinging, budding, withering stars, those stars behind whose well-known names it is nevertheless the eternal needle-piercing of mystery, of the unknown that hurts and bleeds. When the pope was still alive, there used to be some comforting mortar among objects: now it suddenly vanished. There were two candles in the middle of the table, two weary slaves or lapsed apostles who wear the flame of inspiration above their heads like old cabmen wearing long-tasseled nightcaps. So far there had been a billion things between the two candles: invisible, unnameable things, the hooks and nooks of the idyllic topography of certainty — now all of a sudden the air became empty between them, the two candles were but two candles and nothing else.

Probably no living soul in the whole town had heard the news yet. Thus the pope's death was confined to the council chamber, they felt it was they who had killed him: they themselves were death, and if they should leave this room, destruction would pour out and into the town as if from a Pandora box. Death so thinned them to ghosts that they were eyeing one another with suspicion, fear, and loathing. The door through which the messenger had come in was still open: one had an in-depth view of the descending spiral staircase, like looking into a loosened, opening shell. Willy-nilly the councilors were all looking into this snake-shaped opening; from there death had made its way. The staircase-snake could not be shooed away, it clang to the nighttime council chamber like the asp to Cleopatra's candle-lit breast. When the mayor placed his hand on the door-handle, the others nearly gave a hiss: they felt it was a blasphemy to tie up the cut black vein through which death flew. A gust of draught blew from the direction of the staircase: it twisted the candle-flames around its finger like a woman distractedly fingering her pearls.

"We are doomed," said one councilor. "Why?" — another asked, even more hushed. Before answering, the first looked at the mayor, who said nothing, but even his dropped gloves had a "why" shape. "The emperor will take Rome, he'll become pope." "Or there won't be any more popes to come." "Where is the emperor now?" "At Arbento. His soldiers are there anyway." "That was a long time ago. Any salesman can tell you that from Guiccione to Moretta the country is swarming with them." "It doesn't matter where he is: he certainly won't pass up this opportunity. Today or in a week he'll be in Rome." "All his soldiers wear black," someone said as if in sleep. "No reason to lose our heads."

In the meantime the horse tied to the gate was neighing continuously. The first window cracked open, the first unasked-for, hard-peeled bud of the startled nighttime question. A figure in a nightshirt leaned out, waiting: who is going to come out first from the town hall? Is the mayor going to leave the town, unannounced? Is he dying? Is there a conspiracy against him? Did he come home drunk, forgetting his horse? Did somebody tie the uncontrollable animal to the gate in mockery? For a few minutes the nightshirt withdrew from the window and raised his wife to tell her: "I've spoken with a man on the street. The mayor is fleeing because he found out that the plague is spreading here, too. He is abandoning the town to its fate." Then he put on something warm and took up his position at the window. The wife couldn't go back to sleep, her tears were welling up, so she decided to go down to her maids. With her husband she couldn't speak, for her he was the "world" — in times of war, the war, in times of plague, the plague. To him she could not complain. She went down to her maids.

They were already up, with the exception of one, peering from the narrow squat window. Before the woman, her hair all tousled, could say a single word, an idiot-faced servant hooted into her ears: "The mayor has robbed the dowry of his own daughter-in-law and is now escaping with it. He has enforced the marriage only in order to lay his hand on Donna Emilia." The woman felt relieved for learning the truth. The stumbling from death-fear into nighttime gossip made her head swirl. One of the skivvies saw that the half-asleep mistress would now buy into anything, so she threw herself with drunken hiccups, head over heels, into the sweet Elysian waters of lying: "The apothecary was telling that under oath of silence the mayor bought a love potion from him, to make his son and the rich Emilia fall for one another, so that in the meantime he could loot everything. The Donna's maids told us that one night they were tumbling in the bed naked, the mayor's son and the Donna, when a ghost was seen walking the house. Everybody thought it was the spirit of Donna Emilia's husband who couldn't bear the thought that his widow was lying in the arms of a half-grown boy." "The ghost was the mayor, of course," the idiot-looking houseboy blurted out, incensed by such logic. "He was looking for the immured treasures," the maid went on. Bathing in lies quite beautified her: she gave herself over to the opium waves of gossip with such abandon of sincerity that she looked quite cleansed. She indeed looked as though she had gone about naked: the mordant fullness of irresponsibility stripped her bare; she became a Venus rising from the froth of calumny. The idiot houseboy (perhaps thanks to his idiocy) immediately sensed that gossip in the girl was akin to erotic fever and elbowed his way to her, so that the carefree bliss of lying may pour over him, too. The maid felt the seductive, shameless halo of lying around herself and looked at it squarely, to get dizzy and be able to carry on lying: just as dipsomaniacs get drunk not from the brandy but from the willing acquiescence in their own drunkenness.

The mistress eagerly slurped up every word and carried it further with her imaginings: she could barely pay attention to the skivvy, already plotting how she could pass it on. The love potion bought from the apothecary? What if the apothecary sold him poison? The seventeen-year-old boy and the thirty-five-year-old widow are lying in bed — expired? While the mayor is roaming the midnight house, his son and the Donna are struggling with death? What if the blind apothecary gave the mayor himself potion? He is rummaging for gold along the blind corridors, but to his greatest surprise it is not the images of gold and jewelry that invade his mind, but the limbs of his son's bride? While he is fingering secret keys, hidden door-handles, in fact he is caressing the Donna. And when he finally discovers the treasure, the nests swarming with diamonds and sapphires, he leaves it untouched and, disillusioned and like a madman, darts to the Donna's bedroom that he had prepared for his son. By now he is frantically reciting troubadour poetry before the silent, locked door, yelling out obscene cant twenty times in a row without the merest alteration, imploring and praying. In the meantime someone else loots the house, the door is torn down and the dead discovered. What if all the treasure is at the apothecary's already? Or if the boy had indeed drunk the potion and is pursuing the Donna, trying to seduce her first civilly, with verse and the gentle-tortuous etiquette of desire, later uncivilly, with force, like drunken mercenaries, while the father counts, draws plans, searches?

The skivvy looked elevated with the lying: she was afraid of her own conjurings, but even this cowardly giddiness beautified her; she looked at her mates haughtily, like one flaunting a precious new jewel. The mistress, however, was depraved by the calumnious fantasy: tousled, she was rendered even more proletarian in her gaudy floral dressing gown. What if the mayor's son were courting *her*? She knew the apothecary, eternally perching on his improbably tall chair behind the counter, with his snow-white skin, in his black fur coat, holding up to the light his tiny parchment-scaled balance: in those minute scales (which made no noise when dropped) are lovers' sighs, suicides' rapiers, flowers, mellifluous serenades, abortions, marriages. Could this be true — that all she had to do was to walk in?

Cries in the street cut short her reveries. The baker's apprentices opened the shop and crowded around the messenger who was about to mount his horse, but the curious boys detained him. They haggled for a while, but in the end the messenger rode off. The skivvy felt that her Venusdom was about to fade: the apprentices were already loudly blathering. "The emperor has killed the pope," one said. "The emperor, too, is dead," another concurred. "This is the end of the world," a third one concluded indifferently and started into a half-hearted polishing of the doorknob.

The pope! Farewell to romance then. Right now, when she wanted to pass on the news, adding that the Donna is in fact a wrinkled old jade, with a moth-eaten wig (forever askance): the mayor's son fell for such a woman! She had seen the nuptials with her own eyes: the Donna's soiled underwear, her wrinkled back, lead-color rag-bosom (like two stockings hung up to dry), her rheumatic, knotty knees, outward-sticking large toes, her buttocks smeared aside to left and right ... her wig had fallen off, there she stood shivering, unbathed for years, by the bedside ... the wig caught fire from the candles, the whole place was about to burn down ... and that beauteous youth is kissing & fondling that corpse dug up from the grave, with Petrarch on his lips! And it's not even for the money that the mayor is putting his son through this ghastly comedy, but to dump his own illegitimate child on him, only to disown both of them and kick them out of his house ... And all those enticing yarns are over now: it's only the pope who is dead.

34.

Restless waiting, this most expressive of deeds has also been (as
we had ample occasion to see) the most important component in
the mayor's life. For decades he has lived in a veritable chain of
waiting and expectation — one message depended upon another,
that other upon a third, and this wreath of dependence seemed
never to end: one had to wait first for the report of the envoi from
Ravenna, before his envoi could make haste to Ferrara, and even
this one had to wait underway until the first papal corps reached
the town, to send a report to a councilor, who was then to send it
to a certain Naples courtesan — in reality, a spy. A whole series of
overtakings, path-crossings, mathematical functions, delays: and
to wait, agitated, minute by minute, for every one of those, head
swirling under the clock's strikes, like a thin paper flower in a
hailstorm.

The time of the clock and the time of history: the clock in
his studio was like an even, black, gliding stream, a flooding and
molten death-mirror, some pure matter, luminous even in its
mourning clothes, which has nothing to do with the "time" of
wars, messages, espionage, recruitments, and unveilings — as
though history were not unfolding in time at all, but, on the
contrary, as if its objective were to entangle time, to throw behind what is in the foreground, to select and pull out from the
fabric of the past the thread of what is over: as though one set
at time's or the Parcæ's loom a demented baboon, who with a
few nervous, idiotic pawings shreds the respectable, languidly
decorative work of endingness. What do these historical rag-
ornaments have to do with his quiet studio, large pendulum
clock, Atlantic metronome? There is no time in the world: the
time of loneliness is not time, only the swelling of gradually
coloring spleen, its bubbly splaying-out — just as the time of
occurrences is no time either, only the self-refuting, self-ulcer-
ating mosaic of short-span concepts like "before," "later," "still,"
"already," "tomorrow," "while."

Now, too, he was waiting for two men — one was his terminally ill wife's physician, the other a messenger who was bringing tidings of his reputedly raving mistress. While he was sitting by the clock and the minutes, like falling leaves, set on his shoulders, he wondered why people would say that all too symmetrical events, far-too-regular contrasts in character, exist only in artificial allegories, mysterious and moralizing fables: his experience was the exact opposite — virtually no day of his life went by without the occurrence of something naively symbolic, whose regular shape called for schoolbooks of moral examples. The basic rule and order in his life was chance, the more preposterous accident: incalculable encounters, forever fertile dates, events lined up rhythmically and hierarchically — women, wars, rains, decoration, deaths always processed through his life in a symbolic, provocatively æsthetic and moral orderliness, superstitiously aligned. The crossing of the two experiences — i.e., of historical time as hither-and-thithering baboon hysterics, and of its apparent opposite, i.e., that each and every phenomenon entered his life at the most symbolic possible time, place, and sequence of events — is nothing else but the sense of "fatefulness" active in every neurotic and poetic person: one feels that life is the most frivolous, pointless game, but knows at the same time that it flows unchangeably along the trough of a sole predestination. Even in this waiting he felt the working of eternal allegory: to be simultaneously waiting for messengers bringing news from a dying wife and a frantic mistress.

He no longer had any attitude to his wife's sickness, which had started many years earlier, or better said, he could no longer distinguish among his most contradictory feelings: to kill her with his own hands, to have her canonized, to offer up his life for her, or to have her cured at some miraculous well — such different wishes were all of the same hue, variants of ecstatic despair, which only differed in their names, once pronounced.

Notwithstanding this, the day before some change started in his life with her. He noticed that the young physician, rumored to be a passionate alchemist, had somehow fallen in love with her. Somehow: in love with that death which as a physician he imagined to be a fluid that floods the young woman's body like water flooding a sponge, and which — if only he managed to syphon it off — would give him not only the secret of gold, but of all imaginable life. For the last days and weeks the old mayor could have nothing but a moral relationship to his wife: fate, perishing, murderous sacrament, self-denial, impossibility, Albigensian Satan — for him she was something of all those. Now when he discerned a contrasting quality in the eyes and movements of the doctor, in his speech trembling from a haughty damper, he was overcome by a curious shiver, a relaxing sense of well-being. Of course the paradox stood immediately to sight: through the doctor's quizzical love he himself was brought to feel some kind of love for his wife again, which made him at once jealous of the doctor. But if he sent away the doctor, the mirror of those eyes in which his expiring wife started blossoming in unexpected attractiveness, he would never again be able to find anything desirable in her.

The very last precious to-and-froing of psychology, he thought with a bitter smile. All around us the age of destruction, perhaps of ultimate anarchy and blasphemy. Rome is going to fall and the Church will be exterminated, perhaps I myself will hang like a red tassel from a Ghibelline gate tower tomorrow morning or tonight, and yet here I am, fidgeting with such shepherd-boy dilemmas. As if deep down our souls had no sensibility for "fateful, big" events. In fact we live on two planes, neither of which necessarily have anything to do with one another: one is the realm of over-scrupulous, blind, low-caliber routines, the world of microscopic habits, small reflex movements, cell-refrains — the other is the pathetic, nihilistic, broad-gestured realm, swelling with the exotic moral of eternal closeness-to-death: which of the two had I felt to be my self?

35.

When the clock struck again (all Góngorist acrobacies of style aside, he had always felt each striking of the hour to be the gill-like ripping open of a sleeping or dead newborn's navel, starting an unstoppable gush of blood), and there was no sign of either the doctor or the messenger, he rang for his servant. "I'm going to write a letter and you will take it to my daughter. What is the time now — half-past seven? You can be there by eight. Hurry up! My daughter has to be on time for the half-past-eight mass at the Fiore. If she's still sleeping, wake her up. You know that she's not staying with us now; she's at her aunt's. Neither sickness nor the harassing intrigue which pursues me even in my own house is a suitable environment for her. Give me the pen! And stoke the fire in the meantime." The servant brought the quill, paper, and ink and mused about what all the world's domestic servants are bound to muse about, looking at their masters on the threshold of momentous events: about what great lords they are, since it is in their power to turn the world upside down with a little table talk, and about how they are not masters of anything really: for after all they have no power to change the course of big events; they are as powerless as their lackeys.

The mayor put on his greenish eyeglasses and while the servant busied himself with the fire, wrote a short note to his daughter: "My dearest Maria, please forgive me for dragging you out of bed so early for something you don't understand, which upsets you, or for which you will simply consider me an old fool. You know that I've always had mass held for your dear mother at the Fiore and I have always been present. I am now in far too great confusion of spirit, hopelessness, and dull ignorance to be able to

go to confession and take communion. I am perfectly aware that
our priests would say in unison, 'but precisely for this reason,' but
— I prefer to leave this sentence unfinished. You know that I have
always been selfish & comfortable in the extreme. Of this I will
now give definitive proof: when you get this letter I ask you to
jump out of bed at once, go to confession, take communion, this
morning at nine in the Fiore. In my place. I know you are in love,
I know with whom, I know where you meet. I know that, to put
it mildly, you feel no inclination to do this, and I know that if I
talk to you of your mother and her health in this connection, it
would be a very cheap form of terrorizing you, whom I know to
have inherited — *Te Deum laudamus* — every single one of your
father's superstitions, neuroses, motley phobias. Love should not
worry you, you can tranquilly confess — I believe, nay, know that
you are not his mistress. And if you happen to be … but you are
not. I know that the Fiore confessioners make you shudder, but
I'm asking you to go to old Fanelli, to whom I will also write a
note now, asking him to be kind and polite to you. Hugs, Papli."

When he finished writing he asked the houseboy: "Would
Father Fanelli still be at home; does he go out this early?" "I've
always found him at home at this hour." "All right, then go to him
first, it's on the way, and tell him to go to the Fiore to my daughter. I promised her to ask the pater in writing, but it's enough if
you tell him of my request. Go at once!"

36.

The mayor, now alone, thought of the church of the Fiore and
of the place where his daughter used to meet her lover. What
did the church mean to him? The mad transcendentals of the
Church, the objecthood of the world's objects (column! book!
candle! picture! stone and place! outside and in! wine and bread!),
and finally, the eternal pointlessness, impotence, unknowability

of man, spiritual life, of individuality and solitude, of history and judgment. Perhaps he felt it the most critically when he stood up, together with the congregation, for the reading of the gospels, and threw on himself the three small crosses like women throwing powder over their faces and cats, their tongues when they clean themselves: the priest's voice soared high, like the deranged reeds of Asian swamps; music, sound, text, faces, masks all seemed to proclaim that there is, there most definitely is something above us, and that something wills the death of his wife, the destruction of the town, the final triumph of the Ghibellines. And the missal was left open afterwards — no-one read from it, there was no incense around it anymore, no divine good tidings, only leather and parchment, scrupulous art & craft and deathly dull, deathly deaf weight. This is our world: the forever mute, forever selfish world of objects and tools, which trample on the human whim of "goals" with antediluvian power. And in the end I, poor I, the mayor, whose chaotic inside cannot manage to adjust to goals or objectives — it is sheer inability of adjustment, not-belonging-anywhere. A god? What can, what could it ever have to do with me? God and life are mutually exclusive — god is always death's crystal. An object? What can it possibly do to me, what could it have to do with me? He looked around the room: at the fireplace's arch, at the shameless only-mathematicality of the half-burnt logs, the lamp, the oversize quill, the books. Nothing. Nothing to do with humans. Humans have psychology only, but objects & gods have no psychology. Let's leave the gods and objects alone and accept the soul's hopeless chaos! Although he was permanently of this feeling, still, he went to mass every day — knowing that this tragic, sometimes raving godlessness and hostility to god is nevertheless a state of mind whose only possible environment "in style" is the church. His wife's tormenting sickness drove him to despair: after the images, sounds, smells, and dances of suffering that one night or other of his wife

meant for him, morning mass seemed but etiquette, the fastidious codex illuminations of metaphysics — what on earth could
the perfection of Gregorian choruses have to do with his wife's
asthmatic wheezing, what could the schematic poetry of incense
have in common with the garish and stifling smells of medicine,
sweat, and digestion; what could the initialed gospel texts have
in common with the selfish theater of groans? How many times
he had asked God to grant him a sense of abstraction, so that he
shouldn't see the sickbed's horrid, closed concreteness as closed,
to be able to continue both in his logical fantasy and connect
the continuations somewhere in infinity, believing that there is a
connection, a sensible link between the two, *sub specie* ... To pray
for someone? Is it possible? Perhaps it's possible for ourselves;
perhaps his wife herself is still connected to God and is able to
mold such a vortex or funnel from her suffering which sucks in
and swallows the heavenly pigeon with its terroristic gravity —
but it's impossible for a stranger. Suffering itself can turn into
god — there you don't need to pray anymore; physical agony is
the truest transubstantiation. One can imagine how reassuring
the church was for the mayor: had they but seen a fraction of
his feelings, the priests would have chased him out as a heretic
— and to feel all along that with his God-denial taken before
God he cannot help his wife in any way. Perhaps the source of
his all-pervasive pessimism was some oversize infantile guilt feeling — he couldn't imagine God not punishing him and his family,
that He might do anything else with him than punish him. And
because he suspected this to be the main cause of his despair, he
nevertheless dared go to church with the strutting laurel of his
heresies: for he was godless only because he had once thought
God too seriously, too divinely. All we ever do is roam, wander
around one another, having no inkling about ourselves and the
other: my wife's misery means for me human thrownness-into-
doubt in general, but for her it's her own death, for the alchemist

it is Eros and life-riddle, to God it is God knows what, for the priests, morality to bureaucratize, for my daughter, an impromptu confession … Everybody does, thinks, something, but we don't even come to glimpse the sole meaning, the sole reality, of things. In life the most terrible thing is that you can't look at it from the outside: we are always inside and from-within — if only we could lay it down for a time, like a book we finished reading, if only we could step out of it, like from the plot of a book! And because we cannot, we can't compare it to anything; there is no instrument of measurement without us, for God and all trans- and all ultra- is everything but trans- and ultra-, being only something within-our-lives, within-our-world — the "without," the "beyond," can only be an abstraction of what is from-within, never real experience.

37.

He loved the church of the Fiore very much; even now, when the town was on the rocks, he spent much on refurbishing it. The church (the early Christian basilica form) gave perfect expression to each and every inner biological movement — much as it pushed him into unfathomable chaos on the rational plane, to his bodily, "artistic" instincts it nevertheless meant an absolutely classic and utterly harmonic world. The two rows of columns themselves: slenderness and robustness, monotony and linear agitation, perspectival foreshortening and irrefutable symmetry, wall-like closeness & porous staccato, the minimum of "building" and yet, the Cyclopean reality of architecture, the capitals' almost edible bud- and cauliflower-likeness and the columns' arithmetic formula-rigidity in the splendid fact of the "row of columns": these contrasts are not rhetorical opposites, but the gratification of instinctual dualities buried deep inside the human body.

To confront this row of columns with the eternal agony of history! Although, if this early Christian basilica-rayon indeed gratifies some intensely biological instinct, then it must also be closely connected to the chaos of suffering, since death is also something biological. The same life, the same organic body wills, on the one hand, these redemptively harmonic forms that only architecture can yield, and alternatively, the shapelessness of asthmatic suffocation, epileptic fits, disorderly skin disease? Or can one also spot in the harmony of a row of columns the rhythm of sickness, and in the disorderliness of agony, the symmetry of columns? Probably. But, from the perspective of the everyday (and now, when in all likelihood total destruction, the end of his own life and that of the town is imminent, now he truly knew that there is no greater concreteness and no higher forum in life than the "everyday"), the two will forever remain separate. Is it not worth spending money, so that one may see, in their musical purity, the delicate network of the row of columns and above it, the icy, mirror-like smoothness of the wall? The two at once! The line and the plane, which are perhaps expressive of life's most ancient dualism, between dramatic movement and never-born death-silence. However little credit these contrasts are given in learned academics' Plato and Plotinus exegeses, they are all the more commonsensical, love-like, food-like, and revelations when made of stone, bricks, and frescoes. The dark and warm cave of the apse, the eternal completion, eternal within, eternal round-ness and protection after the ascetic strings of column-lines, the roundness, bubble, the apple-shaped cloisters. Above, smooth wall surface; below, mosaic spreading and yeasting like moss or rust; around the altar, a simple marble wall at the feet of the columns, exploding violet, cold, wet flowers. This is the sole cer-tainty in this life, these forms that the church encompassed.

38.

And beside the living-abstract world of forms, his daughter's love. What could it mean, what could it be worth, falling as it did in the shadow of an apocalyptic-looking turn of history? Are we proceeding toward the "events" or counter to them? How can one live in such an absurd world where girls suddenly lay down their forks during supper, leave the table, then (according to servants' reports) cry for a while, alone, in their bedroom, suddenly wrap a shawl around their necks, put on a cape and whizz down the stairs like a spring breeze along the scrawny-leaved branches, stay out until midnight, only to romp in, back to their bedrooms, whistling and with faces transfigured from joy — and at the same time, in the same world, a pope prays all night in front of a bloody, naked statue, speaks in Latin, which is not his tongue, blesses the swords & lances of three butcher-faced mercenaries, fasts, then orders the trumpets to sound the dawn, mounts his horse, sends off a man to kill the emperor's general in the Folegno woods, while sending another to take God's body to a village near Rome, so that his old peasant mother might take the host that her son himself had transubstantiated — at noon villages are already on fire, troops are slaughtered, and they proceed in their bloody rags inside a small church with Byzantine daubings, to pray and to ecstatically declare themselves "history."

This is as human as that, *love*'s lurking selfishness and *history*'s grandiose tall tales — but what has the one to do with the other? Do people want history, or are they merely driven into it? He himself had for decades led a town and during his entire career only for a few moments did he feel that history exists for mankind or for human beings: the whole of history gave the impression of a dreadful fiction. Something artificially constructed, whose great *à-tout* was: always-possible death. *Fictive reasons* for dying — that is what history is. If he was facing momentous events, like now, he was almost driven to despair by the awareness

that none of this was supposed to be so, the whole is just a preposterously frivolous stunt, posturing, blind dime-show histrionics — papacy & empire are not opposites, much less ancient
human needs, but merely bloody pastimes, suicidal comedies.
And when he called history a "comedy" he knew well that the ones
who compromise history are not those who strike deals in the
guise of heroism, not the ones who use the cruciate flag for pro-
moting their linen trade, but on the contrary: those who believe
too well, wholly, to the point of delirium, the heroic nature of
heroism, the cross-nature of the crusades.

And besides that, my daughter. But to be pedantic — is "besides" the right word? Where is the private person (and is there
any person more private than a girl in love?) situated with respect
to history? Inside? near? beneath? outside? above? What is the
right word? One is either a conscientious "collectivist," stylizing
his whole life into an element of collectivity — or he has nothing
to do with any kind of collectivity; there is no third possibility.
Isn't it ridiculous to talk of Pisa, emperor, pope, Italy, people,
Civitas Dei or pious virgins in connection to his daughter?

How many times he had spied on her rendezvous: not out of
an instinct for prying and gossip, not out of senile eroticism, but
in order to see that elemental going-counter-to-history, history-
lessness, which manifests in a kiss, in a flower stuck into a bun,
in a male hat rolling on the floor during an embrace. He kept
a more scrupulous record of his daughter's meetings than she
or the boy — if the time was near, he started skipping documents impatiently, cut reception hours short, & gave recklessly
long leave to the lancers. It wasn't at all difficult to hide from
her — their meeting-place was all flowers, lianas, fallen leaves
clotted like blood. Monday was the last time. It was so fine that
they chose to meet on a Monday: when most people are blinded
back into the prose of work, his daughter, with the pubertal selfishness of love, life, and nature, starts into skivering, kiss, bell-
flower death and defiant reasoning with the boy. The place was

a terraced stairway completely overgrown with brambles and grass, leading to an old abbey. In one place the stairs vanished completely, in another all that remained were three cracked stone slabs, like cake crumbling in tea — while here and there the stairway opened up its rigid bands in the form of a flower-cup, an elderberry flower or peacock tail, only to thin out in a short while again, like old clasps in the forest's thick mane. It was late afternoon, the sky like a green, bronze-, or silk-hide apple — far-off palm trees, Brazilian teas are of such color — and the light was melancholy like a lamp in the mist, or rather, impossible ("couleur de nonentité": shouldn't they try to weave something like this for Paris?) and yet well-defined, plastic, like the profile of an Egyptian statue. Nothing in the whole world can be as plastic, closed, and palpable as the evening sky — this eternal source of "indefinite" spleen, of "contourless" mysticism. The bottom of the sky was dark blue like the funneling base of a calyx, where the unexpected conceit of color makes up for the narrowing of space — on this furious, roaring dominant-band the clouds drifted like flowers or birds, in unanalyzable, over-refined colors, from gold to pink, from pigeon-grey to demonic rust. What does history have to say — of *colors*? What is the pope's latest bull to these, or the secret pact Venice made with the Turks? "Frivolous impressionism": has a more frivolous word ever been said about something human? In the tempo of their proceeding there was something that from the first second rendered the allegedly festive protocol, legal rhythm of courts of justice ridiculous, made the tunes of lancers marching off for the change of guards or to war laughable, made the sequence of calendars, all past and all tomorrow, but a sorry-looking trifle: this was pure swimming, pure hovering, and although it exhaled aimlessness as the bed left by a woman exhales yesterday's perfume, still, there was meaning, certainty, and resolution in it. Yes, this is all that is left in our hand: abstract concepts, neurotic enthusiasms, and mystery, mystery.

How beautiful it was when this sky lit up and ashened his daughter's face to greenish-yellow: green toads' backs, soap bubble blown into a tree's crown, hummingbird-meteors consisting of a single "prrrl" can be so painfully, Lethe-pollinatedly green. Somehow *color* affects our sense of *time* the strongest — a wonderfully beautiful color (where "the hues of hues" and "pure primordial element" mean absolutely the same thing) charms us immediately into the mood that the sight we are just witnessing has hovered before our eyes for millennia; in its presence we feel some homeliness, primordial-fish-idyll dating back to the Pliocene. Is this park indeed part of that Passa-fervata, over which the emperor's supporters, the French, the pope's supporters and his town have been quarreling from the perspective of "ownership"? Undoubtedly so, for it was enough to bend forward a bit to hear in his pocket the rattling of that map folded tenfold, on which this forest and even the stairs featured. That star trembling solitarily at the sky's fringe, like a drop of water that can neither drop nor be absorbed into rouged female lips that have just drunk — can that star be eventually identical to the one in the calculations of the astrologer who tried to lure him into declaring war? And those pale pearls and even paler buds on the trees of the forest (moon-ash?), can they possibly be those fruits measurable by the pound & quintal, which are going to contribute to "the people's welfare," if the forest is conquered? And can his daughter & that boy possibly be: "the people"? How could he, the mayor, keep his seat in these tempestuous times, when he felt with such extraordinary, tumultuous intensity the reality-outside-history of life (dream) and death (life)? The utter unnaturalness of the fact that in the most critical, most barbarous times a splenetic "poet" (he has never written a single line in his life) should be the town's highest-ranking commander, diplomat, and politician — how could he possibly have held on for decades?

39.

The mayor threw a glance at the papal letter lying on his desk —
it was not addressed to him, his spies had stolen it from the envoi.
"... Credebamus devotionem tuam sedulo studere atque esse
intentam tota industria ad ea que honorem nostrum et aposto-
lice sedis prospicere viderentur. Cum vero non sine animi nostri
displicentia intellexerimus nuper te in rebus Janue aliter incedere
quam sit mens et intentio nostra, satis ac plurimum admirati sumus. Nam audivimus te partibus dilecti filii nobilis viri ... ducis
Mediolani non solum non favere, sed non obscure adversari. Hoc
si verum est grave admodum nobis esset atque molestissimum.
Diligimus enim ducem ipsum benemerito et statui eius sumus
affecti, sicut pluribus in rebus perspici potuit..."[2] Is it possible
that there will henceforth be no Christianity in the world, it will
die out within a few years, in Rome the German emperor will
sit on the papal throne for centuries, papacy and Christianity
have been but naïve intermezzi — everything that ever shaped
his life, what defined all his relationships to food, women, prince,
and sickness were intermezzi, outside of which there is nothing
concrete? Is it possible that one could consist at all times exclusively of some intellectual episodes and death? If he thinks of his
daughter, whom he is chasing to a rushed confession, of his wife
who is dying, whom he had betrayed, who is the sole reality, of
his mistress who is raving in her forsakenness like the sad-faced
knight of La Mancha, of the triumph or destruction of the town
— can he find in himself a hair's breadth of thought or feeling
that is not related to Christianity? That Christianity which is
perhaps now threatened with ultimate destruction, which will
never even be mentioned anymore: so the one who has willed
this whole existence didn't will Christianity in the least, but
meant it to be a mere illusion, passing caprice. If the emperor's allies conquer Italy, for years the bleakest terror will follow — what

is love going to be worth then, or confession, for that matter? Some dowry his daughter is going to inherit.

40.

There was a knock at the door: will it be the doctor or the messenger spying on his mistress? It was the spy. The mayor offered him a seat. "What's the news?" "May I then speak quite frankly?" The mayor shuddered with bitter nausea — after such a start there was little point in continuing. He said in an uninflected, colorless voice: "Naturally. Tell me everything: that's why I sent you." Like a gladiator trying to position himself comfortably as he gets behind his shield, so he curled up in his armchair, away from the messenger, trying to build a nest of the armrest, back, his hanging robe-sleeves, his beard sliding down on his fist. All the while feeling that the dumbmost, most pointless doom is going to rush by his ears like drunken cavalry — he felt dizzy at the thought. He would much rather have sent the spy off: there is nothing more disgusting than to listen to "consequences" — in his soul the billion possibilities, ongoing metamorphoses, of thoughts and dreams, the opalescent undecidability of yes and no (which is not necessarily identical to vacillating in the moral sense), and in front of him a strange man's one-only and thus-only deed: what has it got to do with him?

But the spy was already speaking. "The Donna is at the Sagonto Villa, as we had suspected all along, only a lady friend lives with her, but a great many dubious specimens keep coming and going at the most unlikely hours." Dignified company: some strange woman, about whom all he knew was that she was a "woman," obviously "one of those women" who knows perfectly well that men are faithless, but who also knows with what wondrous machinations you can conquer them; she knows great tricks, believes herself to be on the crest of knowledge of people

& of life just because she had had an abortion and had been abandoned by a lover, & is now pumping all this profound wisdom into his lonely, half-crazed mistress. What about the suspect specimens? Is she striking deals with the emperor's allies? making pacts with the Ghibellines? What difference does it make? There is nothing more awful than those two extremes: eternal reflection on history's thousand-and-one secrets smacking of Heraclitus, and intrigue originating in a woman's revenge, which chooses a couple of money-grabbing cripples, epileptic would-be-poets, and hitmen for its vehicle. Amor, amor. "So, have you found out something about that lady friend and the suspect persons?" "I don't know anything more about her — I have the impression that she is a very sharp woman who is trying to rip off the Donna's hysteria — she looks like a superannuated dry nurse: pale, white, grim, with no femininity left, and I think in her heart of hearts she is more vicious than a highwayman. If I'm not mistaken, she is working toward convincing the Donna that the emperor's conquering army is worth her…" "Well, we're not quite there yet," exclaimed the mayor, whom these women's intrigues have unexpectedly driven to wild patriotism: how often was he bored to high heaven by the posturing and gestures of state representation and warfare, diplomatic dinners and the filthiest mercantile bargaining, but yet in this moment with what savage ready-to-martyrdom love he thought of his whole political past: now when he saw it as an instrument of a highwayman's and a madwoman's selfishness. That woman! What does she want? Never had he felt more intensely and more blindly the boundless recoiling from women and contempt for women that from time to time wells up in all men: what does she want to "do," why does she want pros and cons, money and moral, clothes, poetry, husband, death, history — why does she want it? When never has there been, nor can there be, more than a seemly impression, wonderful image, the momentary emblem of fleeting impossibility and pulsing concrete — why does she "act"? And against him of all people, who had pored all his life over the metaphysics of "action," who had avoided all decisive attitudes, who had never in fact wanted anything — is it really against him that two women seek to employ "deeds"? To pick, from among a million variants, one wretched little wick, purposely to run their egotistical, limited little womanly flame along it? When there is talk about the end of the world, the Antichrist, the destruction of Europe, these two want one sole thing — to ruin him? Every living soul has heard from their parents and friends from the beginning of time, "indeed, a passing amorous idyll may have the bloodiest, deadliest consequences." Is that it? Is he to live that trivial ballad now, in his grey old age, at the end of his days? Is thought really as powerless as that: all those hundreds of books on the wall, holy scholastics and pagan philosophers, all his countless sufferings in hidden parks, midnight seas, vanished children's room, by the side of deathbeds, in the lonely vortex of sickness, in the vast gull-rehearsals of liturgies: can all this be mere "association," "the fioritura of mood," "some sort of philosophizing," useless neurosis? Does the truth, reality, boil down to this: the revenge plans of plotting witches?

This bitter thought so irritated him that he jumped from the shelter of his armchair and scurried up and down in the room. "What do they want from me?" — he asked, almost yelling. Could this be possible? That a stranger, a woman break into his house, turn everything upside down, perhaps even kill him, so that in the end nothing else remains of his life but that dumb, deceptive, parodic fact that "he was killed by his mistress in revenge"? For he had never written books, not even a diary, he will hardly ever feature in history, he had always only tried to keep a petty balance, in an intellectual manner, in the background, always dancing on the edge of the abyss. Or is he afflicted with the mania of persecution? Is he in fact taken in by the spy who is trying to blackmail him?

"Take me to the Donna's villa. We'll steal in, or talk, or murder, or make love, I don't know. But in any case we'll go there. How long does it take to get there on horseback?" "An hour if we gallop." "If! Of course we will." He rang and told the houseboy: "The doctor is to come. He shall wait for me here. If he has anything urgent to do, he should by all means leave me a written note, sealed, about my wife. I insist. All others shall wait for me here as well."

He put on his cloak, they went out in the courtyard to the stalls. "Tell me exactly when you saw whom, where, how." But before the slightly frightened messenger could even answer, he remarked darkly to himself, placing his foot in the stirrup, "I must perish, there is no doubt about it. That it won't happen in the pose and with the monumentality and elegance of heroes of legend, saints, and Roman artists, is something I've known long enough. Since my childhood in fact. It is all well as it is." When he was sitting in the saddle and the first breeze of journeying blew into his face, he asked calmly, with an almost humorous accent: "So when did you see her first?" "I saw her in the woods, she was riding alone." "Ah, so she wants the daydream as well! The deed, simple revenge, the bloody bargain, is not enough; she also wants to put on the lofty tempos of pilfered dream. What eternal upstarts women are!" "I asked her closer and more distant entourage about when she usually rides out, and with what purpose — for meeting someone, by chance? But everybody told me that the Donna is half mad, even in town she talks to herself as she promenades." "I see. How I adore this tragic poetry, this Orphically profound pathos, from which not rhymes but hitmen's contracts are born. I don't know if you understand me, Tullio — probably not. All you see is that the Donna had once been my mistress, I left her, she now wants to kill me, and I find that to be against nature. Perhaps you consider me ludicrously naïve, for it looks as if I were outraged to the bottom of my moral self by the simple fact that the abandoned mistress hates me and what is more, wants me dead. First of all, in love it is never man and woman who face one another, but always 'one human being' and 'Destiny': for me the Donna is not a woman, not a human being, no psychological or moral data: there is no such thing in love — but Destiny itself, all that hostile, alien, inscrutable, forever mysterious power that zigzags, clouds, and undulates around my life. If I hate her, it is my destiny I hate, compared to whose darkness and universal hostility the Donna's innocence or, if you will, her truth is of no importance; for me she has never, never been a human being, and I can't take her for one now." "May I say a disrespectful word, from man to man?" "Respect — what a laugh here under the trees, in the forest's anarchic loneliness, among the most comical stanzas of love, on the threshold of a new era in history! Some jokes you are telling me, Tullio. Go on, speak." "All I wanted to say is that, when your lordship made the Donna your mistress — in that moment, and even if for only one moment, you must have taken her for a human being." "Humanity and ethics — you're talking about that, aren't you? And what else do women want but humanity and ethics? Ethics! To perch from morn to night and from night to morn on their bedsides; if an unknown woman passes by under their window, to turn our gaze to the ground and say three Our Fathers, to do lackey and dog-washing jobs for them, heroic pranks with dragons and popes, to deprave ourselves and earn money, caressing their haloed heads in imitatio-Christic sloppiness, to found a religion and in this way dumb ourselves down irrevocably between business and flimsy mysticism. This is what humaneness and ethics means, am I not right, Tullio?" "Your lordship knows better. I spoke as a simple man: I cannot argue with the words that your lordship used in your great learnedness and fury."

41.

The forest was full of flowers and lurking soldiers. Can they really be this close? What's the use of this whole comedy: with flowers, henchmen, spring, and Antichrist? If only vegetative nature disclosed one syllable of its secret, of the mystery of cells, pollen, plasma, reproduction, death, scent, evolution, meaning, meaninglessness, pleasure and beauty, skin disease and leaf shape, chirping and matter! If only we could hear one sole syllable of the meaning of self-mortifying popes, megalomaniac emperors, starving proles and shipwrecked cruciate fleets! But they never, never speak; the flowers continue to perfume the air in their mocking-nostalgic secretiveness, doltish footmen go on sharpening their swords in kips, castles, and churches — at the first moment he felt like a sentimental old maid, at the second he came to realize that soldiers and flowers, history and vegetation are *one* thing — it would be romantic limitedness to see the two as separate. Go on, in, into with your horses, personalities, your physical, sporting health and with your inner spleen: into the flowers' blue-purple, pink sea, into this coldly trembling, cloudily and mistily pearling color-puddle, among the stiff, hairy, matte, sappy, or wilted stems — let the horses' legs be covered in pollen, grass, petals; let them feel, perhaps for the last time, the combined softness of earth, grass, and flower, that mix of solidity and pillow, bed and statue, which can be felt through woods and meadows, through the horse's feet in the horseman's body. Why are you, who are you, what are you? In any case you have been beautiful, flowers. On now, into, among the emperor's soldiers, into the bloody hijinks of holy ownership — if anybody, I have given enough thought to what your meaning might be, throughout my life — if I haven't found it, nobody can, then you have no meaning at all, and I will no longer rack my brains around it. And just as through my drunken horse I let myself be swept over and penetrated by flower-fate and history-fate, so let love-

fate also wash over me: let my mistress murder me, take me into
her bed, do what she likes with me. Have I not always craved
your "life," and is not life precisely this: the totally imbecile risk
and some æsthetic bluff, successful to the point of drawing tears?
Let's hurry up!

Like all superstitious fatalists, he always thought sym-met-
rically. He is going to be reconciled with his abandoned mistress
and rest in her bed till night, but by the time he gets home he
will find his wife dead. Or: in his great hatred of women he will
kill his mistress, and by the time he gets home he will find his
wife, under the influence of a sea of potions, in the doctor's arms.
Or: in the Donna's villa they will describe to him the abandoned
woman's distress so heart-wrenchingly (eventually he himself
will describe them: dictating to the clowns) that he will rush to
church, pray and have mass said for her, and by the time he gets
home he will find his wife dead, murdered by the Donna. Or:
the moment he reaches the Donna's villa, they will assault and
murder him on the spot.

He thought of his library: how quiet is all thought and all
literary beauty, and how thuggish, crude, and mendacious this
much-wanted "life." Perhaps he will be dead in half-an-hour, not
knowing which is worth more, the books or the tempest of deeds.
This is the most fantastic thing in life, that in the last second
before death we are just as ignorant of the matters of life and
death as in the most self-assured, death-remote heyday of our
manhood. "What if I simply killed that woman?" — he asked.
Although his companion did everything to appease the mayor, he
unwittingly answered something rebellious: "There is much plotting against your lordship's wife." "This is what I brought for my
wife, Tullio: from Venice, from Palermo I invited famous professors to cure her, and when none of them could help, I brought in
this fury for free, entirely for free. She will no doubt go about her
business conscientiously. Tell me, Tullio, this one thing: how can
people suffer that such obscene & filthy comedies emerge from

a smile, an odd, banal chance word, a mechanical kiss, or never-willed embrace?" "They cannot bear it either — they are all sick and criminals." "But there are happy people too, not everybody is so mad. I've spoken to many happy ones, I clearly remember every single one." "Happy people?" — the spy smiled on him. "If you say so."

The mayor felt more and more in a madhouse. Wherever they went the forest was thinning, from the clearings one could see the hills and roads around — in the agitated, light-refracting chaos of dust, sunlight, mist and flower-steam strange folks were loitering. Does it go so simply? No fighting at all, the soldiers saunter like women in front of Venetian shop-windows? Some trick? They will take the town and by the time he, the mayor, makes to return, the gates will be closed and the emperor's men will be grinning down from the walls on the late-arriving, ab-sent-minded troubadour? "Now I can find the place. I'll go alone. You shall return and make haste to my wife and daughter. You'll find my daughter at communion in the Fiore. Call her and take her home. Go at once! Farewell!" "Your lordship shouldn't place too much trust in me, I can't find my way easily in times of confu-sion, and one dare not do much because of all the responsibility." "I know and I want nothing special from you, but you have seen me to the latest minute, and I would like somebody who pre-serves my latest moment, handshake, and gaze, to be beside my family. The lords and soldiers in the town hall are only carrying out my orders and yesterday's plans (if they do) — and where is yesterday gone? Good God" — he reached out his hand, and the spy turned to go. He didn't gallop, lest he might draw attention to himself.

42.

The mayor let his entire body and soul blissfully glide into soli-tude like water into a glass. He will not stay there for long; he will at once speak with the woman. He spotted her on horseback on the nearest hill and rode up to her. They were on a height, surrounded by ponds, meadows, rust-colored brambles in the sweet-sad calm of subdued orderliness: one couldn't tell if it was "Italian fatherland" or a studio background to a "Madonna in the woods." The woman raised her head slowly: her look was a curious mixture of surprise and boredom — such neurotic people are so used to a teaspoon's rattle or the purr of a sparrow's wings being an earthquake-like sensation for them that they have developed an excessively efficient technique of camouflaging it, for they are ashamed in front of strangers and of the healthy, so even at the height of some extreme emotion they appear ridiculously blasé, their eyes almost closed, as though they were nearly sleeping. That is their leisureliness. The mayor knew such fake indifference well and it immediately drove him to the rage that he had anticipated for the moment of encounter. "What's the use of this play-acting? Donna, where are you roaming?" — he asked, trying to suppress the irritation in his voice. "Roam?" — the Donna asked in a far too superior, nasally sneering voice. "Do you think one can't go for a walk before breakfast to whet the appetite? Or are you perhaps one of those poetic spirits who tend to roam like the knights of the Holy Grail, or bards? We, women, are much more prosaic than that." In her whole intonation there was some unbearable artifice, which the mayor wanted to extinguish once and for all, so he said quietly but with determination: "Enough of this game. I know you are not here for play or salon-shepherdery, in this villa, in this hermitage." "No hermitage at all, life runs quite high here, if you could see."

The most awkward thing for the mayor in all this was that the Donna uttered each sentence in a different pitch, new psychic background, as if she were not human at all: her questions were no questions but the dying swan's theatrical nostalgia; her denials were no simple nos but some wild, demented, vile hostility.

When she said, "no hermitage," her voice bore such country-fair hullabaloo, fishwife's defiance, that the mayor felt a strong inclination to slap her with his riding whip. What life can one have who lives from one sentence to the next — who has no lasting feeling or thought but keeps jumping from one word to the next as an itching monkey hops from one branch to the next, grinning in-between with that unaccountable triumph of the sick, like one who has uttered some witticism. Nervous persons of course have the impression of "cornering" their interlocutors with each such unjustified sentence, for they are indeed forced to stammer like a Socrates or Descartes trying to speak not to a rational human being but to a whimsical cat, or a fluttering sparrow that strayed into their room.

"Look, Donna, do for once make an attempt at self-abnegation and don't try to contradict me mechanically with each sentence. If you want you can kill me, or send me off, but the present moments are not at all suitable to serve your rhetorical triumphs in every second." The Donna suddenly opened her eyes on the mayor: so far they have been hardly open, out of posture-apathy, a cowardly avoidance of the man's gaze, suppressed tears, and some kind of eye-straining nervousness. Detachment, unreachable Elysium, the deathly sleep of sorrow, purposelessness, sybilline secret, bored womanly power: such could have been the vignettes of those half-open eyes, which the mayor would have earlier liked to lash at with his riding-crop. How does a half-mad woman have the right to claim for herself "poetry" with such well-nigh sadistic obdurateness — excluding from it everyone and everything, the trees, animals, leaving only her arrogant hypochondria to inhabit it? The last thing we needed was that the half-open eyes' Delphic shtick to be followed by the too wide-open eyes' great death-allusiveness.

The woman was pale, white, and powdered — flour and aging pores succeeded one another on her face; under her eyes parallel purple wrinkles, like collars made of five or six threads. One could see from her gaze that she didn't want to look but to stage the wondrous female fact of psychology, eventually to perform "death" as long-ago legalized female pawnshop. The mayor knew perfectly well that in a hysterical person posturing and sincerity, recherché kitsch and real human suffering, are caught in a rather complicated relationship, this being precisely the reason why he could bring himself to bear, for months now, the Donna's scenes: he felt that the woman's madness (and here the most emphatic stress fell on *woman*) was on the one hand the rawest denial of true affect, flower and poetry, alternatively it was nevertheless nature, flower, affect, even poetry, which demands investigation with the Renaissance scholar's and the Renaissance physician's broad-minded understanding, even respect, and perhaps love. For the fatalistic, desperate person there is no difference between Sophocles and Aristophanes: for them, profound suffering and the dimeshow caricature of such suffering are of equal value, so the mayor saw in the woman's flippancy, poetic poses, in the upstart death-metaphoricity of her whole physique, in the last analysis — his own lyricism, his own suffering. A leaning to self-mortification was deeply ingrained in him: for him it was a moral bliss to see the dreadful facts of "feeling," "poetry," "death," which were at the center of his whole life, in such laughable, pathological travesties for which his mistress for months now provided ample opportunities. Of course the world of his affects was always torn between two such sharply contrasting poles: one of them was — to kill his mistress for her uncreditable, mendacious, and pathological parodies of feeling; the other — to glorify her, for she had definitely put him off every kind of love, soul-momentum, grand psychic or poetic gesture.

One could see that she concentrated all her strength into her dilated eyes: her eyes, her thoughts, the mayor, the splint curling from the horse's nostrils, the trees were all absorbed into this mute, black-mirrored whirlpool. In this moment the mayor felt nothing but human compassion and mystical awe toward madness: in this willed, sweated-for, artificial pathos he felt life's dreadful energies, dreadful inertia, that mysterious duality which had always also intrigued him in history: people harbor an enormous desire for action, while in the world meaningful things to do are lacking in the extreme; in them there is an enormous instinct for love, while there is not the slightest live or lifeless being whom we could find it worthwhile to fall in love with — our souls tumefy with unbearably splaying "poetry," while in the world there is nothing even remotely poetic. These black, hysterical woman's eyes close to him: the very Persephonic demons of looking and seeing; they are so black, so open to the point of turning-out, and so demonic precisely because they know that in the world there is *nothing* to see, that sight is utterly and forever superfluous — their gaze is so passionate precisely because they know that everything is in vain, there is no real passion, nor has there ever been or will be on earth — everything has to be forced.

What then is the difference between the two of us — the mayor asked himself — what is her "poetry," and what is mine? Is my repulsion simply the healthy person's repulsion from the sick? or the erudite person's from the uneducated? Is the whole tragic game brought into being by the intelligence gap between the inwardly cultivated philosopher and the upstart Renaissance courtesan? What is more loathsome: hysteria or lack of erudition, sickness or vulgarity — or are the two really one?

"What wondrous eyes you have!" — said the mayor with quite profound sincerity. Although for seconds now she had been concentrating her life and organs into her eyes, the mayor's words were enough for her to tear off this Medusa-mask and throw it away with an idiot child's nervousness. With some histrionic peacock-parading salon-gesture she snapped: "Ah, ah, will you stoop to dropping compliments now?" "O, how regular you are,

my dear Donna: I confess I've played a few hypocrisies on you."
"A few!" — she interrupted. — "How considerate of you! Tell me
rather if there has ever been anything else." "Could you listen to
me without interrupting me?" "Are you telling me to listen to
you!" — and her voice was now ghastly and weeping. — "Have
I ever done anything else but listen, endure, pay attention, humiliate myself, learn and adjust? Are you bidding me listen to
you? I have never dared say a word because I believed it would
not be what you wanted to hear, so I always kept mum."

The mayor knew that from some perspective this was true:
the woman had been good beyond belief, very humble, only that
her goodness and humility glowed and withered in her soul as a
white flower among blue and red ones: no connection could be
discovered among certain psychic traits of hers, she was much
too cowardly to be capable of a unified life — she thought she
would be "clever" if she gave an entirely special reaction to every
phenomenon of life, with the boundless mimicry-gourmandiz-
ing of neurotics: before every flower she put on a new flower-
mask, before every word or person, a new word- or person-mask,
the one which was most alike that momentary person, word,
or flower. What was all her goodness worth then? He probably
hated her most for her cowardliness.

"Listen to me! I wanted to say that you have always given
your most supercilious ah-s —" "My superciliousness — oh my!
So now I am the supercilious one, I with my sack and ashes —
and you of all people are telling me this!" "My dear, dear Donna,
listen to me" — the mayor said and, in order not to hit her for
all her pathetic interruptions, he leaned over and kissed her on
the neck, laughing — "you have always laughed at me when I
was sincere with you and believed everything that was merely
the barrel-organ tune of my politeness. Don't you think there is
something amiss there? And let's not sing Orphic hymns now
about things amiss and death but let's talk sensibly." "Talk sensi-

bly? For you that means breaking into my house to hurl insults at me, to humiliate me, to do me in." "But you must admit that what you are talking about is madness, hallucination, and vision. It's high time you realized that if a love affair is not as smooth as the fairies' nuptials sung in verse, the cause is not compulsorily that the man is a heartless, sadistic rascal whose sole passion is to relish your suffering. One gets the impression that your favorite pastime or opium is this martyrdom." "If only I had some opium now! When my brother was sent by Venice to sail to the East with the Turks, he told me many stories about opium. You see, you are right, you are always right, what I need is opium and for me everything, absolutely everything, is like opium. Can you see that tree over there — for me it is not like what it is for others (now her intonation sounded with that ever more awkward fakeness that one hears when a gramophone record is sped up), for me it is like opium — I cannot live and breathe for two minutes if I don't look at that tree! I have to see it always, always, you understand? Always! Let's ride up there! Do get me some opium, please!"

The mayor was irritated by the woman's whimsicality — nothing is more awkward than to move one's body for the sake of an object which for one person is more wonderful than Orpheus' lyre, but is less than nothing for the other — especially when it is not a real miracle for the first person either, merely something thoughtlessly appointed to miraclehood, "for, after all, some mythic dimwit is entirely comme il faut in love." "Donna, tell me, however difficult it is for you — what do you think of me after all, what do you want to do with me, what do you want to do with yourself? I know that if, as the case may be, you happened to be desperate because of me, you wouldn't tell me, you would by no means tell me because you would think you were humiliating yourself, but you can surely tell me, you know well enough that if I lack anything that's pride — no woman's love ever turned me into a triumphant toy hussar." "What I want to do? As if you cared in the least! You have come here out of smugness, you are annoyed by people telling stories about how I am raving in my loneliness, you're afraid that I might compromise you, I might somehow hurt your adored wife, so you are pulling all kinds of sympathizing and remorseful faces, to comfort me and then leave me." The mayor knew that this simple-minded woman's talk was not her invention, however simple; he himself could never achieve so much logic.

When they got to the tree, the woman hurled herself off her horse with a clumsily brisk movement, her riding-skirt was ripped lengthwise, her heel got stuck in the stirrups, so when she finally reached the ground, she dropped to one knee. At this she gave a disproportionate peal of laughter, without breath, resonance, or mirth, rocking herself to and fro, so that her hair (big, carbonized papyrus scrolls) should get entirely disheveled. "Aren't I just gorgeous? I dressed to kill for the rendezvous and look at me now. For you know that I deceived you, ha ha, I awfully deceived you, you're as easily duped as a baby, a puppy, a starving stray puppy, am I right? How you swallowed, you baby, you schoolboy, that this tree is some 'poetic' place for me where perhaps I'm in the habit of pining after you! I have a rendezvous here, my beau is arriving any time now, he's handsome, young, and faithful. You may look on if that's your wish. Where he comes from — from there? No, from over there. Look!"

She threw herself on the ground and laughed on in her metallic clarinet voice. Her face couldn't adjust to her laughter — it was all a parching of the throat without soul, without grimace. When she was spread out on the earth, making holes in the muddy soil with her spurs, the mayor saw that she was running to fat and this inert, puffed-up woman-pastry was even more at odds with the incessant, enforced, inhaled laughter and the pubertal tousling of the hair in the grass and among the wild flowers. He jumped off his horse to her, trying to scrape toward himself the chortling woman's head, stuck among the brambles, like a beater the felled game that clusters of hounds are already tearing into. When he didn't manage to dig to himself the rather large and heavy head, he started kissing, embracing it on all available surfaces, trying to sober her up in this way. Perhaps in this very moment the pope is murdered, perhaps it's the emperor's hitman or some German bladderbag of a prince in person who is struggling with Christ's savage diplomat rolling among his pillows as he is struggling here with this madwoman: but is it truly against? Do we indeed hate, or love — what is it in general that we want of the other? How little we have to do with one another we feel the most acutely in these moments when we touch their body with our hands: what foreign, superfluous, dull mass.

"Enough of this comedy! I don't care if you have a rendezvous here, or if you want to wax lyrical, to die of affectation or commit acts of strumpetry in line with your arch-nature: I left all my work, my town, my soldiers, my family, to tell you that I have loved you, that I love you very much, perhaps infinitely — but with me love is not 'action,' not household, not living together, no Aranjuez sailing in the free and intimate spaces of dream and dining-rooms — nobody will ever love you, nobody loves you as I do, but please do understand, I beg you, that I am no ladies' man, I can't live, do anything for the woman; if I leave you it is not because I am a Don Juan, not because I got bored, but because I am a ludicrous and hopeless dilettante in living with women. I am a loner, selfish in the word's truest and most sacred sense, and cannot bear that you paint or have painted all kinds of false portraits of me, yarned-together from the colors of gossip, hysteria, & l'art-pour-l'art rascalry: I can't bear that you should be tormented because of a fiction, a hallucination. I have always been of a much more lonesome nature, foreign from all people and animals, to be depraved by you between the most banal, marketplace alternatives of faithfulness and unfaithfulness. You have always recited to me, with transported face and Parca gestures, about how well you understood me, how high above you I stood, what a divine miracle I am — and once your reciting-lesson was over, you expected me to instantly turn into a mer-cenary in his Sunday best, a peasant, an ordinary book-poet, a filthy *littérateur*. I admit that you are right, I admit that from the perspective of the whole of life and nature your need for a banal companion in love is truer, more divine, ethical, and more natural than my conception of love and my possibility of love — I ad-mit that I saw clearly and already at our second meeting that my style of love (my god, what an elevated word!) can never, never align itself to your beastly romanticism and beastly lust for meta-physics, and I should have disappeared with no delay, knowing that if I rest I would inevitably cause you suffering: I admit all this. But you yourself have seen this, you have known all this, and if it is true that you loved me so much, why weren't you pre-pared to — I'll be entirely sincere —put up with even more?"

While the mayor spoke, the woman slowly raised herself and the tiny flowers pressed to the ground under her head also rose happily, with the obedient, commonsense chic of suppleness: as if ten, twenty, thirty flowers had grown all at once from her quiet attention. One could see that she was attentive, but not paying attention to the words, only to the fact that a "grand speech" was being delivered next to her, that "psychic life," histrionic crisis, was present, her very own element, irrespective of content. Be-neath her eyes and around her mouth the small lines of light disgust quivered: she found that the mayor was not pathetic enough, that in throwing a scene he was even more amateurish than in love. When he stopped speaking, her triumphant smile announced that she was solely interested in teaching her com-panion a lesson in much more gifted actorship. The mayor saw this and made a last effort to fix his eyes on the horses sniffing and gnawing the brambles — so his eyes would find some rest. But it didn't last for long, because she fished from her bag a thick book, pulled out from it a pressed flower used for a bookmark, smelled and kissed it with eyes turned to heaven: at this the mayor couldn't help but look. He asked almost with a school-boy's naïve panic: "You don't want to recite poetry now?" "Why not? Poets are a hundred times cleverer than you or I, or the two of us put together."

The mayor said nothing, just went to his horse, placed one foot in the stirrup, and was about to hoist up his sclerotic body into the saddle, when he heard the following stanza behind his back, in an eerie voice: "Hark to my tale of a chaste violet, Your true love calls to me from distant land, Where 'midst silence and in holy dream's realm, Amidst sad musics I sadly pass my days." He looked back: the Donna was smiling at him with a vicious douceur, with which Cleopatra must have looked at a pilloried conspirator. The mayor rushed to her, gave a kick to the book with all his strength, sending it up into the air in shreds, jumped on his horse and rode off, all the while screaming: "Nothing to do with them, nothing to do, nothing to do!"

43.

The mayor lived perpetually in the world of intellectual reflec-tion and of deeds, utterly alien to one another: if he pondered much on a given idea he would soon realize that at its bottom was a way of life, a possibility of life, moreover: a compulsion to act, so he would try to act in consequence (especially in the old days); when he was tossed and turned in the agitated, rough, and always alarmingly unequivocal world of deeds, he invariably felt that this deed was interesting or tragic from the perspective of some idea or theoretical principle — that the only way to bear and situate the absolute restlessness born from the dizzying limitation of "action" was from some intellectual angle of vision. While intellectual bias always prodded him to act in line with the threads of thought just read or mulled over, the world of deeds — as is natural, after all — never pushed him into a particular direction of thinking: all he needed was to set up some naïve contrast of ideas, poems, theories, frescoes, to pit against the humbug of "event." Now, when he was galloping away from his impossible mistress, choking with rage, he felt the same: a wild, beastly greed for some "thinking," which could reset into balance the ridiculously upset, asymmetrical scales of his life. On such occasions he hardly needed to "look for" an intellectual theme: the gaudy misery of "action" automatically tossed him something, anything, which was then to appear to his eyes in its full theatrical, tragic pomp, in the background of dimeshow deed.

I am writing my testament (to have some written work in the end) in the style of Empedocles: and he could instantly see on the shores of Sicily, among palm-trees, snow, azure, and Papua Apollo statues, the romantic figure of the "philosopher" rising from the shabby drama of grotesque love-making with the Donna. Such is the contrast of contrasts: on the one hand, a vacillating, dogmatic comprehension and experiencing of the world with all its phenomena, and alternatively the churning on the street-organ of one puny, anemic, almost fictitious routine (love!), isolated from everything, the world, life, any anything-like thing — and have I ever done other than stumble from the one into the other, not even suspecting that I might as well attempt to bring those two into some kind of harmony. He felt in his fingers the hard cover and pages of his new edition of Empedocles — he last read the fragment the night before and now they suddenly became wild, tragic, living due to the Donna's shameless lying mask.

Aphrodite: the first fragments were about her. Aphrodite — what shall I write about you to my town, my daughter, to the people? You have meant everything: to me, as to the Girgenti poet, you have meant life's simple and complex vegetation, the valency of chemical compounds, the æsthetic suitedness of landscape elements, a gull's tilting wing, a sail, a wave-leaf sucked into the sand, the bouncing in the light of a spark-spirited lizard, one person's tragic mania toward and against another, which boils down to the same thing; you have meant the evidence, lurking at the bottom of everything, that being is being-like, that being wills being, that the momentum of non-being toward being is evident on earth; around us, inside us, in spite of all misery and death, something wants itself, and it is already an aphrodisiac, ghostly, inscrutable, but undeniably "love." I have lived through all your great kaleidoscopic versions, O Aphrodite: the embryonic, blood-core, unicellular nervousness of vegetation, the blind-most life-twitchings — I have experienced the bliss of beauty, the shapeless, Protean eros of artistic pleasure, and the bodily and psychic struggle of man and woman with all its magnetism, absurdity, ethos and deceit.

From primeval matter the goddess Aphrodite fashioned my untiring eyes:[3] this is one of the fragments — and Aphrodite bound together people, men, & women, with the chains of love, nailed them to one another like a coffin with the coffin lid. Yes, these are the two extremes of love: being's self-serving foundation, the blind self-affirmation of all reality (adrenal glands! a daisy!) — and the psychic haggling of man and woman, their nuancing-to-death, squirming among various social orders, eternal shipwreck on the islands of distorted coitus &, for want of anything better, ethics.

All this is Aphrodite — and when I utter the name "Aphrodite," the duality which perhaps quavered eerily in Empedocles is also lurking in me: I see one palpable, concrete female shape, form, the sweet, maddening mass of my dreams and adventures, at whom I glance with that sweetest kind of recognition with which we look at the lover in the morning, if she had furtively

left the bed while we were asleep and is now waiting for us in
her brilliant make-up, but still in solidarity with our embraces
and shared sleep in her loose gown, for breakfast: form, statue,
picture, flesh, person — and at the same time an indefinite concept, broad, hazy, & shapeless in line with its content, the word
Aphrodite is merely a resigned compass aquiver not toward one
sole point but toward the whole of existence, like a vague moth
caught in a net.

Whom have I sought, who had I believed in? In my own
abstractions or some expressive, plastic, great figure: logic or
mythology, dogmas or gods?

Now on horseback, after the mortally offended mistress
and before the Antichrist who is perhaps already triumphing
in Rome, there is not a line and not a single naïve naturalist
blunder of the Empedocles book that didn't mean some significant page of the mayor's life wrung into focus. Already the
idea that the elements that make up the world did not merge
with one another chemically, but are physically juxtaposed: how
this childish contrast expressed the essence of every event in
time, of every landscape, woman, forest in space. The greatest
torment of his life was that of permanently seeing borderlines,
precipices among objects, and when, following his latest conversations with his wife's doctor, he felt an inebriating curiosity
for the secrets of biology — this question intrigued him above
all: the fringes, walls of cells, the outermost layers of the individual organs, beneath which they are still themselves, but beyond which something else starts. How could one observe the
first seconds of embryonic life, when from homogeneous mass
the first otherness is born, the first "near" in space? He felt so
uneasy in his own home because every chair, picture, musical instrument was so awkwardly beside one another in space,
whilst his instinct called for merging into one another, chemical mixing: let the chair become clavicembalo, the clavicembalo,

a picture, and the picture, a vase. How can the foundational
instinct of life (the most un-individualized, most universal
"Aphrodite") balance these two movements: to fashion, on the
one hand, ever newer islands and independent, closed configu-
rations sharply delineated from one another in space (distinct
petals, distinct bodily organs) — and on the other hand, to permanently find joy of life in connection, pulp-like fusion, blood
circulation, mimicry? There is a permanent struggle at the heart
of life, between a tendency toward utmost sporulating-apart &
fission, and the disciplining-back into the sole basic structure. I
can tranquilly say in this will that I have learned & played both
roles well and comprehensively: I have been dispersed in a thousand impression mosaics and I have been equally the slave of
the sole, fateful biological schema of my life and my organism.

Menander and Genethlios have written about Empedocles
that he wrote "physical hymns," taking primordial elements for
gods and gods for the components of nature. Have I ever decided what the "gods" have been for me: inbred superstitions,
learned or poetic metaphors, or nearly empirical realities? The
embodiments of everything that is absence, secret, openness &
question in life, so the Olympus or heaven is merely the revenge-
plasticism of negativity; or are such gods, on the contrary: the
embodiments of everything that is, in any case and absolutely
— of trees, fight, death, love, day and viciousness? Wouldn't it
be a frightful naivety to pose such questions seriously to myself:
is the god a symbol or a reality? Much as symbol and reality are
logically and grammatically two distinct things, they are just as
nonexistent opposites for the soul, for inner experience. God and
myth are, if we stick to grammar and logic, simply the synthesis of "the whole being" and "elemental excitement derived from
existence" — there is nothing more I can say. Pantheism, poetry,
dogma, neurosis are all variants of this, there are no demarca-
tion lines. "This is not God but merely a metaphor," "this is not

religion but only hypochondria," "this is no longer drama but
prophecy": these scathing or celebrating phrases have hardly any
meaning at all, or, because modesty is a gentlemanly virtue, they
have hardly had any meaning in my life. The god is not in the
tree and not on Olympus — he is the concrete undefined. In fact
we always lean toward two god types: the one which we produce
in solitude, from inside our sole personal lives, like a black daffodil (it is often dubbed monotheism), and the other, with which
we try to underline the thousand and million motley sensations
of our impressions in celebration of the outer world: this is the
Olympus, all kinds of Olympus. Empedocles, too, betrays his
predilection toward both types in one fragment, in a few lines —
he first talks about animals, birds, fish, and the picaresque antics
of the list brings the gods to his mind: where there is a catalogue, there must be Olympus, too — then later, when he talks
about *truth*, this mysterious, mythological product of his own
subjective life and his singular Empedocles destiny, he suddenly
thinks of one god: he doesn't say which one, but it's not difficult
to guess that this is the magnified, individual awareness of the
Empedocles destiny.

I, too, have carried those two god-worlds throughout my life;
the one god in myself (I could sum it up as: myself) and a whole
plethora of others, a million whatevers that are not-I, so in the
last analysis: enemies (of course the game can also be played the
other way round: I the "one God" am often the enemy, and the
million impressions, exteriorities, are the allies, the truth).

Few things have given me such pleasure as reading, in those
two-thousand-year-old Greek sentence-ruins, simple words like
"birds," "fish," "trees," "women," "men": as if human words could
only have a strength and intensity equal to the intensity of reality
that we so often expect of them, if they are quite two thousand
years old and if they had been transmitted to us in the form of
torsos, mystical debris. All ingenious poetry is barren and point-

less when compared to this effect: infinitely remote *time* and tragic *fragment* — those are the vehicles of salvation, not truth or beauty.

Have I not felt in every moment of my life the duality of which the Sicilian sage's (what a word!) "opus" left to us such a faithful and unwittingly paradoxical memento of: on the one hand, the finitude of the world's components, their physical limitedness, and on the other hand, the relentless eternity, numbing, opium-like infinity of the world, of existence. In theoretical physics and in theology finitude and infinitude are often posed as a problem — although there is no trace of any problem here. Every living being has lived in those two worlds at the same time, or if you will, in those two moods or thought-frames: flowers have withered, and of flowers there have been a hundred, nay, a thousand, but in any case everybody has had one last flower, beyond which they knew no other; everybody has had a mother, twenty lovers, two hundred books and this sickness, not another one: but has felt all the same that the world of flowers, sicknesses, lovers, and ululating laboring machines is far more boundless and mysterious than to be penetrable — some indescribably distant past, "eternity," is felt in the flower pendulating under the bee, in the mouth budding from a kiss, *&* an equally fatal distance, "future" sailing away into greenish mists, shapeless aim suggests itself, sends off its perfume in the womb flooded by mothers' blood, in the abdicating gesture of kings. This world is both closed and finite, like a hard nut — and open and everlasting, like a perfumed lily.

That's precisely why I have felt death in its crudest danse macabre form, but at the same time was driven to affirm with Empedocles that in fact there is no death, no birth, only the dancing, changing, dissolution and aggregation of elements. I confess that with me the twofold, contrasting perspectives of death never joined in any kind of harmony: on the contrary, they ceaselessly fought, criticized, and refuted one another. Here I couldn't feel "reality" and "metaphor," "nature philosophy" and "domestic, individual life" to be unequivocal: when I stood by my wife's dreadful bed, redolent of suffering, I always had to laugh at the repulsive snobbery with which Empedocles proclaims: "there is no birth and no death, only mingling and separation" — with what academic preciousness this sentence sounded in the abject boudoir of suffering, of wounds, of vomit, of vacuumed excrement! But still, even then and there I knew that from the perspective of the whole of life, in the common flow of all existence, individual death and suffering doesn't matter: the sickness is not what is going to kill my wife and me, too, some time, but that we *feel* this sickness, that we feel it *as* sickness, although it is like the opening of a flower or the undulation of the sea. To feel those two perspectives simultaneously: death as a Christian ethical matter, and death as the vegetative nonchalance of living nature — it is not easy, but I have always had a leaning toward both.

How nicely humorous it is when Aristotle in his *Metaphysics* differentiates between Empedocles' "fundamental ideas" and his "clumsy form of expression"! Is there any distinction at all? Isn't "clumsiness" here the highest, absolute precision? Didn't thinking start on the road toward sterility, pointlessness, and meaninglessness where it turned precise, avoided self-contradiction, and tried to be consequent to itself? Is there such a thing as a fundamental idea and expression at all? With a man and in a world whose essence and sole aspect is this verse: "For one by one all the parts of god began to tremble."[4] My life, the shedding of the landscape, its finery, the gods' great fiction finish-line, time, space — all these are one great trembling, epileptics and shivering, goose-bumps and earthquake: all are the same. And the world can only be felt *so* in the regions of garish blue seas, rattling and hissing palm-trees, giant green leaves blinded into charcoal, the sun that desiccates everything to mummies, and crater-powdering snow: that is the one and only Sphairos with its angina; lost god, the god of the Sicilian landscape, the essence & purpose of lonely Girgenti walks, merchant ships languishing for long Palermo afternoons (each of their sails an autumn malaria leaf), waves splitting into female anuses on razor rocks — that is the true, the only tragic region, the southern choir of luminosity, of the sea stiffer and more supple than a steel blade, of the color, one-directional almost to the point of abstraction, of houses sporulating in filth and Apollo-muscles.

I was awakened to consciousness on the shores of the Mediterranean, those few days that I spent there in my youth are my life's sole real content: at that time naïve joy, whooping serenity — since then, the eternal, phobistic fascination of tragedy. The god of the trembling parts: I see him in the grotto of a well, behind the tiny, almost cracking, peeling-off pontpeplum of leaves, half in water, half propped up against a wall, like a dying gladiator: his limbs are sublime like those of Apollo, but the rich reflexes of the foliage, water, the mossy rocks paint him entirely green, he is like a chameleon or emerald-glowing lizard on clotted earth — he is half agonizing, half sunbathing, his whole body, like a nether-worldly string, is trembling from the dew, from the bees, flies, wasps zithering around him.

If I die, the gods will die with me, if I suffer, the gods suffer with me: this vision, kindled by Empedocles, is the decisive testimony of my "religious life." I have believed in one sole thing, one sole thing did I respect, flee, worship: suffering, man's eternal and absolute abandonment in the world of lovelessness and disease. When Empedocles says that the world is forever reborn and dies again, rises again from the foam to wither again, like a plant — he gave expression to despair, to hopelessness. Our sufferings are not lonely miracles on a point of time, like a wreath of snow on top of the volcano: our sufferings are episodes of an eternal automatism, which through infinite repetition lose all their possibility of ethically-sublime meaning; all people are left with is the animal wailing, the bodies' eternal misery. With this defiant, self-tormenting pessimism which parodies my own bodily and psychic suffering, with this veritable nihilism, I have governed for decades the Italian town assigned to me; I've seen passionate idealists, bloodthirsty soldiers, diplomats and rotting proletarians, I've seen holy priests and meticulous bureaucrats, and I have always been unsayably alone among them, for I always felt behind them this Empedoclean eternal return: they all fought or suffered as if their lives, their city, their age, were an illustrious, important, and definite point in time, whereas all I could feel was that behind us millions of years' barrel-organ of suffering had already rattled in the same way, and equally monotonous millions of years are going to roll on after them, identical-looking, like the waves perishing and charging, one after the other, on the shore — the most beautiful, most sentenced-to-death limbs of the god of trembling limbs.

There is no more maddening duality than this: to be born a self-serving, unique god, to fight in every moment for this unique divine existence, to dream and hallucinate about it, all the while knowing that we are unsayably puny and insignificant atoms in a godless, eternally rattling praying machine. What is more tragic: the once-and-for-all passing of something unique, or its eternal recurrence? The moment I know that my fracas with my mistress, my wife's agony, the decay of Rome, all my inner misery are merely eternally returning refrains — I lose all possible attitude toward them, I look doltishly on it all, like a madman. How well destiny has intimated what we most need for every glass to drop from our hands and for every woman's tongue to turn bitter as poison in our mouth: it has the ghost of mortality walk behind us and before us, the ghost of mechanical repetition.

I have always felt a frantic ardor for the primordial world, for animals, palm-trees, snails, waters, and volcanoes extinct for mil-

lions of years; I have always walked the earth, wherever I happened
to be, as though I were walking in a graveyard — with vast
death-humus beneath my feet, the million-year-old catacombs
of sponges, reeds, lizards, colors, and pulp. In my thoughts I
kissed the conjured-up odd, gigantic red flower and collapsed
on a dome-size snail like on my mother's coffin. We have never
spoken to one another and will never see each other. "Never" —
and after it, the other Danaid-jug: "always." Somebody will play
my role again (because it seems that in existence there are only
roles, no lives), will write this testament with the same hopelessness and the same bleak chance of annihilation-into-nothingness.
And precisely for that reason, because every moment of ours
casts its outlines on the fog-grey curtain of monotony, like the
shadow of a windblown puff-ball on a spider's web: precisely because of that, any carrier of destiny purer than humans — a fish
in the water, a wild animal in the woods, a gull swinging from
its wings, of which Empedocles writes so beautifully (that is, he
names them), are frightening like a wound, and wonderful.

If life is the unending, cold snake of hopelessness, let's dumb
ourselves into the "vital" or into "death," which at this stage are
still one: first and foremost, into Wetness, which manifests itself
everywhere "darkly and coldly" (our salvaged rags: attributes!),
most of all in love. The million waverings of the soul, the incessant mollusk-wrinkling of embraces and kisses, the mucous,
snail-masked oozing of sperm: all this is the play of ancient, vital
wetness, so let's play along with it, let's play it, let's become its
playthings. I have never felt myself to be other than flowing water, lake, sea, turning-statue in an amphora or dispersed in Danæ-
rain, steam, icicle, ovaloid drop or needle-headed froth, wave,
bubble: the tortuous trees "at the height of flowering life," and
the "long-lived gods" have all been forms of water, deltas, springs,
swamps, narcissizing plasma. And water is indeed god-within-
god, so the sage is right in saying somewhere, "as god was fight-

ing god ever more furiously" — because god always means fight, even the god of Jesus' Rome is fight: with itself, with us, fight at all times & with everything, and the forever undulating, fleeting, and mirroring water is always identical to itself and yet not identical to itself, the most consequent element, and yet the most unfaithful to itself. And it is this eternal being-water of our bodies and souls that makes it possible for us to be yet, sometimes and against all odds, happy poets, looking up at life as on a miraculous stage, thrilling drama.

Although over the last thirty years — I could swear — my nihilism and despair have never really abated, a few possibilities have shone through (as on the lead-colored sea would sometimes appear before a tempest, unexpectedly, a parrot-green strip) for seeing life as interesting, thrilling, and, what is more, perhaps even worthwhile — at such times love was not the pitch-black death-flow of the stream-of-destiny, but, to speak in the language akin to Minnesängers, "holdgesinnter, göttlicher Drang der untadeligen Liebe,"[5] and the piquancy of their mystery and wondrousness vibrated above the hosts of mortals like a bitter-astringent, enticing perfume. At such times I was justified to consider myself a poet through the poet Empedocles — water and poem, sea and plastic figure are: one and the same, inseparable.

I also needed water, like Empedocles, because water is the wonderful compromise or evasion (the two are often indistinguishable) of the two contrasting traits of the world that intrigue everybody who has truly looked into it: complete order and complete chaos — or, if we want to formulate it subjectively, we should talk not about two contrasting traits of the *world* but about two equal needs of our own eyes, our contemplative natures: about the succession of our need for symmetry, and our need for zigzagging. Streaming water is not "cosmos," as it is no "acosmia" either — it is not form and not anarchy, Empedocles has lived out both needs: with a woman's obstinacy he would sometimes look on the geometrical regularity of the universe, the harmony of spheres, cones, and symmetrical rings, which revolve in deathly solitude and rejoice in their ghostly brotherlessness (as if the stars, too, were haughty aristocrats, like him) — and at the same time in this universe he couldn't see anything else but chance, caprice, hysteria running away from all powerless gods and humbug-pomp "world-spirit," kitsch, experimentation, fiasco, and isolated success.

I will never forget the images that were triggered in me while reading Empedocles: one renders "harmony," the other, mindless "chance." Whenever I read about "sphairos," a wonderful toy appears before my mind's eyes, similar to the globe that I saw in the studio of my wife's new doctors: gorgeous, shiny brass circles, supple and thin, driven around by some subtle, minute clockwork: in the whole thing there is something sentimental and precious — prisoners would fabricate such line-masquerades out of boredom, on which squirrels can do tumbles or frogs their gymnastics, if submerged in water — otherwise it is painted on every mathematician's portrait, it is the world's most banal heraldic space-filler. But all the same, my own hands and my own soul also rested nostalgically above such a cosmos-birdcage, and occasionally even Empedocles stooped to it.

And beside this, the other "illustration," the one given by Aristotle when in *Parts of Animals* he tries to refute Empedocles' biological and evolutionary theory of "chance": this or that animal has the particular shape of spine because it broke or bent, *by accident*, hundreds of millennia ago. How different this vision from the model fabricated out of circles: a black panther, as it tries to jump into the ditch from a too tall embankment, with that characteristic feline movement of leaving its hind legs on the embankment, pushing its rump high up in the air, and jutting out its whole body, parallel to the wall, toward the depth, like some ceremonial rug unrolled from a balcony, and when it nearly touches the bottom of the valley with its forelegs, only in that moment does it snatch off its hind legs, fastened to the top of the wall, as though rolling up backward, like a papyrus scroll, its backside, spine, and waist all together. This Empedoclean panther, the sooty feline god of chance, also wanted to jump in this manner, but as the height was too high, its body turned, its stretched-out waist got twisted like a corkscrew, and the beast tumbled on the ground with an S-shape spine, crippled and howling in pain, like an overcoat dropping from a broken hanger. The fact that, in this raw form, as evolutionary theory, this is pure gibberish is unimportant; everybody can feel that the very essence of biology is some form of hazard — in the shape of flowers, in the variants of disease there is and will always be some rampant, demented "tyche": the frightful doodle of accidents, surprises, and errors. From this broken-spined, agonizing panther glows out nature's most ancient & ineliminable feature: *error*, the ever-novel physiological *mistake*, which is teeming in the material and spiritual world. "Material & spiritual" — I'm mentioning those two in exactly the right place; wasn't it Empedocles himself who wrote in a poem what was to become the first problem of my intellectual life: consciousness, too, is merely an *accident* of biology; soul, reason, intellect, the capacity to philosophize, fantasy are as much errors and fiascos as the panther's breaking of its spine; and the way the flying sponges & underwater elephants went extinct, so will the disease of the spine's uppermost vertebra wilt and be eroded: the excess of marrow, that syphilis-like mass epidemic — "psychitis."

Chance: this green poison which sneaks into our blood, into our organs of love and vision like a snake — this is the black, secret vein that lurks in the depths of forests, among tree roots, and holds every single acorn, branch, mole more firmly in its grip than the passage of the seasons or the inner, "natural" law. My birth is an accident: if the unsteered sail of an invisible little sperm-yacht had turned one thousandth degree of an angle to the left rather than to the right in my mother's womb, I wouldn't be — there was a time-span within which I was singled out absolutely equally for this worldly, and perhaps the eternal heavenly life, and for never-ever-being — so it is only natural that I should carry in all my make-up, in all my life-history, as my twin-most twin and blood-most blood relation: this naught-possibility, this great, concrete nihil, forever oozing like menstrual blood from my mother's womb. If I stroke my horse's steaming nose with my hand, I always feel my other, equally true, equally biological hand as well: the *no* hand, and attached to it, the no horse, no steam, which could have equally been as that which eventually came to be. While engaged in the work of love, my father has to hiccup or sneeze, because a startled fly bumped against his nose by accident; he nervously interrupts the work, and I end up being nothing for all eternity. How could I seriously believe in my life, knowing as I do that it is perhaps to a fly that I owe the whole world?

If instead of that primrose-yellow crucifix an apple-visaged Madonna had hung in my childhood room, if my father had not caught that particular skin disease but another, if to live next to us had been not three little girls but two boys, if in adolescence I had read not Ezio's but Dezio's book, if one evening I hadn't tripped on the street, hurting my knee and as a result it hadn't taken longer to get home on the narrow side-streets, then I wouldn't have met the girl I met, and she wouldn't have taught me the things which have influenced my relationship to all the other girls, then I wouldn't have married or if I had, I wouldn't have married the woman I have, then my daughter wouldn't have the face she has — she who dropped into this world as uncalled-for as the shiny horse chestnut suddenly dropping on the ground from its loose shell in the forest's deathly silence; then everything would always have been otherwise. The possibility of the otherwise, of the eternally other, glows in every figure living around me, like a blue Egyptian crypt-flame or the cynical, pearly flower of bare apple trees — facing which stands nevertheless, with tragic stubbornness, the belief, impossible to erase, that the very fact that I have been tossed hither and thither and tyrannized by chance every moment of my life is merely chance, and that I have a theologically-fixed, individual fate, independent of chance, all it would take is to gnaw the parasitical creepers of chance off myself with a little effort, and I could see myself as heavenly necessity, like a skivvy staring at her body reflected in the washbasin in the morning, after falling victim to a lodged-in mercenary the previous night.

To care about something, can I care about something? Behind me a raving, mystery-gourmandizing courtesan faltering from tetany to tetany, who is perhaps going to turn all my life upside down in half an hour; if she wants, she may ex-terminate my family. Why? Because a few months ago I drank a bit too much wine in Frascati, dozed off on my horse on my way back home, we lost our way, and on the wrong path, among shrubbery, I spotted this woman as she was reading by a candle: the vision was as perfect as the most exquisite annunciation — perhaps the archangel himself had arrived on exactly such a black, straying horse, incensing with weary mist the bushes retreating fearfully into their cocoons, and all at once he glimpsed a Jewish woman reading in a garden, among flowers artificially paled by candlelight and by a small basin that surrounded the tiny fountain-antennae with slow, tight-fisted rings — so in the sudden, metaphysics-less earthly gazebo of silence and twilight he babbled his annunciation, so quietly that not even a sleeping bee or an alert dog could hear. Such a chance apparition brought me together with this woman, and in vain have I molded my soul, my thinking, from the inside for decades, life couldn't give a whistle about that: everything is at the mercy of a strumpet's hysteria.

And have I not borne in myself, in my uncontrollably im-
pulsive temperament which threatens with an outburst at every
step, the source of meaningless accident, of lightning nonsense:
I spend half my fortune to help a family of poor relations, and
in an irascible moment I lash with my whip at the mouth of the
old woman or the idiot child, and hurl all their money out the
window. I do everything in my power to help another relation
become a priest, have masses said for him, heap spiritual books
on him, push him to become a page of bishops, holy men, theologians, and on a rainy, cloister-hard morning I pour into him
the bleakest nihilism and suicidal doubt. Have I not taken long,
disease-accumulating journeys to ask for the forgiveness of a forsaken, dying lover, to comfort her and love her to her death, and
after the first words have I not torn the pillow from under her
head, as the baker withdraws the baking shovel from under the
bread, have I not trampled on her medicine, have I not rushed
off to the first inn, to drink myself unconscious? Have I not destroyed, everywhere and on all occasions, those for whose sake I
intended to sacrifice myself?

Later when I was tortured by all kinds of sicknesses, when
my left eye squinted skyward like that of Brueghel's idiots, when
buzzing and dizziness made its entry into my left ear like a pan-
icking bat caught up in a woman's bun, or as though a seashell
had been undetachably fastened to it, so that I would incessantly
hear Neptune's roar; when my molars started chipping and gradually turned out of their place, like iron piles from the sodden
earth, when the muscles on my left cheek were so puffed up as if
fermented by yeast, when my mouth concurred in drooping and
my body weakened, quivered, and was emptied, and the mantle
of sleep was trimmed shorter toward both the evening and the
morning, so that my limbs stuck out from under it like a gladiator's from a child's coffin or a bonbonnière, then, O, didn't I abandon myself with relish to my impulses — why should I defeat

such irrationalities, when my body's sicknesses proclaim more clearly than revelation the gloating antics of the one-and-only god: *chance*. Let whatever it wills run its course around and in me, I can have no word, no power in this life: whether I am made pope on top of Rome and shed my urbi et orbi blessings among fans, cannons, and crowns, or die, a syphilitic world-swindler, from the poisonous needles of a demented coquette — it's all the same, I have willed neither, neither is I, I have never been, could never be identical to myself.

"We think with our blood," Empedoclean epistemology proclaims. And blood is eternal whim, eternal secret, vitality's gibberish-brook, its human-denying, human-drowning Ganges: if thought is *that*, then we'd better not imagine it. He also says that the soul dies in the same way as the body: how could it not die, since the soul is thought, and thought is blood, so all raison, cosmeticized syllogism, and Platonic world-ordering are melted into our sclerotic veins planted in the grave — our wrists' blue blood-knot is perhaps a god's torso in the grave, in our heart's cup the ebbing, rust-colored blood-acids are the ends of a biological theory — blood and thought are one, so death and thought also mean the same.

And can the thinking human being be in any other relationship with the soul, with raison, with the intellect, than Empedocles? On the one hand, what shows itself in all human logic, art, and theology is death, the torso, the rag doll of inscrutable determinations — conversely, even in the last wilted, snowed-in blade of grass, in the shadow jumping after the jumping grasshopper, in the palm-trees' courtesan fans, in a raccoon's sniffle one can discern, ever and everywhere, the signs and rays of *thought*, some inextinguishable intellect, one sole philosophical intention precise to the point of mathematics: even man's most perfect thought is but a chance thickening or diluting of the blood in the artery meandering under the neck, mere play, decorative *nonsense*: yet even the less-than-nothing-faced litter-weed, the basest bog vermin proclaim some eternal sensibility, divine *reason*.

Isn't the most possible stance vis-à-vis the rationality or irrationality of the world or human existence this: to weave under the highest intellectual functioning the basis of nonsense, of accidental toy ghost, but at the same time to look at the silliest games of irraison from the perspective of the most scholastic logical order.

And the culmination of all those thoughts, the end of my and of Empedocles' "testament": when I felt myself driven the most deeply into the non-descript gravel of exile, when I was disappointed by everything, afraid of everything, when my most cherished bodily parts came to mean ripe sickness, my greatest loves, brigand murders, and my boldest historical chess moves, amateurish puppet-shows — it was at that precise moment, in those instants of plastic annihilation, that I felt the most divinely, moreover: the most divine. What did Empedocles write about the souls damned to walk the earth? "Now I, too, belong among them; cast away from god I roam hither and thither, because I have joined the furious battle." And what could be the logical follow-up to such despair? Only this sentence: "I wander in your midst as an immortal *god*." What is the use of the gods' casting us off, far away — in vain do they snatch our crowns, clothes, rings from us in their towering, black-shadow jealousy: our nudity, our stripped, bare, ivory-glinting misery becomes a new myth: from our condemnedness a divinity is born, from our blindness a black ray, which rebounds from resentment's doltish-haughty bow directly into the hearts of the deceitful gods. I am god: this article is my last heritage, this is the god of the Impossibility of Gods, the god of god-superfluity and god-fiasco, who was able to float so dumbly among the silky shrouds of tyche as an autumnal leaf-like, flat fish ("I was a mute fish surfacing from the sea," the Sicilian charlatan writes), and I could see the world with its star-arcs and enamored slaves, with its popes and eunuchs so cleverly that in it everything became system, purpose, divine cosmos.

I leave behind no advice, no money, no wish, whether blessing or anathematically vengeful: my life has been entirely and exclusively my life, the mocking game of my accidents, the selfish secret of my divinification: I had not a single moment, not a single idea that could be of use to an other. The "others" are far more other from us than people imagine. The reason why I yet insist to put these lines to paper is that, in case I'm killed by my lover, the papal army or the emperor's henchman, by traitors or heroes, poison or hetaera: may there hover above the imbecile, inorganic accident of my death, not belonging to me, above its dark lake driven to the surface from the depth, the "thought": its arch-enemy, like a thread-thin, glass-transparent willow twig, solitary & leafless, a barely rustling string above the black mirror of senseless perishing.

44.

But the mayor was not the only one to be present at the meeting, so it didn't have such Empedoclean consequences alone: a woman, too, returned home from there, in whose soul the gross fiasco of love no doubt produced different reverberations. Her horse didn't take her home by the same path on which she came: she was surrounded by new flowers, new brooks, and she followed those surprise gifts of nature partly with the most wondrous indifference and blindness, partly with over-the-top ecstasy, as though there had been gods born out of thin air specially for her — for hysteria is an illness precisely because it brings to the surface the most natural, most fundamentally human, womanly features in their most logical and most biological purity (perhaps every illness is the appearance, with exaggerated reality-emphasis, of a reality of nature). This indifference and ecstasy alternating in her soul during her peripatetic reverie is the most womanly thing: on the one hand, to be interested only in people, social relations, business, marriage, profit, the placement of children, and not to give a whistle about sunset, stars, water's caterpillar-wing purr — on the other hand, to be a mother, that is, to be in the very midst and depth of vegetation, of nature (sunset, stars, water), in the fullness of mere-animality. It couldn't be any clearer that the two attitudes are the two crystal facets of the self-same inclination, but in day-to-day life we experience them very much like two distinct, moreover: opposite things in the lives of women. The mayor, too, knew perfectly that the hysterical courtesan's indifference to nature is rooted in the fact that she, as woman, *is* nature, and her ecstatic nature-relish is much rather a core poetry, snobbery pilfered from men, "humans," a Minderwert-accruing, cowardly howling with the wolves. And being perfectly aware of this, his own stance vis-à-vis hysteria was, in the last analysis, a lot more hysterical than hysteria itself: it constantly lapsed from apology to parody, from mockery to homage.

The horse ambled along a quiet little brook. It took unlikely turns, so the northward path by its meandering banks often made again toward the south, like the two prongs of a bobby pin; beside being so winding, in some places it also flared out to extraordinary width, and then abruptly narrowed again. With its black, brown, dark green colors and its human eye-like, rigid surface, the water stood in whimsical contrast to the nearly subterranean anarchy of the directions & forms. One could never tell whether the brook's narrowing within a few centimeters' distance was simply the optical delusion of perspective, or real ebbing: there are few more dizzying and at the same time more benumbingly pacifying phenomena in nature than the overlapping, opalescing-apart, and subsequent re-encounter, of "optical illusion" and "material reality." The wilder this or that curve, the more unlikely a widening of the brook's bed, the more serene, the more idyllic the

mood it induced in the one walking along it: this duality is experienced in the stripping of refined coquettes — the more impudic, in-medias-res blunt their gestures of taking off their various
items of clothing, ducking beneath, above, and through straps,
belts, garters with complicated epileptic flutter like a circus horse
jumping through circles, the more charitable, mothering, sisterly,
and moral the atmosphere we find ourselves in: ultimate obscen-
ity is at the same time also ultimate nursery-ethos. The brook
worked with this technique throughout. The fact that its smooth,
dream-crystalline body showed up a thousand different kinds of
shadows did not disturb in the least the tranquility of the vision.
Along its banks and parallel to it, light green shades stretched
like cigarette smoke in the moment before final dispersion; more
inward, sharp dents, small burrows, like the oblique lines that
bakers carve into the bread; even more inward, shining blindness,
some neutral incandescence, in which neither the brook's muddy,
fishful depth, nor the sky or the surrounding trees were visible,
neither water-reality nor forest-mirror, but only plastic, cold, dia-
mond void, probably resulting from the fact that the light rays
ran quite horizontally above it, although physics is of little help
when it comes to explaining nature. Sometimes a tiny waterfall
formed, only a few fingers in height — here cascading water
abruptly became white; on the margin of the depth it was still
as dark and mute as thirty steps from there, and after the fall it
immediately became smooth again, not a bubble, not the smallest
froth showed on it — comedy actors are able thus to alter their
grimace for half a second. There was no bank — up to the last
minute, only thick grass, then immediately the water, without any
in-between marshy stretch of earth or narrower bed. From under
the water feathery leaves reached out like silvery mermaid arms:
half ballet-movement, half human-accusing agony — among
them, floating flat leaves, green leather-plates: they related to the
jutting-out twigs as drums to a harp. Here and there creepers,

boughs with few leaves bent over to the other bank, hanging deep into the mirror, but curling back at the last moment and somehow reaching the other side; where an oat grain-size leaf touched the water surface, the brook sucked, gulped it down as a catfish mouth bites on a hook; one could even see the water's lips. How many times we press our fingers stretched out like the spokes of a wheel, on a shiny table in such a way that only one or two fingertips touch the wood — so those hesitant leaves don't hover above the water like a bird with stretched-out wings but perpendicularly, with their blades.

45.

She didn't keep a groom in the villa but tended to her horse herself. Now, though, she just absent-mindedly let the animal free in the courtyard and snapped for her attendant, turning from one window to the other: Clara! Clara! Only the closed windows' external lights answered, received jointly from the sun and moon: they looked like puddles in the evening — those, too, first merge into the dust in their greyness and only with the setting of the dark do they start glowing, deranged, like lights holed-forth from the depths of the earth.

An old servant came at the call, rattling before himself the evening's blazon: a bunch of keys and an oversize lamp. "Miss Clara went out to the village but said she would return this evening, and with good news, what is more: with realities, she hopes. Would your ladyship desire cold or warm supper?" "Neither cold nor warm, and I don't want any good news or realities either, this Clara drives me mad with her busybodyship, coming and going, lying. What is the use of a skivvy like that — O my dear, dear Gianni, please don't ever tell her what I said, kiss this cross on my necklace and swear you won't, I don't want her to find out, she's such a sterling good woman, even now she's trotting on her errands for me, to soldiers and spies, but I don't want any of that. If she comes back tell her in what state you saw me, tell her my heart is broken and that I love her more than anything, tell her this, but that I want no-one to do anything for me, I'm a base wretch that anybody feels free to kick. You don't believe me, Gianni, but it's true, I've been kicked with boots and spurs — don't mind me, I only want to die." "Go up to your room all the same, milady. I'll make the fire, make the bed; wait till I bring a new candle. In this village they make them so thick as if each one had been commissioned by the King of Jerusalem for the Holy Sepulcher. You should not go alone, it's dreadfully dark." "Yes I will and hope I'll break my neck, now even the servants are ordering me around, you, too, kick at me," she uttered all that with that lazy, experimental weeping that cowardly children try out for terrorizing grown-ups. But the servant produced a candle double-quick, before she could set out to walk alone.

The villa's stairs could have been of a monastery: wide, moldy, bumpy, with the odd, tiny window at the top of vast, watery-green walls squinting up at the ceiling — extremely cold, echoing and sepulchral. The lamp illuminated those stones with their ash-moss eczema, and the woman's elegant clothes rustling with light — the staircase was distinctly rigid and redolent of death, yet the Donna felt to be very much "inside" something, in exhilarating security, almost eternally protected; her color even rose. A mirror hung at one turn of the stairs — perhaps until recently another woman had lived in the house; from its blackness one could tell that there was some "live" surface against the wall: it was much more determinedly dark than the stone walls. In the lamp's circle of light the wall filled up with greenish embroidery, all kinds of tattered mosaics: the things bearing such a "human" mosaic do not reflect us — only such absolutely dead, empty, & blind things like that black naught-focus at the landing can suffer the faces of humans. The woman rushed toward it like smoke into a well-ventilated chimney hole. "Look, Gianni, how hideous I am. Small wonder everybody kicks at me. Look at my hair, dirty weed, neither black nor blue, it grows down on my forehead, hangs down in front of my ears like a goatee, I couldn't make a parting in it with a plow; neither curly nor straight, neither thick nor thin, it's all waste, all wretched undergrowth. O, if my countenance were trapped now in this mirror, no ghost would ever tread this boudoir-barracks: it would scare them all off."

Stepping out of the servant's role, for a moment the man made use of the seventy-year-old's gallantry: "Only those women heap scorn on themselves who know full well that reality will immediately refute their words." "False, false, I'm a cripple and an idiot, sillier than the dumbest skivvy, I'm stupid, that's why all men worth their salt loathe me, because I am silly and common. Why do you serve me, why do you obey me? Why are you all hypocrites? Do you think I don't know how you and everybody in the kitchen laughs at me for being such a common, sick, hideous wretch." She threw one more cursory glance in the mirror, hoping that in comparison with such violent self-thrashing she would appear more refined and passable in it. "Come, Gianni, wouldn't it be ludicrous if I lingered in front of my mirror image like a beggar, moaning and calling out to my hair: flower and turn into gold, you dirty felt, caressing my wilted mouth: turn into scintillating red currant, and to suffer my hair's & mouth's doltish arrogance with which they cast me aside?"

The servant stuck the candles into the candlestick one by one, lit them from the lamp, then waited for some practical order to arrive beside the hag rhetoric. "Everything's in vain," she said, kicking into the rusty fire irons, "all the jewelry, clothes, makeup, perfume: I'm old, ugly, and stink of the sewer I come from. Don't you know where I was born? On the outskirts of Ancona where all the trash that people toss into the canal accumulates and which the sea washes off the ships' prow — on my shore

the sea itself is the color of swill, it's all clotted grease, oil, rotting hawsers and nets, tar and paint — the brothels' bathwater
where make-up, medicine, patchouli, and urine ferment together
is spring water in comparison. Why don't you say this in my face
all day long, why only behind my back? Well of course you want
to live, you want your wages. You dolt: if you tell me in my face
where I come from and what I do, with the same word you use
in the kitchen, you will get more pay. Do you understand? More,
because I'm the mistress; I will repay you if you humiliate me,
if you heap abuse on me. On my word I'll double your wages.
Just say that word, say what I am. The mayor kicking my book is
nothing — you too will have to do it, for you are a greater lord
than me, so why shouldn't we make matters clear at last." "Donna,"
the servant said, trying to leave. "Donna?" — she gave a shrill,
creaking laugh, "will you call me Donna? Well, if you are too faint
of heart to say in my face who I am, at least I know what you are
to me." With that she jumped to the door, blocked it, and threw
herself at the servant's feet. "Hail, my prince, ave Caesar!" — and
instantly burst out sobbing on the floor like a child who bumped
its knee. "Dispose of me. Shall I dress you, wash your feet, drive
your hounds out in front of the gate, clean your armor, cook supper for you, strip you — command me, for only then will the
disgusting lie that surrounds me finally end."

The servant's head swam for a moment — lo, here was before
him the madwoman whom every living soul pines after from the
beginning of time in their puberty, and perhaps even a bit later
— here was the harvest, the golden age, the mystery-moon strumpet. But when he felt his odd nerve go ting-a-ling at the thought,
he was suddenly repelled by it all, this belated, grotesque bloom
of "dreams come true" and in his grief and fury that after a certain time comings-true only provoke repulsion, he snapped at the
Donna: "Stand up, calm down, you have no right to torture me
or yourself!" And when she indeed rose from the floor, having

suddenly stopped weeping, he added very quietly: "Sit down on that chair!" She, like adult-imitating children, also started whispering: "Paint my face, Gianni, paint me all over as best you can, comb my hair, hang my jewels on me, help me change and you'll see that all's in vain, I'm irremediably ugly." "My dear Donna, you know well that I know nothing of women's ointments, and you can't be serious either. You are upset, perhaps you were grievously hurt, wait now — it only takes two minutes — till Miss Clara arrives, talk it over, have a drop of that hearty wine I brought yesterday, kiss and lie down into the nice warm bed, and you'll see you'll get better." "No-no, you won't get away with it so easily, old Gianni, I don't need your grandpa's exhortations. Come on with the make-up." "But for the love of god, Donna —" "What is it? Don't you know where I keep the paint? Didn't your daughter tell you when she filched from them — half my perfume, half my face cream and powder is missing! Go, get them from the drawer beneath the small mirror! Mind you don't drop the red paint, the jar is already cracked."

The Donna swung a chair in front of the big mirror, slammed down one of the candlesticks beside it, like a bouquet into her ghost-vase, sat down and started ripping open the buttons around her neck. She shook her hair wildly, so it would be let loose, and when her tresses fell on her back, with her fingers she tried to give some shape to the fluffiest curls, as if, after all, she hadn't sat down in front of the mirror to relish in her own ugliness but in her beauty. The servant halted, with all the jars in his hand, a few steps from the chair. "Donna, I'm a servant but I wouldn't like to seem an idiot, a Pantalone, and a dud. I know how the game is going to end: I will daub you into such a masquerade and bogey that when you see yourself in the mirror, you'll chase me out of your house with a whip and set those bloody hounds on me. But I'll play along in this farce all the same: I'm only telling you this to make sure you won't believe it comes as a surprise when you'll set those beasts on me." The Donna paid no attention, only pointed to her face: "Here, here is where you start from. Do you have the blue paint? That's not it, you dumbo, can't you tell blue from black? That longish jar over there, that's it, put it here on the table!"

The servant was at a loss — should he try to make up his mistress as a maid would do, or should he turn her into a savage death-mask? But he soon realized that he needn't worry, for she was continuously giving out orders, pulling his hand this way or that. The odor of paint filled the room: the perfume of thousand-flower gardens and of laboratories redolent of pitch and glue. She was playing with him like a cat with a mouse, laughing, getting a tickle here and there, stripping and chatting. She would now address him as Caesar, now as stupid lackey. Her lips were made red and thick like earthworms and leeches: if they touched, they stuck together, and at every closing and opening tiny vertical paint and saliva strings tautened and slackened between them. Her face was brick-red from the powder and rose-fat, like the floor on the spot where a flowerpot had fallen from great height; below her eyes the lids were dark blue, almost black, her eyelids greasy, on her hands and feet the nails shone with greenish glister.

"This is a penny stocking, get me another. They are in the left-hand drawer. Here, take the keys." The servant took the keys with his little finger, all his other fingers being violet, crimson, black with the paint. "If you stain my stocking, I swear I'll daub your face and won't let you wash it off for a week!" The man rummaged in a drawer and pulled out a stocking that looked like a silver fishnet, made of flexible metal threads — it was cold like a dead fish and surprisingly heavy, in spite of being thin and transparent. The flames burnt with cracks, crumbling, as though the candles were of seal wax; autumn leaves shrivel up and shrink like these sizzling, stingy candles. She stuck her face very close to the mirror, not knowing if she wanted to make herself ugly or beautiful, if she wanted to play Cleopatra or to truly become a skivvy. She literally poked her nose into the mirror, so that it left a dot of chalk and cream on the glass. She tried to burn it off with a candle — in half a second the tar left an unexpectedly and disproportionately large stain on the glass, covering almost all the Donna's face. "Wipe it off with this," she said, throwing him a stocking pulled off one of her legs, "I can't see a thing." The man tried to caress away the still warm stain with his handkerchief. The Donna reached out her bare leg to him — it reclined amid scroll-spiraling, cracking flames, motley silks, brocades and frills, like a fragment of an uncovered Roman statue among clotted earth, torn wild flowers, and tree roots. Its shape and matter showed age, but its color was youthful, like the greenish-yellow skin of half-ripe goat-udder grapes. Both were silent, as though intuiting that the leg is something beyond life, love, hysteria, and mankind — glowing form that was to be watched with awe. He slowly pulled the stocking on it, like a glove on the dead crusader's hand on the bier.

46.

In the deathly silence all of a sudden a trumpet sounded: a brisk, abrupt tune, like a crooked arrow on the meek-furred hide of silence. "Ha, ha," she laughed triumphantly, kicking aside the old man who was still fidgeting with the stocking, so that he fell among the open paint jars under the mirror (as mugs and flasks go, those were quite big) — "my knight is here, he's come for me. You didn't paint me in vain, Gianni! Bring my dress, the tight-fitting blood-red one, where is it, good heavens, look at yourself, what a sight you are, you old dolt! Get out, wash your face, go and tell the knight to wait for a quarter of an hour and come up after."

The knight had long been loitering in the villa's garden, waiting for the Donna; only now did he lose his patience, or rather, he would gladly have waited on, had it not been for his henchman who asked him to signal their presence. The knight was the very young Juan Bautista de Leal, whose mission was to find out on behalf of the imperial army stationed in those parts if the hermit courtesan could potentially be used in conquering the mayor and his town. The young Leal was utterly unfit for this role. He was famous for being passed around as a painters' model, such was his beauty — they mostly immortalized him as Narcissus gazing into a pond, and those idealizations of his self moved the boy so much that he shunned women and made love to himself. He was an orphan boy in the care of a rather grim general, who felt repelled by him, but in order to be good to his promise given to his dead friend, once every two years he tried to make a man of him, overwhelming the boy with all kinds of petty political and military functions, which invariably ended in yet another Narcissus fresco in the refectory or studio of the enemy town's podestà. The young Bautista Narciz had an all-year-round flu, according to his adoptive father, because of standing for long hours stark naked in the painters' attics, showing off his scrawny pubertal charms. This disorderly lifestyle made the youthful Narcissus pale and weak, so he tried to acquire a healthy military ruddiness with the help of all manner of ointments: next to his rapier hung a powder-case (in rigorous armor style) and from the string of his gloves, his rouge. When not in uniform, he usually wore white: the kid was all T-shirts and pompoms.

He arrived with two attendants to the villa where he had been once before. He sat on his horse doubled up, tired: his feminine, arched amphora-legs going on forever glowed afar in their stockings reaching up to his hips, like a moonlit, snowy branch — his trunk was wrapped in a wide, rough ranker's cloak, which one of his henchmen threw on him out of mercy, he was shivering so badly in the icy rain. "I say, tell me, isn't my nose too red?" — he asked one of the lancers. The man pulled out the de rigueur

travelling mirror, held up a candle close to it and waited for Juan
Bautista to stare his fill. "It's preposterous, the way people talk to
me! If you had only heard my adoptive father this morning, or
that Donna yesterday evening! Why am I living among the likes
of them? Among old military battle-kites and mad courtesans?
What is war to me, or love? Self-important intrigues and passions! Do you think I keep blundering at everything because I am
clumsy? Only my father believes so, out of a soldiers' pardonable
naiveté. I keep blundering because I find those peanut self-styled
businesses trifling and ridiculous. I am an artist, therefore absent-
minded." "But that is precisely why senor Mazo sent us to attend
to you, lieutenant: so that, if you should pore too much over the
fine arts, we should warn you. Right now, why are we waiting
here in the rain to no avail?" The mercenaries could address the
boy in a tone of derision, for they could see every day how the
general treated Juan, no better than cats, canary birds, harlequins,
and women. "No point in rushing things." "But upstairs it's most
certainly nice and warm by the fireside and you are freezing here,
sir." "I'd rather freeze down here like a flower than roast upstairs
in the arms of a tasteless wife of Potiphar. Aren't you bored of
women like I am?" The truth was that Juan was afraid of the
Donna — her violent, hysterical manners, her gestures, threats,
raw coquetry scared the sneezing little model out of his wits;
he felt in the claws of ghouls and spent the night before weeping. One of the mercenaries heard him from the room next door
and even saw him through the keyhole writing a letter, which he
handed to an envoi before daybreak. The mercenary immediately
stole the letter from the envoi, fearing that the brat might commit a new howler, but the latter was entirely innocent — sharing
his fears of death in distichs with some painter friend and remi-
niscing about the sunlit seaside days of yore that they had spent
together. "All right, I don't mind, give the trumpet signal if you're
dying for that wish-wash porridge that the kind house-folk are

going to feed you in the servants' kitchen." The mercenary blew the trumpet.

In a while the servant appeared. He carried a lamp that was not burning — he blew it out at the gate, lest the strangers see how wildly his clothes were daubed in all the colors of the rainbow. "Will your lordships dismount and come inside. In the small hallway there is a comfortable armchair by the fire, be kindly seated there, lieutenant — in a quarter of an hour the Donna will be ready to receive you." He helped the powdering brush-like Juan off his horse and whispered in his ear, half in goodwill, half in malice, "You are going to find the mistress in a spiffing mood, lieutenant. And magnificently prepared. When you look at her, bear in mind that I myself painted her face. Your lordship is knowledgeable about the art of the brush anyway. But don't you whisper a word about this." "But pray, what's wrong with her? Is she in a temper? Is she raving?" "Your lordship knows full well that with women it's impossible to tell if they are sad or full of spite. I think she had some altercation with his lordship the mayor." "Good god," the lieutenant cried out in squeamish disgust, all the while trying to balance his feet, propped against his spurs by the fireplace, "what a day. Have you a mirror here?" The servant wanted to send for one but Juan waved him off: "Leave me to myself for the quarter of an hour. Then come for me to show me the way upstairs."

Juan was shivering with fear. He pulled out the medal with the Madonna from under his shirt and started praying to it in a whimpering tone: "Sweet, dear Virgin, You see and know full well that of the things which surround me here I want nothing, they have been forced on me. I know that You also see how I wallow in the sins of the flesh, but please do not make me perish by the hands of such silly women and even sillier soldiers — I am trying to go off my vices which, precisely for being habits, are not such great sins, as the priest explained, who is Your devout worshipper. How much this base bodily habit of mine is a thing almost beyond my powers is eloquently proved by the fact that, even now, now that I'm praying to you in penitence and in terrible fear of death, even now the desire to do it blossoms in me. But it will go away now, I'll grow out of it, You will drive it out of me, or my relatives are perhaps going to try heavy corporal punishment on me and even send a priest to my mew to put me to confess — so, considering my will-power weakened by vice, albeit not strong, the intention to confess is nevertheless always clearly present in me, without which Your holy Son will not let off my refuted sins before my death. And in fact it is not true that I don't really want to free myself from the eternal defiling of my body, and that I don't want to confess all that much in the nearest future: I say so precisely because sorrow, remorse, and the penchant for self-mortifying is far too strong in me; although I want to be cleansed at all cost, out of ascetic modesty I lie to You that I don't truly pursue my wish to be cleansed because I reason that if You believe that I don't want to be cleansed, You'll mete out greater punishment on me and my mystically exaggerating, refined conscience dictates that such is the punishment I would deserve. But Your wisdom is not blind to the fact that in this extreme exaggeration of my mind & morals I am far more virtuous than my sorrows and confessions would show, and although my wakeful consciousness wrestles with cleansing and confession, deep down in my soul, unfathomable even to myself, it is impossible to struggle against them, so look not upon my will but upon my deepest depth, which alone is worthy of Your heavenly gaze. Pray for us at the hour of our death, Amen."

Young Juan lay back in his armchair, musing: he saw before his mind's eyes the last painting for which he modeled — it depicted him at the depth of an entirely dark forest, chemisteried-together of mirrors & charcoal, spring leaves and deathly acids, with silvery body — or rather, not silvery, but genuine silver:

the painter found that that cold, glossy metallic skin renders well
the coldness and closedness that separates Narcissus's body from
the surrounding world, from women, preserving it all inward,
for itself. In the picture all healthy youthfulness and deprived
perversity, all David freshness and sodomite cosmeticizing-into-
abstraction fused: from flu to onanism, from hermaphrodite to
heroics. Shall women destroy such a boy? Juan almost saw the
picture in front of him, hanging on a wall, and felt that it was
imperative to present to it a final sacrifice of farewell from his
body. He checked the doors and locked them, then proceeded
to the sacrifice. But it seems he didn't check the hall door well
enough, for toward the end one of the doors suddenly opened
and Juan found himself face to face with the old servant. "Ha
ha, I've been busying myself a bit," he said with a hoarse and not
too embarrassed giggle, "small wonder if one is left alone for so
long." "Noble knight, I beg your pardon, I'll bring a basin with
hot water to wash yourself before the Donna arrives. They are
preparing dinner in the kitchen, there's plenty of boiling water,
I'll be here in no time." The servant went and came, indeed in no
time. "I say, I'm not in the habit of doing it on my own —" said
Juan, smoothing his hair back with a forty-year-old demon's calculated nonchalance. "Ehmmm," said the servant, slightly taken
aback, but regained his composure, "pull the big screen over
here, lieutenant, we'll take care of it behind." "What's the use of
a screen, you can lock the door you've just come in from." "I will
lock it and no mistake, never fear, lieutenant, it's just that, even if
there's no living soul in here, in such a big room a man like me is
somehow ashamed. It's as if there were someone —" The lieutenant dragged and laboriously opened the screen, and when he finally managed to fold the accordion, he started zithering, having
put up a wall between himself and the anemic fire. "No need to
fidget with it any more, lieutenant, we'll be done in a second." The
servant started the office, unusual for him. "Perhaps you'd better

take off your sword, it dips into the water and will get rusty." Juan took it off and dropped it carelessly. "Dry me quickly, I'll catch a cold." His legs were steaming in the cold room.

In that moment a sound of guitar or dulcimer was heard, together with the creaking open of the door, locked a moment ago. "Good god!" the lieutenant cried out in panic and leapt aside, fortuitously knocking over the basin and landing in front of the screen in a state of undress, also sending up his sword in the air. For the time being no-one could be seen in the door, only the music got louder. "My body is the sea and Venus incarnate, On my longing's blue fever-sea I toward you drift: Desire-tide and longing-sails swell against your shores, Sweet youth, and my tempest to soothe, no power is strong enough." The sickly Juan was used to having blurry visions and hallucinations after his Narcissus-sacrifices, so he harked to this articulation of un-expected pathos with the rigid pose of the blasé, seasoned ex-perimentalist.

47.

The next moment the Donna appeared in the door. She wore a long crimson dress, skin-tight like the shirt of the drowned, cer-emonial to the point of burlesque; from her neck a guitar hung on a black ribbon, her face was thickly painted, her eyes were bathed in tears and vapor. Some kind of somnambulist, vacant conceitedness crisscrossed her body, the mime-like shameless-ness of posturing, lie, would-be Sibyldom: her eyes were almost completely shut, so she had to throw her head far back to be able to peer out under her eyelashes; her mouth opened slightly, like the initials of "desire" in the beginner's alphabet. Despite her ex-altation and Orphic would-be twilight, there was in her some prosaic sassiness, harlot's hauteur, almost in mockery of whoever would yield to her mystical apparatus.

Juan was standing there with trousers pulled down, his shirt hanging loose, wet and steaming. "I feel sick, Donna, I'm ill, I'm dying!" — he said in his first panic and threw himself on the floor, feigning a swoon. "Yes, indeed," the servant concurred, panting, "I told the lieutenant to wait for the Donna here for a quarter of an hour, and when I came in to attend to him a few seconds ago, I found him stifling and breathing heavily, tearing at his clothes; I don't know what it is, maybe his heart is failing, or a snake got into the house, for the Porto swamp is close — I've often heard it from the other servants that snakes got into the villa — so I stripped the lieutenant. I didn't find any snakebite on him, but wanted to wash him over with scorching water all the same. Let's take him upstairs to the large bedroom and lay him in the bed!" "Oh, quickly, oh my, that such things should happen, woe me, Clara would surely know what to do — isn't she back yet? Something must have happened to her too. Come on, hurry up, wrap him, call for help, or no, you and I will carry him upstairs, dear, sweet boy, fair youth, like a child" — and at this she kissed Juan on the mouth, who behind eyelids kept shut with much effort was convinced that the fatal poison had just been smeared on his lips.

"Perhaps your ladyship could lay down that instrument and leave the volume of poetry on the table, it will be easier to hoist him up." Juan was agitatedly calculating if it was wiser to pretend to come to right away, or to wait until they got upstairs — will they not haul him underway into some deathly pit? But the next moment he was up in the air, he felt his head between the Donna's knees like a nail in the pliers, and his legs were firmly grabbed by the servant; his head almost knocked against the ground (the woman treading on his long tresses at every step), while his feet poked up toward the ceiling. O, "l'initiation à l'amour," as the French officers would put it — that was it doubtlessly, the very it. He furtively peered into the mirror at the landing: the sight was uplifting — the Donna and the servant almost touched, so the lieutenant was folded and flattened into a V between the two; he could have stopped the servant's ears with his heels, and felt the Donna's green-varnished nails digging into his armpits like the Holy Inquisition's instruments of passion; his bony organ of sitting bumped into every step, like the tongue of a rattle into a dented wheel. When the servant felt an imperious urge to throw the little cretin over the banisters, the Donna whispered to him from her scented mouth: "That I love above all else, to feel a mother. My darling, my one and only son!" But in her great abandon of spirit her muscles apparently gave way, so she dropped the chevalier. Juan yelled out in pain; blood gushed from his forehead, and that drove him wild.

"Where's my sword? Intrigue-mongers, traitors, hetaeras, hangmen — I'll kill you all! Why are you standing there like eejits? Are you surprised that you didn't manage to schlep me into some torture chamber? Or are you just catching your breath, darlints? My sword — where's my sword!" "Pull your trousers up first, lieutenant," the servant said and went down to bring hot water and a towel for the second time. "O, what a misunderstanding, what a tragic, deathly misunderstanding, lieutenant Juan, how entirely worthy of my whole underworld, fatal life: I was always, ever misunderstood by all, when I was more motherly than the most caring of mothers, they believed me a mercenary; when I spent entire nights kneeling in front of the altars of saints, they believed I was coming from the brothel; when I wanted to offer up my whole life for a fair child, they said that for pay I was procuring children for sadistic old child-molesters. But in pride and humility I bore my woman's lot, and am not resentful of you either. Juan! You are sick, you fainted and now I, clumsy wretch, hurt you again. Against my will! Forgive me, let me support you, come, I'll heal you, I swear!" "Wasn't the thing you bumped my head into rusty? Won't I get blood poisoning?" "No, no, you won't, dear, sweet Juan, my own, O and how happy I am that you are now talking more calmly. Come, here's the bedroom; you'll lie down, I'll stay with you, my sweet everything."

48.

Juan's wound was insignificant, the bleeding stopped almost instantly when the servant applied some yellow powder. "Look, it is for you I put on this dress, for you I'm wearing this hairdo, this scent, this make-up! For I wanted to make myself beautiful — and I am beautiful. What else do we need in life but your manly youth and my mature, womanly beauty! It would be madness to squander away your goods on girls who can't appreciate you at your true worth: I know I'm the one you need, for I am a full-blown woman, clever and beautiful, femininity blooming and bearing fruit in the fullness of experience, beyond which you couldn't possibly wish for anything else. Shall I undress you? Or would you like me to go out and leave you to undress on your own?" "I'm not lying down, I'd rather just sit in the armchair over there." He threw himself into the chair with legs stretched far out in rigid parallels. "Aaahhh." "Now, now, don't throw yourself about like that, for you'll start bleeding again. Would you like some wine, my sweet?" "That would be nice!" "Tell me, do you often faint like that? Have you seen a doctor?" The little lieutenant was getting more and more annoyed by the Donna's insistence — he imagined that a real fainting would never generate such a sickly and ghostly atmosphere as a feigned one; comedy is more frightening than death itself. "The dickens only knows what it was. Let's drop it altogether. I have the impression that its cause was not at all natural. One can never tell in such spying, warmongering, brigand times." "In these brigand times you're not going to die on me, Juan, I know that and you can safely trust in my female intuition more than in any god. If there is to be any death here, it's you who are going to mete it out, and if there is to be vengeance, you are going to be triumphant — you're going to be forever, my Apollo." The boy started going numb from those senselessly exaggerated words. He kissed her hand. "Ego te absolvo" — she whispered, as though there had been no better à-propos in her life to those grave Latin words.

Now when she looked in the mirror, all she could see was her own beauty. Her long, narrow, blue eyes arching, Egyptian-fashion, almost to her ears — black, white, red strips (there was blue in it, too!) resembling marble veins & homespun, on which the lashes bent like caterpillar feet faltering on a leaf edge (one could observe a curious optical illusion: while the eyelids were fluttering, opening and closing too often, the lashes seemed to hover in the same place, quite independently of those movements, like the shadow of hard-stemmed grass over a rushing blue streamlet); around her nose she could see the tiny constellations of freckles, whose brownness merged into one single brown spot at the corner of the eye (one can see earth-strips of this color on thin March ice-crusts or muddy meadows); her elastic black hair, which galloped across the room, streamlined like a pert Nike; was this the woman whom the mayor dared humiliate? This beauty — that cripple? This life — that hypochondriac? This triumphant reality — that scum, that intellectual?

She dug her claws into Juan greedily. "A non-entity, a petty poseur, a selfish, sciolistic pseudo-politician insulted me to death a brief hour ago. If you could only see that physiognomy, Juan: a gout-ridden, shriveled-up, schoolmasterly old fogey with a dirty goatee, in his frippery — a veritable masquerade." "The mayor, isn't he?" — the lieutenant asked with profound disgust. "Himself. You don't know him, do you? Happy you. He moves in the world as if history were revolving around him alone, according to his ratiocinations — but we, women, eternal & timeless women (at this she pinched, with an intimidatingly mercantile gesture, the

fold of flesh situated at the crossover of the chest into the waist-
line — new linen is fingered like this at the marketplace), we know
that it's around *this* that the pope, the gods, theology and money
revolve" — at which she pointed at the mirror with her grossly
sharpened index, at her own effigy; Juan, perching behind her in
the room, appeared in it like a dead silver fox on her shoulders.

The image, the *whole* image, was indeed beautiful: the big
mirror's greenish semi-dimness, a mixture of smokily hovering
midnight space and nothingness glimmering into crystal sheets;
the woman's Aristophanean harlot-mask; the candles' steam-
tufted little S-pokings; and finally, Juan's white glove-nude. But
of all that the woman obviously saw only her own invisible beauty.

"Can you tolerate that *this* is insulted, this hand, this leg?" She
was about to lift up her skirt with an instinctive movement when
something occurred to her and in the pose of the Sleeping Beauty's kitchen aid who froze in the act of wringing an ear, halting
her stiff skirt in her stiff hands, she asked the boy: "I hope you're
aware that I am young?" Juan answered as if from a schoolbook,
but embraced as if not from a schoolbook: "I'm no idiot. What
is this if not youth?" — and with improvised flurry tried to grab
one of her preposterously young body parts, but only managed
to paw a protruding pin that tore the skin on his hand.

"I'll show you my youth," said she and started about the business of undressing with such desperadoism as a slightly tipsy
mariner who has to jump into the sea to pull out his captain who
hasn't paid him for a month. In the meantime with one breath
she blew out the candles (standing at a considerable distance
from them): the flames were first torn off the wick, flying off like
butterflies or autumn leaves, and were extinguished only after
that, as though drowned in the mirror's deep waters. And Juan
watched, staring at the "youth" like at some deduction that a passionate Saracen arithmetician scribbled on the blackboard at the
Sicilian university of Frederick II — quod erat demonstrandum.

49.

He saw that narrow, tall, black building they rode by the night
before, next to the well smelling like rotten eggs, which allegedly
cured venereal diseases. One could hear from afar the water's
gurgling and murmur — one could even hear its muddy *warmth*,
for cold waves never splash against rocks with that sound. The
slender hospital resembled the music teacher of *The Barber of
Seville*: black, lean, both abbot and song, both death *&* joke. The
building stood in the well's spume-curve, boiling water washed
its steps like the base of Venetian palaces; its color was golden
green like spring sprouts, *&* torches spread their light in its vapor.
It seemed that people never slept here. One of the attendants
told him how the hospital was furnished — one of his masters
died there, probably because of some much-too-evident "youth."
He observed the patients as they were introduced by the soldier.
They were divided into two large groups: one kind was rendered
bigoted and hallowed by their purulent disease, while the others hardened in savage fornication, so that the black sickness-sty
was more monastery-like than an Albigensian castle, and more
of a bordello than the lowest Carthaginian kip. From the hospital came such a racket (at half two at night) that you had to
strain your ear to hear the frothing, fizzling sulfurous well. The
bathers were loudly conversing with those who leant out of the
fourth-floor windows — the ones who tripped up at every step
in the muddy pool yelled at the top of their voices, the wind was
slamming the windows, the moribund threw apple-cores at the
bathers from the roof and the balcony that consisted of three
wire X-es. Not far from the gate, immersed deep in the water and
only airing his toes and the crown of his head, a bespectacled old
Pantalone read aloud from a book in Latin; the mercenary told
Juan that the old geezer had a prayer-book made of stainless tin
sheets, so he could continue reading during his bathing cure. He
sometimes lifted a leg out of the water — his skin barely showed,

but a few thick hairs growing around his shin were as big as the
nails or arrows driven into the martyrs' flesh on village crucifixes.
In the side pool (in the "Venus puddle," as the patients called it)
love raged supreme: they were clasping and smooching ecstatically,
happy that for once they needn't fear disease. Sometimes priests
(half undressed because of the steam) howled in the direction of
the boundlessly fornicating and diving-copulating, at which either obscene answers came, or deathly silence ensued — the love-
birds submerged in the water as though they were made of lead.
Not even water-rings rippled above their heads: the shadow of
the tree bowing deep down on the surface, laden with midnight
elderflowers, stretched so quietly above them as a sarcophagus lid
on a cathedral floor. Under one of the trees a raving "holy man"
and a drunken doctor were haggling: the patient flourished a
relic and the doctor, a surgical instrument of some sort, and Juan
couldn't have decided which of the two was the greater supersti-
tion: myth, or science, Olympus, or the laboratory? There was no
end to the struggle: the alchemist physicians would sometimes
tear down the monks' chapel, at other times, the zealous brothers smashed the doctors' fantastic jars and tubes. There had been
yet no director of the hospital who had not caught the disease
from some ulcerous-loined but all the more fairy-visaged patient:
the women would have stoned to death any director who dared
stay healthy among them for more than a few months. Pageant
and gang-askesis mingled there, and Narcissus watched with
bemused eyes those few, startled nightbirds that fluttered above
the hospital and the Venus puddle — how clean, indifferent, and
harmonious they were.

50.

"Well: I'm beautiful, aren't I? Would you have thought that I am
so beautiful?" In her words there was no vanity but only childish
would-be-objectivity, almost sculptor-like pedantry. Juan kissed

her, so he needn't look at her, feeling in the meantime that this hysterical rapture at the sight of her is more beautiful than beauty itself; we relish not in women so much as in the way they relish in themselves. With his cretinous little finicky head Juan knew well enough that when one is faced with nakedness, what follows at the stanza's end is either disease or murder, so he slowly removed his mouth from the woman, like a slackening poultice from a healing wound (so it wouldn't hurt) and asked with an actor's irony: "Whom shall we kill then — the mayor? I know that your Greek nakedness demands a phallus, so here's the only one that women love: voilà!" — and at that he pitted the whip-thin, long rapier, so far propped up against the wall, against her body.

"Here — let's see the wedding program!" "Program? Let's not start with a murder — it would be too simple. We've got to torture that bloody old lascivious snob." Juan found it wonderfully strange that one could emit oaths when undressed: he thought it was an act bound up with the wearing of clothes. "You're going to write a letter. One, in which you tell him that the seeds of his wife's sickness were planted in her by a mysterious pursuer (you're going to write in his name): if he doesn't lie with her tonight and so doesn't catch the disease from her, he's going to contract it within a week from somebody else, under much less blissful circumstances. He is free to choose." Juan was staring at the nude, at the "youth": shoulders and an anonymous letter? *Stimmt.* Hips and such idiotic grand guignol fantasies? Yes, the connection was logical. Breasts and disease sadism? Of course — is there anything else that fits these breasts (Potemkin domes themselves, puffed up for the sake of one wart-point) better than flimsy intrigue, low-caliber vengeance?

"Another letter is going to calumny his daughter: his daughter is plotting against his life, she has long converted to Mahomet's faith, last summer she was living in a secret harem in Venice." "So am I to rhyme all these virginal lays into shapely epistles?...

Don't you then need this?" — and he flicked the rapier into the fireplace: it was almost as thin as a knitting needle, so it soon glowed into a red line in the ingle. This was Juan's first mystical experience in months: the red-hot rapier-string in the twilit room. That strumpet could say whatever she liked, any nakedness could exhibit itself in the window, any Narcissizing broth could swell up from his body: heroism, purity, geometry, and holy one-god *did exist* in this world as long as there lived such rapiers, swords burning with cherub rigor and joy. Tears filled his eyes like rain the cups of bell-flowers: they were full but didn't tilt over. "Yes, the rapier, death is merely romanticism, kitsch, and poetry: you're still young, that's what you need." "Merci. If you insult me like this, it will no doubt inspire me to write those letters." "Inspiration? I'll pay you handsomely. Do you think I want this for free? I'm sober, that's my problem. Unsayably sober." And while she said this in her singsong, she checked her own "unbearable sobriety" in the mirror.

51.

There was a knock on the door. "Clara?" — the Donna asked with shrieking joy. "Yes." "O come in, wait, wait a second till I put on something, come in then, or wait rather, half a mo. Juan, go now, it was scrumptious to be with you, wait, I'll give you another sword (the old one was like saliva anyway), do wait for me downstairs. Clara, so you're finally back —" "What? Shall I go? Now, all of a sudden? Why? On that door? Why can't I stay?" "Stay, sweet child, stay on then —" and she pushed him back into the armchair with a kiss.

Clara entered. Aging, withered face, like a cough. "My dear Clara, this is lieutenant Juan. He's going to destroy the mayor with slow torture, frightening, ghastly letters, which will preferably arrive at the dead of night: I know the mayor, he's a nervous

man, sickly from the inside, perhaps they will even manage to
drive him mad. He kicked me! Of course you don't know yet —
he kicked me, with his boots!" "Go on then," Clara said in dull
voice, looking in the void with her colorless sockets of vision,
"no point in delicacy. My friend," she said, turning to Juan with
her head, but not with her eyes, "is an angelic spirit: she understands everyone and shows mercy to everyone, she gave herself
entirely for free to Italy's richest overlords at the height of their
office, just as she would offer banquets afterwards for the poor
and read poetry. Luckily she met me, I do my best to make a man,
that is, a woman out of her. As far as that's possible with such
a saintly little nymph," and with that she planted a dry kiss on
her cheeks with a barely visible smile, like a cook turning over a
pancake above the fire while half asleep. "I love her like my foolish child. In her angelic eyes I am of course nothing but the devil
incarnate. Well, mister my knight, this is the point where you
stick in a quick compliment — refute my devilish appearance!"
"Madame..." "Point de trouble," the grey-complexioned Clara said
without as much as a twitch of her face, and the French word sat
on her body like a lily-of-the-valley on salt rock, "we're past it
now. The ideas with which she wants to cause the mayor's downfall — enfin, since this crossed the mind of my holy flower — I
myself could have carried out just as well. But when I found out
that a handsome officer might be involved, why not let him? For
I can certainly present a little sex-medallion to my only daughter,
history and politics (it was at these words that she gave her first
real smile) are, after all, a better backdrop to this whole affair
than an old hag." At this she absent-mindedly pinched the hem
of her dress as though she were about to tear a leaf. "It's not easy
for me, poor pseudo-maman. For on the one hand I like seeing
my daughter romp freely, more virginal even after her courtesan-
pageants than an aborted child — youth is so lovely." With narrowed eyes and a slightly visible tongue in her cheek she leaned

close to the Donna and with the toe of her shoe lifted high her dressing-gown: "By the way, I think this belated commentary is a bit superfluous, don't you find so, lieutenant?" The boy came to with a shudder, at which the death-mask rattled on monotonously, as though asking for a statistical detail: "Quoi? Pudicity? No trouble, you needn't be ashamed. Nous avons une compréhension excessivement large: this is our pension. Quasi. There's a great many French soldiers in Milan, that's why I sometimes lapse into Gallic."

She pulled out a bottle from under the table and drank a bit of wine, then observed, with the swallowing-rims of the last draught still audible in her voice: "Youth is lovely, but I resolved to make a woman of my friend. We're going to compete, lieutenant: you're going to trigger renewed virginal allures from her, while I'm going to sober her up, age her, make her matronly. But we're going to get along well. Don't you fear that I'm going to monopolize you now & again, with the step-mothers' terrorism, stealing you from my daughter?" "Don't ridicule me by always forcing me into the most banal complimenting situations." "So the only possible thing that occurs to you in connection to me is a compliment? Is there a greater insult than that, jeune homme?" "I'm keeping mum." "Don't hurt him, Clara dear, don't hurt my genial little lovebird. He has just come to his senses — he fainted while waiting for me."

At once a profound silence ensued. Clara rang the glass with her ring, looking for the first time, sharply, almost rudely, the boy in the eye; she curtly asked or rather, stated, "So you're sick." "These diagnoses and definitions are a bit far-fetched, mesdames: now a lovebird, now sick. Accuracy isn't paramount, but … tout de même …" "Look, lieutenant, sick or lovebird, frivolous or accurate is of no importance. You shall love my daughter — don't laugh at me for calling her so — for she means everything to me." "How much more a woman is worth," the Donna sobbed, "than that old, untalented mayor: he'd sacrifice all his subjects for a phony aphorism. The bastard!" "Don't praise me and don't trust me. I stink of selfishness. Lieutenant, let's write those letters! How far are you from your troops, and how mobile are they?" "One and a half days. Mobile? When they like, they're forever and excessively mobile; when they like, they're inert. It will be darned difficult to drag history, as you mockingly called it a moment ago, from that modest nook, into this intrigue." "Leave that to us women," said the Donna, her tears not entirely dried up, now puffing herself up in the mirror like a leech: "Behold, beauty," now peering at Clara's ingle-less ash-face: "Behold, wisdom." She bathed in this cheap allegory like in a narrow bathtub.

While they proceeded to compose the letters in three, Juan resolved to steal the huge jewel hanging from the Donna's neck in the love-dark that was to follow, to burn the letter and bribe with the jewel some hitman to kill the mayor; he would live to his dying day on Capri among painters, far away from women. When the letters were ready, Clara got up and told the lieutenant: "Light a new candle, your sword will be a perfect fidibus now, and lead me to my chaste bedchamber. My friend will wait for you here."

The corridors were freezing cold. Juan's teeth chattered like jingles on tarantella dancers' tambourines. When they were at a safe distance from the Donna's bedroom, Clara suddenly squeezed the lieutenant's wrist and told him all in one breath, imperatively: "Lieutenant Juan, let's drop this comedy. My friend is filthy rich, all her fortune, money, and jewels are in this villa. We've got to rob her. You'll bring your troops here with the pretext that the mayor is here, the town's military commander, or if you will, here are the most important political and military documents. With a bit of cunning you can lure here someone from the mayor's town, some petty foot soldier, into whose pockets you can smuggle all kinds of fake battle plans, so that if your troops come here to charge the villa you should also find some political delicacy. For all I care you can bait the mayor himself. The soldiers will set the house on fire, service d'histoire, the Donna's money will be ours, robbery: politics — murder: politics — all the filth that's going to pass: politics, & we'll flee far from here and nobody will ever look for us. If you betray me, if you stir, you're dead. I, too, have my 'troops,' mais… pas assez du genre ‹ histoire,› vous savez …"

52.

When the mayor got home he was received by a trembling, tearful servant; he knew at once that something was wrong with his wife. "What is it?" "The doctor is at the dear lady — the blessed madonna's back had to be cut open down below, the doctor said this was the last attempt he had to make, but — pardon my saying so — there's not much hope." "Yes," the mayor said in that colorless, forcedly polite tone in which he dismissed the envois who deny military or financial aid in Old Greek or Latin distichs and odes. He slowly pulled over the armchair whose legs slid as easily on the polished floor as mercury on a mirror, and sank into it, exhausted.

Nothing to do. He took in hand, with one sunset gesture, all fate's documents, loves, gods. There was *one* secret that kept intriguing him in this reckless inertia: how was it possible that man could be annihilated so easily, so completely? Now he realized that, although day by day he had woken up with a spleen and gone to bed as a nihilist, he had never truly been a pessimist — he never held evil, the destruction of love, state, and god, to be real, merely self-frightening fictions training one for death, his own toys, so that the joy to follow might be all the greater; but now, when love, politics, and morals flared out one after the other, with superstitious grossness, among fate's candle-extinguishing fingers, he indeed sensed *the great reality of meaninglessness*, of naught. For the first time he despaired: what he had imagined to be nihilism so far was still, nevertheless, the apology of divine providence.

His wife was going to die — he couldn't as much as exchange a word of farewell with her, the key with which the doctor had turned the room into an operating theater had locked her off from him, from all possible meaning of life. But even if he could go in, if he could speak: what would it be worth? Could the complicated secret that the mute suffering of marriage grew between and in them, be made to disappear with a word or embrace? Could he take that untraceably complicated tapestry of homage and boredom, gratitude and cheating, carnal pleasure and morality, which characterized his relationship to his wife — to her deathbed? Is there a more disheartening opposition than between analysis & agony? Is there anything more humiliating than to see the myriad hues of morality and poetry from the perspective of the gruesome simplification of death? What was the use of spiritual life, of the wealth of nuances, of the prolonged scrupulousness, search for truth, discussion and remorse, when in the eerie solitude of agony his wife suddenly appears an inaccessible stranger? We have never told one another anything and if you die, I'll be standing by your grave like a halfwit who has chatted, made love, eaten and suffered with you for thirty-five years without ever having uttered a single syllable that spoke about ourselves, about the essence of our relationship. Of course, all this is an illusion: neither I nor you nor our relationship has an "essence"; life consists precisely in developing in us all, equally, this neurosis for non-existent "essentials," while at the same time piling up, with baroque zest, the evidence of inessentiality. In everyday life we are incapable of looking at the core of our destiny with our wife or neighbor, because prose wears off our sensitivity to such issues, our petty errands distract us, the well is far too turbid for us to see anything in it; but in times of great crises, at the theological curtain-downs of illness, death, political downfall, being discovered with one's lover, on the other hand, the agitation is too great, the change is too annihilatingly blinding and all-powerful for us to be able to address the theme of our destiny — at such times the well is too deep for us to glimpse its surface.

What lacerating debate & tapestry was woven in the mayor's mind between goodness and awareness, love and knowledge — on the one hand he felt that he was unable to get close to his wife even psychically, for neither the realistic details of the past nor the fate-charged, mystical emptiness of the present offered a key to knowing her, charting the "meaning" of his marriage; on the other hand, he felt that he was infinitely damaging, fatally hurting and insulting her even during her agony with this resigned or cynical thought of his, laying down her "eternal foreignness." He felt that through this thought he shrunk to a filthy little intellectual, a Jewish analyst beside the divine moral unfolding in his wife's death. Symbolic reduction was inescapable in these impossible moments: death, suffering, was triumphant ethics itself, boundless agape — while his own impotence, psychic loss of color was the eternal pettiness lurking in raison, the childishness generating philosophies, the radical "evil" of "truth."

He kept asking the servant mechanically: "Was she already feeling very sick before the doctor arrived, or did she get worse while he was already here?" "Already before his arrival, she was perished alive." "What did she say, what did she complain of, did she ask for me?" "She didn't talk much, was hardly conscious most of the time, sometimes pressed her eyelids shut, then suddenly released them and then the whites of her eyes rolled like abacus beads on wires, sweat poured down her whole body and she wanted by all means to hide with her handkerchief what in her weakness she made on the pillow or sheet."

Never had the mayor seen something so clearly as his dying wife: "This is reality, this is reality," he kept repeating to himself obsessively; aren't danses macabres right when reciting the skeleton's eternally triumphant carnival? Shouldn't he as mayor have forbidden all comedies and tragedies in the town, that were not danses macabres — have all books and poems confiscated that were not like Toscanus' *De Morte Universali*? If he had done so, everybody would have held him for a hypochondriac fool, perhaps his red-mugged generals would even have locked him up in the lunatic asylum: but is it lunacy to proclaim the all-annulling primacy of death? Is his wife's agony lunacy, is the power that renders all thought superfluous and laughable lunacy, that hails from this vicinity of agony? Is it perhaps going to be the eternal fate of the world that, whenever someone calls a simple reality a reality clearer than daylight, and lives in accordance with it, he will inevitably be called a mystic and biased? Death is the only consistent reality, if I am to take for the surest marker of reality the *foreignness* situated at the greatest remove from my subjective penchants *&* prejudices: it is in the vicinity of death that we really feel that life is *not* about ourselves, not about our intelligence, feelings, history, and pleasure, but about something primordially other, anti-human, outside-of-human, which doesn't as much as acknowledge our existence.

What inflamed foci of humanistics are aglow in the dying person's body, and what awe-inspiring power of utter dehumanization: his wife's partly-blinking, partly-relaxing eyes, trickling excrement, heavy breathing meant, on the one hand, a triumph even in their perishing — the indefinable (*&* perhaps sole) *moral* residing in suffering renders such bodily parts so plastic that in comparison, the last ointment appears as an unnoticeable abstraction: this degree of being-condemned-to-death and to-damnation, this murderous absolute of the denial of the human that brandishes itself in agony, nevertheless exalts the *human*, even infinitizing him; suffering, unsurpassable, mathematically sharp despair is something so utterly perfect, so classically mighty and homogeneous as a Thousand-and-One-Nights magic crystal — trees, stars, waterfalls, gods' snobbery with "specie aeterni" are all insignificant when laid beside such an upward-hitching female eyeball. In this moment the two temper-sentences, that "this alone is" and "this is impossibility itself," have the same meaning and justification. Bodily death is something so absurd that it is the only god that demands respect; there is *one* certain polytheism, the polytheism of death: all human beings have the duty to worship themselves as gods carrying the fantasticality of death.

Death and realism belong together like the hands and the fingers: what an abstraction the female breasts that had undulated in our embrace like a leaping hare, how colorless and imperceptible in comparison to the breasts that death scoops aside in its onward march, like a snow-shovel scooping aside two worthless clogs. In this sense death is a birth: abstract girls, theory-women first get a truly human body in death. Although the mayor was not by his wife's bedside, he could feel almost in his body how the dying woman was becoming more and more physical, how she was putting on herself, at breakneck speed, the divinifying cosmetics of "the human." All around, the world paled with its blooming lilac trees and doomed papal state — of the whole of existence there remained only fingers, toenails, lips, armpit hairs, shell-like ears.

All human attitudes were impossible. To pray? Death does not tolerate foreign gods by its side; from this frenzied atmosphere of suffering the cowardly gods flee and trail off: Jewish and Chinese, Greek and Papuan, hot on one another's heels — even the darkest corpse-demons appear like petty, æstheticist, rococo frippery when set against the single dying person's apotheotic sanctity.

53.

The mayor, whose entire life had been spent in anxious contemplation of the battle between pope and emperor, in his imagination watched with dark satisfaction the exiled pope, slaughtered bishops, pilloried thirty-voiced Gregorian masses and churches turned into stables; at least people would some day draw the conclusions from their suffering and found their simplified theology on their own corpses. His childhood communions, theoretical warfare for the scholastic cause, his profound remorses of conscience and scrupulous confessions, *comme-il-faut* "shredded" gothic art, its nervous askesis-epochs, his never-ending conversations with priests, his toying with, and fervent prayers to Jesus and desperate fight against the unacceptability of the Old Testament: such was the catalogue of his "clericalism" — and what was all this worth now, by the surgical table? Nothing. For the first time he had to confess how primordially improper his whole life had been. In fact all great religions stem from primal *non-knowing how to believe* — he reasoned with his usual egoism and nose for paradox; there is the Catholic and the nihilist version — Catholics seek to cover up primal despair with frantically analytic dogma-mosaics and precision-veil, whereas nihilists appoint the void itself to be "the sole, simple god," with whom we stand in a sole, simple, unmediated relationship. Of such heresies he had often heard recently.

While he saw his wife's yellowing eyeballs in the glassy-florid birdcage of tears and pink veins, he found out that the human soul was naturaliter anti-christiana. What can I bring you, my dying bedfellow, in place of my outmoded wedding present, if not the world's greatest blasphemy? Take it from me with all my heart. But as only those who don't even intuit the death-ness of death can pray by the deathbed, so only the entirely myopic can remember their shared past with the dying, as though anything else could belong to death's biology and logic but the present, the death-present irrevocably and equally excluding both past and future. One doesn't so much feel his memories, his past, to be real & death, to be annihilation, but the other way round: what had been so far is shameful, impossible-to-expiate mendacity, posture, mask and flatus vocis, and what is now is reality, but it is inaccessible to our organisms weakened to fiction. Naked woman: while inside the doctor tore off your smock in order to cut into you with his hopeless scissors, I am peeling off your moral garment — divine future in front, human past behind you. O, which is the more awful solitude: that of the dead, or of the mourner?

The mayor harked. He heard an unknown, half-melodious, half-idiotic voice: neither animals nor humans nor any kind of object could produce such a sound. The word "harked" was plain wrong: he felt that he had been hearing that voice for all eternity.

54.

For a moment the doctor reached for the small jar on the table with his freed left hand when he heard the woman's moan coming from her profound slumber, and he immediately pressed some more sedatives into her mouth and nostrils. This all-renouncing, sick, beyond-human sigh made him feel almost giddy during the operation: it was like old clocks' carillon, like the sinking underwater of some heavy object — on the one hand, in it the whole world breathed its last, on the other hand, it was childish and insignificant, like a newborn's whimper when the teat falls out of its mouth. But who could enlist all elements of this woe in which the erstwhile society hostess' salon "ah" was just as recognizable as the shapeless ventriloquism of death, that strange, never-heard sound which we can also eerily feel with our tongues after high fevers or swoons, as though in place of candies we were sucking ashes. The sound showed the same tragic compression as the whole body: life's most embryonic reflex movements and socially conditioned postures, small everyday gestures succeeded one another at regular intervals, sharply delineated from one another. Perhaps this mingling of the two kinds of movements is the saddest thing about agony: the unknown twitchings of the most primordial life, and the useless little gymnastics of the evanescent moment — who can tell which of the two is the more meaningless and pointless.

The young physician was now standing face to face with the "vital force" whose investigation he had set as the goal of his life. What did he see, what could he learn from the woman's grotesque reflexes? Nothing: the center of vegetation, the most basic source of life is inaccessible — all we see is a few shoddy movements, ghostly caricatures. Nothing else.

55.

Before he came here to the moribund one, he attended the appointment of a professor at the university: a quite young, posturing, and mundane colleague of his was adorned with the purple mantle, black beret, and gold necklace. The physician was conscious of the difference between the two of them: there, superficial observation and lightweight positive successes — with him, some manic will-to-penetrate-the-depths, which resulted in great pessimism and desperate giving up of therapy. There is hardly any middle way: half of the doctors are cheap positivists — the other half, mystical alchemists. The one kind leaves the naturalist who worships the reality of the real just as unsatisfied as the other.

The whole university congregated for the ceremony: the servants, pharmacists, and nurse-nuns were all present, so the epileptics could go ahead & faint, the women go into labor in their squeezed-in, filthy dens — not a soul was to attend to them in the half-basement hospitals: everybody gathered in the splendidly lit upstairs aulas. The young doctor was nauseated by the abundant Latin hexameters, Aesculapius statues and symbolic objects, he was annoyed by the senescent, bearded doctors' naïve theorizing; he loathed the fair-haired youngster who read, in cocksure voice, his inaugural address about *The Exclusion of All Philosophey in Medical Science*, and because he had the impression of hearing some clamor from the hospital which the flutes and violins of the inaugural music couldn't quite cover, he simply ran down the winding stairs to look out for the patient.

Indeed, there was an old, constipated woman lying on the floor downstairs: for the cure applied to her was to tie her up with ropes that cut deep into her skin, to an awfully heavy leaden chamber pot day and night, and now the already half-idiot auntie tripped up and could no more get back to her "feet" (that is, her chamber pot) than beetles turned on their backs can clamber back to their feet. What could this insane little body, shriveled up with solitude, have to do with those Latin hexameters, odes to Aesculapius to eight voices, and mantles purple-scintillating in cascades of candlelight, which filled up the aula to the brim? He would have liked to hoist up this wizened, bound-up old woman, this frightful muse-jade of suffering, carry her upstairs into the aula, blow out the candles and tear the mantles and gold necklaces to shreds — so that nothing but *suffering* would be there, the doctors' first and last concreteness: after all, the aula was no ballroom and no baroque theater stage.

It didn't escape several of the old professors that the young doctor was absent from the ceremony for a few minutes — one of them even called him aside and accused him of arrogance and boastfulness, who, instead of feeling in seventh heaven for the privilege of standing among the luminaries of the faculty among the aula's sacred marble columns, showed such demeanor as would provoke his expulsion even from the village barbers' guild. He was otherwise known to be in the habit of meeting charlatans from the outskirts at midnight and their conversations were, horribile dictu, not carried out in Latin.

While he listened to this lengthy sermon, he was still full of spite and trusting in his own furore of observation, wild nose for the most ancient layers of vitality: what was to him science's methodology-etiquette, when he saw reality itself, which could not be approached with science, poetry, charlatanism, or theology, but only with a *chance* human spirit-constellation born once every thousand years, and which consisted of the untraceable fabric of the above-mentioned elements. He believed that he was one of these precursorless and successorless accidents, and with ironic stiffness planted a kiss on the freshly anointed sniveling brat's forehead.

Instead of returning to the hospital, the gull-bonneted battalion of nuns proceeded to the church after the professors, where they prayed loudly for the new professor's happiness. When the pale host appeared above the heads, the physician raised his head (provoking a new scandal), because he liked looking God in the unleavened eye rather than blindly dodging Him (the hand-bell knocked the heads off the "believers'" necks as some candle-extinguisher puts out the flame from the wick): what would that Body have to say about this whole comedy? What would the primeval vitality of creation have to say about these "methods" distorted into articles — and the suicidal humanism of salvation, about these cosmeticized fogeys preoccupied with themselves rather than their patients?

56.

He was boiling to go to the mayor's wife, to whom he was bound by the double binds of love & knowledge. A more tragicomic situation could hardly be imagined: the theme of his love was in fact the perishing body, that dark erotic aroma of sickness and death which can sometimes turn even the ugliest girls into Venuses: when this bouquet vanishes, love probably also disappears — yet he felt that through this woman he would render concrete and expressible all his shapeless intuitions about life and healing which had preoccupied him since childhood. If he can summon to the classroom before the faculty's elders & youthful finaglers this woman whom all knew to be suffering of an incurable disease, and exhibit her cured, healthy body like a bunch of freshly picked flowers, then his truth will have triumphed over the university's pedantry. He would have liked to perish together with her in the love-heated torpor of Lethe, and at the same time to hand her back, with his innovative medication, to that womanly life that would be independent of him in the future, in which he wouldn't even like to know her any more: with a noble pose he would like to disappear from the town and from the country. In him the daimonia of the boudoir alternated with the daimonia of the operating theater.

Sometimes she felt better: she emerged, pale, from the waters of fever, like a long-flooded seaside thistle after the tide in the drying morning sun. The mayor was in the town hall, the servants were downstairs in the kitchen; the windows were all covered, fire hummed quietly in the fireplace, by the bedside there was one sole, lampion-like, yellow candlestick: at such times they forgot everything and lived solely for intimacy, for the love born from the melancholia of sickness and the kindness of healing. The source of all neighbourly and erotic love is compassion, the pity felt at our own "condition humaine" or another human being's individual misfortune: from the meaninglessness of destiny these two people huddled together in the odd, invaluable moment of accidental peace. At such times he completely forgot the university, healing, the divine kabbalistics of the kidneys and capillaries; he didn't care about the chemical structure of reality and the imprint of destiny in the skin's cross-section: the daemonia of the boudoir was the polar opposite of all these. Although their whole love was utterly bodily, flowering, as it did, from sickness, the body itself hardly featured in it — they were first and foremost moral beings, figures of neighborly love, of immaterial

attraction. If he thought about it he chanced the distinction between a "procreative" and a passive "humanist" corporeality: the
former was restricted to coitus and was thus *abstract* rather than
physical — the latter, involving the whole body, was that mor-
bose-idyllic resting in the blissful-splenetic fact that we have a
body: and love germinates from the latter. This all-sensitive doctor couldn't escape the great metaphysics of "pampering" — that
wondrous feminine atmosphere that is composed of menstrua-
tion, housekeeping, death, and pietism. The woman's body was
transparent like glass, the doctor could hear not only the moral
music coming from her but also the hammers and strings: this
physiological transparence was so eerie that he hid from it with
a child's cowardice into the same woman's lap.

Her room was always perversely tidy: this tidiness had
nothing to do either with puritanical symmetry or mundane
prettiness; this was the female onanism of housekeeping incarnate,
one of love's most inescapable vortexes. A flower, a bottle of wine,
a small sandwich, a kerchief placed under a lamp triggered quiet
Bacchic suggestions in the doctor's blood. And above all of them,
mortality hovered, the disquieting Paracelsus truth that "der Tod
kommt nicht morgen, sondern heut":[6] that all these sweet nuances, these sugary proportions and richness of the living body
and the mute object world were all in vain, and the more crowded
they are, the more clearly they proclaim death — death, which,
however, is not an awful physical blunder in the world during
the pseudo-convalescence, but a love metaphor.

And with all these things they were in an unmistakably moral
relation, in the mellowing mood of hypochondriac Jesus "pax" —
their adultery was full of tearful lambliness, Samaritanness, and
Madonna-vexation. If there is a true enemy of the scientific pursuit of truth, it is these dark idylls blended from death *& kharis*.
And the doctor was fully aware of its danger and barrenness. He
believed nothing of it, so it didn't elicit real pleasure in him, if not

for the fact that he came to know the tormenting emptiness of
even the greatest "felicity" found in a woman. He wrung himself
across into the medical perspective: to see in woman not a moral
companion but a dehumanized, experimental flower of life, of
nature in general. When she fainted, when he performed smaller
surgeries on her body, he almost flogged himself into sadism in-
creased at a "histrionic" degree: he cut and pierced her like superstitious old hags thrusting their needles into their enemies' wax
effigies — he wanted to avenge himself for the crippling amorous
impotence of idyll & Lethe. He couldn't distinguish his desire to
sophisticatedly kill the woman from his desire to genially heal her.

Now as he was performing the last and apparently utterly
hopeless surgery, he was in the latter mood: he felt that what he
was doing was no true science but some kitsch allegory of "re-
search," but he couldn't get away from it — perhaps not even the
most righteous were entirely free from it. Life and death were
gesticulating on the table before him, stripped of their mask: and
he saw in despair that he didn't know an iota the more about
them than the methodical pedants — the passion with which he
wanted to penetrate the core of all the secrets didn't make him
any cleverer than the doctrinaire. Did he behave in such a superior manner at the ceremony for this? Or does he have to search
on and on, so that what today is merely a romantic presupposi-
tion may become reality in the end? He felt that the greatest reality was at all times such horror and chaos, such complexity and
polyguity that science can't even get close to it — as Paracelsus
writes, "erschrecklich ist er, greulich und streng."[7]

57.

The mayor was surprised that he had managed to preserve his solitude so far. In one of the rooms to his right councilors, soldiers,
and messengers were waiting for him, buzzing extras of chaos and
jurisprudence — to the left, relations and acquaintances worry-

ing about his wife. What shall he do with them — which is the greater humbug, family or the town, blood relations or politics? He didn't see any other reality before him than the reality of moral and biology: for him there was nothing else but those dribbling, light blue, quite turquoise suppurations that he used to wipe with a handkerchief from his wife's abscesses — and "moral" was in fact nothing else but the eternal question, impossible-to-erase & frenzied page margin around the blue purulence, "Does it have any sense, is there anything else beside it, or is this all"?

For the mayor ethics always consisted of these two parts alone: the superstitiously intensive, lyrical world, shot through with veins of nervousness, of amorous fidelity and infidelity — and the question whether it was worth it at all to speak of ethics. Was it worth regarding oneself or the other person as anything but the chronic tube of blue suppuration? Of course when he reduced man to a mere hormone rattle, with him it wasn't mere "materialism" or godless fatalism: he could well imagine all these things to be replete with divine good intentions, luxuriating transcendence, it was only that he was utterly tone-deaf to them. He felt that his love, the vows of marriage, his eternal cheatings, brought him into some real relationship, beyond purulence, with his wife, but death, the selfish triumph of puss again rendered that illusory. Are both merely sham fictions — moral life and biological functions? Is fidelity just as much of a caricature as blood circulation? Is the whole thing a blue-black farce? Is the sole lesson and palpable part of life, that in moments of crisis nothing has value, nothing is certain? And which is the sicklier neurosis, which is the more obsessive obsession: the notion and experience of "certainty" or, on the contrary, "uncertainty"?

The young doctor was heaping these same questions around the woman's cooling-out body as chips around a cut beam: his bloodied fingers were literally caught up in her veins and muscles while — giving up all hope — he wanted to breathe a farewell kiss on her powdered face. Voilà! The two gestures: the operating hands among the bowels' forever tuning-down strings, and the mouth on the skin cosmeticized to a beautiful mask. Which was the more human? For one cannot shake it off saying, both are equally human: our brain demands one sole "worthy" one, wants to see the essence of man and of life gathered into one navel-whirlpool.

The doctor was very surprised by the inward squeezing that surrounded his hands in the woman's pelvis, as if it were not the soul exiting with Elysian slovenliness and impatience from the dying body, but as though all the inner organs were rushing toward one point, if possible as far away from the face's pallor, from the glassed-over eyes' (for them) pretentious humanism as possible. What strength there was inside the body that he would have remained forever ignorant of, had he just looked at the moribund woman from without! In fact he felt two movements around his fingers and wrist, like muddy rings and greased-over bracelets: a noose-like, squeezing force, the narrowing-down to bursting point of muscles and veins — and a waterfall-like, sweeping, one-directional cascading, as if he had dipped his hand like a childishly impotent dam inside a stream that carried away pebbles, fish, and leaves. The woman's whole body seemed to be emptying out with that eternal, one-directional greed and yet remaining full, shown by the paradox spiral of a revolving corkscrew: it's as if all the organs were piling up, pushing toward one single sieve, and at the same time a tree-like knot formed between his fingers — the lines running in infinite *parallels* need only a speck of dust to be instantly drowned in closed rings. Did he feel the topography of death's energies, or those of life?

58.

The moment he kissed the dying woman the mayor entered with terrible racket. This had to be so, the doctor thought: there where life's most essential questions turn out to be forever unanswered, and what is more (and this is the very point), such questions whose sheer raising seems utterly senseless (the question of questions: isn't it an absolute error to "put a question" at all?) — there always occurs some kitschily symmetrical human action, some ludicrously placed "point," as though all the intellectual barrenness that life means for the true intellect, attempted to compensate with the artistic proportions and clockwork punctuality of dramatic scenes.

"It's all right, doctor," the mayor said, "it's all right. Here beside death nothing matters: the greatest fidelity, too, is nonsense, just as the basest perversity, too, is sacred theoricea. Despair has no perspective, moral, or science. If you want to become a great professor, write two books alone: one about there being around us some enormous reality — or, if you happen to be of a doubting persuasion (and, since you are a realist, you are most certainly so): that there is some awful illusion of reality around us — women, royal crowns, gods supplanting one another, diseases, arms, the whole gamut; and then the other Summa, about how to all this belongs absolute (*absolute*, you understand?) uncertainty, annihilating doubt, the dizzying Saturn rings of doubt."

The doctor pulled out his hand from the woman, his kneeling famulus quickly slapped on it a vinegary towel like a butterfly net on a butterfly. "I couldn't help her. She's dead." "You are crying, while I am preaching. I'd like to send you out of the room, doctor, but I have no right. I've been unsayably mean to this woman: I couldn't bear to be left alone with her. My marriage to her has just started now, in this very minute — it's not the human drivel of fidelity and infidelity, of coitus and sacrament, but the secret, the greatest this-worldly reality: the marriage of the secret, the barren fertility, in my womb, of ignorance planted in my body."

The young doctor squatted at the mayor's feet crying like a four-year-old little girl and lay his head in the mayor's lap. "You are so clever and good to me, my lord, I don't deserve it." "Am I defiling you, my dear wife, by caressing this clumsy child, valuing the sentimental pose of 'understanding everything' more than your corpse sharpened into morality? But what else can I do? I feel that the only act worthy of you would be suicide — for, even if I had lived with you like a saint all your life, even so, to live on after your death would be: the sin of sins, basest of baseness — there is no more repellent ethical downward slide than to dare *live* by the side of a dead person. And because I don't choose immediate death here, though, I feel such loathing for myself that I can go on play-acting at will: as compared to the filthy betrayal of staying alive, everything else is merely a pardonable game."

While the servants bandaged the bleeding woman, the mayor said with a blasphemy canonizing himself holier than the saints: "Let us pray." The prayer consisted of two parts, or rather, "perspectives": on the one hand one single, tragic breathing-in of this world, this life on earth, history — on the other hand, a bitter prying into, and homage-bearing critique of, the netherworld. This world: all the tidings, stool-pigeons' reports, military gibberish and church legates speak about the imminent and ultimate end of papacy — with this pope Christ and the whole of Christianity falls. He had never before seen Christianity so much, so dishearteningly to be *merely* an episode in history, with its dogmas and ethics: how could he pray to a god whose last and final datum is perhaps filled in with red ink, in that very moment, by the German emperor? Even if he had ever believed, his faith was bound to relics, bishops' effigies, church ground-plans — if these are scattered, torn down, he will be left with nothing: pure spirituality had never been his kettle of fish. And when he thought about the netherworld, if he attempted to imagine that Christianity is, after all, not a nerve-intermezzo of pubertal Europe, he could see nothing else but his wife's, his mistresses', and his own certain damnation: after the sea of suffering he had to undergo here on earth, yet further and infinite torments. These two, mutually exclusive imaginings (Christianity's historical downfall and his personal damnation) harrowed his soul equally, for both were plastic metaphors of his shapeless despair looking for some form: in his self-mortifying atheistic spite he wanted Christianity to be merely a biological reflex, a short-lived, insignificant neurosis in the life of mankind, yet he nevertheless wanted it to have sufficient power to hurl those who lived in its era, which lasted but a few brief moments, into eternal damnation, infinite perishing. He felt that even if he was to be damned he would have no cause to feel remorse for having neglected anything that might have served his salvation here on earth: he had indeed wanted to believe so entirely, with all his nerve-endings, that he couldn't possibly be charged with superficiality and negligence offending the Holy Ghost.

He looked at his wife's distorted face, at the doctor, into his own soul, and offered up to destiny, like an officiating priest bearing aloft the enflamed chalice, that great, near laughable metaphysical ignorance that filled the room like hanging fog.

59.

In the meantime the doors were thrown open and the corridor and the room's threshold filled with people. When the mayor slowly lifted his head from the prayer (as a thief lifts a muffled key from a lock) he felt a profound justification of his entire governance: he felt that it was more logical and lifelike to represent, at the head of a town or a state, history's core nihil and its tragicomic nonsense, than with however Machiavellian egoism, the state optimism, or with some naïve theoretical mysticism the "city's historical mission." He would have felt it entirely right if every single burgher came there now to kiss his hands — no better father could have been found for his people than himself.

Two councilors helped him to his feet. For the first time tears sprang to his eyes: so far both he and his wife had been destiny's puppets — now, between the two supporting elders, he became the icy-bedded widower. One of them growled into his ear in muffled voice, "We stand by you," while the other only said modestly, "The Venetian ambassadors are waiting outside. Forgive my speaking about this now, but I have to ask if you'd like to speak to them, or if we should send them off now and call for them when you feel ready to receive them?" "It is all the same, my friend: they can come here, now, anywhere." The first elder interrupted: "Pardon me, but they can't possibly come here now: you are hardly in the state of mind to negotiate with them. Especially not with such selfish, narrow-minded merchants." "You are wrong, entirely wrong to believe that I would make a melodrama out of the settlement of debts and the transporting of grains: if you will, I've always negotiated the most arid business in a funereal mood, just as I could never take any suffering of mine so seriously (so *intellectually* seriously, mind you) as to not stick scrupulously to the relations that are best expressed in numbers and legal articles. You are convinced that it is gross histrionics if I receive them here, but it is not. For the moment I cannot leave the room. Bring that chair here." The chair was pulled over, while three councilors hastened to summon the ambassadors.

60.

On a side-door a freshly laved, red-robed priest entered with two Franciscans. He searched the room with glinting beagle eyes; when he spotted the woman's corpse, he made a sportsmanlike "aha, it's here" gesture, pushed the two monks ahead and with his crackling, rustling robe hastened to the mayor. "Wait here or pray in silence. I'm going to trade with the Venetians here."

Are there still priests around? The mayor had immersed himself so much in imagining the destruction of the Church that he could hardly believe his eyes when he saw this flustering eminence at the door.

The Venetian ambassadors were slowly approaching on the corridor: one could see on their faces that they couldn't decide what diplomatic grimace to display — should they express their "sincerest sympathy" for the mayor faltering on the edge of insanity, or should they keep their cool as people who are aware that the whole audience by the catafalque is a shtick, political buffoonery for obtaining certain interests. The mayor met them halfway. The three ambassadors expressed their sympathies, threw an uneasy glance at the woman's covered-up body, and when the two monks and the bishop suddenly knelt beside the bloody-edged bier, joined them and knelt down before the woman. "Get together, two follies: Venice's ephemeral politics and the female body's pointless physics." The whole scene was like the symbolic wedding of life's two flummeries — it indeed asked for pulling the unbreakable ring of schmegegge on both parties. The mayor remained standing and caressed the kneeling Venetians' shoulders like dogs. "Come," he said after a while and, not waiting for them to get up, went back to his armchair. The ambassadors' etiquette condolences refreshed him: while genuine feelings always disheartened him, social hypocrisy, the playing-out of formalities, always inspired faith and optimism in him. He let himself down flexibly, almost swinging, between the armrests. The Venetians were still kneeling (they seemed to whisper together) with their backs to the already seated mayor, who addressed them: "You will no doubt harshly criticize my act of mixing my private life with the affairs of the town, which in an entirely superfluous way (& as you will probably say, mendacious) creates a theatrical situation, to which I can only reply that with me this is no game but, at the moment, my only possible simplicity and natural freedom

— on the other hand, if it's a pose, you'll yet have to realize at some point, on your deathbeds at the latest, that only in posturing and well-balanced kitsch can that flavor and inebriating scent of reality be felt, which is all our nervous system and reason expect from reality. Be seated, drink a bit of wine."

In the meantime the Venetians got up, foreheads reddened by the "prayer" with bowed head, and looked at the servants offering wine. They started suspecting that the mayor had indeed gone maboule and were already formulating in their head the witticisms to dot their reports of the event when they dish up the anecdote to the doge. One of them spoke: "I can't imagine a more awkward and less gratifying task than to cruelly shower on your shoulders the thousand worries of the town's fate when we should hand you over to your boundless grief, so as to somehow find peace with the Lord, destiny, and yourself after the inevitable grapple with solitude. This is not our first meeting, that's why I dare commit this seeming lack of compassion: you have always been a man who wanted truth more than comfort, and even the darkest reality more than the infertile rest of midnight sleep. Perhaps I am taking advantage of your manliness even now, when I'm about to present reality to your eyes, forcing myself (and believe me, *forcing* is the word) to forget the blow that you received but a few short minutes ago. You know that the emperor is conquering Rome. You have always wavered between Rome and the emperor, and although everybody who have at least once spoken with you or read your letters know perfectly that this wavering was by no means a feebleness of thought or action, far less business-like calculating, but that profoundly manly philosophical insight that truth is infinitely complicated and its components are not to be found inside one party or one city's walls, but scattered under many different flags, religions, and legislative interests: although everybody knew and will know this perfectly about you — still, we have to confess that it had been a politically well-nigh unrealizable system and now, in the present historical moment (and please don't regard this as arrogant criticism, for it is not, but rather, a humble, affectionate request from a friend), in the present moment this approach is simply absurd. I had to call profoundly wise and manly (although you raised your hand in mocking disdain) your thesis that it is not worth the name of politics that which doesn't take into account, with analytical scrupulousness, the near untraceable complexity of truth — for its application to real life demanded greater intellect and heroism than anything else. There are many who know you only as a nervous negotiator and impotent brooder, and in the famous chronicles which are read across half of Europe you feature so: but this is the opinion of the plebs and of petty critique-mongering literates — we, your friends, know that there was far greater heroism in your negotiations than — I am no longer afraid to utter the word — in the deeds of many a commander of the Crusades. But now the situation in Italy has come to such a crisis that your admirable (and this we say with the greatest conviction), one and only truth is utterly impossible: diplomatic experimenting has definitely come to an end, the world is simplified to one sole brutal alternative. If you take up the cause of Rome: the emperor will wipe you out in a day and make slaves of you and your people. If you felt an urge to suddenly switch to the emperor's side, the way is barred: I say it under oath as the supreme truth that, thanks to a few of your 'benefactors,' the emperor is expecting you to change sides as a false trick, so he would see your change of tune merely as an even more telling evidence of your pro-papacy stance than if you were to commit suicide and (what is a far greater sin) genocide, committing yourself openly to Rome. You are in debt. Join us: if your path to the emperor should lead through us, you have a winning cause — Venice is the emperor's favorite state; neither Cologne nor Augsburg are dearer to him than Venice. We will pay your debts, & your people will be happy. Could you, are you allowed to, sacrifice, for the sake of a historico-political truth (which we all know to be the *absolute* truth), the happiness & future of a people that wishes to live?"

The mayor had long wanted to answer: as during his whole political career, even in this moment he was less preoccupied by expressing his own thesis or truth as against the "thesis" of the Venetians, than to play off the Venetian ambassadors' manner against another manner, their gestures and style against his own character traits, grimaces, and intonation. But he had no opportunity to do so any longer.

61.

From the corridor came a noise of fretting, whispering, here & there the slamming of doors, ever louder, ever closer, the odd military-sounding, startled order-word followed by exalted, yet muffled female syllables, & by the time those in the room could have done anything, the last lover appeared in the door: the Donna. The mayor hardly even stirred in his armchair, he only tightened his grip on the armrests and said to the Venetians in a sepulchral voice that was at an equal distance from loudness & quiet, "The Donna will answer instead of me. But if you report this comedy to the Doge, kindly point out that this act is not my composition."

The Donna hastened to the center of the room; she wore a full-length, dark green dress, splendid like an outfit tailored for a royal ball & pathetically simple like the garb of a penitent nun. With her left hand she grabbed the belt's string as though it had been a rope destined to the mayor's neck. "This is so much like you," she recited in a nasal voice, "the death-chamber and diplomatic salon in one, great theater with great mimes, as though the whole of life existed solely to provide you with coulisses for your puny dramatic delicatessen. You need dead bodies & states —

it is with such fates you cosmeticize yourself. I, too, had been foolish enough to step on your stage as a mad, hysterical extra for a while, but I've had enough. I thought I would torture you for long, with cunning intrigue, but I got bored of the plan: I came to tear off your mask with a single move. How those Venetian lords stand about there, taking the petty interior decorator in dead earnest — how proudly this dead body lies here, although she had been less than the lowest skivvy in the eyes of his lordship the mayor!"

Of course the guards at once ran at the half-mad woman, but the mayor sprang from his chair and roared at them: "Nobody shall touch her! Let everybody hear out my glorious history."

There was a great flurry, the councilors and relatives, like swarming bees, buzzed to beg him to cut the lowlife scene short; the Venetians were loudly quarrelling with each other; the young bishop was giving frenetic orders to the servants and monks to lift the corpse off the table and carry it to a quiet, distant bedchamber.

The Donna continued: "Heaven forbid that you silence me, for his lordship the mayor loves dramatic turns of fortune. I myself am an actress, an amusingly twitching little plaything in his puppet theater — why should he renounce the spectacle now, pray?" "For the love of God, be silent, unknown Donna, for the sake of this dead woman," the bishop intervened in his girlish pubertal voice, "let us not all go mad, when every single word and decision is fateful. These hands and knees are in the habit of bending before the Highest One alone, and now I am wilting my interceding arms before you — let us not defile the dead, our city, the bereaved widower, Venice, and above all, yourself, your own femininity." "It was the mayor who defiled me, and this swindler Madonna who stole death's pose on herself," the woman screamed and with a drunken gesture grabbed at the dead body that pious hands were lifting off the table.

Chaos & scandal reigned supreme. A never-felt, trance-like calm overcame the mayor: there can be no greater confusion than this, and all the idealism and vileness, fanatical thirst for logic & sensual liberty that had long rendered his life an ungovernable circus of self-contradiction, had now crystallized into one solid, plastic block: he held it in his hand like Columbus the blissfully finite globe after the seas' infinite chaos.

The ambassadors were gesticulating at the open door — seals, ringed hands, a greying head, rustling of parchment, swearwords in a foreign dialect — wasn't the Donna right: hadn't he been attracted all his life by these decorative "impressions"?

On the corridor, white-mute Roman statues: what an infinite void stretches between the festive historical marble head and the living person wallowing in scandals! Venice, the world's Cleopatra-faced Händler: drenched paradox of water, east, pose, terror, Byzantium and stock exchange — what did they want? What were they talking about? the well-being, fate, future of the people? is there a people? Is it worth sending hundreds and thousands of galleys across the sea to transport grains and bring in flour, so that the "people" could live in prosperity? There is no people — there is always, ever one sole person in the world. To eat? When we don't know if God exists and if we ourselves exist? To instigate to join the pope or emperor, Venice or death — when we don't know a single letter of the hidden text of the whatness of "pope" and "emperor"?

There stand the bereaved relatives, one of them already has a knife in his hand to murder the corpse-defiling mistress or myself: isn't this insane hetaera just as much a secret of destiny as the wife? Is there value — is there morality? What do those glitzy lances want, the soldiers, the awful, bloody torsos of *order*? Does order keep madness in check? What does order justify itself by, in the face of madness? If there were some real order, some absolute guarantee behind my lancers' savage-stiff rayon, then let them club this epileptic coquette to death — but the lances are only straight and parallel, death-filled and scintillating — they don't mean order but the very absolute lack of order, the sickly, fruitless nostalgia for order, the imagined (and always only imagined) opposite of madness. Discipline, legal canons, the phalanx of arms, syllogism, the symmetrical theses of dogmatism: they bear all the imprints of primal madness just as visibly as this hysterical woman. And there is truth in this hysterical woman, too, some irrefutable positive trait of life, some mathematical absolute. She is right, she is right: I have been attracted by salon allegories; I've been a ha'penny gourmand. In half a minute I will perhaps die of that knife, and yet what am I distracting myself with? I'm looking at the lances' nervous tracery in the room — the soldiers are all crumpled up under them, but the drawing escapes from them, straight, like reeds from chaotic mud, or the whistling spirit from the corpse. And among the lances, the coquette's face — outside every relation (for this is the only experience of life: every attitude is absurd and impossible before every phenomenon, object, or occurrence of life), with the gross stain of vengeance around her half-open mouth and half-closed eyes. It is all well, for this scene had lurked in all kisses, "happinesses" (what a word!), there can be no follow-up to enamored love. He suffered a lowly (lowly?) woman to defile his dead wife: this blasphemy (for he felt it to be so all the same) filled him with such bitterness and pain, in it his own moral insanity appeared with such apocalyptic precision, that without this ignominy he couldn't have loved his wife so truly as he now did. What little amateur "yeses" these quidnunc priests were beside his wife's monumental "no"! But let's leave distinction aside — I think it is an awful mistake to distinguish between yes and no.

From the window one could see the garden. Under the bushes a blackbird hopped and shuddered with its wings, now & again rustling the leaves petrified to silence. Sometimes it spread its

wings and the feathers stuck out like the thumb and little finger holding a decimal on the cembalo — in such moments the
thought of flight hovered above it like a scent above an opening
flower-cup — but then it drew them in, like a fan closing with a
stutter, and continued picking at the ground with its beak. With
superstitious clarity the mayor decided that if the blackbird remained in the garden for another half minute, his life would yet
have a happy ending, but if it flew away, he would be killed. He
was counting the seconds on his pulse while the bird hopped in
the garden.

II. The Pope

1.

The pope's older brother also lived in the town. The ninety-year-old priest almost never slept. Now, too, he was awake, fully dressed, sitting close to the balcony door. The moon cut into the room with a sharp, green stripe: this death-shimmer lay across the old man's knees like Christ's body on the Pietà Madonnas' laps. Around him the houses were all smaller, looking like plants swaying underwater. The old man harked to a distant blare.

This have-nothing priest could have easily become a cardinal or overlord while his brother, the pope, was still alive, but he turned down all offers. Not for being a dyed-in-the-wool ascetic, but because he loathed the ways of the mundane world, etiquette, and intrigues. He didn't take any interest in theological debates, was bored to high heaven by the dug-up ancient statues; to him diplomacy, women, and kings all appeared like caricature and drivel, so he would invariably send back his brother's donor-letters with a guffaw. Only once had he gone to the Vatican: right there in the antechamber, even before taking off his cloak, he found a huge wall-mirror so much to his liking that he asked for it. For a while the two brothers joked, shuddering, who should confess whom, or if both should confess the other, then they parted and hadn't seen each other since.

The old priest had contact with two people alone, his niece and his nephew. At fourteen, his nephew was a composer already famous in all of Italy. His niece was a famous travelling coquette and actress with a Sophocles mania. The priest shared his quarters with the boy who was now asleep in the next room. When he heard the blare in the street he also heard some kind of grate at the door. Sitting in the open balcony door, he was neither on the street nor at home. Because his house was much taller than the surrounding ones, his rooms opened not onto the street but onto the clouds, so to say, between the earth and the sky: the roofs boomed from afar under the sky weighed down by the Moon & the poppy-petal-shedding stars, like the accompanying tonalities caressed by the left hand in the low registers under the resonant theme intoned by the right. If from the room he heard the bell ringing or a fidgeting with the door handle, he didn't feel that somebody was trying to get into his room: there was no room, only incandescent-smoldering clouds, bragging midnight meridians close to God — can stars have door-handles, could a doorbell break down on the Moon? He waited for the skivvy to let in the early-morning visitor, but then remembered that he had let her off the previous evening, so he got up grumbling and went toward the door, scraping off his foot-warmer with impatient, trembling hands, like a mound of fallen leaves from a garden statue.

The priest was pale and lean, with a huge aquiline nose from whose shell-like openings big, thick hairs hung like huge stamens, or like the last remains of a toothbrush; his face was slashed by deep wrinkles, as though put together from melon cloves; there was no connection between the territories this side of a wrinkle and beyond, all mimicry ended at the edge of such a dark and rather unwashed-looking precipice. His mouth was enormous and blood-red like an actress'; between his ears two thread-thin, red lines fluttered incessantly like the drifting reflection of a rope tightened on the banks across a rippling pond. His hair was the most colorful of all: silvery-white, moon-moldy, greenish-blond, dirty-brown, hyena grey — like a buffoon's wig. When he made his only visit to the Vatican, he had already arrived at this degree of motleyness coupled with an equally aggravating tousledness, so the pope immediately commended him to the care of a stodgy Franciscan. The monk then literally ploughed and harrowed his head.

Through the glass the outer world entered the squeezed-in apartment like a stage: when he stood in front of the mirror in the room, he truly got *out* into the freedom of stars and clouds. Reflected in an inverted perspective, or one steered to the side, the landscape truly became landscape. In the huge mirror, at the bottom of the image the room's individual objects appeared, dark brown and padded with the warmth of dreams — a chair, an old clock, a pale jug's bulging belly; as if the chair and the clock were two old peeping Jews and the misty-venereal jug, the bathing Susanna. The jug's oval said everything there was to know about love: the moats of the breasts (two bird-eggs resting lukewarm in the nest of shirts, camisoles, blouses), the face's oval, the shoulders' seal-slides emerging from water, the blunted doubleness of the anus. The ticking of the clock perfectly expressed the essence of his love: wizened old gent, lean, pedantic, calumniating onanist — the ticking, the mechanical circulation of minutes in his body simultaneously meant the barren clacking of desire, the theoretical rattling-down of merely-imagined, never-materialized seeds, & the never-ending *Nacheinander* of the words of voluptuously-phrased gossip, sharply and precisely-chiseled prickly pearls of intrigue. The chair looked on Susanna quite differently: its armrests were clumsy, modest attempts at embrace, its flatness a prosaic ratiocination about a manageable wife, whereas the slightly flaring-out legs, the sigh-statue of (by far not pessimistic) "no use, no use."

This was at the bottom of the mirror, the history of Susanna with junk-shop Andersen characters: otherwise the whole reflex-stage was occupied by a giant cloud. This cloud best resembled a strip of smoke which, very thin when it starts from the chimney, at once spreads, bulges, until it fills the whole sky, and by the time it reaches us it has thinned again, even if not quite as much as it was at the outset. Examining the relation between thinning and bulging, the most interesting thing was that one couldn't

tell if the cloud had swollen abruptly or slowly, gradually: if
one followed the image step by step, the change seemed gradual,
whereas if one glimpsed it in a flash (like the priest getting up
now to open the door), it appeared disproportionate, a dragon
irrupting from space-womb, whose Nereid-tail is not connected
in any harmonious way to its elephant belly. Otherwise the sky
was perfectly empty, with this lone cloud: once his niece had a
blood-red gown without any adornments, save for a black acute
triangle whose two sides started from the left shoulder, flaring
out to human width at the hips, and at the knees already curled
backwards, so that the two points almost touched at the skirt's
back; underneath they suddenly narrowed down again (between the knees and ankles, that is, disproportionately low) and
again converged in one point at the feet, like at the top on the
shoulder. One is used to such whimsically galloping, swelling-
squeezing forms in Baroque painting, but nothing prepares us
for seeing them in nature. For each element of the picture in
fact belongs to the style situated at the farthest remove from
essentially untamed Baroque — sweetish-velvety, caressingly
tragic Biedermeier: the sky's near tickling navy blue, the cloud's
rust and silvery fringe, the rooftops' drowsyish lemon tint, the
lurking Moon's spike-like rays — it was all "The Night," the 1803
edition, the very it. And although it was filled to its last atom, to
the point of kitsch, with utterly banal melancholia, the whole
was nevertheless tremendum mysterium: Greco griffin, swaying
death-trail (between a G sharp and the E under it in Sarastro's
aria there is a more tragic, extreme, and wilder fall and distance,
than in however recherché a five-octave interval).

The cloud now covered the Moon: in the darkness of its face,
in the muffled security of its shadowing the back's scintillation
and luminosity could be felt; how gorgeous such a cloud's back
must be, its foam-glacier turned to the Moon, its waving steam-
tresses, as light penetrates them — the cloud is forever stripping,

removing one mask and garment after another, so that its naked limbs can be washed over by midnight light — it stirs relentlessly, changing its limbs, bathing, turning them; it quarters itself, offering up to the wind's fawning bed now its bun, now its ankle.

The cloud's face turned toward the priest was also a kind of Susanna, bordered on the left and right by moonlight's curiosity-frame — however it may shine, it cannot get in front of the cloud, to its face turned to the Earth. On this picture Susanna is death itself: death as sailing-off midnight foliage, dazed migratory bird — and the peeping elders are human curiosity incarnate, gossip-craving, rationalist, forever off-the-mark boudoir eavesdropping. All this was visible inside the room, above and among the furniture: the little room's fragments falling into the mirror knelt under the sole cloud-diagonal like much too concretely portrayed donors on the stairs of old triptychs' transfigured Madonnas.

2.

The priest quietly scuffled to the door and opened it. "Angelina!" It was his niece. "It's me," she said in her voice thick as a man's, flashing her teeth in a laugh. "If you only knew how I came! with whom! and why!"

She was extraordinarily tall, in pitch-black dress, red leather gloves almost reaching up to her shoulders, and in a huge black hat adorned with thick plumes, their fringes dropping to her forehead like a frou-frou magnified for the sake of a scientific experiment. Near her slenderness the priest seemed hunch-backed.

"Are you awake at this hour?" "I'm always awake. For years I haven't been sleeping. Why should I? My blood circulates so slowly that it doesn't need any rest anymore. Only death is slower. What brings you here, Babylon?" She started pulling off one glove and quietly asked: "Is the child asleep?" "Yes. You needn't whisper, he does my sleeping, too, and quite profoundly." Angelina pulled off her glove, tautened it like a string and said: "Our old man is dead." She slammed down the glove and started peeling off the other one. "What?" — the priest asked. She didn't answer, only gave a prolonged, quite melodic "Hmmmm." "Who?" "Pius." And with a bitter smile, throwing her right hand high in the air from the wrist, as though conducting an orchestra toward the highest notes, then dropping hand, glove, and voice, she dryly repeated, like one who doesn't utter the word but only its negative imprint: "Pius." "My brother? Is that why there's that hubbub in the street?" "Yes." "But that's impossible… then we must… then… when did he die? What happened? Do you know for certain? Rico, Rico…" "Let the boy sleep, what do you want him for?" "Rico" — the priest uttered his childhood name tenderly, with an animal's whining sadness. — "Rico! Rico!" "Pius! Pius!" — Angelina sarcastically imitated in the voice of bootlicking courtiers, puffed-up secretaries, and all-important sycophants.

"What's happening in Rome?" — the priest asked, blinking at her from the thousand-branched tree of his grief (which he had grown around himself for shelter in a second) — "riot?" "I have come with the emperor's soldiers, more precisely, with the mercenaries of the duke of Sigmaringen. They said they would march into Rome: Rome is already as good as fallen." "They killed Rico, the bastards." "Poor Rico, nobody cares about him anymore." "Pius!" — Angelina said again sarcastically, as though in these moments the sheer name were the most deserted island on which Philoctetes were wailing in his eternal agony. "Who on earth cares about Rico now? The cardinals are only preoccupied with their own candidacy, they keep whispering, chirping to one another, allying themselves with the emperor, plotting against bishops, spending money — from morning to night mendacious sigils boil and froth on mendacious letters, the arms of secretaries grow leaden-heavy with all the scribbling and candle-gripping, the plebs are roaring, the soldiers looting: there is no truer *dona eis requiem!*" "Rico was a famous man" — Angelina said with an actress' gusto. — "Everywhere I passed the bells were tolling for him. Sometimes I got ahead of the news of his death and then the black carillons danced behind me on top of their insatiable campaniles. But most of the time the news travelled before me, like a rolled out black carpet, and at such times there was nothing to do but sink my feet into the fabric of official or sincere grief and deathly terror." "But this is madness! To leave Rico in Rome!" "Why aren't you a cardinal?" Angelina asked in rude reproach. "You're right, I should be there; that's where my place is."

3.

In his imagination he surveyed the Vatican halls and chambers that he had seen on his visit, the clerical and diplomatic official-dom whom he knew personally or from hearing, and the possible causes which led to his younger brother's death.

Where does Rico lie? Where did he collapse? He was per-haps sitting in the garden, alone, near his favorite bush next to the small fountain's Madonna statue, and his death was signaled by nothing but the breviary's quiet splash as, dropping from his hands, it fell into the water. There floats the prayer-book like a fallen leaf or water lily: Saint Peter's drowsy life. Young priests spot it, daren't say a word, only mutely wring their hands at the path's end, too frightened to stir... Or perhaps he had been long ailing, preparing for death on a ceremonial bed among Eu-rope's extras: among a host of black-robed doctors, organ pipes out of rigorously lined-up phials of medicine, money-grabbing pseudo-relatives and cardinals ruffled by prayer? Did he think about him — did he write a will? And now, in the otherworld, does he see some connection between his clamorous, belligerent bulls, and the risen Savior? Is it worth at all wondering if he had cared about him while alive, when there are no relatives, wives, children in the underworld anyway? O, this is the most hideous thing about death, that the dead deny us — on the bier each one of them suddenly becomes a heartless metaphysical upstart, they are ashamed of ever having been earthly, of having once whined after some girl, or worshipped a father. And now Rico, too, is haughty like the rest of them.

He saw the bed in which he had slept; once the pope was very tired and went to sleep early, while he remained sitting by his bedside, not like the elder brother but like an old nurse, a superstitious hag. They were alone. Even so, they couldn't feel very homely, for documents, charts, were piled up even on the nightstand; there were more crucifixes hanging on the wall than clocks in a clockmaker's. The pope was indeed the world's first priest: here one could find the mathematically highest quantity of church things, objects, and files. And this was of course the very essence of spirituality — you had to be a fool or a heretic not to feel it. Did he receive the last ointment there, in that bed? O, how envious he was of the oil that touched his hands and feet! Then, when the pope had fallen asleep, it was he who kissed his brother's hands, his feet, who straightened his pillow. The pope's life appeared to him as a bitter-sweet, sometimes tragic, sometimes childishly playful world: the struggle of one person, armed with spiteful kyries, weary prayer, glittering lances and cracked etiquette, against the world's universal folly. Was there any point in the struggle? Was it possible at all? Does the thought, which is so all-powerful in him, also burn deep in his brother's heart like a secret, but perennial lamp — that the sole reality is the family members' desperate, unavoidable blood-love for one another, as compared to which the love of God pales and carnal love is dimeshow parody. On that night, in the Vatican's silent, pitch-dark garden, like some stealthy worm holding vigil by the slumbering seed, the aging priest knew well that this was the most sentimental — that is, the first & last real — moment of his life.

CHAPTER ON LOVE · II · THE POPE

The pope was asleep: the emperor's gigantic letter lay under the night-light, its sigil dangling to the floor like the tongue of the hanged; its foldings were fresh and sharp, as though the meridians of a globe had been carved across the text: trumpeting that its contents concerned the whole world — and the pope didn't pay much attention to it then. The sweetest and deathliest in this moment, lit by one night-light, was the priest's feeling that his love was folly: enormous sentiment, bigger than anything in the world, but his lonely affair only; the next morning he would steal out through the back door to give his place over to fat lackeys, murderous generals whom nature designed to be butchers, saints, and thirsty inquisitors. (Once he had spoken with an inquisitor who could never get enough water — his whole body was a single bone-mast that he never managed to imbibe.)

O, if only he had rested there for good after that night, like a furious dog: why didn't he bark off the morning visitors? If he knew, with absolute certainty, that his love was the summum bonum, why wasn't he valiant? Why didn't he become the pope's captain, diplomat, courtier, canon jurist, cook, confessor, supreme theologian, organist, physician? Why did he leave him to others? A folly. In his grief he forgot about God and all the saints: he felt that with the last ointment the court notables washed off or covered up his brotherly kiss on the pope's hand, as women cover with powder the rashes and blackheads on their face and shoulders.

What swollen-headed and fanatic specimens bustled about Rico! Some only cared about God, hanging tied to heaven every moment like a puppet-theater marionette; some burnt with a flame for the Church only and wanted to draw abbeys and chapels from every hillside in Europe like charlatans who promise to smite the rock and draw water from it; some cared about their own families, some about everything and some again, about nothing. But there was nobody to care about Rico as Rico. And he,

224

old fool, had let it happen, for a lifetime! He should have kidnapped the pope, brought him back here, under Monte Solario, to the cradle, to his toys! For it was only his wits, fantasy, theoretical abilities that made him a pope and kept him on the papal throne, not his blood: he was no real aristocrat, nor tiger, nor a fanatic of love. He had often confessed that to his brother. Did he perhaps also tell it to some stranger on his deathbed?

But if he had been ill for long he would have called for him; impossible that he should have forgotten him. Was he killed? At this thought his whole body started sobbing. He saw nothing and nobody, only the silly child playing with boats on the shore, who now fell into the water. There was no more history, tragic fate, human passion, God's will, or any other such ceremonious, æsthetic, and learned whatsit here, only silliness, unfathomable silliness. To die! Why? Did he die for the Church? Martyrdom? Did the pope have the right to offer as quarry to a manic emperor the body on which the one-and-only brother's lonely, idolatrous kiss blossomed like a scentless, obdurate flower — the body, on which the savage sigil of the *concrete* bled: did he have the right? He imagined that the emperor had the pope poisoned: not for a second did he hate the emperor, it didn't even occur to him — only his brother did he hate, for betraying the family, himself, his brother: for the sake of an abstraction. Because there was no need for this, this death is not asked for by the Church, by Christ: this was nothing but realized superfluity, grinning nonsense. O, if he weren't so old and could go to Rome to the bier! Where is the corpse?

The corpse? One moment he couldn't at all imagine his brother as dead *body* — death was only some kind of moral quality of Rico's, a newfangled role in his high office, which didn't touch his body; "he is no more" — this was not a biological quality or state. And the next moment he realized that it couldn't be entirely so, and then he imagined the expression of death so horridly on Rico's face that he nearly went mad with terror and frantic, vengeful despair. He had not seen him sick, so he couldn't lead his imagination step by step down the chromatic slope to the final stage in the body's wilting. Where was the corpse? On his bed, in a nightshirt? In the garden, half-dipped into one of the ponds? On the chapel's "intimate" bier, or in Saint Peter's, on top of the "European" catafalque: invisible, only the blazons, tassels, & crowns rain down from the black pyramid, like those mysterious summer showers when no cloud can be seen on the sky and yet one gets soaked? Around him the macaroni-thin candles, springing up into incredible heights without bending, with disproportionately tiny, dot-like flames, set so densely that with their grid they devour the church's inner contours, fashion-ing new routes, new clearings... Or did they perhaps haul him into some cellar? Is he bleeding deep in some forest? O, he should run there and implore him and God to make him at once a cardinal, so he could become his successor, to protect his memory from history's assailing humbugs!

4.

A short letter, the last the pope had written to him, lay on the nightstand. In it he reported the hanging of a brigand captain in Rome. "Tomorrow they are going to hang Tiburzio. You know well that these days are most painful for me, perhaps not so much because I am sentimental, a tragic courter of mercy, but because I was born a logical being. I don't know how much in this sentence is divine justice, how much is my lyrical-effusive despair over human destiny, and how much is diplomacy for the ears of rowdy dukes. With all that, I have not an ounce of doubt that I have done everything that was humanly possible, now as ever. Sed mors: mors."

How curious that this should have been his last sentence. In history it is perhaps rare that an occurrence takes place in an indifferent moment: the thing either happens at the moment that is right to the point of stylization (as now, after that sad "mors est mors"-type letter) — or in some absolutely, glaringly inappropriate time and place (apoplexy on coronation day, et cetera).

Death at once turned every word of the letter into hypnotic blossoming, he saw and heard his brother's and Tiburzio's dialogue — Tiburzio's, who was likewise dead, and the pope's, who was heading to Tivoli. Had he got there in the end? Did he die there?

5.

— Nous voilà: this is the stage. Now and then I will perhaps lapse into French, partly because I'm expecting the king of France's envoi early in the morning, and partly because you, Tiburzio, are a hanged man, and for me the hanged are forever linked to the *Ballade des Pendus,*[8] and I'm mixing you up a bit with Villon, although you've never shown much talent for poetry.

— My dear pope, I don't know why you bring up the issue of talent here: you are far too talented, as I know well, to take the slightest interest in the difference between the talented and the untalented, or even notice it. And the sheer fact that we started conversing here, I, the hanged brigand on Castel Sant'Angelo's rather exposed gallows, and you, the living pope in the Tivoli night's living blue — this fact is enough to prove that our dialogue is a much more elemental necessity or reality, for the scrupulous factor of "talent" to be even mentioned here.

— You are wrong to believe that my remark was meant to belittle your worth (don't bear me grudges though if I smile at the word "worth" in connection to you). Otherwise you are right to consider our conversation of the entirely general, not to say, *sub specie aeterni*, denomination.

— How else could I? You are the pope, God's lieutenant, and because the abstract notion means precious little to such a basically vulgar person as myself, in effect for me you are, that is, you were, God. You sentenced me to death because I looted Rome: there is no-one lower than me, there is no-one higher than you. And still, you will talk to me. Why? Conversion, confession, absolution is out of the question: I'm dead. To speak of interests, that you might be talking to me out of diplomatic *finesse*, is laughable — they'll toss me into a hole this afternoon and basta. I'm no longer even a human being: the dead are never human — the dead are either the only god in which blind proles like myself truly and unquestioningly believe, or the fabulously négligeable quantité négligeable, if you allow me to lapse into your French: the perfect, redeeming non-entity. And you, my pope, as far as I know you, are not in the habit of having conversation lessons with either lower-rate gods or higher-ranking non-entities. If you speak, you most certainly speak not as God's lieutenant to the expired highwayman, and not even as a human being to another, but —

— But?

— Why are you asking me for a definition? It's you who are the jurist, the poet.

— Are you insulting me by not adding after jurist and poet, "the saint"? Never mind, I'm not going into definitions either — it is a fact that our conversation has a distinctly, how shall I put it, transcendental flavor.

— Le dernier luxe d'un pendu, le premier devoir d'un pape.[9]

— Yes, something like that. And since it has a transcendental character, we are in the realm of shapelessness and of unanalyzable, un-logifiable things. Without the least intention on my part to blend in any legal, sentimental, or philosophical taste, without consciously striving to find between us anything that goes by the name "common ground," it is nevertheless true that to inspire my dialogue with you is some common trait in the two of us: at this moment, when you are dangling, dead scare-angel, on top of Castel Sant'Angelo, and I'm listening in half doze to the blue buzz of the silence and the woods in Tivoli, we are both proclaiming, with howling evidence, the two eternal aspects of life, human & animal, of vitality.

— How nice, how genteel, how refined cultivation is, O pope: I, poor dancing corpse (I feel my body as an orphaned clapper whose invisible bell is the transparent jar of all non-existence) become all at once a symbol of "vitality," a characteristic of life. What a pity that only convoluted intellects can see this point, and I not at all! Since you stooped to talk with me, you must be a great saint and a great humanist — but you will have to brace yourself, because every so often I will be a wee bit prosaic, to put it mildly — although I feel that death had inordinately refined me even to myself.

— And you are laughing at me, that at the height of my preoccupation with the living-most features of life, and a quite ecstatic height at that, I should choose a moral & physical corpse as my companion. Be assured though that the strongest of all my instincts is the one dubbed "instinct d'apostrophe" by the French diplomat whom I am expecting tomorrow morning, in this very garden: all my thoughts select with an absolute biological infallibility the person appropriate to them. Now I have chosen you.

— As a symbol — for instance, the eternal gallows-bird, beside you, the "eternal divine"?

— I don't know to what extent death has refined you out of existence, so I cannot know what you mean by a symbol — a poetic plaything or, on the contrary, the most real, "heaven-realistic" core of reality? I'd like to tell you something about appearances: you are dead and yet you continue dancing in the wind — you pendulate like a clock's swinging bob, like an elongated insect that holds on with its mandibles to a twig, but its body keeps swinging hither and thither, as if the irritable, frivolous wings

had not yet noticed that the mouth had already made its decision, whereas I am alive, but I lie in the grass mute, struck still
by night's wondrous presence, as "dead" as in the most optimistic
imaginings of the king of France and the German emperor. It
just occurred to me that this *appearance* might be important for
that "aeterni" whom we are in the habit of citing in the formula,
"sub specie aeterni": what if your biological, subjective deadness
is secondary, and the only thing that matters is that you *dance* in
the wind — what if my own life is but a meaningless fiction and
the "true" reality that expresses me is my stiff lying in the grass?

— Everything can be asked, O pope, and you are so mundane
and logical, such an affectionate heart and sophisticated brain
(you know of course that the two cannot be separated from one
another), that you give even the most non-sensical, the most
chimerically impressionistic questions a rational coloring. For
that's it: either we look on the thing from the concrete banks of
life, which means I'm a prime cadaver and you are in life (and in
the prime of life at that) — or we look at it from the shore of
death (or, if you prefer, the "transcendental"), and then life, death,
appearance, reality are all utterly meaningless notions, for on the
shore of death everything may as well be the other way round,
any old how, everything is both true & false, indispensable and
superfluous. Are you sure you are not going to mix up the two
perspectives in the present company, and will you not speak,
as you have so far, half in life's, and half in death's jargon?

— How pedantic, how over-scrupulous you have become: I'm
almost moved to like this. But you'll have to put up with the fact
that there is nothing to do with those two perspectives but mix
them. Why I consider you to be living I could hardly explain to
you, it is so glaringly obvious. My first argument — which is going to make you laugh so loud as to drive the guards of Castel
Sant'Angelo half mad with the horror of ghosts — is that you are
frightfully present in my thoughts, adorned with such tropical

wealth of realistic traits which you could never imagine. And I, in this lonely, sea-blue, virgo-blue, nihil-blue and *cara-mia*-blue Tivoli night know too well that there is no point in making distinctions between my consciousness, soul, the subjective world of my memory, and the objective world of the forest opening and closing, cracking and fermenting around me — in this forest night all the "human" is a dreadful folly, and all "human personality" is but an optical delusion.

— It seems that death's pedagogy has a most incomplete grip on me, O pope: death may have brushed apart my physiognomy most horridly, I have precious little to do with people, but when you decree the insignificance of the "human" with such tyrannical radicalism, with such pugnacious clatter of Peter's keys, pardon me, but I can't keep up with you.

— To keep up with me and to not keep up with me? You can talk as long as you wish, little "homo" Tiburzio: you are here, every bit as concrete as the trees, and if your memory lingering in me is not reality, not plastic life, not existence and ontological à-tout, then the trees themselves are hallucinations, and the galleys of Venice are but a dismissed lackey's neurosis-shreds: non-existent. I know it irrefutably that in one and the same world there cannot be watertight hallucinations and realities, and in turn, there cannot be "subjective memories" or "objective facts": either everything is uniformly real, or everything is uniformly nothing. And yet, there is no "nothing," because I am. Life and death: these are not distinctions. Both life and death are simple realities of the same hue.

— O pope, now you are: either so pedantic, of so low-caliber prolixity as no-one in this chosen century of science — or indeed so divine that man can do nothing with your divine perspective, just as a humanly human person here on earth in general, or even if no longer on this earth, but still entirely earthly (as yours truly dead) can never get anything out of an entirely divine god. So to my chagrin I cannot participate in the conversation, which at the beginning gave me great pleasure. I was so lonely in my death on the gallows that I was driven to hypochondria, planning to write a medical treatise on the illnesses of the dead: what effects a flu has, for instance, on a cadaver dancing in the wind and rain? But you are leaving me alone again: I can't call pedants even in my death, and, given my profoundly human nature — even if I did have the good will and brigand loyalty — I cannot savor gods.

— Don't think this is pedantry, or worse, overdone ex-cathedra mysticism: it is not. Don't believe for a moment that I'm here to console you with ridiculous would-be resurrection; that I'm trying to push on you my lyrical runnings amok as reality: not in the least. I simply feel that in this world all phenomena are always present, the dead stay alive, the cut-out forests continue spreading their foliage, the yesterdays are here today, too, anachronisms are full of white-hot actuality, the abandoned mistresses are eternal concubines; everything, always, is *here* and *now*. I don't mean this in the elegant sense of the psychologists and naturalists, that in my soul yesterday is present in such a way as to impact the today, that it has shaped it, been absorbed into it both consciously and unconsciously, that "lurking" in the present historical situation, the whole European past is present, that in a rose's petals the myriad morphological memories of the bud are enclosed: I don't mean it so finely, so "truly." But much more superstitiously, roughly, realistically: you, Tiburzio, are present alive, or at least *both* alive *and* dead, the dead Tiburzio and the live Tiburzio can get to know one another if they will, for it only depends on them.

— Yet another prosaic interruption: provided everything, always, is alive, is reality, provided the goal of the whole of creation is that everything may always be alive, then why does nature *enact* death forever, for a million times? Then why did you sentence me to death, why did you have me hanged? And if you have already seen this death-humbug to its conclusion, then why did I feel it to be death nevertheless: why did my wrists, knees, elbows start boiling at the tightening of the rope, like water frothing on fire? why did I feel my tongue gush forth from my mouth as if I had thrown up into a vacuum a sunk object from the pit of my stomach? why did the contents of my rectum pour out with such magic ease on the stones of Castel Sant'Angelo as water pouring from a plate? why did I feel that the leash of my eyes had suddenly been cut and they rolled apart — they were just as seeing, just as sensitive as before, but they were no longer calibrated, not in their place: I hadn't as much as closed my eyelids, I positively felt them to be open, but my eyes rolled far away, inward, down some inner slope of my skull, and there was no-one to set them right again anymore — tell me, why does nature perform these horrors with every person, sea-wave, fruit, and animal? What is the nauseating concreteness of agony for — if it is not concrete?

— You have put your question very politely, Tiburzio, and I will express my gratitude by myself being impolite with myself and speak harshly, not in the form of question but of accusation, saying: if I deny death, I am no Christian. And indeed, tonight, here in the gardens of Tivoli, among the blue fish, blue statues, blue fountains, blue tree-crowns, and blue stars, I wanted to experience "the absolute humanist's absolute nocturne" — half in experimenting, half out of an animal desire, as it usually happens with intellectuals. When I sentenced you to death — I performed a moral deed, I believed in God, believed in death, in morals in general, in society, in society's myriad distinctions. These were the two protagonists of the judgment: the concrete person, homo humanus, and morality as the former's sole specific distinction. For reason, the capacity for thinking, imagination, and creation is not a special human function, but a universal biological one — the distinction between syllogistic trains of thought, frivolous chains of associations on the one hand, and the sporulation of plants and cells, their growth and proliferation on the other hand, is nil — a mathematical deduction and the morphology of a parasitical plant, its inner structure, impulses, and rhythm are, in absolute terms, *identical*. Thus the essence of this homo is not reason but *moral*: not as moral instinct, not as the organic attribute of every single human specimen, but as a side product automatically resulting from deeds, from interaction, unavoidable in general in the historical existence of humanity. If I now compare this present blue Tivoli night with the daylight of my studio where I had signed your death sentence, I can see that while there the protagonists had been moral and homo — here they are existence and human-lessness. One couldn't wish for better words to take the place of homo and moral; of course in place of "existence" and "human-lessness" (these being fundamentally non-practical concepts) one could look for other approximations, like "life" and "dehumanization," "mere-æsthetic" and "anti-psychology," or many other items from the pale but yet indispensable museum of imprecision. In the morning the "human," that is, moral, still meant everything — now, in the suggestiveness of the night, it cannot mean anything. Night is vital, beautiful, and above all, human-annihilating: these three things mean the same, are identical. And I, just like many of my scientist & artist companions, have been dubbed "humanist" precisely because every now and again I hark not only to moral but also to the Tivoli blue of the night, and lo, it turns out that the service of beauty can never be identical to the service of man, of the well-delineated homo humanus: beauty annihilates all affinities for the human and thus for the concreteness of death in people. If you say human, you will needs say moral — if you say beauty, you will needs say human-less. In other words: if one is a "humanist," he will be ab ovo "*de*-humanist."

— If you see this so clearly, why did you insist to talk with me? Could you have been so optimistic or arrogant to imagine you can lure me, poor pendu, from the world of "moral" (as you will call it) to that of "beauty"?

— I don't know myself what I imagined, for when I called you I didn't know that in fact I wanted to experience life, that is, everything merely as "absolute metaphor," for the length of these few Tivoli-blue nights, forgetting about everything else — or if I wanted to have an exam of conscience, a courtroom confrontation of metaphor and moral. I had better implore you, for I can see that your "morality" is very strong: allow me to see your corpse as metaphor, just as much a decoration of life as the blue-skinned butterfly-fish in my ponds. You are of course aware that in my life the antithesis between moral and metaphor is by far not identical to the worthless antithesis between asceticism and contemplative pleasure; asceticism is merely one trait of the thousand-contour picture of morality, whereas contemplative pleasure is a well-nigh ignorable element of metaphoric life.

— I'm caught in a conundrum, O pope: I feel equally inclined to offer you my agony as a ballet movement, my death as organ-point, my eyeballs hitched upward as benobled flowers — take them and behold, what a lord I, the brigand, am; take my whole perishing home to your salon or library, as a metaphor. But at the same time I cannot betray my highwayman and plebs colors: I couldn't bear it, however much aware that you are worlds removed from tarting-up æstheticism, that my whole life should become an ornament in a vacationing pope's midnight park. At gunpoint, I'd probably stick to my republicanism rather than be turned into a metaphor.

— A republican? Are you trying to gentrify your robberdom with this word, so unexpected to me, or has death turned you into a philosopher of history and uncovered to you surprising connections between adlib robbery and republicanism? I don't know if it sounds like philosophy of history or down-to-earth ratiocination if I tell you: there are only two enemies in the world, God and the anarchist. God goes by a thousand names: sacrament, objectivity, king, Ten Commandments, unerring pope — likewise, the anarchist goes by a thousand names: robber, scientist, equal right-er, commerce, art. If human cunning has given so many names to one role, why shouldn't you now and again call yourself a republican, for the sake of a more refined elegant variation on the monotonous brigand? The two of us, being the two types of history (you on the gallows, I, on Peter's holy throne) represent two fundamental nostalgias: you, the nostalgia for the perfect meaninglessness of life — I, for the perfect meaningfulness of life. Perhaps it might be more logical or biological if we changed places: you, the constitutional apostle of nonsense, could preach the thesis "life = metaphor," while I, the situationist apostle of civitas Dei, might hold sermons on "moral above all."

— Finesses, finesses: you have sentenced me to death and will have to continue sentencing me to death, there is no Tivoli-intermezzo, no human-less nature — be consistent.

— Why are you torturing me, why are you throwing your weight around, why do you keep reminding me that you are the problem of Christianity, its enemy, thus its king: how ridiculous my fights against the all-too-French kings of France and too-German emperors for the conductor's baton of Christianity, when you are the ruler, with your suffering, nothingness, distortedness, your being-eternal-temptation and eternal-death, with the coquettish and riddle nature of foul infinitude.

— You sometimes embarrass me, O pope — I don't know whether you are adjusting to Vatican or to import Spanish etiquette, or if you might indeed be experiencing something like tragedy.

— What have you been, what are you, Tiburzio? Unstoppable well bursting from the earth, the reckless pulse of nature — or wickedness incarnate, one of the puppets of primum malum wriggling among us? The legitimate consciousness of the people, aggrandized to the point of caricature, a political symbol — or a simple tool, mercenary in the hands of some duke run wild,

a Malatesta or Colonna? My relationship with you, the black li-
aison of the death sentence, is unquestionably a moral one: the
product of human *interactions*, embroidered with imperatives —
but you, what are you, in fact, by yourself?

— Are you racking your brains again, senile gourmand of
distinctions, what am I: a force of nature *or* primal evil, emerging politics *or* the old tune of business —isn't it likely that I am
all of these put together? Even if they don't share a name, the
whole gamut is one: nature, Satan, politics, & business — why
shouldn't it be one?

— This monism run amok is but the mannerism of death, the
monism of death in you. I won't touch your corpse, but I'd like
to dissect your soul.

— If someone talks about dissection, analysis, could anything
else come to my mind but love, and once love has fortuitously
come to my mind, I can clearly see that your dilemma, O pope,
between Tivoli-blue metaphor and daylight gallows moral, is
identical to the dilemma of love.

— How come?

— Do not all great loves go to the dogs by starting out as æsthetics and complicating into morality? Isn't a female face a metaphor and isn't marriage, not to mention an extramarital affair,
morality? You are trying to do the same in reverse with me (great
overlord as you are, you can afford such whims): I have been morality to you first — and now you are trying to pronounce me an
ornament.

— Wouldn't it be the most polite and factual thing imaginable if you tried to depict to me with the best of your capacities
the fateful threads of morality, of pro and con, of death, of responsible action, of mundane and social networks — and I, the
godless beauty of the Tivoli night to you?

— Shall we then stoop to tableaus?

— No, I want something a lot more dramatic: you shall speak,
live, act in such a way as to have me condemn you to death again

and again, so mercilessly and eternally and forever to death that afterwards I might feel an even more maddening thirst for a world where there is no justice and no human beings.

— Pope, the way I see it, you are entirely on my side. Tell me, why did you sentence me to death at once? Why didn't you order your sculptors to make giant wax effigies of me, to have them burnt and melted at the two gates of Rome? We would both have fared better — I, because I am dreadfully superstitious and the mere imagining of my lifelike doll-copies melting in the fire raises goose bumps on my livid back. I've seen such things in my dreams: strangers who wore my face as a mask, mortally wounding all the ghostly issues of individuality, of the "I" with their ballroom shtick. And you would have fared better because the burning of the puppet would have quenched your thirst for moral action, the "judgment" function would have functioned, and at the same time the *puppet* is a metaphor, theatrical toy, so it would have perfectly drawn you inside your sought-for present world.

— Puppet, puppet: who knows which is the puppet-most puppet — your living body, your painted wax effigy, or your swinging corpse?

— How sweetly relativist you're being now: to the right in the grass, your tiara, to the left, glinting cups, plates, forks, in your lap notes in elevated Latin. Don't you find it childish to take out your crown in the garden like a toy?

— Childish? On the contrary. Perhaps it is childish, but then in some things children are right: I am always a pope, in my dreams, stealthy heresies, meals, papalement et papissime pape, as a pamphleteer put it, and someone who is so inwardly pope cannot for a moment go without the external accessories.

— All right, all right, so is it also papal that you tie a ribbon of grass across the crown spikes, turn the crown upside down and pad it with leaves as though it were a small basket, to trap lizards in it?

— Are you trying to discover the differences between the "intimate pope" and the "hieratic pope," Tiburzio?

— Perhaps I am. Lofty intellects as a rule superciliously toss aside such discoveries, although they alone are interesting. Now, when you sentenced me you didn't raise such questions in a splenetic voice. You were sitting with four cardinals in the Sala Giuliana, all five of you aligned along the wall, adhering so strictly to the wall that you couldn't be told from a mural. Why did you sit like that, why not around a table? You couldn't even see one another — you had to peer at each other, leaning out far from behind the gigantic armrests and partitions. I'm sure morality, justice, demands it to be so. But precisely this form, all those rituals and all the stiffness round the truth, the countless featuring of God, oath, death, balance with equal scales, make me see from here, the gallows' favorable "belle-vue," that moral, justice, are every bit as irrational, chaotic, not to mention anarchic, as your Tivoli négligé and Tivoli thirst-for-metaphors. And so — glossing over for a moment the very different practical consequences of the two — it is hardly necessary to set up as alternatives, moral and metaphor, homo humanus & vital "dehumanus."

— This is perhaps true from an intellectual perspective (and can a hanged man, long gone cold and stiff, be anything else but an intellectualist?), but does it alter in the least the tragic fact that there is a tormenting and apparently eternal struggle in my soul, in my feelings, between the two worlds?

— You needn't talk with such lachrymose aggressiveness, O pope: neither do I myself take intellectual vindications and viewpoints very seriously — if one took such things seriously he could never take a single step forward or backward, for all intellects worth their salt would be reduced to declaring, at the third step, the reverse of the first, and perhaps come round to repeating the first step at the sixth, and so on, without the least intention to casuistry. Isn't it a bit our case here, too, in our unmolested, and therefore compulsively self-contradictory, eschatological chirping?

— Go on reminding me of the morning of the sentence — let metaphor and moral mingle, let one sole positivist nude — suffering — rest between my hands.

— Suffering! voilà le juste conséquence de votre nocturne absolue d'humaniste ou des-humaniste. I can't get rid of the fauteuils glued to the wall: how did you feel in that weird mixture of isolation and community? All you saw was me; you saw not one of your cardinal-judge colleagues, & they, too, looked at me, each alone in his sacred hutch, not seeing you and their fellow judges. The giant, insulating armchair no doubt immersed you fully into the lyric and auto-erotic bottomlessness of your subjectivity — but the awareness that along the wall, four more such unchecked subjectivities were aligned in perfectly *identical* cases — this abstract perception of the others must have warned you a lot more glaringly that there is no free individuality, only society, the others, majority and minority, justice. And I could look at all of them at the same time: on the five simultaneously glimpsed masks I could better observe the birth of justice than you or anyone else. Open to me, closed to one another: and how open! As if the armchairs had not been aligned against the wall in a straight line, but in the indecency of opening-up to me, in a concave arc, like the naked sand of an oval dune jutting into the sea. For me there is no "moral truth and justice" without such stage settings.

— And what psychological benefits did you draw from this, Tiburzio?

— What a characteristically intellectualist fantasizing on your part: to presuppose that while you were formulating my death sentence, I was making psychological observations of you. But you are right: the faces, the furniture, the gestures, are deeply engraved in my memory.

— Tell me your memories!

— You were suffering, pope: perhaps not because justice and mercy struggled in you, but because at that time, too, your present struggle was going on inside you, between the world's theological meaningfulness and its biological meaninglessness. What happened there in fact during the drama of judgment?

— Before telling it, Tiburzio, allow me to interrupt you to muse for a moment over all the horror and weight of the word "judgment." For this "judgment" is the most characteristic, most typical word of moral life, of life decreed to be meaningful; the blooming, viola-filled Tivoli night could have no more exact opposite than this "judgment," the courtroom trial, the choosing of *one* possibility concerning your fate.

— All right, I will keep mum for a moment, scrupulous master of rituals.

— Go on now.

— I find it especially easy to go on, because this momentary silence has been something symbolic, etiquette-like, and it was one of the protagonists in the grand comedy of judgment: the symbolic liturgy. The other protagonist was your inner chaos, the chaos, the metaphoric vision that you wanted to live to the fullest tonight, and which I have spoilt. Identical chairs, and your human portrait: that is, some symbolic "order" and the absurdity of the vital — at least it was an absurdity as compared to the armchairs' symmetry. The chairs' uniformity, the theatrical lucidity and stiffness of the legal articles, the symbolic inhumanity of the priestly garbs, the mathematical strictness and biblical flow of crucifix, candles, the legal protocol all served to lift the portrait, the sentencing judges' personalities, that is, their interior psychic chaos (can an interior be anything other than chaos?) into some un-individual, objective "order": chaos into ritual, interior into divine, nonsense into sense. But in this you were wrong: there was no contrast between the strict order of the armchairs and the interior mess of the judges' spirits fidgeting in them — the kind of order (although I'm not sure whether there is any other) that ritual, uniform, conventional actions represent is not the antithesis of chaos but, on the contrary: its innermost necessity.

— What? Are you trying to prove that order is the need of the lack of order? That symbolic symmetries are the fruit of chaos?

— Precisely. In other words, I want to explain that you should no longer see an antithesis between Tivoli's blue anarchy-foliage, anarchy-fish, and anarchy-Venuses, & the courtroom's rigorous armchairs, scales of justice, absolute candles, moral initials and sacred bulls. *One* sole instinct wills justice and chaos, the justice of sentence and the frivolity of metaphor.

— What? How?

— I'm going to explain this with a pedantry unusual even with the hanged. Man's most ancient vital instinct is probably a plastic instinct, an instinct of palpation: he wants to feel space and in space, positive forms. Visuality, sexuality, palpation, perspective: these are but different facets of the same instinct — the ancient thirst for space and forms splits into women, vision, grasping. But this ancient instinct (& it is an instinct precisely for that reason!) is ultimately paradoxical: it quenches its thirst for palpation, its form-need with the eternal to-and-fro of waves, their shapeless washing-all, so in a sense it is also an *anti*-formalist, form-hiding instinct: love-making is at once a will-to-sculpture and a will-to-become-water. The courtroom's uniform armchairs, legal symmetry, the rational plasticity of the ethical, philosophical, legal concept of "justice" are the product of this chaos, the exigency of vital chaos, the theme it can embrace. The concept of "justice," the order of syllogism, all the correspondences of logic, the whole Euclidianism of geometry, the meanings of rituals, tradition-crystals are not meaningful and intellectual orders, or at least they are not intellectual in the way you imagine them to be, of being opposed to, or situated above, the vital and chaotic: on the contrary, they are the most immediately vital. The order of the philosophical system, the satisfactory nature of justice, every single atom of the experience of demonstration relates to your vital center, your chaos-focal point, O pope, as a flower's regular shape, a crystal's structure to the life-instinct in general: for is the petals' regularity a matter of intellectual function, after all? Are they not precisely the blazons of the life-force's anarchy? You perceive the formal order, symmetry, the sensual links of correspondences in truth as *intellectual*, although, if you allow me to use a swearword in my own brigand idiom: every system is erotic and *only* erotic.

— I'm convinced that it is true, Tiburzio. But my problem is not the antithesis between the traditional scheme of judgment and the Tivoli night's flower-anarchy, but the antithesis between the inescapability of morality, the eternal obligation-to-judge, the issue of truth, of justice relating to practical human interaction, and the freedom of flowers and metaphors. I myself have long intimated that "order" is something sensual, erotic, that the re-frain-monotony of ritual and logic, of geometry and tradition, are not intellectual but vital. For when I wanted to give myself en-tirely over to this night, perhaps I wanted that precisely accord-ing to the thoughts that you exposed a moment ago: precisely for being a dyed-in-the-wool intellectualist, I sought to liberate myself from the animality of order, the beastliness of logic. Life is forever undulating, streaming, rolling from formlessness into form, or more precisely: with formlessness in form. The octo-pus swimming by is the most apposite symbol (if it is not dare-devilry to choose a symbol from nature's infinity): all loosened snakes, decomposition, scattering-apart, and at the same time a frantic sculptural creation from itself, from the water, the rock, the quarry, as if it wanted to embrace the form of forms, the most absurdly form-like form, to identify with it — the caricature of its *form*-insatiability is its looseness. And whoever has once felt to the core this chaotic form-hunger of vital powers, not only in the octopus but in love-making, in the bell-flower's regularity, cannot but experience the same in the laboring-clarifying precision of logical definitions. This is true, Tiburzio, but it is the problem not of morality but of the systematizing intellect. And it was rash of you to take the ritual of judgment & the Tivoli garden's floral libertinage to be one and the same thing. Although I, as I assure you, suffer not from the dichotomy of intellect and life, but from that of morality & life, perhaps forever incurably — I neverthe-less see an opposition between this courtroom order & the Tivoli flower-vegetation (which you see as the two versions of the same life-instinct). Perhaps because I see too great an abyss between eros and subjective well-being, between sexual instinct and the instinct of self-preservation. To put it briefly: what you say of the logical, legal order, of the vital instinct for order that finds its expression in the former, that instinct is erotic instinct — the phallic world of form, plasticity, symmetry, all belongs to it. But my Tivoli relish in the blue freedom of fish, flowers, leaves, stars (a relish that is *not* identification, *not* congeniality or consubstan-tiality with the fish and stars!): the satisfaction of the instinct of self-preservation whose essence is arguably that it eludes form, logical regularity, scholastic order, geometrical analogies, identi-ty-accumulation, in which it can see nothing but the mendacious after-images of onanism: it is mendacious if it makes intellectual claims, while being merely "order." For me Tivoli is two things, the transparent sea-blue of its flowers has a dual value: a value for the intellectualist, because they are not "true," not "composed," not "ordered" — and a value for the moralist, because they are not good or bad, and from the relationships and actions con-nected to them no consequence follows that would force one to renewed action. Impressionism lived to the utmost degree: this might be the sole nostalgia of the true intellect, for as soon as it gets close to the system, to aggregated truths, in fact it will have fallen into the claws of pornography — and ultimate amorality, that is, independence from the ethical questions, for if it is moral, then thought is absolutely superfluous, because the essence of thought is that it should liberate itself from practicalities, that it be free, absolutely of course and not in the idiotic political, censorial sense of the word. You may rest assured that I will continue suppressing and throwing to the Inquisition all those books and writers in whom I discern the slightest trace of heresy: by the freedom of thought I mean not the freedom of principles, political and religious views, but some kind of freedom of function, the unanalyzable, non-mechanical mechanism of eternal self-contradiction, turning back upon itself and flying-apart, whose very essence (as opposed to so-called "freedom of opinion") is, that it cannot be *one* thing, it cannot be definitely *this* or *that*, but is always and wherever: anything and everything. And the way my infinite impressionism can put up most naturally with leading the assemblies of the Inquisition, my contemplative capacity, independent of ethics, gets along most naturally with sentencing you and your likes to death.

— I didn't set up distinctions between an instinct of woman-love and a separate one of self-love, like you: I called Tivoli absolute-impressionism and Vatican absolute-systematizing the two variants of the same vital instinct. And I believe, O pope, that you are proceeding quite arbitrarily and unjustifiably when you consider this intellectual experience of yours, which you characterize first and foremost with the absence of form, composition, and order, to be entirely independent of the erotic instinct. You know I harbor no childish ambitions to eroticize you through thick and thin, but allow me to say that I find your self-assurance in saying that your impressionist technique is the manifestation of a vitality fundamentally different from the formalist one, a bit on the bold side.

— How nicely we are theorizing! Why am I calling you "Tiburzio" and you me, "O pope"? It would be much more appropriate if we called each other "O Socrates" and "O Alkibiades."

Otherwise our dialogue went both well and not well. I wanted metaphor instead of moral, and yet became neither metaphor nor moral but a rational conversationalist. So it didn't go well, for we didn't get to the bottom of the question of questions either theoretically, or with a view to the practice of my midnight siesta. But it did go well all the same, because it proved that a dialogue, if the smallest bit of the ambition of true thinking is present, cannot be "thematic," cannot be about this or that given subject, for if it does, it is no longer something properly intellectual, no longer a true dialogue, but barren paraphrasing, trifling ornament. Who you are, Tiburzio, whether a metaphor from life's textbook, or moral sigil in the hands of God the judge, we cannot decide, for we have thought about it. Whether I myself could be a metaphor, whether I could be a carefree, empty, truth-less and moral-less entity, like this azure moment of my garden, is likewise undecidable. There are two worlds: the eternally-fermenting, justifiably never-to-be-concluded world of thought, and the solitary, self-serving world of phenomena: the gallows, the gardens in Tivoli, the Vatican courtroom. What do they *mean?* Quel mot inutile!
  —Amen.

6.

And there remained the things, without reason and sense. There remained the Tivoli gardens; all the secrets of the roots in the earth, the mucky-blunt, snaky-diplomatic, or arteriosclerotically broken roots; thick tree-trunks with rough notches, girlish-slender twigs with their slippery-smooth bark, and the million varieties of leaves: hanging bunches, toupee-undulated, peasant-edgeless, coy and decadent, quixotic & smudgy — but who would be disposed to get down to analyze their "sense"? For even listing them in the most arid catalogue is by default myth and metaphor, the *name* alone is enough to strip them of their virginity, of that mythical (dementedly mythical) and practical (dementedly practical) feature, of *being-there*.

After the pope and Tiburzio concluded their exchange, stark-simple *is* took over: ubiquitous self-evidence, which in fact is the secret of secrets. What is this blue night? Satan's moralizing stage? The holy mirror of angels? The ha'penny staffage of piquancy? Death's sacred fluid? The most maskless face of chaos' one-and-onliness? The divine inquisition chamber of remorse? The atheistic fête of biological freedom? What are its consequences; of what is it the result? Who could know. It can be anything and everything, if we think about it — and if we don't think about it: it is so absolutely just what it is, that for man such tension of unglossed self-evidence equals naught.

Why are you here then, identity-harlots: leaves, ponds, stars? Only to make us suffer the alternative — that you are either *anything*, or *nothing*?

It's difficult to imagine a lilac bush so that it means nothing, is in no intellectual or emotional relation whatsoever, but the pope, good pedant as he was, wanted precisely that: to see the eternal garden, eternally independent from man. There was something disconcertingly and befuddlingly fearful about this independence. He tore a blade of glass, caressed a lilac bush, powdered his nose with the pollen of some golden-yellow wild flower, saying: "So we have nothing to do with one another — you are, as I am, but our relation is nil. You can't be the object of our cognition ('cognition': encore un bon mot, n'est-ce pas?), the symbol of our emotions — you are foreign, our paths can't ever cross, not even in infinity. And perhaps both you and we are going to live beside one another, mute and barren. You will bloom a million years from now, in the garden, by lovers' feet, but we will never know one another."

And the hanged Tiburzio? Does he have anything to do with truth or justice, history, morality? One can't tell: it's a fact that he is "something dead," and death is an eternal component of existence; it's a fact that on his face and body the traces of infernal suffering bloom — but why, and whether it is justified, or lunacy: who can tell? If we thought about it, any variation could be considered with equal logical credit. Let's stick to the naked inventory: to the corpse decorated with the arabesques of suffering; just as the Tivoli gardens' blue-flower-shedding is not "the biological," so the hanged man is not "the moral."

The pope was shivering next to the two nihils — that of thought, and that of objects; in the world of such metaphysical angst it wasn't easy to think that in the morning the French ambassador would arrive to blather and gossip against the Aragonian family for an hour and a half. But he realized that this mood was the kind that by excellence inspires one to political action: precisely because thinking is an unstoppable, eternal game, pro and con at the same time, the psychological organ of all-possibility — but precisely because the things, like the gardens or the corpse swinging on its rope, are absolutely foreign, self-serving, mysteriously closed-in on themselves, there remains nothing to do but act, which is at an equal remove from the illusions of *cognition* and *object*, which is not a judgment and *knowledge* about the gardens and the corpse, neither is it *identical* to the gardens or the corpse, but a functioning independent of those.

Poor Tiburzio: apart from its bloody rag, your corpse had been hitherto covered with associations, like fragrant, dense creepers — now those, too, have fallen off. There is a "matte" democracy in this ontological picture — corpse and garden, being equally meaningless and equally eternal. This lends your exact appearance, this fatal lack of cause and justification, this your being right-in-front-of-us and right-here: every vein of the flower is fully visible, every whiff of its scent makes our nostrils tremble, for not a single atom of it is absorbed into the broader canvas of some meaningful cause or intellectualizable purpose — every stiffening of the corpse's skin, the muscles' every accruing of weight, the blood's inner degrees of clotting, the organs' closing into sleep all appear to us in their ultimate precision, all their potential and energy is invested into the being-*here*, the ontological *now*, and is not spent on answering the "why is it so?" type of questions, on feeding the possible commentaries.

And *this* is sentimentalism, the unweepable bitter weep: *this* precision of the gardens and the corpse. It is not the blurry images, not the smeared-apart nights and corpses steeped in mist that are pitiful to see, but this precision which solely stems from being unmotivated, from being absolutely remote from any rational touch — and is there anything more tormenting than this perpetual cohabitation with blooming flowers and exsanguinated corpses, without for a moment entering a relation with them?

And the third loneliness: the courtroom in the Vatican. This, too, is eternal milieu: one man judges another — this theatrical conceit is unavoidable. Let us therefore build it up, again and again — the identical-looking wooden armchairs, as though true judges existed and were indeed capable of secreting justice evenly, as bees secreting honey; we shall always place the candelabra at the table's two ends: the proportion of their branches, the candles' pale and sweating wax carcass, the flames' uncertain, nervous, and often merely metaphorical light (as opposed to the armchairs' dynamic uniformity!), the ceremoniousness of their distance from one another, the gravity of their facing one another, their half-portrait, half-mask gaze are all indispensable on the chamber stage of moralitas militans; the clock shall always be at that exact place on the wall: with its pale clock-face, infinitely elongated numbers, almost imperceptibly swinging pendulum, sepulchral chiming: all time's bureaucratic postures and stealthy flowering-into-death shall be together in the room; the law books shall be filled with five million rules covering a million cases, as though their articles indeed had a sincere penchant for realism; their idiom shall be stiff and ceremonial, it shall cover thought and serve it as the finest armor does an invisible body; the parchments shall have their conventional folds, the sigils shall have preposterously long strings attached, so as to signal that everything in the world is connected by an invisible but unbreakable umbilical cord to some lurking ethics — and the sigils shall be red, almost cynically scarlet, flexible, foam- & meringue-like long after having cooled, their heraldry and Latin phrases mathematically complicated and riddle-like — in order to signal all hell's hunger and watchfulness and that pernicious enigma, invented to spite us, of ethical life.

All that, because the meaning of things is hidden; because their justification cannot be explained. What is the most authentic feature of morals, what is purely divine in it, what purely biological, what is purely historical à-propos, what fiction, what fatefulness: who knows? Yet, undeniably, there's a power in the world (although in place of "power" we should employ a term of broader meaning and character) that prods certain beings to fashion such Vatican courtroom architectures: eternal armchair, eternal candles, clocks, bulls.

7.

(Epist. I. pont. max. P. ad fratrem)
In those days I was still a layman — to use an imprecise phrase: "I wasn't even considering priesthood." Lay and church, ancient calling and chosen profession: do these distinctions make sense when set beside the enormous phenomenon that is my biological existence in its absolute metaphysics-lessness — that pressing and howling feeling of metaphysics-lessness which is the foundation and forever glaring postulate of metaphysics? All metaphysics is "non-evident" at its roots — existence is so much the highest conceivable tension of meaninglessness, openness, unre-

solvedness (both in the philosophical and emotional sense) that we must give first place to this fantastic lability among the much-desired "positivities."

What is my life? I couldn't render it with a metaphor, although I feel it to be one and homogeneous, but as all our fundamental intimations, inner perceptions of essential things, it can only be infinitely complicated in its expression: of rhythm, image, sex forms, dramatic movements. My life is first and foremost a whirl-pool or geyser: an uncalled-for eruption from my mother's blind womb. Think, brother, of the womb-darkness, one guardian of which is the nerve-tickling of carnal bliss, posturing with theo-logical affectations, and the other the maddening pain, plung-ing from one deathly spasm into another, of childbirth. I burst forth from this darkness as storm and non-entity — and can this stormy nothing have a "calling"? lay or church character? Can there be a difference between my worldly youth and papal old age, when pitted against this primal irrationality-geyser?

If I was born a priest (and since I am one now, isn't it abun-dantly clear that I was born one?), it means that priesthood was already ablaze in every blown-out-of-proportion gland of my fe-tus caricature — and I know, even if I'm incapable of giving its impromptu rational analysis, that this conception has nothing in the world to do with Geneva theories. I conceive of life as much too predestined for any "doxa" to be able to express it. Just as summum ius summa iniuria, so the most complete self-evidence of sense is the most perfect senselessness: if every cell of mine is one brick eagerly pressing itself in line for the pope in the mak-ing, then I cannot have any "role" in life but can only be life itself, a force rushing by, nameless wave in a tide that no vision can encompass.

I am I: not a lay jurist, not a Basel humanist, not an itching codifier of dogmas, not a beastly dumb fetus, not the crusade's amateurish hero, not the pope, not your brother, not the inquisitor, not the courter of hospitals: but simply "I," a single life-line beyond or below robes, professions, masses, bedrooms — some matter, some energy, some all-permeating, utmost uncertainty, some singular unit that fatally excludes everything from itself, some ecstatic punctiliousness in death's etiquette.

I am far from my chapel, my basilica, my cardinals' college, so I can speak freely, that's why I'm telling you: perhaps I could have confessed people all the same when I was still a layman, so much is man a single tragic furore, he's so busy weaving the asphyxiating silk cocoons of those special graces already in the maternal womb. And the landscapes, the "accidental" coulisses have all been present there too, in the secret collisions of sperms — the sizzling river of Basel with its bridges that resemble sleeping-in courtesans, the tiara's slender-blunt shadow, Rome's walls looking like half-baked dough — are those landscapes? Aren't they, too, me? They, too, preserve the itinerary of the sperm's hazardous splitting-growth — Rome's walls are heavy in the way sperm was heavy, are strong the way my mother's opening pelvis was strong — spring's perfume that hovers in my room now has the smell of the blood that soaked my uncalled-for body in those months.

Layman? Do you know what my nightly pastime is? To call for my most accomplished artists and order them to draw and sculpt scenes of women in labor: Madonnas barking with pain (blasphemy? no, no), secret lovers clasping, wretched childbearing machines, illegality's obsessed, the pale martyrs of legality. Isn't this paradox comedy the best symbol of fate, where pain and bliss overlap, and death licks precisely those bodily parts that were the shadow-and-honey-giving petals of the blind moth of pleasure? I can't get away from the scenes of childbirth: this is the most howling liturgy of nonsense, the irrational, mad fountain of my papacy. Mothers I can only conceive of as snake-haired maenads, death-gazed sirens, however pious, petit-bourgeois, and selfless they be: they are maenads with the gushing venom of suffering, with the obdurate tradition of "woe," who give us not life but death: shrill mother and baby cry out, a blood-Nile mires the valley of love; blood was my first garment, too. Do mothers believe or do they swear during childbirth? Do they think of anything at all, or does pain turn them entirely idiotic?

No matter: I'll tell you a "lay" adventure of mine that many know, you too, probably, but today is my birthday and on such occasions my fate always seems more fateful. It was in Basel, I was a jurist and a poet, enamored of the res publica and res *nullica*. How the law and emotional anarchy were then related in me would be difficult to analyze: perhaps in those days worldly justice, lucidity in matters of business and civil discretion were so sensational that such legal prosaicalness appeared romantic, a revolution, and could thus be closely bound up with poetry. What is more: poetry was filled with Horatian mediocrity, while the exotic, the mystical adventures, were precisely the lucidity of the law, the "suum cuique," the "equale," and such like.

In those days I had a lover, a French girl, who was lying by my side in the bed one morning. Piquancy? no, not at all. You have never been a layman and as a priest you have always lived a holy life: let me go back for a moment — with no melodramatic touch of nostalgia! — to that morning. The girl lay there in the greyness of dawn like a jasmine. A jasmine: because the jasmine's scent is dizzying and sweet like all the promise-embroidered secrets of the Orient, and the flower is simple and simple-minded like the innocence of peasants (in case innocents exist indeed) and the geometers' poorly, basic plane figures. Such is every nude at dawn: they are still replete with all the mysteries of the night — if you will, with the most redeeming metaphors of existence, "thanatological" guidelines, or if you will, with kitsch, posturing, the histrionic impotence of lying, but at the same time also with a new, morning reality, the treacherous, aquarelle-like daemonics of the praesens: who could accurately depict the morning of love-making? The melodic pain we feel for the past, midnight pleasure which is curbed by daylight: the house fronts' reborn faces which are left behind like stones from the slurped-up fruity flesh of dreams, the cold ebb and tide of waters, the flags' senseless cracking, the ships' merciless arcs in the harbor, work? And at the same time, that equally melodic joy of being able to tow in that female body among the house fronts, the waters' diary-grey, the flags' military stiffness and the ships' mercantile gills? If ever dream and reality, memory-opium and reality-fruit could stand in perfect balance — that would be around the mistress' morning body, where every perception, memory, and every splinter of the milieu carries with equal credit the role of reality in one moment, and in the next, that of irreality.

How many steps: the meeting, the evening love-making, the renewed love-making when waking, the morning love-making. You know well, my ascetic brother, that in refreshing these memories I'm not guided by any shade of poetic affectation, humanist libertinism, or adolescent will to shock. I'm writing all this as a physician and as the slightly blasé subject of suffering — this, too, was part of my fetus-embroidery, so let it stand here — for some, a metaphor, for others, "mea culpa," for others yet, physiology — for me, the indefinable initials of destiny on my life.

My bedroom had one window-door opening onto a balcony: through it came in a tall railing, tall house-fronts, the early morning, and the too-early racket of a fast river. Dawn is the supreme secret: nowhere is man and landscape, man and his creation, in such well-nigh ridiculous canon as then. Everything is clear, the outlines are positive, the waves shamelessly loud, but because it's only half past three, we have every right to sleep on, to feel our limbs still dumb, to wear the mask, or ancient face (O monde diplomatique des synonymes!), of mystery: simultaneously to relish the doubtful day and doubtful night, of the one, the unmistakable precision of contours without any action, and of the other, the inner anarchy, perversity, selfishness, and crippledness without any external sanction. The woman changes from one moment to the next: now orphic, now menial, now supreme nude, now a snoring dog.

Jasmine, jasmine: I can't get rid of this equation. White, un-adorned petals, like a Romanesque chalice: they are not even ma-terial, but the trace of two joint palms walled in the air, cup-shaped, like the shadows of a distant, half-hearted caress from which yel-low, honey-bearing stamens were born — the woman was like this. White? green? yellow? grey? Her body's inner luminosity and the silvery commonsense of dawn disputed the bed among them-selves: fever-paleness, virgin-grey, bed-staleness, dawn-greening, moon-white, daylight-epidermis — how useless are those rhetori-cal syntagms when I try to evoke the colorless coloratura of the dawn's, the bed's, and the female skin's colors! Let alone if I wanted to depict the body's weight: its hovering above the bed, its leaden, sigil-like sinking into the bed's waxen obedience, that halo-like ethereal feel that its proximity lent my muscles, that snake-like pressure and rheumatic burden which the same proximity meant at the same time? Did we embrace or pull apart, clutch the other or kick the other away? Who could tell? That yellow stamen in the jasmine's midst: at once wholesome and decadent. Then I was truly in love and believed that there is no greater happiness and no higher god than the limbs of a woman we made love to, in the morning: in my hands everything still lives in the fantastic mag-nifying glass of touch (touch is the organ of fantasy by excellence), but dawn also throws to my today's eye the sleeping Venus in her animal ennui and moanings, and I hold in the dreadful black net of past touch (in jest) the small butterfly of vision — one god, one god, I said, frightful and a believer. And then, in the moment of "impression," I had to find out that there is a love more love than love itself. Somehow like this:

Someone knocked at the door. At this hour? Who could it be? Only death news is brought so early — who could have died? I was perfectly sure that someone had died, for there was not one happy instant in my life in which no suffering penetrated — perhaps because I sought it (not out of asceticism but out of mathematics). When the quiet knocking was heard at the door, at the same time from one of the open windows across the street came a clock's soft chiming: I have never heard the noise of time bloom into endingness with such fatigued petals — the time-"point" was like the slow opening of a perfumed fan, all opium and melancholia. How different was the stranger's knocking: the sharp hailing-down of impatience, one point after the other: *man has no time to bloom struttingly, as the clock does.* This strange chiming of the clock, a gift of a boom, filled me with a renewed mood of amorous and brotherly love, I couldn't tell why. I felt the clock's chiming, with its underwater feminine pudicity, to be so personal as though I had been offered a glimpse into the distant home from where it came, right into the bed: at that moment I realized that time, this most anonymous wave above us all, is nevertheless a more individual, more personal "secret" of a home than its most beautiful woman's body could be. Perhaps it's all a game: the body of the woman sleeping by my side molded ev-erything, even the distant clock-chime, into body shape; I don't know. I took one more look at the transparent mistress before taking the death news: let me feel for one last time love for what it is — a fleeting form's fleeting-by, the memory of an absurd psychological constellation, the blend of visual draft and anxiety-feeding destiny. Love is this: Japanese prints — lots of blank pa-per-space, here and there a blot of color, a letter. How beautiful was this alternation: between the palpating-all of love-making and our souls' finicky impressionism. At this moment the whole woman was indeed a "breath": if a flower, then one sole petal fad-ing into green; if a pond, then one sole B-voiced wave; if a scent, then one single drop of perfume on the embroidered initials of yesterday's handkerchief.

I opened the door. A wizened little old man stood on the threshold. My kharis-greedy eyes saw in him at once the pathetic tracery of poverty and goodness. "Tracery" — how cold and overbearing is the word against the little man's sad reality! It was also clear at first glance that I cannot but be unfaithful to the woman sleeping in the next room — here was the new Venus: the poor man. He was a beggar. He wore huge, upward-curling, stove-pipe-like shoes and his trousers were creased at the knees; his posture was so ramshackle that he seemed not to stand but squat. He was half bald; his eyes ran over with tears. This was prima materia: this chemical belief of mine hasn't changed since. Sentimentalism, hysteria, misery, affectation, disease — all are mystical to the same degree, whichever may draw tears. In the old man's gaze infinite tragedy and infinite harmony fused; his poverty and homelessness were so enormous, his experience of people's heartlessness so pitch-dark that his manners nearly turned into some kind of feminine etiquette, amiability, or downright cosmeticized angelicalness — the spontaneous classicism of despair.

He was like a page from the Gospels come alive: the metaphysics, poetry, god of poverty incarnate, around whom flickered the flame-tongue problem of "love."

The poor man: do we ever really think about the fact that our god chose poverty for his dwelling-place? For us Catholics it is not the landscape in bloom, not the stars and not the soul's chaotic mysteries that is our fertile soil, but poverty: poverty and divinity are indistinguishable, and with some sleight of hand I can affirm: I am a "worshipper of the poor," the way some pagans are worshippers of apes or fire. For Christians poverty is not simply the domain of charity, not a place for exercising virtue, but an intellectual foundation, the very raw material of theology, its sole possible dough. Poverty is not a social issue, not a historical aspect and an effect of chance, but a perpetual ontological given, which God declared to be alone worthy of him with all his life on earth. We must swim in poverty from morning to night, spying on poverty's interior climate and fauna, independently of the individual being of poor people: poverty itself, in all its natural, that is, theological wholeness. What is the effigy of poverty, since it is an effigy of god, the most analogical of all analogiae entis, for this is what Christ chose — certainly not in an attempt to emphasize his religion's social features, but because it is poverty's psychological-chemical compound that is the most suitable for taking in the divine. The poor man is always first and foremost a theodicea: I looked on the humble beggar as on a god revealing itself.

And I *believed* in him: the most redeeming, forward-propelling feature of my "coup de foudre" love for him was its being a rational love, set against the love for the mistress whose very essence was perhaps the sheer impossibility to believe in the woman as reality — that she is only an impression, which becomes all the more fleeting, the more passionately willed she stands before me. Beside me were the two greatest inspirations of love: irreality, doubt, the colorfully budding-levitating mask — and reality, the divine matter of love, its sensible object.

The poor man was praying to me with clasped hands: "Forgive me, my gracious lord, for waking you at this hour, but I can hardly keep to my feet, I'm very ill, for months I've had no work at all, I'm sent away from everywhere I go, I have no bed, not a bite to eat, I'm very thirsty and cold, I beg you, milord, let me sleep in a nook and give me some rag, I'll work for it, I see there's a small garden here and the grass is tall, I'll mow it nice and even, I'm very good with the scythe, and I'll dust all the rugs in the household, I'm a strong man, I'm only reduced to this because I lost heart at all the hunger I endured, you see, milord, I only lost heart, but I'm strong, if I could get a bit of stale bread and warm soup."

Dear brother, this slowly oozing sentence uttered through tears is one of the foundations of my life. The words, the old man's voice and face, my feelings, the meeting of our eyes and hands: the supreme law, the sole Muse of my cathedra.

First of all, the old man was the goddess of "haven't" (there's no helping it, our world is made so that "woman" will always mean some more refined sensation, that's why I'm calling the eighty-year-old a woman, a nymph or maitresse): the picture of human lack, negativity, material, and sentimental fiasco, a lack far too universal to generate revolt or philosophy. His tears oozed slowly, but it was precisely from this slowness that have-nothingness' true spirit, its god-bearing atmosphere, emanated. His "haven't" was an autumnal haven't: of the worn-outness of mists, swooning leaves, not too high fever. Shall I call this inner sparingness in his pain "resignation"? Where are all the haughty nomina when one really needs them?

He called me "gracious lord": he, the eighty-year-old Madonna, me, the twenty-year-old beau who had just jumped out of the warm lily bed of doing-nothing. Me, a lord? And gracious? To him, poor man, the whole world, all nature's rainbows, history's and society's whole richly capillaried maze was restricted to this sole motif: master and servant, the rich and the poor. And he couldn't see the relation of the two in political bloodshed or commercial contracts, but only in "grace": if he wants to, he will give, and if not, he won't. I have never seen the fact of "master and servant" in such frightful veridicity. Who can suffer it, who can let it be that such old men full of goodness be servants? What is worldly legislation worth if it doesn't punish those who refuse to help the beggar, who is: metaphysics offering up its nakedness?

"Gracious lord," I looked myself up and down with all the asphyxiating inebriation of shame: I was wearing a long yellow silk shirt, its cuffs and collar negligently unbuttoned. Stammering with ardent love, I grabbed in my hands his fists joined in prayer, caressing them like frozen birds that I wanted to bring to life: "My sweet uncle, I'm neither a lord nor gracious, I'm a nobody — how can you join your hands like *that* in front of a boy like me?"

How polite he was; perhaps the only Christianly polite person driven by the dual mystery of "haven't" and "gracious lord." The most painful of all was that in the accent with which he uttered "gracious" there was *forgiveness*, as though he had realized resignedly, yet wisely, that it is not the fault of the rich that he is poor, as though he knew that one who is poor is neither human nor an animal nor a plant, but some eternal disturbance in creation, which is understandably not much cared about. Why, why did you forgive me, foolish old dryad, for having trampled the streets of Basel up and down on my hunt for lovers, instead of chasing you with Gospel love?

And you were sick: of course, for sickness and poverty come together in the one common morphology — one could see in your whole being that you bore suffering *in its entirety*, with an old wives' instinct for synthesis. Sickness: I thought of the woman lying in bed and of the pleasures of love. How can suffering and joy fit in the same body? They probably can't: the woman is one greenish-white blot like a water lily, uniting in herself the weeds' puss-emerald *&* the icy gentility of flowering — and a blot of color cannot get sick. Imago! The poor man is sick precisely for this reason, because he is not *only* body like the mistress; the poor man's tattered shirt, threadbare shoes, rusty stove and tin cup are identical to his body, and is not such a pile of rags and rust: sickness? What could possibly get sick on a slender nude? Its greatest death is a movement, its darkest poison, if the shadow of a fraying curtain falls on it. My mistress' body didn't merge with anything, either lace or bed sheets: it always remained an island that shook off the world. The poor man had grown into everything, was mathematical function grown into biology.

I wanted to visit the whole species: like a greedy hunter who, inebriated by the flutter of one bird, is driven at once to shoot down all the sister birds in the whole world, so I wanted to drown entirely in poverty's yellowish froth. Give me yet more poor people, all of them and nothing but them! Finally I've got you, Archimedes point, viewed from where everything is irrefutably nonsensical.

He was out of work: is then work really such an essential phenomenon? The poor old man wanted to work — for him this was redemption, happiness, the supreme goal: that someone can serve others — resting was out of the question: it was work he wanted. Work? What kind of work? To mow the grass, dust the rugs, the kind of work whose result we don't even notice, the kind of work that for us sinks into indifference — that for him would be a calling. But isn't work precisely that: the care for invisible trifles, worrying for the marginal? Is this awful lack of proportion understandable — between the evenly cut grass as effect, and the whole life of a slave gardener as the cause of this effect? Isn't there some madness, some dizzying vortex?

There is either work or conception: "work" always absorbs the whole of life, pushes one into poverty, and is of minimal value (is the grass even? is the rug clean? What nonsense!) — the "conception" (by which one means the soldiers' military deeds, politicians' state-shaping legislative gestures, artists' music, priests' soul-nursing) is always biological momentum, rushing pathos, physical exhaustion to death, meaningless goal.

And yet how much childishness there was in this grass-mowing project, as if it wasn't his livelihood that depended on it but as though he wanted to play, get in touch with mythical desire & amiable snobbery, with the grass of the "lords" — as if he had really asked: "Uncle, pray, may I hold this flower for a second?"

What was stronger: the paradox of work, its human significance, or this childishness? — How conscientiously he would mow the grass, how innocently he would comb it, believing with all his heart that something utterly just was happening there: "The one works, the other pays for it." I hated in advance those arrogant women who would trample the grass which my lachrymose saint trimmed with his softly clacking scissors. I have always been a man of "conception," of "creation": when in my imagination I saw the weeping little old man bowing over the grass, the very words "conception" and "creation" filled me with disgust, let alone their meaning — as compared to work!

And on top of all that, his strange statement that he had "lost heart," as if loss of heart were not a poetic mood but a skin disease. In this word, "heart," was summed up poverty's passive classicism, that I have already mentioned to you on several occasions.

Here I went over the words of this poor man, one by one, in the paraphrase-style of official and clerical "food for contemplation": indeed so that you should pore over them. What is the meaning of work, what is true work and what is play; is poverty a social phenomenon or an intellectual one — who could settle that once and for all? I didn't even get as far as their analysis, for I was standing in the midst of fantastic emotions, and emotions are too homogeneous and absurd to be analyzed. But pray, try to experience, now and then in the silence of the small hours (and don't worry if you force it) the mysterious themes and relations of have-not, work, sickness, loss of heart, master and servant, grace — forget about my letter's convulsive tautology and let the sheer fact stand before your eyes, in the eerie nakedness of living things.

When the poor man came to the end of his supplication, my whole body was one big tear sac swollen to bursting point, and *hatred*, hatred against those who have not listened to him. "They send me away everywhere": this sentence, spoken in general, sketched before me the most individual portrait possible: of the

stonehearted who should be executed and tortured. Perhaps
this hatred of those who send off the poor man was even stronger than my love. "Wait, sweet uncle, I'll immediately bring you
something." I stole back to the bedroom.

By the bed lay, on their sides, the two high-heeled shoes like
shells from which the animal died out, or flowers whose stamens
had been torn out, and now they stick into the world blind or
unsexed; next to them the silk stockings, which perhaps best
expressed the demonic degree of woman's irreality: I could well
remember when, before pulling them off, my mistress boasted
about the fineness of their fabric; it was already dark in the
room — only the moon's prehistoric blade lay across the night
and she called me to the balcony door, which almost sizzled with
moonlight. With her long fingers she reached under the stocking
above her knee and pulled it apart, off her skin — as if it weren't
a homogeneous texture, but only silk threads combed next to
one another, greyish-pink almost-strings across the moon's silver — it was well-nigh unbelievable that something so extremely
elastic and ethereal could (the moment she pulled out her hand)
cover her leg like thick moss. Three forms were flickering in the
air (and I'm not writing this in frivolous pursuit of artistry, nor
from lapsing back into my humanist routine): the silhouette
of the net-amphora stretched on the leg, the forcibly expand-
ed silk sails adhering to the hands' shape (like a bat's wings to
certain bones) — and finally: the hovering fabric between leg
and hand, knee & fingertips, free and moon-negative. *This* is
woman: those form-nuances, the thousand fineries of space
and color: leg-shape, free net, crippled glove — this, this is the
chosen antithesis of poverty's harrowing concreteness.

The poor are the only *human* beings, I realized, when I gazed
at the stockings' deflated silk rings. On one chair lay my mistress' new dress full of golden flowers and gemstones. Next to the
dress, a veil: at the back the dress was cut so low that she covered

it with a veil. I gave this gold dress to the beggar: he could live off it for years. I also gave him a short note with which he could prove that he had not stolen the dress but received it from me.

He didn't go into a frenzy to thank me: the extraordinary gift is so remote from the imagination of the poor that they can't thank in a manner that could be worthy of the gift. I confess that I had expected such thanks though: of course not because I was so taken with myself, but because gratitude's sobbing ecstasy could have provided me with the nearest occasion for lovemaking with poverty. Come what may, I thought, I'll somehow settle the affair with my lover. I knew well that it wouldn't go down without a violent fight and hysterical accusations, but I was happy to suffer for the poor old man. How anxiously he treaded down the stairs, how kindly he kept explaining that he told no lies when saying that he was out of work — so much wildflower-like forsakenness trembled in his big, downward-curling mouth!

Is it settled with my gift? Shouldn't I keep protecting him? Protect, this is an important word: he was the absolute to-be-protected: his whole body was dewy and nervous with such sensitivity that the fact that the staircase railing to which he held on didn't kiss back his palm, that the squinting lamp didn't shed more light in front of his stumbling feet seemed an act of brutal hostility. Every object, color, or smell which didn't mold to this little old man with such servitude of mania as my whole life was: abject, and to be destroyed. How could I then let him move among those objects? I ran down the stairs after him and when I caught up (with what humble frightfulness, roe deer-like trust-mistrust he looked into my eyes: one could see that gratitude dumbed him down to the point of pain, yet at the same time he was searching my face with an old entomologist's thoroughness not directed at humans), I said: "Dear uncle, if you need anything, call on me any time, I'll always give if you need money. Anytime."

He didn't know how to express his gratefulness otherwise than telling me among tears his woes again, by now his melancholy "role" in my honor, more or less in the same words. There was something deathly moving in it: the poor who has already forgotten all human speech apart from the words of begging, and when he wants to thank one, he can only utter again the unbelieving prayer of supplication, a bit more ceremoniously than before. A word of his, however, pushed me to blind hatred again: "nobody believes what I say." Not believe him? Who do they believe then? I again thought of the net-stocking stretched on my lover's fingers: do they believe that? "What I say": because what such a poor old man *says* carries a huge significance — for him, speech is always the leaving-by-testament of his whole life into one tragic musical tone, with him every word is a secret-most last will, unlike with other people who dabble in wordshed. Old men cover a long way to the word, for them the word is something sacred, a ramshackle boat with their whole life for cargo — who are the madmen or devils who have no respect for that? For that very reason I would have liked to shape a statue-paraphrase of my whole life to match his words — I didn't know with what expressive gestures to signal to him that I absorbed every word of his, uttered with Sisyphean laboriousness, with the pious attention they deserved. With one clumsy movement I kissed his hand, regretting it in the same instant, knowing that he would take me for a lunatic and so, morally speaking, all my kindness would have been in vain: he would not leave my house with the conviction that good people are still to be found in the world. And how much I wanted him to recognize in me a human brother, not a madman.

Racked by doubt and utterly shaken by dizzying love and hatred, unsatisfied, I stumbled up the stairs. Where does this overwhelming torso emotion, dissatisfaction, come from in the vortex of all love? Perhaps from feeling that love is too big a thing to exist, to have a purpose: love collides with death. The speed of love is higher than that of light: it flashes through the whole of life at once, illuminating a father's, mother's, lover's, poor man's whole life in an instant and thus must see that love does not vanquish death. Is love (and we can't speak of true love in relation either to parents or lovers, this I learnt for good from that *poor man*) an earthly or celestial feeling? How maddeningly it is diluted by death proves that it is earthly. This beggar is going to die — what is the use of the whole love, living for the other, if the other dies in the end? Love wants ultimate good for the other, but can only yield laughable little drunkennesses as compared to death. Then isn't this woman worth more — I said to myself, walking to the bed —, for carnal pleasure doesn't run counter to death like the goodness that helps the poor, but with death, and in death.

I wanted to lie down next to her, but, hearing the soft click of the gate, went out on the balcony to see what the beggar was up to. I saw him plodding toward a large red gate: I knew that house well; it was my former mistress'. Why is he going there? I was hurt: the golden dress is not enough for him, he begs on as though I had given him a cracked kreutzer. I waited to see what would happen: out of some weird sadism I wanted my former lover not to give him anything, so that I could sob loudly over the old man's imagined suffering and hate that woman freely before God and the world. At that moment I spotted her crossing the street and walking toward the gate.

My lover of old, the new lover: when I write these characters and concepts it occurs to me that lately my whole life has narrowed down to two things, nouns and wonderments — that is, I have reached the point where primitive man and the philosopher with a plethora of rationalist tricks up his sleeve appear very alike. Lover of old, new lover: there was a time when a dichotomy like that would have ignited me to white-hot analytical excitement — and now? I won't deny it, the furore of analysis is well alive in me, but I don't use it — I'm waiting, for perhaps one

day a redeeming perspective on the things of the world might
open to me, when I could analyze again with due scholarly and
poetic right, although that is probably going to be an analytical
ease that feeds not on the things but on itself, and exists entirely
for itself. But let's drop the unctuous and the ironic prophesies.
It is true that whenever in the evening I want to jot down something for the *Rerum Memorabilium*, I always end up writing only
nouns and red circles in my notebook; if I'm walking, things like:
the river, the tree, the star, the bridge — if I get to my writing
desk from the cardinals' college, things like: the truth, the vote,
the jurors, mercy, dogma, man — if I receive ambassadors: the
etiquette, the war, the entirely interior, the entirely exterior, the
king, the people. I repeat, perhaps I'm jotting them down in this
way because I want so much to analyze them to bits or together,
that I'm postponing the task to more quiet times. But perhaps
all this is really old age's acquiescence in the existence of things.
Acquiescence? What if it is really revolt? Isn't there greater revolution and anarchy in the passivity of the old than in the heroics,
parading from one moment to the next, of youth?

The lover, the river, the king: how is it in fact that these
things are? "*How* is it": this is the essential question; *why* they are
is only asked by the useless sparrows wallowing in the puddle of
the intellect. What is wonderful and problematic in the world is
never *why* something is the way it is, but *how* the thing is the way
it is. How the river is a river, the pope a pope. Those moments
are beautiful when there is nothing else in my mind but a naked
noun: "the river" — and in my heart nothing else but excitement
and wonderment made up of worship and doubt, love and savage
distrust; in my eyes nothing else but the living fact of the river:
shades of green, physical calculations, the dead nonchalance of
fish, boats, mirrorings, rippling, sliding-by, mud-smell and cool-
ness, in brief, all the undisguised secrets of a portrait. Is there,
can there be more?

The soul of "creators": the soul of moral-, god-, music-, image-
& battle-creators — if they indeed live off creation's absolute
inspiration, then shouldn't they by default reach my non-creating
creation: the naked noun, the wonderment that sends a shudder
down the spine, the infinitely tight-fisted and yet all-generous
reality of the fact? *Rerum Memorabilium?* What I write down
of them is neither "res" nor "memorabilis" — the sole interesting and important thing in my life has been life itself, and what
is important in a diary is not what it tells but the fact that it is
a diary, that there has been this, too, in my life, that I wanted to
speak about my life. There you cannot rescue anything, amass
treasures, single out from the memories and objects, "eternalize"
them. Only one thing can be related to "eternity": moral life,
virtue. "Value" is what is already here redolent of immortality:
everything that grew into the intellect & the instinct for beauty
will be lost.

You see, with such polished, academic ideas I chose to intro-
duce that scene from an adventure book when I spotted my lover
of old. It goes without saying that like everybody, I, too, loved
the woman of old, whom I have abandoned, and with whom I
no longer had any connection, a thousand times more, for she
was in an ideal position, the best imaginable one between two
human beings: complete knowledge without any practical consequence (even now while I'm writing this I get dizzy with the
elysian thought: I *know* a living being absolutely, metaphorically
and scientifically, and I needn't *live* against or according to my
knowledge!), utter plasticity and closedness in her entire being,
while around her hovers all the metaphysical dream-perfume of
the past, of time — perfect bondage, for we have only one kind
of common life-story, in one sole, forever unalterable order, as
compared to which all my life's periods will appear the more colorful and free, the more liable to comforting heresies: "quinze
joies du ..."

Of course when I saw her facing the beggar, I didn't think of any of that. I saw the beggar address her, ask for alms. Is he mad? or does he really want to relish the fact that if she should not give him anything, in this moment it would be utterly indifferent to him? Whichever way it was, the moment he addressed her I felt a convulsively sharp inner pain which I can, however, only characterize with the simple word disturbance. There was some terrible disturbance here, which was of course nothing but the characteristic disturbance of all living life: there was a disturbance between my frenzied and idyllic charity, the water-lily sailing on the lake of dreams in my bedroom, and the woman of old. Suddenly I couldn't feel anything; there were so many feelings inside me. What's the use of all these feelings? Fear that she won't give; pity for the beggar; pity for myself, because from now on I would have to hate the lover of old and so the main value of her being-past will be lost: the free and conditional feeling-variations that can be linked to her; and above all, *what* this feeling was at all: what are they in themselves, and what in their contradictoriness? Is love simply identical to feeling, and feeling, to becoming eternally self-contradictory? Why do I feel, Lord, why do I feel? (You see, I said and continue saying: *why*. It wasn't all that wise to have preached against the instinct for causality.)

What, then, is my love? Eye and adherence? That I glimpse some phenomenon and completely adhere to it? "Eye" and "adherence": with a bit more of affectation I could also say: perception and mimicry. Love is nothing but too active remembrance of perception, an impotent adjustment to the object following the impression; in any case, a special form of remembering. In love everything is terribly clear and objective, one couldn't decide which in the function of love and its objects is the dependent, and which the independent variable. And then comes an utterly crippled, lazy, impotent foundering at this hyper-clear vision, the halting or treading in place.

Nature displays the most peculiar blending of dynamics and sloth, kaleidoscope turns and unanalyzable inertia. Lots of mountains, lakes, crystals, and flowers owe their "beauty" (how problematic & relative the word is, even in this milieu!) to the fact that their cells have grown lazy, halted, piled up in one spot: the capricious boldness of one moment was followed by the boredom of a million years of routine. Love is perhaps such "boredom" after the terrible drama of the first perception: the beloved object (human, idea, landscape, etc.) does not turn problematic, but on the contrary — we try to *clear it away* from our consciousness by nearly identifying with it, or at least completely adhering to it: we wrap ourselves around the lover to hide her from ourselves.

Of course a plethora of love-definitions and hypotheses came into my mind: some of them were completely intellectualist, some (like this one) strove to see in it a biological inertia-instinct, to somehow loosen or grind the eternal tragedy-core in its midst. According to some, love is the absolute affirmation of things, simply the precipitate hallelujah of acquiescence in things — and according to others, love is the organ of sense of the lackingness in things, the rich mirror of the world's negativity. Whatever. For even then the mutually exterminating hunger for formulae and the incredulity in formulæ ran together. I knew that here I was facing something bad and that its cause was my emotional life, it was for this reason that I wanted to settle the diagnosis of my disease as fast as possible.

She didn't give the beggar anything. I was still completely aswim in charity, and that woman was simply the puppet of not giving. You know how much I loved ornate externalities, rhymes, and cosmetics in my youth — perhaps the sheer fact that I only loved the make-up, the dresses' frills gushing like eternal fountains, the hairdos' algebra, and the various hues of face powder in women betrayed my ascetic leanings even then: it was not the female psyche (mot assez bouboubou) or the female body that interested me, but these abstractions: the card game-rule-like figurations of color, form, proportions. Suffice it to say that I have never hated these colors, forms, and proportions with such blind fury as in that moment. The woman who, for a thousand reasons, remained a formula for me, the heraldic sign-complex of a circle of emotions, suddenly became: *human* — so it must be when in a book of mathematical theory the doctor suddenly affirms of a complicated formula, with a face so livid to match catastrophe, that this formula *lives*, has turned reality. Only in an ethical relation can we sense human beings as *human*: the intellect and especially sex, æsthetics and historical impact completely dehumanizes them. Under my very eyes thus a human being was born.

She had a tall, shiny black bun, mauve-pink complexion, a stiff grey silk dress: the whole woman was like flowers loosely stuck next to one another in a half-designed bunch — face, hands, bun, gaze, tread were scatteringly mixed. For an instant I looked at the sleeping woman in the bedroom; propped up against a chair was my long rapier, so elastic that it sometimes swayed like an ostrich feather. I put on a cloak, grabbed my rapier, and ran out on the street.

What followed was the act, the murder. I killed her.

You may know yourself, albeit no great friend of "observations" (you have the habit of uttering the word with an accent to make people ashamed of it), what an act is? Something that upsets one like nothing else, and which is naught for all that. Acts have no ethics and no drama, no analysis and no assessment, no color, shape; they don't belong anywhere and to anyone: they terribly are, and are terribly invisible. I have never been more consistent than when I killed that woman, and haven't been at more interstellar a remove from myself and everything than in that moment.

When I got out on the street I couldn't see her, she had probably already entered her small palace; but I saw the dawn,

I knocked into it like into a stone wall. This is always the most immoral time span of our lives: in those moments the whole of yesterday and the whole of the night means definitely and irretrievably the past that we no longer are, that has dropped from us like clothes — but the new day is still far from starting, it's still mute and untuned, one can still live nothing in place of the past yesterday and night, so this is utter freedom, complete independence from our future and past, contentless present, the best prompter of every mad intention and shapeless hypothesis — if the grey precision and inhuman lameness of dawn hadn't surrounded me, perhaps I wouldn't have killed her at all. This was a "scena": the coulisses schlepped me in it like victorious procuresses. My house, the house of my former mistress: were they indeed houses at dawn? No. They were rubrics that I had to fill in: at dawn all milieus were left completely to me; if objects were conscious they would say that one cannot speak of the independent life of an object (house, river, cloud), everything hangs on the milieu, and this milieu (from their perspective) is the man strolling among them at dawn, equally disconnected from his past and future.

It's curious that I should explain my deed, which was first and foremost an ethical frenzy, with such mechanical motifs as the suggestion of dawn. The cause is simple: I explain it so because I am *explaining*; and since it is an explanation, it cannot be but such a fictitious whatsit, which probably didn't belong to the act at all. When it comes to such dreadful, long past crises, one cites at the same time one darkly-glittering chip of irrationality or another in its terrible crystal-solitude, while twisting and turning the convoluted ratiocinations of the long years that followed it: he wants to rush back to the act's forever-submerged blind actuality, and yet wants to lift the whole thing into the analytical garden of the *intellect*.

When I got at her villa's gates, I could hear the key's grating in the lock; I pushed in the door. It was not she who fidgeted with the key but a servant. He must have asked me something, but all I was looking for was her, now going up the stairs. When she looked back I was already behind her and stabbed her in the back with my long rapier. I judged; I was righteous. I felt that my act had nothing to do with any kind of justice and judgment, because "justice" was inside me, it is always the single person's inner perspective that can't be channeled into the world, to another person: my hatred was not satisfied with the murder; my feeling and this act, my sense of justice and the pile of meat groaning on the stairs could never have anything to do with one another, but it was precisely my solitude and senseless forsakenness under the foreign bell jar of the act that drove me on even more; I believed that my act was necessary in spite of everything, precisely because it was so self-standing.

There is a melancholy humor in all writing where the intellectualist tries to somehow digest the indigestible *act*: this humor, as you will probably discover, abounds in my lines. After the dull thudding of her corpse I ran to the gate, out onto the street and with the key snatched from the lock I locked the gate from the outside. Why did I do that? Perhaps out of cowardice, in self-defense, or perhaps (more likely) because, by locating my murder to an enclosed place, I could lend it sculptural or technical plasticity, not to say, turn it into a reliquary. My rapier was dripping with blood. I heard a noise on the street — I spotted the old beggar as he was savagely trampled by a naked woman. My new lover believed that the old cripple had stolen her gold-flowered dress. How smoothly insulated the different aspects of this thing lay next to one another on my consciousness' peasant table rubbed with blood: the fight between the naked woman, who had rushed out onto the street, and the sick old man, only separately a picture, only separately a moral caricature — singly it was what it was. Yes, yes, it was necessary that once life stand before me with its most truthful face: in the collision-point of terrible ecstasy and terrible senselessness. The cruel woman was dead — but the act's pathos tore me out of every human relation, was nohow related to cruelty. I killed for the beggar, and the beggar is quartered by a wild hetaera, not in spiteful fury, but in the drunkenness of panic. How her skin still bore the night and the memory, the ash of my subjective gaze, that skin-solitude that can be assembled from gold, pond, moss, butterfly-scales, which could be a rightful symbol of everything that was not "act."

My bloody rapier, my ceremonious, howling nonsense still needed sanctification: I started out toward the nearby church. The windows popped up like bubbles or cherries spitting their stones: woe and curiosity bathed me like the fire raining down on Sodom. By the time the armed guards appeared I had entered the church. At that moment I heard a dreadful crash: they had forced the gates of my dead mistress' house open. I couldn't see anyone around either when I was walking to the church or inside: my imagination sculpted and daubed up and apart the faces and gestures. But so it fits an *act*: to an act nothing visual should belong, an act is like atmospheric pressure that kills: it kills but is invisible, transparent like the most chiseled nothing. Only noises: now, too — steps from which one can feel some great weight that renders them insecure and gluey: a servant brought the lady's body.

In the church communion was in course: a wizened little priest muttered the "corpus Domini nostri Jesu Christi" to a couple of sparrow-framed, toddling crones, I held the bloody rapier aloft in front of God's host-face: I came to show how much I love the poor. My murder was a kiss, a kiss on the beggar's face — I, being a soul, the cosmeticized subject of all kinds of toy psychologies, no longer felt the connection between my drive and my act, but the host-bodied god did. He had no psychology. I'm committing a shocking blasphemy here: will death strike me down on the spot in punishment? Or am I a saint, an archangel descended on earth? I knelt in front of the altar railings. The priest shook so badly that his ring chattered against the chalice, like a drunken servant's bell. I held up the rapier high in my right hand, tilted toward the sky (the blood didn't drip to the floor but trickled down under my shirtsleeve, drenching me down to my armpit), I stuck my tongue out on my lower lip (it felt wooden!) and asked for God's body. With a deathly sin? I have confessed this a thousand times — but what was the sin and what the sacrament here, I don't know myself. Everybody froze in the church. The woman's body lay like a bundle of clothes. The priest wanted to run. I blocked his way. Yelling like a madman, he shoved the host in my mouth, like one who tosses a damned coin into a well.

Now when I have told you this horror-burlesque in a nutshell, my nouns come to mind again. And then the impossible life and the equally impossible work: my two nightly Parcæ. What a tempest this scene was, and yet it is "isn't": in fact it wasn't even then, it isn't now, and it will not become "handiwork." You wonder perhaps how come the thought of "work" still flares up in me, but I can't help it, I can't forget the strivings of my youth.

I'm writing this letter from my Tivoli gardens in setting dusk, close to a white Hermes statue. This white marble flower or ice torso is my lamp. You know the pupil-less eyes of Greek statues — now, among the darkening foliage, this whole statue is such a mute and ghostly eye-white: it illuminates with its blindness. As yet there is no candle around me (how desperately even torches sizzle and wriggle in the evening breeze: for my skin such a gush of air is the tender caress of grace, but to those hypochondriac flames it's already agony's violence), only the statue: with its muscles' harmony, in its fragmentariness. By being both a fragment and proportion he is what half-kneaded Adam must have been like — on one side, a still-dead sea anemone, on the other, a blessed angel nude. Its mistily blue marble doesn't shed light; its surface is gritty and cold, doesn't resemble the Moon's white light; it glows with its closedness. Or does it shed darkness? Perhaps it's not yet evening, it only emanates from the grey torso, like death's Hellenic scent. The sky is still golden-green, and in this pathetic-sharp yellow the trees' rarefied or dense crowns appear gorgeous: no longer green but not black yet, far too analytical to be silhouettes, and far too unitary to bring to mind the notion of "leaf" — this is the most beautiful state of trees. All spring's contour-shedding, the freshness of matter is still aquiver in our imaginingly palpating fingers (our whole body), and yet they stand above the virginal horizon of silence (instead of altitude above sea level one might speak here of colorfulness above silence-color) as if they were eternity's otherworldly caryatids, who support God's celestial kingdom with relentless mummy discipline. During daytime there was no separate sky and earth: now they split all of a sudden. How only-earthly the earth is, how only-sky the sky: and curiously, now that they have abruptly separated, foliage and star, garden and outer space are in a much more fraternal relation than during the day when flaming noon wrapped them up into one common bunch. The most beautiful thing is that now every needlepoint-size crack on a gigantic-crowned tree is visible: its green-black mass is pierced through by the yellow sky, creating a strange union of weight and porousness for our eyes. Darkness makes foliage heavier, loaded boats, yet the glaring yellow sky makes them net-like, similar to that stocking that lay by my mistress' bed. The slender little foliage sits atop a thin-trunked tree like the black sketch of sparks at the end of a rocket-gun: noiselessly it shot into the sky. How much sky is there! Now toward the evening the sky becomes like the sea: every house, tree, appears to be standing on the shore of an infinite sea; the sky somehow becomes positive, a palpable, landscape-like infinity. The moon, and the crickets' chirp into the breaches between the stars, makes air-thin mist-scarves visible around the trees' necks. Does this deathly garden idyll, the Hermes torso's glowing melancholia, the sky's sour gold, the trees' carbonizing buds, the crickets' abstract polyphony, have anything to do with my life, my past?

My nouns and the Hermes are identical, I think. The many gods of the Greeks are so many nouns: the sunset, the plants tarred to poppy-seeds, the cricket, the layers of silence descending around me like transparent glass coulisses: these are my unattainable nomina — and with the Greeks such grammatical signs were gods. That's why the religion of the Greeks seems to me the religion of doubt, the catalogue of non-knowing: the god of water, of the forest, of death — these are nouns: water, forest, death. And such nouns are always the trace of some renunciation, the coats-of-arms of impotence: "undoubtedly there is some water, some forest, and some death in the world, but we cannot know what they mean among themselves, how they are interconnected." For me it remains forever a mystery how one can believe in nature religions: because every single godhead is nothing but an anthropomorphic question-mark about the enigmatic fact of water, forest, and death. The flight into any ontology and existentialism is but a masked form of doubt: the divinization of water as terrible water-*ens*-, of forest as forest-*ens*-, of death as death-*ens*- (this is the consequence of ontology) happens only for want of some better method, it is no solution to anything. And yet the world has to be resolved, explained: I can't quench this instinct of mine, so laughable in the eyes of many. When I think back at that mad scene of my life, of course I feel the temptation of the ontological-mythologizing, noun-establishing and Hermes-epigone method, for it would be infinitely comfortable and cheap: to give you half-baked hymns and meticulous external descriptions of the poor man, the hetaera, the rapier, the communion, the frenzy, the sin, the act, the sacrament, the love, the law.

So actuality, kitsch, and horror would disappear from history: all its elements would be some eternal trait of the world — death would no longer be my lover's personal accident that came as a result of my murder, but a tragic factor lurking on earth since the Creation (the dry "factor" will for once serve here), "eternal" deathlike-ness. But that is hogwash! My Christian restlessness cannot bear it — my morals and logic join forces against such things. This event is not some impersonal ontological "pattern" woven from the world's eternal threads, but my singular, very own personal problem, secret, damnation, question.

My life's true companion is not the Hermes statue but the murdered woman's grave: has someone really died because of me? By me? And I am alive — if this is a life: to serve one foreign death. At the same time I affirm, on some ecstatic plane, my act, because I feel it to be the divine punishment of the incapacity to love, but forever pray for the woman's soul. You say that there is no opposition in this, yet I know there is. She died, I am alive: this cannot be changed, she was once and died once, and I willed it so. What can one do here with Thanatos' plaguey lotus-postures, the ontologized death, which is the most ontology-less possible? That event is verily not "eternal" but one single moment torn out of time, some eternal openness (if something need be "eternal" here); by having been once, it's some tormenting and lacerating asymmetry; the possibility of the complementing version is lacking — for instance, that she be alive, and I be dead. Because of the fact that everybody lives once, one single destiny, everybody leans out in a distressingly certain and dizzying arc from the world of reason and certainty toward *absolute* torso. Some measure is lacking, to which I could relate my days and deeds: my own life appears to me like foreign landscapes — I'd need a point in them from where to look at it, a point that is *not* a foreign landscape but the old, familiar one – but it is impossible; I'd need one certain event in my life which could be the "foundational" event, the essence of destiny, as compared to which the others would be mere toy functions, but there is no such event. In vain the lily-white Hermes stands before me as the way, the secret, the theft and the news: my ways, secrets, thefts, and news are my singular life's singular accidents, which are foreign from any pre-historical convention *narrowed down* to god.

"One": this always means cut-offness from everything, blindness, meaninglessness. And so I am going to die, without having learnt anything about my life. In vain I lower my head into the rationalist waves of my Catholic faith: the life-events remain, in spite of all, "singular," without variants, and this is frightening.

Secrets have no end: this "sacrilegious" communion of mine after murder, with which I wanted to force God's hand to sanctify in me the murder of the cruel person, became the germ of my calling for the priesthood, or rather, one of the most shameless unveilings of the foliage that had long been growing in me. It was a sin, and it made me a priest; it was a sin, and it is my only feeling of sacrament. A dead woman visits me every night, and if I had some joy that day with which I'd like to sleep in, she takes it with her, leaving me shivering in my bed. Whom shall I believe? This victorious dead, or the God who chose this dead to make me the prince of Christians? Adieu.

8.

(Epist. II. pont. max. P. ad fratrem)

Yesterday evening when I went to sleep, or at least wanted to go to sleep, I was desperate that in this dreadful heat I'd have to attend the Duke of Benzano's academy celebration today, but now that it's behind I'm very glad for having been there. I have perhaps never felt the irreality and all-importance of my role so clearly, so tragically, and nevertheless so reassuringly as there. Why did I go? First of all, I like the Duke, not as a person but as a black panther, as the virtuoso of instinct & the most beautiful of animals. I like seeing the beast and the god side by side, his coquettish-black stockings reaching up to the hips, and the tiara. I am a worthy lieutenant of God, for I am absolutely detached from the world: contemplation, estrangement from everything, hysterical bouts of desire to intervene and create, the barrenness of spleen render me so. Perhaps you, my dearest ascetic brother, believe that it is merely the fad-whim of a new "style" and new spirit in me when I say that the carelessness lingering deep down in my world-weariness (or on its surface perhaps) is a greater Petrus calling, more jealous guarding of keys than of those of my passionate and ascetic forebears. One is either in the world or stands outside it: either a politician or a nihilist. Those who have ceaselessly propagated God into shrewish emperors and councils bursting with rationalist high-handedness, have perhaps done good service to God, but were not divine — I, who feel every historical act except mystical threading-oneself-into-God to be inwardly meaningless, I, who bear flags without an atom of faith, make alliances without an atom of faith, look upon the comedy of peoples with the most worn-out pessimism, perhaps I don't do much service to God (although one should never take it for granted): but in any case I am divine.

Don't misunderstand me, dear brother, do not believe that with entirely ridiculous peremptoriness I would call a certain impotence and nervous exhaustion, divine. But: my neurotic disillusionment, my incredulity toward historical personalities, lay heroes, lay victories and defeats, contracts and hypocritical pseudo-councils, my constant alienation from them is: a human analogy, grotesque aspect of the divinity's standing-above-the-world.

How could I not shy away from it — from things like the Duke of Benzano's classical soirée. I like the duke — but for me the thing ends there. I don't want the dinner, the fancy cakes decorated with the keys of Peter in sugar crust, the duke's whores, whose dressing gowns are embroidered with the heraldic motifs of my blazon. But the Duke is a sworn enemy of Venice, and I am another. I can't bear those merchants: the city has been ordered around for decades by Turks and Jews, and they behave in their frescoed palaces as though they were all scrupulous purists or saints. Being what they are, drapers, rag-and-bone men and procurors, pedlars and ha'penny hawkers, why can't they give up their posturing, the vacuous histrionics of their betrothal with the sea, the arrogance of secular processions, the humbug of the "republican spirit"! I have always loathed Venice with its clamorous Annunciations and even more clamorous Jews and eunuchs. Like me, my frivolous little duke, too, loathes the merchants in them: his hatred of merchants is an aristocratic pose, cretinous pride, an animal's animal reflex — my loathing is ethical, of St. Peter, coming from God: but I need to make use of the animal for the sake of the divine. So I need to be on good terms with the duke, who in a propitious moment will overrun that bog town: I feel that the reason why water continues flowing in its canals is to remind them of the Flood that befell the world because of the sins of men.

This duke isn't particularly moneyed, but Leone of Aragon definitely is. Leone of Aragon is an old fogey, terribly pious (the work of my soul-ravenous Spanish priests), whom my duke would like to ensnare in his net. He invited him to his celebration today, to which he answered with a snort that he wouldn't dream of taking part in a heathen, blasphemous, immoral fête where they recite verses on Venus and explain Greek sophists. The duke knew that I was close by, so asked me to come over: if the old Leone should see the pope there, he will hang his fears and happily answer the invitation. The duke wants to build palaces and commission paintings, and for that he needs Leone's money; and Leone in his turn needs me to soothe his anxieties. And of course I try to tighten the relationship between the two, so that in the end the money would not be spent on stones and paint but be used against Venice.

So for me the whole evening appeared as a political act, but — as has happened so many times, perhaps always — it eventually turned into an intellectualist act. First of all, it made me completely indifferent to the "dilemma." For I was, or at least could have been, wavering: should I deceive Leone, should I exploit an impertinent little beast, or should I suffer that three filthy bankers haul the steering wheel of Peter's ark? I didn't pore much over this dilemma, for no dilemma is worth poring over (in point of fact one cannot even do that). History is the jungle of contradictions, of not bifurcating but thousand-branched alternatives; the rite of exclusion, par excellence, of thinking and intellectual solutions — there is no way for me to solve a dilemma, for the solution needs my thinking, and the moment I see before myself the strumpet-gestured Venetian galleys, the duke's permed black toupee, or Leone's sleep-rusty, blinking face, and at the same time perceive the fermenting uncheckable freedom of thought, associations, of logical pros and cons, of opinions, perspectives, rational sporules — I have to laugh out: pray, what obdurate limitedness could want to go about the case of concrete cities and persons with this tool — the limitless, irreal, unbound tool of *thought*? Isn't this the most irreconcilable or irreconcilabilities: thought existing in a mode of absolute thought on the one hand, and historical masquerade, person, city, or situation existing in a mode of absolute history?

Of course one always has some "practical" reason, juridic, diplomatic, and commercial, but it differs from my "real" reason and thinking in the essential trait of being entirely artificial, foreign from my personality, bowing to conventions and lacking in emotions and intensity; not endowed (from my point of view) with any intellectual valences, as if it were not the functioning of my brain but of some primitive history-sensing organ.

The evening was beautiful, especially the old Leone and myself. I made my entry with considerable pomp, with many attendants and trumpets. They weren't used to much pomp in the ducal castle. The halls & chambers were almost empty, from bedroom to kitchen everything had a crypt-like atmosphere. The slender duke ran hither and thither in the cold, bare-walled rooms, in one person he was the master, the specter, the lover, the furniture, the wind, and the statue. In this thin boy and in this castle resembling a disused monastery all the ascetic traits of overlordly vileness were manifest. His legs united in themselves the preposterous thinness of a roe deer, women's ovals, and the muscles of horsemen — not accidentally did he wear stockings without hose that reached to his hips, the whole man was legs going on forever: running up and down, jumps, dancing, hesitancy above the ground, phallus-compass, being in more places at the same time, flight, assault: the frivolousness of space. He had creole complexion, a smooth face and dark hair, which stood on his head in giant rings: these were so thoroughly regular, complete circles that one didn't know in what manner they could be attached to his head, if they had roots at all. In addition, they were soft; it was hard to imagine how they didn't collapse. The whole man was like the slender, glinting, & sharp line of a rapier, its tension at once of truth and intrigue.

The old Leone, too, was beautiful: all bed-covers, with doctors squatting by him, and religious scrupulousness. You know that I'm not saying this in cynicism but because I am unable to see portraits in any other way but from the perspective (or, more precisely, the perspectivelessness) of "figura figurans."

And I? I was sleepy, I lazily poured my beard over myself, and brooded every now and again on life's inexhaustible strangeness. The rather erotic poetry and enthusiastic apologies of sophistry read out in Leone's honor were the non-plus-ultra of nihilism and the Sodom of thought. But because his blinking eyes saw all this time my bearded, golden-tasseled, and fanned body on a throne, he was put at ease. And I for my part realized that all the "liberated" thinking of those humanists is phoney dogmatism as compared to what lurks in me, to the conception of thought that increasingly pervades my whole being. But although I was more "nihilistic," to use a sufficiently misleading word, than all those pedantic libertines and academic doctors put together, my religiosity, my moral stubbornness, ascetic desires were much, much stronger and stricter than those of the shivering, superstitious Leone.

From the astrologists I learnt a certain inclination to symmetry. Now I compiled myself some sort of horoscope while listening to the eros-less distichs: I am the peak of all that is hieratic, the plastic guarantee of the world's meaningfulness, the guardian of order, the place where God's hand touches the world — and I am also (and this is *no* contradiction) the most tragic (and here tragic doesn't by definition mean pain) connoisseur of the psychology & physiology of thinking, the one to experience the most sincerely, and stripped to the bone, the soul's inner and eternal disorder, chaotic freedom, emotional and intellectual gibberish. When I want, I'm holier than the saints whom I have canonized (they know in heaven in what way I mean it and won't misunderstand me) — when I want, I'm viler at heart than any sophist. But I know that my sophist layer is first and foremost something *unreal*: thoughts that don't belong anywhere — and that is what scholars & the more aggressive poets, the kind who strutted at this academic rumpus, cannot ever admit.

If I am the iridescent arc between tiara & anarchy, what is Leone, what is the duke in the horoscope? Leone is equally far removed from holiness and from anarchy — or rather, he is the crippled form of holiness. And this "crippled" isn't meant to deprecate or mock, but is much rather medical or tragic. However anthropomorphic, holiness, grace is nevertheless distorted here on earth — when I watch Leone's sick, piety-feverish body on the stage's edge, it's as if I saw the abstract schemata of "homo" and "gratia" pressed into one formula. I, in whom holiness and anarchy are poles closed on themselves that never traffic with one another — Leone, in whom the poles of homo and gratia are, on the contrary, continuously trafficking, colliding and mixing, and that's why he becomes a torso or gnome.

There remains the duke, whom I have sufficiently sketched for you, my dear brother, my sweet moral guarantee. The duke is pure beastliness, the animal's reckless punctuality, history's venomous butterfly. I feel at home among such butterflies, just as I feel at home among self-mortifying friars and vision-drenched hermits; the milieu in which I am forever uneasy is the world of jurists, especially the French. After the brigands and saints these colorless "justice"-insects are extremely alien to me. I know that I am in fact torturing you with these letters, my dear brother, you are afraid that with such thoughts it will prove humanly and morally impossible to steer Peter's ark with purity of heart, in such a way as to please God and bring happiness to myself. But it is all right if you should be afraid: then you will pray for me more often and more fervently to the Lord Jesus and the Blessed Virgin Mary, something that your tightrope-walking, giddy brother is always in great need of …

The humanists' "liberating" thought is half-freedom, pseudo-freedom: and do they imagine to attack the Church with this pseudo-freedom? My freedom in thinking is absolute freedom, that's why it cannot refer either to the Church or to the world or to anything: it is simply (as the French ambassador likes saying about the state of Naples) "décomposition totale." And this was the decisive thought, this was the essential at this ducal fête — I sensed once and for all that thought is what prepares *dissolution* in the body of a human being; it's the organism's relentless training already in life for post-mortem decomposition, falling-to-atoms. Starting from today, for me the "absolute intellect" will not be a scholar, a poet, nor a vibrant thinker, but a decaying corpse — a carcass rotting not in the earth but in the air. And as corpses hanging on ropes are not in the habit of heroically strutting on the battlefield, so my disintegrating thoughts will not become "principles," "heresies." My inner freedom is a flowering: the flowering of the corpse from which no pride but only the humblest humility can be born, whose fundamental conviction is: to talk is either God, or no-one.

Warm embraces,

R. P. P.

III. Forest and Anecdote

1.

In the meantime Angelina lit a candle and started scrutinizing herself in the mirror. Her dress was dusty, here and there green leaves stuck to it. She was not particularly preoccupied by the fate of the world and the family — she felt that it didn't touch women, especially women like her. To her all the palaces opened, whether they were Guelf or Ghibelline; Christ and Antichrist were mere ornamental frills, like interior decoration or cutlery, or the difference between the French and German language. She was sapient enough to know that, however many times men might betray their faith, God, emperor for their love, they still believe in faiths, gods, and emperors a cut more than in their love. So if with half a day's horse ride she crossed from ducal castles sworn in to the pope to an imperial town, she did it not with the belief that she, love's expensive errant, stood *above* the battlefields of Italy, but simply, outside them — on the roads left empty by battle. What was exciting about it all was that she saw the battle from very close, more clearly and loudly than anybody else, yet had nothing to do with it: the flame of love was upright, although a thousand storms were raging around. This made kiss *logically* pure: with everyone she was in a relation merely of kiss, didn't mix with anything. And most men (as a rule, politicians or soldiers) who took her in for a while loved precisely this purity in her: that thing which was definitely not war, the chemical compound that is incapable of mixing with anything else. She was simply always the glass-clear, glass-sharp, living symbol of "it's not what was meant before." The love that she gave was not "higher" than history ("what was meant before"), neither was it "lower": it didn't cleanse men with Elysian pleasures and didn't inebriate them in animal orgies either; it was simply the mysterious pause among the other things in the world.

Her passion was acting — the last time, too, in the castle where she learnt about the pope's death, she had been playing. A mute role at that, for virtuosity: of Iole in Sophocles' *Women of Trachis*. When she looked at herself in the mirror and wiped off the dust and leaves from her dress, she was involuntarily repeating the Iole movements, like a pianist who after a concert will for a while finger the cutlery following the musical score.

Her last lover didn't please her. She went to duke Martino Montanaro's castle to pay a visit to the warrior she hadn't seen in a long time, but to her embarrassment didn't find him home — he was fighting somewhere against the imperial troops with the pope's army. Of all the masters there were only two persons left in the castle: the duke's very young brother and his somewhat older sister. The sister was a portly, blond, sluggish, phlegmatic but determined woman. She had never sinned against any of the ten commandments, but morals didn't interest her in the least: she was snub-nosed, ate copiously, wore light yellow silks and loathed all jewelry, with the sole exception of topaz. She was as prosaic as a mug of sour cream; the three poetic versions of gold sat uneasily on her: her hair radiated palely like a slumbering wheat-field toward evening, the silk of her gown resembled a god's ingle-like skin, and finally, her topazes were transparent, incredulous and all-resolving, merging weight and nothing, as if a queen's face radiated at once all the Apollonian haughtiness of power and its lesser-than-air nothingness.

The sister knew who Angelina was and why she had come. She told her that Martino was abroad, but that she should stay with her for a few days. They supped downstairs, in the guards' hall; there was no-one, all being away with the war. When wine was served (the sister drank a lot, Angelina didn't touch it), a shadowy-faced, bearded man came in: the sister introduced him as a famous painter working on her younger brother's portrait. So the brother was mentioned: Gasparro. A scrawny, pale youth who reads and stares at a Venus statue all day long; when they took a walk in the garden, the lamp was still glowing in his room and some clavichord music was heard. Angelina intuited that he must be a cretin, but the music was beautiful. She asked the painter to show her the picture; he did, and humming, with the artists' habitual incisiveness and exaggeration, analyzed the nineteen-year-old boy's psyche. How demonically deep-set his eyes, how pale his lips, how bright red the lower rim of his eyes, how much Greek he has, how well-versed he is in Latin versification, how dearly he loves flowers, with what pathos he talks even in sleep of some beautiful lady-in-waiting. "A cretin," Angelina thought to herself. Before going to bed, the sister delivered a curt laugh: "What if he had a Venus instead of the Venus statue?" Angelina took the candle and retired to the guest room. She took off a few of her clothes, then went to Gasparro's room.

She was with him until two o'clock in the morning, then the boy went out of the room in a nightshirt and left her alone. Bored, she started cleaning the Venus statuette with her handkerchief and a bit of spit: it was soiled, with that leaden, repellent mark of eunuch lips. She felt a sweet, unknown quiver in the boy's bedroom: she had seen a great many male bedrooms, but this was not one of them — it was rather like a female bedroom as men like to imagine it. She pictured herself a man, and in jest scrutinized "women's" secrets. She was grateful to the Hellenistic little teener for feeling her own femininity within her femininity for the first time — poetically, melancholically, as in a dream. She opened the window wider so that the dark tree-trunks and the moonlight-budding shrubs could catch from fleeting time her beautiful moment, as a green net catching an unexpected fish.

At that moment the boy returned with a towel: "Go. I have confessed. I no longer want you." Smiling, Angelina took the towel from him. "Is there then an absolution-tap in the bathroom?" — she asked. This may have been her first blasphemy; so far she kept superstitiously off it, as off wine. She returned to her room; around four the boy woke her up; she let him in. In the morning he took communion — it seems he had confessed again. Around noon Angelina took the brat on her horse and rode to Caretto: the boy felt as if the devil itself was carrying him off on its apocalyptic horse — but, as this was no temptation but overpowering, he sank his head in sweet resignation between Angelina's chin and shoulder. All love's cruelty and rapture were together on that small landscape: concavity, eternal valley, eros' sole Phidias conceit, and the strict, deathly triangle of the neck's muscles; and even of valleys, two kinds — the one sloping toward the breasts: the full, cushioned valley; the other arching toward the neck: the empty, hovering skin — which was the truer fountain of Venus?

In Caretto she had a company of actors: with them she played *Women of Trachis* for Gasparro's instruction, who was by then half-mad. Heracles was no more than a sniveling imbecile cripple: his death-bed, like an ornate tray with fancy meat at a regal banquet; it was served obliquely onstage, on an oval cot, with the Nessus shirt underneath: an enormous female silk dressing gown, and an identical-looking gown on Iole, the captive slave girl, to show that Heracles was killed by love. Heracles was reclining in his nakedness, powdered sky-blue and sprinkled with flowers. His wife was a withered old jade in a kitchen, among steaming pots and dough-kneading skivvies. Iole was a dancer in a leotard reaching to her hips. On the stage's left was the horrid-smelling kitchen of "morals" and "family," on the right the whimpering Heracles marinated in the enormous red dressing gown with a small toy hydra, a fluffy lion that jerked when you pushed a button, and above, on the tribune between the two, the Trachis ballerinas headed by triumphant Iole. The women brought a small waxen Hercules statue and lit it; the wax drops trickled down on the lips of supplicating Deianeira, like a sigil.

2.

With that she left Gasparro and set out toward Monte Solario. On her way she met vagrant soldiers who led her through a thick forest toward her destination. She had never enjoyed nature so much as she did now.

The soldiers' palaver was a curious mixture of political excitement and total indifference to politics; they made thus possible for Angelina to relish the buoyant, seesawing opposition between historical lie and natural truth, or true history and lying forest. Here and there the forest was so dense that all her protruding parts bumped into some natural phenomenon: her left knee into a stone, her left foot into some tepid creek (which was so shallow that when she stepped in it she had the sensation of stepping on a half-woven silk fabric on the loom), her hair got entangled in the brambles' malicious comb & the foliage caressed her with green scales, dewily chattering bracelets — when she was so much in the midst of nature, under it, as it were, diver-like, it was passing strange to hear casual talk about diplomatic intrigue. Never before had she been so *inside* something as on this secret-forbidden journey of the mercenaries: political prohibition enhanced the forest's benumbing-buzzing mystery, the artificial political map its naturalness.

It was a rebirth: a rebirth of muscles, of lungs. How significant did each step become, they had to be calculated in advance, balanced, suspended; on every half meter she received a new harmony, a nettle-staccato through her stockings, high-vaulting bines into the feather of her hat, an unexpected mud-trap under her turreted heel: suddenly she couldn't have found anything more comforting than this zigzagging forward-hesitancy. In the depth of the forest she managed to completely forget that there is a beginning and end; here only "very-midst" existed — frothing, bubbling in medias res. The air stood among the leaves in exactly such lazy patches, steaming, quivering bags as time — now they suddenly trod into warmth, as into a forbidden nest, now cold strips harshed against their faces, like withdrawing seabirds' wet wings. Silence was profound, some lower silence that could only be noted under four or five ledger lines, which people never use in this pure form in their daily lives or in their poetry, just as they never use pure alcohol: but here they drank it up greedily into their empty lungs, took it in their mouth, made of it a negative mask of their ears, wadded their clothes with its furriness. Do trees dream, or are they insuperable lucidity? On a twig, glinting bud-symmetries: so precisely that such precision presumes the acutest attention from nature — but on the other hand this too-regular setting is so immovable and motionless, so unveering from itself, that such a paralytic absolute of self-identity gives the impression of death, non-existence, vain, idle meaninglessness. Eternal changeability and hypnotic monotony — are they perhaps not the contrast that stands at the foundation of all human life?

How the color of the air kept changing: now it was entirely black, as though space were nothing but the porous shape of pitch-dark earth, an earth-ribbon, earth-dream, and earth-twilight that wrapped the flowers, waters, lizards, trees with its staid moss — in the warmly misty, velvety night only a light green leaf flashed here and there — Cranach senior used to paint in this way his reviers and paradises: uniform black beneath everything, then on it tiny gold-green half-circles or leaf-contours, veins. There is nothing more beautiful than a bit of foliage half-glimpsed in the forest's stone-deaf midst: blue, trembling mosaic cloud,

trunkless boughs — small, gold-glowing jewelry-splinters with-out
a thread; sometimes, quite close, a flower that shudders away from
our step like a bowstring, with giant stamens, propeller-shaped,
in- and outward-bending petals, on which the almost blinded eye
gropes the tremblingly reborn allegorical statue of "proximity" —
at other times quite distant foliage, beyond its height and dissolving into the air, there where the forest lets the sky's forgotten
luminosity penetrate: uncertain, grey patches, so tilted that they
project their swimming obliqueness on the whole lower forest,
on our limbs — from that one side-lying leaf-froth (it relates to
"real" foliage as tinnitus to actual ringing) we at once feel in our
entrails the globe's oblique falling over on its trajectory.

At other times air was light blue — one's body, chest, heart,
past, the gluey word- and sentence-islands of the mother-tongue
floating in the mind were all deep amethysts held up to the lamplight: the light blue consisted of reflected sky, dusty leaves, inter-
spersed-tossed bell-flowers, sweetish vegetal fatigue, filtered-to-
death sunset vapors benumbed in their net: it was a mixture of
incandescence & meekness, sharp tyranny & melting evanescence.
In such places they felt that they were walking underwater: even
the birds seemed to be fish really — the forest was so dense that
flying was out of the question, all they could manage was muffled
falling: they sank, rolled from one leaf-ball to the next like a ball
rolling toward a halt on broad, low steps.

And again the air turned bright green: as if every pebble, cloud,
and bark were a huge green lizard's gold scale; the landscape was
all smallness, density, moss, impossibly thick grass and blindly
"zzz"-ing beetles.

Angelina remembered the flight to Egypt: although the forest
was tranquility incarnate, for man this far too "objective" degree
of tranquility could cause only disquiet — the thrill of the flight.
To flee forever, even when there is nobody to chase you, and
nowhere to flee: there is *only* flight. She thought that her whole

life was mirrored in an orphic dream, but she was in fact all agog, in ecstasy.

At a certain point they reached a small lake and stopped to rest. The body of the water was extremely small, but wanted to reflect everything on its minute surface: pressed on one another lay the arsenal of motifs of the whole of nature, as in the stretto passage of a fugue. The sky's unexpected, glassy convexity, on which the perspective thrills of remote, remoter, even remoter, remotest were so concretely visible, musical scale-fashion, as the annual rings in a tree trunk; the shadow of watercress; clouds, the Moon, already fraying into the evening with its sun-red half-petal; the disconnected, cold ingle of a star or other; the pitch-black foliage of gigantic trees; the inverse minor viaduct of distant meadows; the Japanese-calligraphed bird-wings, rushedly sketched with a ballpoint pen; its own rainbow qualms; the wind's capricious mimicry; they were all in this tiny lake in the middle of the forest, as a memento, as a crowded refrain between the forest's past and to-recur darkness.

By the small lake stood one gigantic, balding oak: how convulsively its branches twisted in all directions and yet how proportionate, statuesquely classical it was all the same. The base of the trunk was whitish, it glowed sharply in the middle of the lake's black parts. In the tree's whole distribution of foliage one could distinguish some concrete human gesture: as though one scattered something in the air, every single foliage-knot was a handwave in different cardinal directions, the painter's solitary brushstroke on the canvas, but in such a way that the tree brings to mind, or rather, to our muscles, not the painting's colors but the painter's muscle movement: every foliage was a transient gift dropped into the air, a floating jewel or lace on a barely-clad, transparent, mythical nude. The person lurking inside was felt to be now a sunset-redhead Aphrodite, now a serene, bearded old gent; its knotty branches, rusty leaves, whitely bared trunk, rhythmic baldness indeed gave the composite impression of nymph lovemaking and Olympian-loveless male peace.

Its reflection was reabsorbed into reality: on the real leaves the reflection was reflected; the water's cool colorfulness, optical freedom, and sharpness trembled on its quiet boughs: in the shape of self-identity returning the kiss, twilight dew.

3.

The mercenaries were rudely distrustful: they intuited that they had to do with an uncommon, uncertain woman, who was both much more aristocratic and useless than them; her beauty exceeded their sensuous capacities, they hardly realized that she was a woman — in their occasional rough-pudic innuendoes they mostly tasted the humor of how they would treat as a woman some creature who was in fact no woman but a stranger.

On horseback again, they were talking about one of the Vatican's secular diplomats who escaped on the day of the pope's death. Angelina asked why they said "escaped" — was he threatened, had he committed a crime? They shillyshallied, like ones in the ken, although in fact they knew nothing.

Angelina was interested in this affair because the man was the only one who had ever proposed to her. He was a lily-livered milksop with soft, brushed-back fair hair, a flattened and nearly transparent, violet-bloodless sharp nose and small, pouted, sparrow beak-like lips. He always wore black with glaringly white lace collars: he picked the kisses from Angelina's mouth to his own like someone picking orders of merit from their velvet box to stick them on his breast — the whole man was a symbol of calligraphy. Angelina could imagine him turning his coat in a blunder; he could have been ashamed of his scented impotence, and in a blind moment committed some entirely maladept crime against the Vatican. What if she had been his wife? It was hard to imagine here, in the midst of the ever more colorful, ever more resonant silence's bubble. What will his fate be? The emperor will pay him, see through his lack of cunning at a first glance, and send him off to the shore of some organ-voiced sea: there he can have his lace collars ironed at heart's ease, and his conscience remorsing again and again.

As a true actress, she imagined a truly dramatic fate for him: he walks up and down, all alone, in his seaside chateau gotten for his treason, with long, yellow, pointed goatee; the whole castle is full of winding stairs (twenty–thirty becharmed, petrified sea serpents): his pallor is half the pallor of repentance, half that of envy, that the emperor had entrusted another man, some brutish soldier, with his home affairs while he was in Rome. He writes epistle after epistle to the emperor, on paper paler than his countenance, offering his services, to which now and again a cursory answer comes from the protégé general (Latin pleasantries mixed into Swabian insults) — and at the same time he confesses and expiates, tightening the noose of his grief around the neck of some poor Dominican dogsbody. The stairs are always the best confessional, and since the whole castle is the vertical tissue of creeper-like stairs proliferating, accordion-fashion, on top of another, you can confess anywhere: the priest stands three steps higher and the count, below him. In the meantime he is plotting against the life of his military rival, so that if his repentance was unsuccessful, at least the *fullness* of sin should obliterate his sin. He gets to know the simple-minded, beautiful wife of a fisherman — he watches her for hours as she scrapes off the fishes' scales with her dirty knife: behind her, the sea's rabid Nordic blue, on her hands the scales' broken, bloody silver, his nose is filled with the sour, lent, rotting fish-smell. He sends off the fisherman and takes her to the castle; the poor woman is dazzled by the brilliance and refinery. After much toil, the count manages to knock a misshapen child out of this illicit affair — the woman can't give birth in the blazon-clouded, blazon-showery, vast bedrooms, they have to take her down to the fisherman's hut, she goes into labor underway, the midwife is nowhere to be found, she is lying sweating, barking, blood-drenched and half-dead under a tree; for a while the count hops around her impotently in his silk hat, snow-white lace collar, dead butterfly-shaped, oversize shoe buckles, man-size courtier's ashplant, then leaves her all alone. Locked up in his bedroom, he is waiting for the death news. To his greatest surprise both mother and child survive. He sends the child (the cradle of all kinds of neuroses) to Rome, with the intention to make a priest out of him and so expiate his crime. The son turns into a savage, ascetic hermit, the father never sees him, it is the poor woman he sends to Rome every second year. The woman is driven insane between her two families: her husband is lordliness, her son, holiness. O, you foolish, blind mothers — Angelina thought, imagining the "countess" in the rented rooms of filthy little Italian inns, as she clutches her husband's letters on her way to her son, with the intoxicating conviction that she is the humble handmaid of the most ravishing and most mysterious destiny. The boy is a student of theology: a morose, splenetic, unfriendly teenager whose self-abnegations please neither God nor Satan, being merely the clockwork-like ticking-on of a crippled body, born to suffering. His father's Ciceronian epistles present him with fantasies of martyrdom; he had fantastic fish engraved into his sigil blazon. Some Italian charlatan deciphers the old count's cherished dream and proceeds to milk him: in florid words he eulogizes his son's saintliness, what miracles are rumored, how fond the pope is of him, how he preaches, how he turns over the supporters of the emperor to back up the pope. After plundering a few legendries, he gets to the point: the son wants to have a marvelous new church built, but it costs money. Money! This the swindler also tells viva voce to the poor mother: her own statue will stand among Roman church columns thrusting skyward like artesian fountains, surrounded by St. Peter's bounty of fish, made of glass: the mother of the pope-to-be! The poor woman completely loses her head: at night she dreams of fish, of Gospel fish as they swim, like a thousand crystal-glittering wicks, among a half-built cathedral's budding columns: the prophecy of her son's papacy is glaringly obvious. The father sends the money, but his rival finds the charlatan's letters. The rival wants to put out the count, because through his son he incites to insurgence against the emperor in Rome; but the count, too, is prepared to go to any extreme — his son is going to be a saintly pope, this blinds his tortured conscience: before his rival has the chance to plot against him, he poisons the emperor's protégé. Shortly afterward the news reaches him that his son abandoned the priesthood and founded some heretic sect, for which he was dragged before the Inquisition.

4.

She felt a curious lust to ruin in her imagination the man who had asked for her hand in marriage: in the forest's all-powerful silence the histrionic intrigues and impotent dreams got a sharp coloring. As the setting sun's yellow, melting everything into miracle, covered the lake, like a book's left page covering the page on the right, she felt that perhaps, after all, the Deianeira caricature that she had showed to Gasparro was unjust; she imagined the wives of these simple mercenary soldiers and of these pictures she composed the portrait of the poor fishwife going slowly insane in the lordly mésalliance. For a few seconds she felt in herself the mystical rhythm of demos: poverty and motherhood, which alternated like night and day, ebb and tide. Perhaps the difference between a flowered-to-death maternal womb and hers is the same as the difference between a washerwoman's rough hands and her own, sterilely manicured ones. Whom should she believe? The Danaida-lilting secrets of nature, of the lonely forest, the soldiers' and diplomats' motley fictions, or the laboring and starving mass of the poor? To go into labor? When one can bathe, naked, in this warm nymph-lake? To fight? When sweetly, murmuringly good-for-nothing eros hovers above the lake's gilded title page? What does she have to do with the contrast between blunt-nailed, dull Deianeiras and pathetic mothers splaying into holiness?

5.

The painters' bathing nymphs came to her mind. Bored, she cleaned her shoulder-length red leather gloves. Nymphs in a lake: the fusion on landscapes of infinite pudicity and infinite freedom. Every single bathing nymph radiated her essential being-*non*-Susanna: the security that no-one is, no-one can be watching them. If these pudic girls, covering their bodies with Vestal frenzy, can feel so free, can be so naked and playful: it means that they have to be infinitely distant from all male and human gazes. Stripping naked in a room, or at the enclosed pond of a castle's gardens, already seems daring: doors can be forced, walls can be climbed. Even more so if someone drops off all their veils in open nature without a blush: how enthralling it is for the spectator! The foundation of the game is this duality: the absolute possibility, unhinderedness of the apparition of naked women, and against this, the mythological girls' perfect certainty that here they can be almost forever alone, unseen. And the spectator witnesses that which is the very glaring, suggestively incandescent, velvety-humming, eternal unwitnessedness: they see the invisible.

If we look at the landscape, the trees' dream-silver, the sunset's violet kiss on every ankle, its procuress-finger on the ever more tautened string of evening desire, the waters, the grove of ruined Corinthian columns — then we slowly believe the painter that no mortal can ever glimpse this landscape, this true core of

nature, and such fairy-tale valley of the supernatural: and yet we
see it, the painter sees it; the painting's whole raison d'être is, that
we see and uncover it. Nakedness and perspective: nude, alone
not on a bed but on the whole planet — instead of an intimate
boudoir, an intimate empire. And these bathing women always
bathe at some preposterous hour, all their gestures trumpet the
fact that they don't need to bathe at all: neither for hygiene, nor
for erotics or sport. Somehow the landscape converts them: they
become the ineluctable crystals of landscape-dream, its side-
product, simple counterweights in structural balance, and although they were created by such primitive technical need, they
are the unattainable embodiment of amorous beauty and bliss.
The gigantic trees, which become infinite and unfathomable
because the naïve painter had drawn each of their leaves separately, countably (an impressionist painter's foliage will always be
more finite and shabby than the vegetation of a miniaturist or
a contemporary of Poussin), breathe such a mystery of solitude
around the pink nudes, that one indeed has the impression that
these women have no inkling of love: they, too, mean solitude in
an inhuman butterfly form — and yet their forsakenness, ignorance of love prods the viewer to a rape of the Sabines. For man
is seduced to the point of madness by two types of women: those
who want love with the greedy clairvoyance of passion, with all
the flaming objectivity of bodily experience, with all the blindness of childish love-faith — and those who know nothing at all
about love, are sexual tabula rasa, but whose absolute ignorance
glows with some blood-boiling warranty, that if ever they learn
what love is, they will want nothing but that. To this latter type
the classicist painters' nymphs belong, whose life Angelina would
have liked to emulate in those few moments of dusk.

6.

One of the mercenaries told jokingly that his wife bathed the dead in Rome, perhaps she herself would wash and prepare the great Pius for his last journey. (No, she cannot imitate the nymphs, the waters willed otherwise.) In a cellar a couple of sturdy women are washing the pope in a shallow tub, so the only point of his body where water covers him is his sunken belly, his arched chest gets underwater only when they splash it — and even then the left and right water-threads barely touch under the ribs before falling back again. The cellar vaulting is low, everything wills the horizon of death: the pope himself shows only his vast nostrils and bushy eyebrows. Above, at the cellar door, a little blond officer stands, young, arrogant, with feet planted wide apart, and in his boredom trails his riding whip in the grooves of the iron door's blazon up against the first obstruction. Now and then a captain comes to ask if they are ready, then the little officer shouts something to the women below, who cannot help wondering how much the pope is like any other man, and how he is unlike any other man. When the body is brought up on the winding stairs, there are a great many soldiers at the door and among them, trembling priests, young monks, captive cardinals. They are bringing up the body on the narrow staircase: why are they taking it upstairs? To throw him into the depths again at the burial, like God's great, damned seed? The whole scene is like the raising of Lazarus, but at the end in the cellar's opening there appears a corpse. The soldiers are clumsy with the body, the women are handy and strong, their arms jump up and down around the half-covered naked body like black porpoises around the sinking ship's ribs which glow with eerie light: as they climb up, the pope's head now disappears and only his naked footsoles stick, white, into the night; now his tousled brow rises again and his belly caves in — as if it were made of wax and being melted by a candle, like the Heracles statue in Angelina's mime-show, or made of paper and starting to soak apart in water. Every now and again the soldiers' torches drip on the freshly washed body, the women meekly protest, as if someone had trampled a flower in their garden. Above, they are waiting with excitement for the reversed resurrection: a few priests had lighted their candles and are praying on their knees.

Does she have a right to the life of the nymphs when she hears the voices of those distraught candles, like the buzz of an insect caught in her ear? There is something horrifying in the dead body's "expressive" gestures as it is rolled left and right, and which now express nothing: for hours perhaps he had wriggled impotently, as the poison started working on him, twisting all his strength around an armchair's left armrest, then unfurling it slowly, like a thread trascined by a dropped ball of string — now, in death, at once it makes passionate gestures: lashing out left and right with its arm, throwing back its head like a fury, then tossing it on the chest again, like one tossing a corner of bread next to the plate; it bends its knee in acute angle, dropping its soles, like a sigil, coldly on a stair or other; it is gesticulating like a mummer whose role is done. In one moment Angelina felt that there is nothing in the whole world but this large corpse schlepped up-stairs on the basement stairs — and in the next moment, that it was madness to talk about the dead, for this forest knows nothing about death: all death is hypocrisy, the hallucination of fools.

7.

The water stirred: in the mirror's unbroken proportion the black shadow of a small fish flickered. That is what we should catch, that was the only imaginable problem — she almost felt it, first the vain clutch's strange, hardly believable emptiness, then the captured fish's icy S-wriggling in her hand, with such persuasive power of the rapid succession of movements, signaling escape, that she should finally be convinced that a fish belongs in the water, not in the hand. The convulsive fins and tail, the expiring gills cry out for water with such infinite impatience that Angelina believes: catching it was a mathematical problem. To see a fish out of water: to watch our going insane with a lucid mind.

8.

Did they perhaps set free the inmates of the Inquisition's prisons in Rome? Some poseur with a liberating, haloed bunch of keys, or a cynical halberdier, drunk rioter? Curiously, the ones in there didn't want at all to play at catching fish and throwing them back in the water: they are old, young, fanatics and doubters. The emperor's party expects them to kowtow; the poseur expects the Latin ode (salvator veritatis oppressae... ha ha!), the mercenary the ransom money from the well-heeled relatives. But the two freed heretics rush to the pope's corpse and cover it with kisses; they regret their revolts and errors; there is only one young madman who runs upstairs, barefoot, into the Inquisition's courtroom, where a couple of frightened cardinals mutter together, red tonsure poultices above their grey heads; the madman leaps on the papal throne, swears and blasphemes with foaming mouth, the priests watch paralyzed or scurry up and down, until a soldier bursts in, knocks down the madman, and hangs him on the chandelier's thick iron chain.

The huge armchairs lie scattered about: there is nothing ghostlier than those giant rectangular chair backs with their embroidered blazons or icons; upright steles, accusing, irrefutable shadows, fate's cruel extras. At once they appear unmistakably anthropoid: the armrests spell out comfort, their undulated form with almost sodomite fawning, as if every one of them were a paradisiac serpent come to life. The hollowing-in of the padded cushion evokes the humorous form of the most compromising human bodily part — while being superhuman: the chair's back is the savage stylization of the man who sits on it (or rather, who will perhaps never again sit on it), his knocking into an almost smothering and meaningless symbolic space — as a large ring cools a hand into a heaven-bound relic, so these large rectangular chair backs plagiarized the whole body into death's lofty stiffness. Light enters the room behind the chair backs, making them appear even blacker. The chandelier swings wildly: the emaciated body is perhaps swinging exactly above the documents which anatomize, with judiciary pedantry and protocol dryness, the pros and cons of his teachings — the spellbound magistrates stare, with bulging or covered eyes, at the question: what connects the objective legal procedure, dogmatic precision, to this hanged madman? Is it worth submitting to the trial, weighing things sentence by sentence, conjunction by conjunction, when at the bottom of heresy lurked this madness, this blood-throated Medusa? But the height of torment is that the magistrates kicked into a corner feel that madness and brutality are not the distinctive privilege of the heretic but simply, of history, of life, of all complicated politics, moreover, of all simple, basic human action, too: in human action, if it is action and movement, there glows, like a potentiality that can flare into reality at any moment, perfect dementedness and perfect cruelty.

9.

Did they perhaps forget entirely about the little Sandro Fermo in the midst of the tumult? This Sandro was something like Gasparro: pale-faced, with a thin appetite, eternal Eros-victim, without the slightest possibility of escaping his predetermined role. And the one who wanted to marry him through thick and thin was the only woman of whom Angelina had ever been jealous. She, Flora, was very beautiful, but somehow didn't manage to get married.

She represented that mysterious (or for Angelina at least, forever exciting) form of beauty which is equally inclined toward coy, pink homeliness and violet-mendaciously flaming demonics: in an opalescent mirror it discloses the "homely virgin's" incandescent-expiring, eternal sadism, and the blood-bathed lesbian maenad's eternal thirst for idyll, her babyish, philistine homesickness. Of course, these moral contrasts perhaps only depend on a peculiar blending of powder and make-up: when she compared the opposition between demon and bourgeois Vesta to the opposition between violet and pink, she was not citing a metaphor but evoking complexion and shade of face blush. There are women who can quite miraculously find (but then perhaps their complexion helps them) that ambiguous shade in make-up that leads from slight, pudic blushing to provocative flirtation: precisely because there is so little make-up (of course, here "little" has nothing to do with "ladylike conduct") it is so provocative — a lot of make-up, woman painted into a mask, does no more correspond to the awakening of the first erotic possibility but rather, to desire prepared into barbarian mythology and loud caricature — but tender make-up is still the poetic symbol of puberty's first, half-onanizing, hardly social erotic thrill, which draws attention not so much to the woman's objective reality as to the greater reality of positive pleasures to be concretized in the boy's body (at this age the erotic-tragic opposition between woman as absolute dream, poetry, irreality, and medically crude, primitive, mechanically direct and "ready" phallus blossoms) — as against which the veiled-off woman already alludes to conventional, long received amorous gymnastics, its half-believing, but mostly forced mysticism. In her hair, too, there was some kind of "sisterly" softness: her haircut was a mixture of childish, fumbling, naively over-decorating vanity and "great"-womanly nonchalance. In the quavering balance between plumpness and thinness, too, there alternated sit-at-home roundness and freely-roaming Artemis' skinny

line-and-bone chastity: already in her girlhood (if these wicked
"respectable" women had indeed ever been girls) she had something characteristically young-womanly about her, some warm,
housewifely early aging, a form and degree of prosaicalness that
covers every muscle-flower and muscle-leaf with its strange, tepid
dew. Her nose, mouth, ears, hands were all one cunning shade
bigger than they should have been, preserving all the meanwhile
the skin's little-girlish transparency, the refinedness of forms:
they were "*large* miniatures," "*large* small objects," in the strict
sense of the word, and this was decisive in the representation of
the dual portrait of quiet girlishness and vampire-leaning wom-
anliness. One never quite knew if her bored gestures betrayed
the idling-away of some sensuous impatience, or on the contrary,
of end-of-day fatigue accumulated with matronly handiwork.

Angelina's beauty was its fundamental opposite, or at least
something essentially different. Her beauty was "glaring æsthetics," the equally intensive superlative of woman as natural phenomenon and as artistic miracle, while Flora was the superlative
of the beauty of *love-making*: her beauty was love's dynamic beauty, beauty in *action*, spliced together from poetry and awkward
materials, pitted against Angelina's paralyzing statics. Around
her face always hovered something that was never to be seen on
Angelina: the sentimental novel; Angelina was logical and frenzied gothic incarnate: she was "the beautiful woman" in all its
Aquinas pedantry, colourful and plastic accoding to the whim of
color-splashing wood sculptors; Flora, of whom she was jealous
precisely for this reason, was: pudicity, pastel-ethics, the perversion of tears, the whole of Greuze. Angelina's eyes were green,
those of Flora, grey: complete with the ostentatious, Circean
mist of melancholia *&* sorrow.

10.

Flora was somehow left on the shelf; her younger sisters were all married off and by the time her turn came, both she and the men got bored of their dances, she soured a bit and also got impoverished. She lived with her mother who harrassed her to marry from morn to night. Sandro Fermo worshipped this Flora who was just about to start wilting; she of course wasn't in the least inclined toward him, but for want of a better alternative would have consented to marry him. But the boy was a non-entity. At that time they again created lots of new jobs in the Vatican, which could be bought at various prices, and Flora made up her mind that for the sake of her dying mother she would gather the money for a medium-priced position. Fermo's parents were have-nots and swam in tears for weeks on end when they learnt that Flora offered to scrape the money together: all day every day the two shaky old parents spoke of nothing else to helpless little Sandro but that he must needs thank Flora for her self-sacrifice. Sandro was a dutiful son and had a good memory: he kept thanking her. When now and again Flora paid a visit to his parents, out of gratitude they soaked her nicest clothes with their thankful tears. Flora suffered from the role-playing but was past the age when this could have caused major ethical convulsions — she was twenty-nine, and at that age all girls dull, or revolutionarily romp into, the self-same flat moral insanity. Her dying mother had some money on the side, but would not spend a penny of it on husbands — she wanted to leave it to a poor priest's younger brother, for allegedly a saint asked it of her in her dream, & this small fortune could be the foundation for the poor boy's ecclesiastical career, and of the flowering to European fame of a ramshackle little south Italian bishopric. Flora spent long evenings with the priest by the light of one crooked candle, by the filthiest & swampiest bank of the Tiber, to beg him persuade her mother out of this hallucination & renounce the inheritance. Of course the priest didn't need the money at all, but he didn't know, didn't dare state, that her mother's hallucination was only hallucination. What is more, in a short while he started hallucinating himself: this was all that Flora's erroneous strategy yielded. She thought of stealing her mother's money and to eventually lead her husband to her deathbed: the pope's "first lord of the bed-chamber" or "upper master of audiences" or "serving college sec-retary" (these were the jobs up for grabs). Later she ran left and right to relatives, bearing a thousand humiliations for a man who meant nothing to her, for a dying, maniacal old hag who wouldn't give a penny to help her. How many times she panted the air in front of too slowly opening gates full of why, why — ? Sandro spent every afternoon and evening at Flora's: lately in two with the dying crone, while Flora was begging in some faraway palace. Sandro, too, would have liked to escape — he had long forgot-ten about Flora, love, everything: his head was filled with this dying, reeking old harridan who chattered non-stop from four to nine in the evening. At nine Flora would arrive, often soaked to the skin, because they let her stand in the rain like a statue and started exposing her financial projects: credits, interests, mort-gages, loans without guarantor, alms. For whom, why was she doing that? — Sandro asked, his stomach still turning from the old woman's vomit that out of politeness ("you must be attentive and nice with dear Flora's nice mama" — his parents parroted before he left) he had wiped up half an hour earlier. For whom, why? — Flora echœd above her bills, additions and subtractions, still shivering from the rain and the relatives' affectedness. If her mother were to die now: wouldn't she & Sandro run apart from one another, happily, in the bliss of freedom? Amor, amor: in the dark garden of the villa a statue of Venus stood where she waited, she knocked it over into the mud, so her dress got splashed all over — she looked at these mud stains now as a warrior looking on her wounds and gushing blood: it soothed her. "Why aren't you more attentive, brush up your dress, go!" — her mother rattled in one breath. Sandro's parents moved outside Rome into a small house they inherited and commended him into Flora's care. For the first time in his life, Sandro was staying without his parents: in his giddiness he started trafficking with the damsels of inns and pubs. Flora wasn't much troubled inwardly by this state of affairs: she bought a huge key for Sandro's door and locked him up.

It was this laughable key that brought together Angelina & Flora one evening: Flora was constrained to pay a visit about some business to her half-mad uncle in the house on the Tiber banks and lost the key on her way there; Angelina passed by and found it. They talked well into midnight on the riverbanks: by the filthy black river the white key almost glowed on Flora's lap, like a wick. Angelina decided that she would somehow raise the missing three thousand gold ducats for Sandro's position, what is more: for the same money would gift him with a far better position and title.

11.

Around this time Angelina was on good terms with a Jew who had fled to Rome from the Inquisition in Portugal, and who was financially connected to the Vatican. He lived in a secluded villa rather far from Rome, in the middle of a forest, pitted among scattered crucifixes and freshly-planted Madonnas. He paid Angelina exceedingly well. He wouldn't light a lamp even in his chamber which opened onto the courtyard: only the small coals in the fireplace illuminated the room. His favorite pastime was to try on, in front of Angelina, the great many masks he had used on his flight from Lisbon to Rome: dazed by this histrionic feat, Angelina, too, tried them on. The Jew was always cold — many times did Angelina stand in a shift perforated with a hundred flower contours, and in some black-bearded, red-nosed mask by the window (the mask had a small tag with the exact date and place: "worn from Dec. 8th to 13th betw. Lunago and Montebarro" — it was quite a pedantic diary), while the Jew was shivering in a thick fur-trimmed coat, almost crouching into the fireplace. This secretive Jew had a decisive word in the distribution of those positions. Angelina didn't whisper a word about Sandro, simply asked for the money and gave it to Flora. If they ordered a blazon to be made in haste for little Sandro Fermo, it should include a huge silver key, a black mask, and a pillar of coins, Angelina thought. Of course the 3,000 ducats were again in the Jew's hands in a day, for he was the Vatican's secret banker and the upper highest distributor of the position fees, their airer and layer-to-rest. Angelina again asked for the 3,000, had the Jew's effigy made after a stolen portrait, and after a night of banqueting put it on in the morning in the bed, so that the fugitive, hypochondriac banker nearly died from the shock. And he immediately left the little villa-refuge for good.

And now the pope was dead: Sandro could barely enjoy his new title and his marriage (if it took place at all) — isn't his fate a key again, this time not Flora's but of the emperor's mercenaries? She imagined his pale face, reflecting total forlornness, as he gazed down from a slit tower window on the pope's half-wrapped body, hauled away, locked up, and far away from all help.

12.

She wondered why now, as she was standing by the lake, strangely disquiet, *young* boys came to her mind, young lovers, loitering among the dark blue shadows of childhood? Her beauty, reflected in the water, was complete. The two black wings of her shoulders, resting right & left, warm like moss sinking into the evening, and almost resonant, like the twisted depth of mysterious black shells; the small cut of her dress, at whose point, instead of a brooch, a white patch of her neck and breasts appeared — although her body was smooth, on this point (because of its luminosity) it was like a blooming flower, its petals half shut and crumpled, half wide unfurled-apart; her arms were thin and sharp, as if the main nerve that runs from shoulder-blade to wrist were wrapped around, funnel-fashion, by a single big, black, slender leaf, as on some flower-stems; at her wrist, a handkerchief was somehow stuck into the tight sleeve: fuzzy fruit at the end of a stringy bine, which the wind will immediately take off, like the dandelion's noiseless tuft; her hips, which were so narrow to seem not the meeting, in one circle, of two semicircles arching toward one another, but two circles sectioning each other: the right hip-bone reached beyond the left one, and the left hip-bone reached beyond the right one; under her hips the long skirt, tight down to her ankles and down below suddenly scattered, widening to foliage, like a pack of cards dropped to the ground, or a slender tree-trunk's vertigo-ridden, hypochondriac roots, crawling apart in all directions: her beauty, pride, loneliness, was indeed directed *not* at children but at men — why does she then think continously of those pale eros-apprentices? Gasparro, Sandro?

IV. The Youth

The corporeal form, brethren, is transient and what underlies the arising of corporeal form, that too is transient. Sensations and feelings are transient, the sense organs are also transient. Perceptions, mental formations, and consciousness — all these, arising from what is transient, cannot but be transient. All distinctions are transient, all things lack essence. (From the Buddha's teachings)

1.

And the little Cugnani, whose last letter she still carried in her handbag? Was it the forest's loneliness, the Moon stealing like honey into night's transparent chalice, which wanted to suck Angelina's coquettish stamen-curves clean of death's honey: did that protect and glorify those brats pining away in love's misery? How did that letter speak — how spoke Cugnani?

… On that morning I was sitting at the window, looking on the garden where I had courted my bride. That night it had rained, the tree-crowns were cleaner and brighter than usual, but also more tousled and tattered from the wind's bites: my childhood virginity must have been like that — a white banner, but in tatters. I have known you for two days, Angelina; I have known my bride for three years. And tomorrow is my wedding. I did court my bride! I don't know if you had ever been courted, and if yes, by whom and how; but I don't know if courtship consists of anything but tiresome bickering which nips in the bud the slightest remnant of the gift for happiness and desire. At the beginning I strove to reach some form of happiness with my bride, but later all desire for that expired in me. My love life became one continuous self-defence against à-propos miseries, insults, insensitivities, delusions. If we had made an appointment for a walk, I woke up imagining: she would not come; if she shows up, she would faint in my arms and I would be unable to help her in the middle of the woods; or that I should die all of a sudden; that a stranger should jump out of a bush, take my bride by the hand, and the two of them would walk out on me, laughing; that when I kiss her for the first time, a riot starts in my bowels with all manner of disgusting and laughable sounds and smells; when I want to make love to her, I lay her half-naked back on a hideous toad. If against all odds she came to the meeting and nothing of the above came to pass, I couldn't even rejoice, for my protective visions against deception were so strong that reality seemed merely an awkward, barely noticeable fata morgana as compared to the determinate plasticity and blinding colors of my self-mortifying dreams.

The cold smell of rain came in through the window as into a suicidal lung, and I could hear my bride stirring in the room above me — she got up from the bed, clambered back into daylight from the unpleasant folds of covers, cushions, and sheets, as a deaf silkworm climbing into the half-gnawed mulberry leaf. I felt only gratitude toward her, not some affected, posture-ascetic gratitude for having perfectly extirpated happiness, but sincere, childish gratitude for having estranged me, perhaps forever, from happiness. Unhappiness, aphrodisiac nothing, became my companion, as comfortable, warm, and familiar as my old clothes: if sometimes smaller joys flickered around me, I started shivering with cold and hiccupping in the most bodily sense of the word, so transcendentally different did their substance seem, and I ran with constrained philistine neighbourly love back into the atmosphere of familiar barrenness that my bride exhaled. I knew the fiascos of love, both bodily and psychic, as a pianist knows his instrument: it fanned my vanity that I, too, should know, professionally so to say, some craft (is pain an art or an industry?).

A young man is not a body and not a soul but the will's great cancer, inflammation, predestined to happiness: he has no heart and veins, doesn't eat and doesn't sleep — if he loves a girl, even his most hidden, most primitive-zoological, dumbmost internal organs identify with the vision of the girl; denying all biology, medical definitions, this body is the buffoon or demon of spirituality: it wants nothing but to see one woman's image, forever — its navel, spine, blood clotted in the heart ventricles are all: eyes: and the eye is not body. It's easy for a woman to overpower something that is mere thirst for vision. I managed to stifle, for good, my organism's frenzied hunger for sight.

It was at that point that I got to know you. I knew well that you could be had by anyone who pays the price, but love knows no difference between faithful and unfaithful, hypocritical and sincere, honourable or dishonorable woman; never once had I quarreled with my bride because she might have been unfaithful to me. When I looked into your eyes, in which all the darkness of my garden (*of the leaves one by one*: your every glance, every slow oar-movement of the lids in the otherwise unrippled lake of sight, was one more black leaf, undesiring desire, the shoot of velvety indifference) merged with the greyness of some unknown, distant-to-the-point-of-self-irony, *&* nevertheless certain goodness — could then the question even occur to me, if you were "dishonorable," or "a saint"? When I was standing in the hall by the stairs, watching you from afar, while you were talking with my father and other high-born gents, all I felt was that from you one can receive such a form and flavor of happiness that I know not: you are happiness itself, one doesn't need to do anything with, or for you, you don't have to be staged separately, designed with dull male-fatigue into the willed drama's willed act — for your presence is happiness. My bride completely lacked this "horrible présence": between the two of us something always had to *happen*. That you were some sort of miracle and fateful in my life, I knew from the fact that when I looked at you (having no inkling that you, too, might be watching me) I felt as if in a second I had caught some deathly disease: I had dined a short while ago, but all the food nearly escaped into the air through my pores, and my stomach, which a moment earlier felt heavy, suddenly became so empty, shriveled, and wilted, that this unexpected emptiness tilted my balance. I fell against a servant.

You are either clever or not: if you are clever you won't consider it "tasteless" that for me fate always reveals itself in the form of such stomach-vacuuming, such annihilation of the entrails and appetite — it basically means that for me, *happiness is essentially an ascetic phenomenon*, happiness means total detachment from the earth, from life, in a matter of seconds: my body suddenly shuts off any biological function, my ears want no more sounds, even the most marvelous music nauseates them and makes them ring, my hands shake and shrink from the touch of any object, especially cutlery. My body dried up, my gullet became a rusty rattle, I couldn't swallow, for that, too, is some "inward" movement into the body, and my body wouldn't suffer it now. I was excluded from myself.

Two things were certain: this was the great pathological flowering of happiness, and it was something that I *cannot* bear. No more could I defend myself against it, of course: whether I accept or refuse it, I can be only unhappy. My body was so desiccated, my joints so worn-out, that I had to crawl into the nearest servant's room to drink a sip of water. The servants knew that the young master is very agitated when he drinks a lot of water; now, too, they were half-jokingly, half-seriously discussing my hapless boozing. My gullet stopped, my mouth was brimming with water that I couldn't press into my body. At last (with a screech of old locks and picklocks) it turned and as if through a gaping wound, water poured into me. At such times I felt water not with my throat but with my skin; my entire body was a skin bag containing nothing else but air and water. This was my baptism into death. The water was cold, so I faltered back to the hall all ashiver. I caught the last of the farewells. You suddenly turn to me, pull off your glove, reach out your hand, press mine, look at me at length, then go down the stairs to your boat. You took off your glove for me? It was as if you had been naked — your glove was in itself an evening dress with a huge lace collar, sapphire choker, with veil-like, shiny-shadowy finger-stockings. It was then that I said (there was no way you could hear me, I was so hoarse), "From you I could be happy."

Have you ever intuited the unavoidable paradox of men, Angelina, that they always take the principal argument for life from the foretaste of death; from melancholia swelling in an instant to an avalanche, the proof of happiness; from the stifling night of impossibility, from murderous amorous absurdity, the positive effigy of reality?

I knew that I am not like other men: for three years I have trained myself, with excessive logical punctiliousness and emotional cruelty, to go off the mere imagining of happiness, so my organism is particularly incapable of bearing even smaller joys — but I feel that, even if not at such a pathological degree as mine, everyone has this susceptibility to the only trustworthy marker of happiness: death.

You stepped into your boat: all your gestures and glances, all your clothes were so *inside* me, and all the oars, servants, evening sunrays were so *outside*! At that moment I felt that I've never had true impressions before: the objects, colors, sounds which I put into verse, and which I played apart on the cembalo, were but external wallpaper on me, loose masks which you peeled off with one caress. But you, you thrusted yourself into me: inside, into the place of my stomach. This simple bodily alternative sounded loudly in me: instead of stomach, eyes on the inside — instead of feeding, sight. This is the most basic opposition of life: frenzied contemplation that wants to see only, and the biological functions willing to live, moving in the earth for earth. Curiously, love seems to be rather "in the earth for earth," that is, a materialist phenomenon of life, for its goal is the ensuring of life's continuity, and yet it always provokes the most unlivable emotions, chasing us to the Styx boundary of death, first and foremost with this "reductio ad *oculum*," as it narrows-enriches our whole existence to this inward looking. And it is this looking which indeed has truly, bodily inner interiority: desire is nothing but the unbearable numbness that comes from the stabilizing of the inward-turned eyeball. I often speak with priests, pardon me if I lapse into Latin, you surely know the language too: identitas imagines et mortis — this is love's optical, fundamental law. Every single nerve concentrates its power so much on continued seeing you in imagination that the organism has no time and resources left for anything else.

When you took off your glove and all of a sudden your fingers were inside mine (how marvelous is such a handshake: that deathly-lifelike mix of the fingers' restless, personal contours, and the palm's warm, animal-amorphous mass — the fingers are so human by excellence, so spiritual as forever-meaningful eyes, while the palm is so prehistoric-animal, only-material by excellence as an anus), then I felt first and foremost goodness, blessing, grace, something that the Madonna & the apostles must have felt when the Holy Ghost came to them: the annihilating suggestion of some higher ethos. But the tragedy (if you will, we can call it comedy) of goodness is that, while one can certainly not live without goodness, one can't live in goodness either. History without goodness (that is playing out around me here, among Venice, the Turks, the pope, and France) is unbearable nonsense, posturing and beastliness, discredited heroism, the automatism of business and inertia — but if I imagine the Ghost's bulky celestial pigeon in the middle of the Ducal Palace, as it makes the Doge's head swirl with its feather-shedding inspiration, then the Doge will faint without a word, or fly into a monastery, or downright die, provided he doesn't go mad: there is something so absurd in the divine that man cannot bear it (heresy!).

I have once painted the descent of the Holy Ghost, in memory of your redeeming handshake! The Madonna is reclining by a lake, her bronze-red, wet hair tramples into the earth the surrounding, ornate little flowers, above her head the Ghost flares with the celestial intrigue of goodness, as a poppy fading out in a dying man's last glance: gratia plena — she's nearly turned into a corpse. Around her, the apostles: Peter, dropping his nets, around him dying stranded fish scattered on the ground with wriggling tails and lashing fins, he himself crumpled up like an unread papyrus scroll in the fire — above his head the red Ghost is the melting sigil. In the air, an unknown hour and tempest: neither day nor night, neither summer nor autumn — one fruit is overripe, on the next twig the buds are barely shooting. One of the apostles is preaching on a rock, in a tongue unknown even to himself, in his eyes, madness and despair, he knows that he is lost for himself, life is over on this earth.

Then what is the earth for, if it can't be borne with or without ethics? What is the body & woman for, if we can't live without her and can't live with her? Probably the fault lies with my sensitivity: for me, goodness is something so femininely exotic that the moment it appears, it turns into an illness in me. O, how I'd like to relish to the last drop, to the bottom, the pathological cup of goodness which you have offered to me without asking, without a stuggle, Angelina: all its moral, physiological, psychological, æsthetic shades in a way that befits the young, the clever, and the dead! In every woman's bodily beauty and facial physics the secret relation of beauty and goodness is the main prodder: unwittingly one feels female beauty to be the most ethic-less, standing at the greatest conceivable distance from the possibility of goodness —

but in its becharming, seductive impact one nevertheless finds some kind of moral satisfaction; in the fact that woman is so annihilatingly attractive he finds a moral phenomenon.

To eradicate individual life for a mere vision of woman: there is something vertiginously just and ethical in it, in spite of all its deceitfulness. Here more than anywhere else it is revealed whether "meaningless" morals or the meaningful one is the true one: doesn't the ethical radiance of love culminate precisely in man's feeling that here any morals is mere hallucination, at most a metaphor, here every feeling is mania, here absolutely everything is swindle, albeit to a divine degree — and precisely this all-permeating irrationality becomes the true ethos, true reason: it is worth sacrificing everything for the great beauty because somehow, according to one of our minds, it is not worth doing anything for it — morals (or more precisely: moral atmosphere, the goodness-*landscape*) is for me always the unwitting logics-mask of utter meaninglessness: the momentary reciprocal mirroring of life's idiotic and divine face.

What was the most mysterious in your green (black? blue? brown? grey?) eyes resting on me: this unexpectedly petal-opening goodness on your demonic body's lean branch, or your true, womanly demonicity emanating from this goodness *and it alone* (and not from your body's beauty, or the scarlet romanticism of your profession)? I think it was the latter. In that instant it was clear that there is some kinship in Deo between the guardian angel's celestial caritas and lesbian females' sensuousness: in both, the widened fish-mouth of love-hunger opens toward the sibling. In your handshake, etiquette couldn't be distinguished from shamelessness, poetry's venom from blasé prose: your movement, the pulling of your glove, was so much the form of forms as a dance move, but doesn't the human heart throb stronger at the height of ritual: shedding its body-*mask*, finally unveiling its mask-*body* — wasn't that movement the infinite of simplicity:

as it started from a shadowy wave of your shoulder & with your skin, it reached my skin — so that, because of its simplicity, the world became empty around you.

The water, as its fish-bodied plein-air sent a babbling flash, now and again, into the hallway's carpeted, motley-windowed dusk, was complicated & incoherent; the boats' swinging needle-points superfluous, more than what and how much they ought to have been; the stairs, which up to that point had meant for me the most puritanical architectural minimum, now appeared stiflingly complicated, full of deafening, nauseating side-noises.

The relation of goodness and nudity! Was this handshake so simple for being a last, parallel ripple, flutter-breathed in my direction, of the distant whirlpool of goodness? Or did it seem so replete with the dark green shades of morals because it was so "simple"? What did you express with your gloveless handshake: that you see and consider me a man, although my appearance and whole behavior is entirely childish, or that you wanted to caress me in a style that befits a child precisely because I was a child? I still relish that sweet, benumbing uncertainty, whether what passed between us was due to the child's being-child, or to the man's manliness; for goodness, the sensual degree of tenderness (Babylonian lamb!) are so evanescent rarities in the world that one can never decide if they are childish or grown-up qualities — if they are more closely bound up with the chaotic dreams of the cradle, or with the hero's bitter lucidity.

Nuditas charismatica! How could this puritanical handshake so insulate itself from the rest of the things of the world? Is your anatomy simple, your dress simple, your goodness simple, your symbol-technique simple? The greatness of love is precisely this: to conjure from something infinitely scarce (like this handshake) some infinitely nuanced nuance, something fixed, great, certain, and statuesque: to see the ephemeral as being ephemeral with such frenzied clear-sightedness that it ends up a Doric column.

The great lovers know that they took on the religion of trifles —
this is their rapture and torment, they will forever sacrifice their
lives for those qualities of woman that are closest to non-being.
What lies at the bottom of this all-beginning-of-love relation: between woman's fantastic irreality and her fantastic importance? If
I cast the anchor of my admiration to such places, as ephemeral
as almost to recede into non-being, why is she so important —
and if so important, why do I continue to hold her irreal?

Then you stepped into your boat: from the hall I couldn't see
the gondola rocking at the stairs' lower end, and could only observe the movement with which you lifted your huge skirts above
your ankles to step into the boat. I imagined the two invisibili-
ties: your flashing ankles, and the dancing boat — your ankle
was sharp & strong as a nail, the boat was uncertain and yet reassuring like a chord dissipated into time with a tremolo line. It
was strange to see you start suddenly trembling among so many
hard columns, stairs, and corniced walls, with that foreign, non-
human hesitancy that has nothing to do with the inner crumbling of those who are about to faint. Your face was red, your
gaze determined as the starched visor of a jockey's cap, but from
beneath you the fugal parasite of water-movement crept forward
with generous, invisible petals. You scintillated: "behold, reality"
— and disappeared: "behold, lie."

I have said to myself a thousand times that the feathery
shadow of a fan doesn't quite equal womanly goodness directed
at my ethical insatiability, that a body flickering away on invisible
water is not yet the opening-up to me of the primordial, redeeming, and *true* irreality of life; that every smile of yours is a whole
rosary of torments destined to me, that every piano-key shadow
of your voice sounds the promise of the bleakness of lonely hours
spent and to spend without you: in vain I doubted and in vain
I explained, I knew that you were happiness. Happiness itself:
not hedging, furtive pubertal eros, stolen, maché love that brings
dissatisfactions and laughably big consequences, not scruples,

not æsthetic, not idealism, not "the love," but: you, you alone, in the destructive concreteness, murderous puritanism of your bodily solitude. *This* is happiness: when we have no thoughts, plans about, with, and around the woman — when we are not approaching the woman and not distancing ourselves from her, when we are not her suitor, husband, lover, neo-Platonist, when there can be no question of will, life, me-you — we are paralyzed like the dead in whom everything died indeed, but he continues to *see* through his transparent coffin. How could I have known anything — when would I see you, who are you, what do I want, what is possible and what not? You alone were the world, me, everything: why should I care about you, what have I got to do with you — we are not a story: we are *"we are."*

On the objects scattered around there still lay, like flowers tossed on a banquet table, lots of human things, the shrinking-unfurling scent of times about to pass and about to begin, one memory or other like entries in the catalogue, one perspective or other, like the primitive shadows of man and destiny on things: but all this was laughable, morbid, and superfluous when compared to your presence, which was not an impression, not a memory and not reality either, no hallucination, but the only something that was something. When I face such realness I feel that all the sap of my body wants to leave me: my esophagus fills with bubbles rushing upward to my throat to burst open with prolonged, squeaking gurgles, leaving their place to the next. This is perhaps a puppet-theater parody of the flight of the soul. At such times the only cure is to lie on my back on an entirely even floor: the organs in my chest-box weigh down on my esophagus (at least I feel so, independently of anatomical fact) and the asphyxiating bubbles in my whole body stop. I suffered a great deal from those bubbles, but I love them, because they are the most precise of all the tools I have at my disposal, with the help of which I can "depict" and serve reality's frightening veridicity.

I see my reality-enamoured, reality-shunning disease in ever newer similes: my body is a dark well without inner anatomy, no heart or bones, only one tiny flame, and when I see a very feminine-ly woman, this flame starts longing to get out of me, it keeps ascending, closer and closer to my lips, pulling upward and turning inside out the whole black wall of the pit, as one button will sometimes tear a whole dress with it: my body wants to turn toward true reality with its innermost part, at reality's fête the only possible mask is the body's *inside* — bowels, blood, organic night. While your beauty is all on the skin, is the divine thinness of the exterior, celestial "superficiality," I want to strip down to life's central organs to be worthy of you, and this vomit-like inner gurgling of mine is nothing but the inside's migration toward the outside.

These bubbles also served to make me mistake life for death before every great experience of reality. In my body's dark tube the many acidic beads rose like a pale-pink thermometer column — are they life's beads in death's vase, or death's sparkling air-pearls in life's crumbling glass? Love is the life of life but in such a way that I can neither eat nor sleep — I lose weight, get sick, die. Isn't it madness to call these two things "life": the life of the individual, and the life of the race? Love is the life of the race and my death — and since it is my death, can I see race as life, shouldn't I feel all that (rightfully) to be: death? I loved and love these bubbles popping into my gullet, because they always made the beginning of pleasure coincide with the beginning of suffer-ing, and without knowing exactly what the true meaning of suf-fering is, I half-know that it must lie close to the heart of reality, so in some fancy way it is: value.

There are two lives: the life that serves health, and the life that serves love; the distance between the two is unbridgeable — they are like two distant lamps, we see clearly when the one and when the other is burning. When love's candle flared up from nothing at the sight of your beauty, Angelina, then the bubbles crowding in my esophagus, growing into one another and bursting, were nothing else but the sudden switching-off of the source of the other, non-love life, the sudden becoming-meaningless of the sap of "health" — my eyes, hands, gall bladder, legs stopped functioning all at once, the "humors" of life that were already underway and headed somewhere were extinguished, and were now hovering, swimming about and souring, forsaken, between their starting place and goal, into biological nothingness. The individual's biology is permeated with chemistry, functions, sap, organs, and thousand-balanced, dynamic action — in contrast to this, the biology of love (for instance in its most lucid moment: in the desire for the extraordinarily strong woman — a desire that is *not* of love-making) means one sole, intensive connectedness, an abstract mania that in fact annihilates all biology per se, the freezing of the whole of "life" before beauty, the defiant triumph of non-life. Sexuality has *nothing* to do with biology, if not in the form in which biologists themselves affirm, in high-faluting sentences, "death, too, is a phenomenon of life."

When I went up to my room and lay down on the hard floor, I felt it truly: in my sizzling bubbles the "life functions" were deserting me to leave their place to something that has no need for the body anymore. What do you want with me? You were like a frenetic magnet that first tears off my skin, then my inner organs, as a hand picking the grapes from an ever more ghostly-skeletal, torsoed bunch: you took away my body, not in order to give me "soul" or some such thing, but in order to definitely *cripple* me into your rebellious trinity — love, happiness, death. I was looted as never before: your benign smile hovered in front of me and I had to remark to myself with a touch of irony that real goodness, the apparition of true neighborly love, kills with a more primal fury than the most horrendous Gorgon-head. Peace radiated from your gaze, restfulness and sincerity, green-tide silence forever rippling toward me, the eternal, & hierarchy-less disquiet of promise and the red overtaking of already-fulfillment; secret was more of a secret than ever, on your eyelashes I saw the foreignness of objects incandescing, like inexpressible tension that will immediately explode, and at the same time I was at home, like an exile in the dreamed-of children's room, at the goal, yes, yes, falling into yes: I couldn't take this utter only-to-be-accepted-ness of your being, your truth ripened to the point of hallucination — I threw myself inside you like a suicide jumping into the well, but I was still holding on to the unsevered cord on which I could, and will yet climb back: from love, back into life, from happiness, back into "biological functions" — from kissing, to eating.

You tore off my body from my ribs like sempervivum from a rock; you crushed my muscles & bowels like colorful Gothic stained-glass windows, leaving only the fishbones of the lead frames, so that I should be ecstatic, lifted into that beatifying sweetness of "feminine goodwill" that I have always longed for and will long for — but I there on the floor, with my croaking throat, arms extended in crucifix, was nevertheless defending "prose" from ecstasy, which cannot but annihilate me. I have no strength for happiness, Angelina: my childhood, when my organism was still flexible like seal-wax kissing the flames in air (hot foam, red froth, rootless flame, blue gases and golden lianas!), my childhood knew nothing else but suffering: my heart knew syncopated throbbing, my lungs, torn breathing, my skin, the creepers of small wounds, my eyes, sqinting, my feet, stumbling — to these ailments all my joints and organs aligned themselves, they became the precise caskets, vases of the forms of suffering — the forms of happiness will never again fit in. Suffering causes incomparably less suffering than happiness coming from you.

2.

On that day Cugnani had lunch with his mother. His mother had recently married for the second time: it was hard to imagine two less compatible people. She was tall and lean, with completely white hair — ascetic, cruel, sentimental, and logical; her husband was a huffing, stout little merchant with a trimmed moustache, who needed the old woman's title to get at politicians and through them, to foreign merchants. The huffing little merchant was even now at some business meeting: as far as Cugnani knew, something about a Turkish prince who had created a secession in the Turkish army and was willing to ally himself with Venice and the pope against the sultan. They rarely dined in three, and now it was almost certain that he wouldn't see his stepfather for days. He knew that the meeting took place in a small room at the back of the house, which looked on a small canal: the representative of Venice, his stepfather, and the Turk.

He knew that room well: it was dark and luminous, for the darkness of the canal, of the courtyard, the outward darkness of the streets penetrated among the rooms — it was not a dark "room," but a glassful of the city's darkness. It was an intimate & depraved place, and for this reason the chosen place of his pubertal amorous trances: through the windows, the red plaster of the walls opposite, peeling off in strips and bunches, almost tilted in, the window-panes could get entangled like the pages of two books opened into one another: the green creepers frothing from the windows, rooftops and garden walls grew one long snake bine around the Cugnani house & that of their neighbours opposite — one couldn't tell in which direction the small bridges built in X, V, and even O shapes were sprained; the slowly gliding, fish-mouthed water surfaced now here, now there; sunshine flashing among the shades' joined blazons tore apart the stones grown into one another and started into fairy-tale construction work; at dawn and in the evening the sunshine flung at the windows was reflected and exchanged among the houses opposite: all this in the most profound silence — the city's street anarchy was the stage setting of a boudoir.

Love always wriggles among home and elsewhere, the most familiar warmth and tormenting female foreignness; we don't know if we are groping for our own body's most dreamlike pleasure-moment, in our attempt to find a near-transcendental degree of an onanic grip — or if in a female portrait we are attracted by another person's pure otherness, the fact of the "human" as eternal unknowability.

This room with its Latin pouring-out-onto-the-street and bedroom-like, velvety secretiveness united in itself the two poles of love: it was both love as his own body's satanic intimacy, and love as the foreign world's forever-foreign, forever-freer freedom. When Cugnani got there after a long flight of stairs, he felt that he was in the midst of the palace, its very core; the surrounding corridors, too, were dark, brown, and golden (like candles that don't shed light but merely put the sigil of golden loneliness on a corner at night), and when he opened the door: at once he found himself on the street — as if a dissecting physician suddenly discovered the dead person's *face* in the corpse's entrails: the cause and root of the organism was, yet again, the portrait! Here silence was deeper than anywhere else; three palaces' corners piled up here, the slowest, most sluggish parts of living palace-bodies; on the walls, the windows flapping like caterpillar wings, on the rocking little boats tied in front of small, rusty iron gates only a meremost minimum of life showed, as a disentangled thread of hair blown hither and thither by the wind on a sleeping body. Water, bridges, red walls, creepers, gondolas: these are so eternally the symbols of dream, love, solitude, reality, impossibility, redemption, or rather, their exclusive bearers, mimes and gods, that Cugnani couldn't imagine how one could discuss politics and commerce in that squeezed-in wardrobe.

Where do certain places, like this one, get their essential, distinctive, miracle-death-beauty character? And where does their incomprehensibly *unitary* harmony come from? Because when one enters here, everything radiated the undivided melancholy of materialization, severing in an instant our connections to past and future, other heres and theres — it was the merged plenitude of time and space, the divine romanticism of "being somewhere," the benumbing wave-slope of "being now." Does the color, smell, or thought that covers everything originate in one unanalyzably small detail? Does one crooked bridge railing possess the magic to wrap up trees, water, windows in the *unity* of irresistible beauty? Or is it the other way round: are all objects and details equally unfamiliar and surprising to us, and is it that seamless, giant mosaic of foreignness, this "democracy of irreality" that confers unity on them (the essential trait of such milieus)? On the whole: are these the most remembering instants of memory, or are they the first true appearance of foreignness, of our most basic and absolute ignorance vis-à-vis the world?

Great melting pot of object and symbol: the bridge is more concrete than ever, its own objectivity scintillates and trembles in our consciousness and in the world (is there a separate soul, and a separate world?) as a white-miracling, lonely Venus on the bluest southern sea: and yet the bridge is no longer a bridge but the indescribable interior form of our most ancient longings, the mist-spreading embodiment of all our delusions, symbol, prophesy, the concentrated and proven whatsit that is eternally inexpressible and impossible in our lives, therefore eternally the only and the most important thing.

But where did this encounter originate — what made this room in an instant the place of rendezvous between the objects' electric object-hood and their most fleeting symbolism? What is it that provokes the duality: "this landscape has resolved my life," and "this landscape has annihilated my life into mystery

for good"? And above all, what is it that does *not* make life-and-
death dynamics between radiant certainty and opium-dazed
doubt tormenting, enticing, but rather, reassuring? Do the ultimate things tremble here — God's infinity, the crooked mirror
of love? Or the utterly small things: neurasthenia *&* hallucinations? Or the two together?

Every color fits here: the brown suffusion with shadows,
the yellowish-grey, gradual lightening around the windows,
the bone-color of the small balcony's stone pavement, the
water's brown, muddy, "glub-plup-glub-plup"-voiced color, the
water's other, light grey-light blue shade (further, where it has
pulled off the silk glove of shadows), the red wall shedding its
peel (dull and vulgar brick-color), the foliage's green, the sky's
steamy whiteness — so many colors, and yet all at once they are
in some picturesque *unity*, beyond harmony (moreover, having
nothing in common with harmony). They are not even colors,
nor meanings: but the only possible form of positivity and
concreteness. Every one of them encloses time in its melody-like
purity; these colors stretch out, growing ever more silent, true,
or lying — but they are continuously underway somewhere.
Perhaps they realize a mysterious form of time's inner rhythm:
they touch neither the abruptness of surprise nor the phlegmatic
historical time of usage — they are a mathematical mean of
"endingness," to which our body responds, as if to an unknown
chemical substance, with pleasant swirling of the head.

And in that room they discuss — commercial contracts?
Commercial contracts are the polar opposite of this milieu not
for being commercial (even if poetry is not commerce, commerce
is nevertheless luxuriating poetry), but for being human — for
being action. Cugnani couldn't have imagined anything more unintelligible than diplomacy and business in the desperate hour of
happiness from woman. The world of objects and the world of
action, or in other words, the world of love and the world of hu-

mans, the world of states (Venice) and the world of movements (the *triumph* of Venice). Love is something eerily concrete, like the bridges you could see from the boudoir, which connect the houses as arched lines do the same musical tone through several beats; Angelina is, he has found her; politics is irreal, always a plan, is not about human beings, is not for human beings, it is abstract and eternal quest.

There is nothing more dizzying and more awkwardly pleasurable than to leaf through history books, or attend a political conference in the first great hour of amorous desire (*between* the first sighting of the woman and the first rendezvous): we can never *not*-understand something so perfectly as then; we can never wonder at the fact that both love and history (these two things of an utterly alien content, style, subject) are human: that one and the same soul is capable of sitting by the water and seeing his life resolved for good from one dirty little wave which beats against a bit of wood with its determined hue, determined little stink, determined little splashes — and is capable of weaving plans of alliance with the French, setting a trap for the pope, pawning galleys, baptizing Turks, plotting the emperor's papacy. Man is made up of contrasting parts, but this may well be the contrast of contrasts: the redeeming, passive enjoyment of the world's one chosen moment of landscape and of time (the great life-"mood" beyond sentimentalism) — and action, activity with a political objective.

Even if meaningless, the question is not laughable, for it is so biologically ancient: which is the more valuable, which lies closer to God's intention of bringing being into being? Indeed — which of the two is the more divine: the landscape's "static" poetry, which is mute and inebriates all the cells of the body, the objects' object-like loneliness and object-like plenitude, love's psychic, lyrical nihilism — or the mathematical drama of moral deeds' man-pitted-against-man: mathematical, because here the objects' passive reality-swelling is supplanted by the abstract contours of actions, and the concrete by streaming intentions. In any case emotion and reality stand on the same side: in our most sentimental moments we are the most closely related to a flower, bridge, smell.

3.

Now, too, Cugnani would have liked to retreat into this boudoir, but because his stepfather had his business meeting there, he started for his mother's bedroom. On the staircase he glimpsed the painting depicting Mars and Diana that his mother had bought a week before and which he doted on, because the sleek nude best expressed the never-to-be-realized erotic movement. For Diana's left leg was drawn in full profile up to the hip, so that the right leg behind should have been either completely concealed or, if you will, in absolute optical profile; yet the right leg was almost completely visible, but not the way anatomy and optics dictate: it appeared from the back, something evident especially around the two flesh globes under the hips — the left leg ended according to nature in an entirely flat, plane circle, but the right leg (which the richly layered shadows swelled into more spatiality), on the contrary, ended in a three-dimensional sphere: it was impossible to see, from one and the same viewpoint, such hieratically flat and naturalistically statuesque legs. And for Cugnani this unwitting error of perspective was precisely what meant the non plus ultra of eros: the left leg's sharp-cool profile depicted eros as absolute image, precise vision, the fact that love is always based on some engraved, crystallized ornament, drawing, physiological *formula* — while the thigh culminating in shadow-foliage depicted eros as *embrace*, as swimming-style penetration of the female body's spatiality, the duality of statuesqueness and penumbra, squeezable plasticity and wave-emptiness enough to make one seasick; as opposed to the momentary planimetry, which can only ever mean an instant-point of beauty (= formula), the dark wrestling of possession, jungle-like "pleasure time."

This is the supreme erotic attraction of most nudes of the Old Masters: they combine two or three perspectives, fashioning criss-crossing modulations from the different tonalities of love, primarily (as here, in the case of the two shins) from the two basic tonalities: woman *glimpsed*, and woman threaded into *embrace*.

The other beauty of this Diana was that her waist, up to her neck, was disproportionately small and thin as compared to the two funneling shins, the thighs and globes: thereby placing a special accent on the body's being-bred-for-love, also signaling that on a female body shins stand for the most soul-less animality, the mass, and at the same time, through their delicate, arched shape, refinery, nearly-affected Platonizing "style," "beauty." The blossoming and shapedness of the body radiating up- and onwards from the ankles culminates somewhere around the hips: as if its sole purpose had been to reach here, to shoot broad leaves and fruits into the wreath, and after reaching this love-making goal, its momentum suddenly abates: the trunk, arms, the breasts looking like elongated little drops on the verge of dripping from a melting icicle, the inert head sunk above the breasts — are merely the reflex of a distant erotic momentum, its distorted echoes.

4.

This Diana was the plenitude of love, but had nothing to do with Angelina, because Angelina meant not love but *woman*: while his distracted feet sank slowly into the rugs concealing the stairs' edges, his hands glided, inert, along the railings, the painting's silver-green shadows remained meaningless for him. He thought of the girl with whom he had so far been in the habit of living; an outsider looking on would have said, "so far he liked one girl, now he suddenly started liking another." One, another: one, another! Do these two words indeed mean anything here? Is there anything, however minimal, in common between the girl he was used to, and Angelina? Nothing. Perhaps one of them can be called a "woman," and what he feels for her, love, but then the "other" is not a woman and cannot be compared to the "one," and what he feels for her can be compared even less to her match. Unfaithfulness? Although he felt concretely that ever since he saw Angelina his former lover didn't interest him anymore, it was precisely the stroke-like, sudden, complete stiffness of non-interest that rendered the former lover all too real: this sudden ceasing, silencing, molded her into unalterable form, like a chord suddenly cut off mid-air — the object of our attention up to this moment (woman, or sound) ceases suddenly, therefore what remains is pure attention, the soul's bare pointedness to a goal, which we feel more palpably (because it is in our consciousness, muscles, the chemistry of our nerves and irises) than the object itself that drew our attention. What he felt in relation to his former lover, or rather, what manifested itself in this relation: the duality of familiarity and irreality; and what he felt toward the "new" woman, Angelina: the thrilling duality of unfamiliarity and reality — these are mutually eliding, not exclusive things.

First and foremost, in contrast to the woman of old, I *see* the new woman: the gist lies in her visual sensing, the maniacally cataloguing perception of her perceptible parts and relations; I *don't see* the familiar woman, my relation with her is not the relation of spectator and vision, but the relation of those who live and act together the joint life and action. The woman of old is always associated with action, the new woman always with an image. Action *&* image are alien: one cannot even speak here of unfaithfulness. If I could get to know the new woman in such a way that from the beginning of her relation with me she should be not primarily an *image* but some *life*-activity together with me, then one could in fact speak about unfaithfulness. But when the exclusive image-likeness, of the relation's beginning (reductio ad imaginem) starts falling from the new woman, and she, too, becomes as familiar as the woman of old: it is then (if by some circumstance the woman of old should still be present) and only then that one might in fact speak of unfaithfulness. Because we cannot call love in the full and pedantic sense of the word anything else but the world of emotion of the days following the first glimpse (vision!) and first being-in-agreement (ethics!): the short period of too-precise image-likeness and of sweet, naturally Christian, gospel love, goodness emanating toward one another. Imago ac Charis.

Let's observe closely the first moments of so-called unfaithfulness — what luxuriating æsthetics (although the word is but an approximation in this context) & luxuriating ethics the new woman means, as compared to the woman of old! From under the new woman's black hat, small but stylishly elongated, youthfully curlicueing but stylized-blasé red tresses run toward the ears: love, the new consists in the fact that this image as image pleases us above all — there is *no* mention at all of the woman, "woman" in fact always means the woman *of old* — the new woman is always one isolated visual fragment or other, is not really woman, not really love; something that, in its virginal image-likeness, is equally distant from all expressed sexuality and from all expressed æsthetic. We have no shared memories with the new woman, perhaps no shared future either, she is pure "pleasing": when after the new woman we meet again the woman of old, we face time spent together, shapeless "history," something we know, remember, what is scattered in time and space: in contrast to infinitely fragmentary, insulated fragment (the new woman), a branching, amorphous "situation."

5.

Cugnani's mother lived an uncommon life. She withdrew into three relatively small rooms: a dining-room, bedroom, and parlor. Her dining-room was furbished with ten big candles, her bedroom with a man-size crucifix, and her salon with a sole, giant palm tree. She liked to have an early lunch and lay down immediately afterward — not dressed, on a sofa, but in her nightshirt on the bed, and she slept without waking until midnight, sometimes until two in the morning, woke up, dressed, and stayed up until lunchtime. Everybody knew that her husband had been poisoned with an apple: the crucifix in the bedroom was a memento of that. For here only one arm of Christ (the left one) was nailed to the cross, the right one hung in front (holed), away from the wall and into the space of the room, as if the nail had fallen out, so half the body peeled off from the wall like a young, half-felled tree that the night storm had entirely winded off its propping wood. Christ's face was not visible, so low did his forehead drop to his chest, indeed down to his Adam's apple — the cervical vertebra was sharp as a roof: one slope was the back, the other the neck, and the two formed a crippled triangle. In his hanging right hand Christ held a big red apple, the apple of Paradise, holding it out to a mirror: in this mirror an Eve appeared, carved on the ceiling and smiling a smile of the dead, through the veils of death, lakes, blue-thickening time, of eternal human error-nature. In the corner was the "bed" — a few pillows, duvets, silk and velvet rags on the floor.

In his childhood Cugnani had often peeped through the keyhole to see his mother's early afternoon or noontime stripping. In his mouth he still had the taste of food, and these tastes were like small advance-hooks of the afternoon time to come, which ineluctably towed him, powerless little fish of minutes and evening waters, to life, so that his mother's voluntary withdrawal to the bedroom, this forever unintelligible mix of chapel and stable, remained unimaginable for him. The preparation for sleep contrasted with the streets' full sunlight, and the erotic thrill contrasted with his mother's withered old age. He will never forget the sighting of lingerie on her bony shoulder: under the window the waters rippled with such daytime splashes, throbbing deeply and broadly like a big, shapeless green heart, rolling the conceited, fragrant rings of life and noon against the walls; the shadows' huge creepers and Egyptian umbrellas caressed the walls with the lazy life-trust and worn-out elasticity of the body that has just eaten, and from these walls the warmth that had impregnated them since morning was exhaled with the melancholy faith of "it's worth, it's worth, it's worth": everyone's body longed for this non-human, celestial, star, and vegetal warmth with their skin, while his mother turned her back on all that, seeking the artificial, impossible warmth of the bed and duvets. With what paradox meekness noon and the afternoon floated above the not-yet cleared table: in this or that yellow reject of light on the floor, early dawn was still glowing with its unripe gold, the virgin wick of first light: clumsy desire, acrid piety; and in the walls' warmth, in their porous-loose, yellow sun-squares sunset was already breathing, the untied ribbon of evening lights, buckle pins escaping from the holes of belts. This was the boudoir's lighting as well, with the disharmonious musical tone-heads of a few inserted candles, equally falling from dawn's slightly stiffened refrains and the sunset's deshabille promises.

6.

His mother was extraordinarily tall and thin; when with arms stretched above her head she took off her daytime shirt, her fingers always got entangled in the small chandelier's branches, starting a peculiar, low-sharp clatter, like a bird flying against a windowpane: the thump is quite sharp, but the point of contact is the softest feathers. The birth of Venus: the curtain, the shirt was not dropped but lifted — in this, too, Cugnani saw something unnatural, although in puberty every glance, movement, and push of nature is the embodiment of the unnatural. From some of the windows and balconies opposite, rugs hung into the lukewarm wind, smelling of dessert, in the side-streets dirty shirts swayed, holding up the "praevalebunt" banners of human abjection with devilish glee, and his mother's lifting shirt was somehow a kin of such afternoon concerto-yawn textiles. So nakedness is not necessarily a sister of the night, or its very essence, like the glaring Moon: for a long time, precisely because of this maniacal grafting of thoughts onto the night, Cugnani had considered "naked woman" to be just as much a celestial body as the Moon or the Ursa Maior. Now his mother was inviting him to partake of some great Copernician erotic turn — while being not eros: his mother is, after all, his mother. The thought of incest settled on his body like a necklace warmed up on a stove tile. "The natural and the unnatural — is there such a duality, and if yes, are we not mixing them up?" Who has not asked this of themselves in their early youth? Perhaps the greatest pleasure of this peeping through the keyhole was that uncertainty, sensuous as much as moral: the excitement that felt its goal now to be in its grip, now dissolving into nothingness. The boats sailed on quietly under the balcony; each one was like a pedal in the palace's cellars: the straight-lined, strutting-proud crescendo of swimming, the unexpected edge of oar strokes, always closer than calculated, the tiny petals of scattered human voices on our soul brushed mute, the stirred water's erupting stale odor (smell of pressed flowers lifting all of a sudden from a book we open) — at once they lifted the palace into the air with its furniture, his mother, so that for a few instants they could tremble their own reality freely, like unmuffled strings.

In his mother's stripping there was some gothic disfluency, opposition to any natural rhythm: goal, water, the houses' melting into time, the chirrup of distant gossip, the slow swelling of death, the clumsy discretion of the maid clearing the table were all kindred, tranquil, & obvious — but the lifting of the shirt in zigzagging angles was a revolt, a heresy. He felt disgust and happiness at the same time: perhaps here originated his body's peculiarity, that love always threw itself into the pit of his stomach, upsetting his digestion to the point of excess. Nausea irrigated and scratched his throat when the shirt suddenly fell from the height, like a dead bird dropping from among the chandelier's rustling-chattering branches, and stooping, his mother sank her shoulders into her nightshirt's mist-cave.

The first birth of Venus: what is it? what are all the things it can be? and what are those it cannot? A rejection of mothers, provoking of disease, sleep-sickness, incest, the sudden inflammation of the moral sense, death-drive, onany, feeling of loss and lies, nihil, nihil, then again the desire to childishly become a child, artificial dumbing-back into idyll, dad-mom, for some Venus to step again into our dreams on the evening pillow, who is neither our mother nor our sister nor some little girl nor our own sexual organs nor brothel drag nor the cliché of sin, but some nauseating, unjust, undeserved suffering, suffering from the uncalled-for, undesired, by anybody ever unwanted fact of sex.

After he had vomited his fill in a nearby room, without pressing his palm to his forehead (he felt as though the knife of martyrdom icons had cleft his skull), he ambled out onto the street, to the canal bank amid the afternoon's warm, dark green shadows, holding on to the image of well-known bridges, unchanged equestrian statues, psychology-less church facades and orange vendors beyond the realm of sex, so that, sidestepping the ghostly image of his naked mother, he could steal back into the previous, infantile times.

7.

During today's lunch they hardly exchanged a word; his mother saw clearly that Cugnani was in turmoil. He couldn't feel anything else but his mother's love for him, and he never felt this love, its spiritual nature, more sensitively than now, when he felt love for Angelina who appeared, then disappeared.

The mothers' love for their sons — & the love of the sons for their lovers — why shouldn't we for once look to the bottom of those? — Cugnani asked himself, quietly sounding the bell of his china plate with a peach stone. Both are love, both are the religion whose sole doctrine, rite, salvation, is another person. Does there exist another god in whom we can positively believe — other than the *other person?* Cugnani slowly rolled the stone into the middle of his plate and looked into his mother's eyes. Her whole body was ramshackle, wrinkles, bones, too loose clothes, patches of white hair sticking out, jewels which miraculously preserved their youth independently of their wearer and were therefore alien, contorsions of the muscles that knew nothing about one another: like a coral convulsively branching apart and together again in time's rotting, turbid waters. What does this coral want, this leafless, barren thorn-bush of love? For it was full of thorns, needles, rapier-points and truths, starting from her gaze. "She loves me," — Cugnani thought —, "and I love Angelina" — but in her there were no needles and true things, on the contrary: she was all melting, amoeba-like play-acting, flexible adjustment to reality. "Reality": does the word mean anything in relation to Angelina? "Fiction" — does it mean anything in relation to his mother? The mother is connected to her child by a biological link, therefore the child is no "reality" for her, no portrait, no sculpture, no flesh, but the immaterial goal of bodiless, blind-abstract worship; lovers are not connected by blood relation, their meeting is haphazard, foreignness almost disembodies their bodies and precisely for this reason, because there is no biological umbilical cord between them, they can become "reality" for one another: human being, face, guaranteed world. The blood relative is always fictitious — there love is so great that its theme frays into nil; the foreign lover is always real — there the *reality* of woman is so much stronger than love, that love becomes nil in comparison. So the theme of eros is complete, divine *reality*; the theme of parental love is abstract "*for* somebody": which of the two can hope for more satisfaction in this world?

If he searched his soul he could smell in it the closed-petaled flower of barrenness: here, in love, everything is in vain; if he looked at his mother as she watched, almost disfigured with worry, the evident signs of his lack of appetite, he experienced the same: there, in child-worship, too, everything is in vain. Why don't they ally themselves —charity's master-barren?

8.

The daytime candles combed themselves pale with the wind's gap-toothed rake; the manservant was asleep on a chair in the corner. "What's wrong with you?" — did his mother ask that? Always, immediately that word: "wrong"? While his mother was arranging the leftover fruits into renewed little symmetries, on sudden impulse Cugnani told her: "I'm very cold, I'm not feeling well. Go to bed, I'll come upstairs & lie down in your bed, can I?" "Come. Wait for me outside until I undress."

What would Angelina say if she saw this? He felt like the alchemist who mixes in his test-tube two kinds of love, the love of mothers and the love of lovers. They must ally themselves, conspire — he couldn't get this idea out of his mind. There is infinite difference between the two kinds of love, but they are infinitely akin in their futility. For years he had stopped peeping through the keyhole, but now he pressed his warm eye against the draughty, cold opening: his savage symbolism-hunger now poisonously, irretrievably stylized his mother into a big, wriggling puppet of "the love of blood relatives" and watched her movements in the bedroom with the experimentalist's self-mortifying pedantry: identifying the lethal symptoms of "love" in all her pantings, falterings, in the catching of her clothes in the furniture. She wore a girlishly cute, long pink dayshirt: the shadowless expanse of silk suggested to Cugnani's eyes a fish-elastic pubertal body; a fold here and there, instead of engraving black grooves above the body sliding here and there as it undressed, conjured on the shirt, as though by magic, new colors, lights more surprising than luminosity, and if the shirt crumpled with however small a wrinkle, the opalescent patch created there immediately poured out onto a disproportionately large surface — it literally "poured," resembling not optical spreading but the slow splashing of liquids. Perhaps these are the two main virtues of silk, that shadows are supplanted by colorful luminosities, and the disproportionately small fold pours huge light-rays over the body: but these two features were too girlish, springtime, what is more, infantile — it was unbelievable that his mother wasn't rejuvenated by them. On the upper fringe of her shirt lace bounced and boiled with thick froth — the whole writhing body, with its head covered, was like a tree in spring, on which not a single leaf is open, but it is in bloom, and the blossoms are torn by a cold, sun-filled breeze with March brusqueness.

"Bloom, old woman!" — Cugnani cried to himself. And she did bloom indeed, but as though the flowers did not pop up on certain points of the still wintry-icy twigs: it was as though the boughs had split lengthwise and the petals had poured forth from those cracks like rich trimming turned inside out: the silk's long folds, now tautening, now slackening, sometimes abated to humble U-s (how curiously close those two opposites were to one another!), and wrapped the mother-tree in the springtime flame of blooming (oh, schéma en fleurs!): higher and higher did the shirt rise, zigzagging left & right high above the bun, so that, tumbling over the held-up wrists, it fell to the floor. Cugnani felt that the pink silk's drunken wriggling up higher was the filling of all useless loves' wine in an invisible glass — everything rose with it, the colors of the world, history's yarns, God's fancy incognito. As the upward-creeping tones of an instrument give the impression of "triumphant falsity," "impossibility's reality-dance," so this burning shirt wrinkled and crammed up to two meters' height also thinned to an ambiguous picture-scream and statue-scream, becoming a kin of the Spanish baroque crucifix on the wall — both were the agonizing coloratura stunts of a deranged love.

Christ's body was yellow: yellow like the warm, unhealthy wax of the candles that pale around noon, yellow like the sunflower's blunt petals when the afternoon pulls its strings across it perpendicularly. For Cugnani this mourning yellow meant death, god, all conceivable religiousness, the color of reality sufferingly perceived as suffering: perhaps king Midas saw the mouth found for a moment before his death in the night to be so pale, undulatingly, and luxuriatingly barren — first it was red like a half-baked little parody of the Holy Ghost, but when he touched it with his dying mouth, it, too, became gold, unfeminine, his murderer — around him in the steaming, coagulated, and mendacious night everything was golden-yellow, the sea waves showed up an overcrowded junk shop's yellow statuettes in silent nooks and crannies, the branches, stirring tremolo lines all followed the pale metal's fever and hideousness: he was looking for redemption in this last, redemptive little doodle and now it, too, turned yellow, like the Moon that, run out of oil, shrinks to gold. Christ's body *poured* onto the cross: he had no real anatomy and sharp-edged theology, it was only a pouring, some thick, snaking, yellow cascade that falls on the earth from on high, and as a running brook does with the rock it meets on its way, this embraces the cross' wood hewn as a dam rushes around it, froths on it, only in order to leave it behind with fatigued ebb-wrinkles.

Here everything was together: God as the paradox of paradoxes, God as beauty flaring to tragedy, God as the drunken feudal overlord and vasal of suffering, God as the bloody charlatanism of enigma, God as man's most human, most programatically humanist profile, God as love's Spanish bombast & its hypochondriac Jewish metaphor, God as silence, as the booming-released dominant of flower-mute peace (O, Augustine's dichotomies: how much you are the only possible things, whether I take you for stylistic routine or for true God-structure!) — and beside it, his mother with her animal-ethical love of the child, with the theology-less, unwittingly atheistic Cugnani-worship.

The two dances fit into the keyhole: God's slow haemorrhage into the world, the yellow thorn of his savior body in Venice's weedy, Doge-flowered, Doge-swampy, fleeting body — and his old mother's greedy fidgeting with the shirt that she nearly tore in her excitement, waiting for her son to come to her cold bed. Christ's naked body (all real reality and all vacuous, histrionic co-quettishness is naked) with its sticky-evanescent limbs was like that star which unleashes the Last Judgement, which would not fall from the sky like an August meteor, but melt: the yellow dot (and this is the terror of terrors) will become a small yellow line, as if it were not the star itself but its ghostly arpeggio, smeared onto a quivering wave.

9.

Love! What is it then about it, how do they grow together, in what roots do their diverging flowers meet? What is love? The ontology of ontologies, or minderwert household drag? All, truly all love has a *common* denominator in this world — be its adored object God, a parent, or a whore. "Christ, my mother, Angelina" — Cugnani said to himself in front of the keyhole, trying to squeeze them together with trembling fingers. He "knew them well," but none opened up to him.

He knew well the deathly neutral taste of the Host in his mouth, knew well the transient flash of the upward-turned chalice above the officiating priest's head, knew well the underwater plasticity of the priests' heads sieved through the confessional's grid, he knew in his knees the blade hardness of altar steps, the haughtily wilting shadow of the statues of evening saints — but what was the gist here, the certainty beyond psychology's boring nuances, reality beyond theology's baroque-glittering truths?

He knew women well: the superstitiously comforting plasticity of the "human being," the great, spiritual legends of love and faithfulness and the redeeming fiascos of beds, that mix of meaning and meaninglessness, pleasure and sickness, debilitating dreams and roadside invincible prose with which only women can acquaint us, and yet — was he left with anything concrete, did the humbug-compass of the phallus gain a moment's credit?

He knew his mother well: as, sick and feverish, she scurried up and down the streets of Venice to find him when he didn't get home one evening, with the mad irrefutability of self-sacrifice in her insurgent eyes — he could never forget that grotesque and sacred run that she squeezed out of her clumsy stork legs after a galloping potato cart at the time of the conquest and famine of Venice, to feed her son — but what the truth, ancient justification of this blind love is: he knew not.

All movements of God, lover, mother are replete with mania, puffed-up metaphor, the suicidal and histrionic ornament of all manner of pathologies — could this be the essence of life, the eternal goal of reality? And yet, when we realize that it is always love, "true feelings" that compromise everything on earth, crocodiles and composers, dames aux camélias and Buddhist myth-stuffings alike, at the same time we feel that this eternal venom-source of parody is also our organ of reality: the sole useful finger exercise of objectivity.

Man's all-time favorite word for reality is "comedy": and they are right, especially if we examine the love-actions and emotions of God, mother, and lover. Life is doubtlessly comedy if entirely meaningless, and it is all the more so if it has some absolute divine meaning which we, humans, deny and distort to the point of ridicule. Love always juggles with two balls: objectivity and comedy. Love is a peculiar world of objectivity: for what attracts and entices us is always something external, something which is absolutely wanted because it is absolute *not*-I, but an external object: to God, man, to my mother, I, to me, Angelina. And the great seriousness of "objectivity" becomes comedy because man wants to assimilate, fasten, ensnare in his net, this external reality: his only goal is the other thing's otherness, but he can only attain this purpose by stripping it precisely of its otherness — when God makes nearly a god of man, when the mother almost creates an inner organ of her womb back into herself out of her child, when the man in love can have the woman play (as a hired actress) the decorative and all-too-subjective formulae of daydream.

10.

What is the most sincerely world-like trait of the world? The lonely waters, lonely trees, the secretive clouds, enigma butterflies? Women alone, gods in the taboo-frame of death, lovers placed, instead of the common bed, on top of distant pillars, like mutually repelling, deranged stylites? Is then reality the fact that everything is isolated, everything is lonely and self-serving, can only be understood by itself and from itself, and cannot be compared, however superficially, with anything other? Or does the essence in the ode-ringing, mewing, tantalizing attraction, curiosity for one another, of all these distant islands and things drowned in their own reality, lie in the desire of every single one of them to become every single other — in one word: in "love"? What is worthwhile reality: *things*, or their *relations*?

Or do the two make up reality together — the face of a beautiful woman is only half of reality in itself; it is only the mythological hunger of the man in love that transforms it into a spatial statue — and love, too, is only half of reality in itself; it is only the woman's isolated face, embodied foreignness, impossibility, irreality, that renders kharis and eros complete reality.

Why did Cugnani forever doubt all love? (Of course this is not about doubting God's or his mother's love for not finding them sufficiently "great" or "sincere.") Because he was surrounded by the great illustrations of sterility — in the Bible as much as in the labor rooms of maternity hospitals and in brothels? And if he doubted and doubted for this reason, why would he still consider love the sole treasure and meaning of his life? Perhaps for seeing that this sterility, the obvious disproportion between love's huge drama and its huge pointlessness, is the most possibly human: the very last, highest possibility for man. This is unquestionably a melancholy fact, but resembles neither disillusionment nor pessimism. Love is the plasticity of the impossible: woman is the secret kernel (as man is for God, the child is for the mother) where nothing and everything hover in quivering equilibrium like the two scales of a shaky balance, with that vibrating shame with which shiver the horizontally opened wings of butterflies settling on a flower.

"If you are here, great mania of love, let you blossom and live!" — Cugnani said to himself with that inward gesture with which a steerless boat is pushed out of harbor. — We can't go on brooding forever on what you are. Simply the externalizing of the fact that there is God, too, apart from the world, the eternal noticing of the "openness" of existence? The fruit of nature, organic life? Biological clockwork, like the opening of a flower or the rotting of a fruit? Or the historical episode, disguised in the drag of morality, of the sentimentality, hypochondria, and sensuousness grafted onto Europe by the Jews? No matter. I live from it and die with it."

11.

The world is full of pictures of the Madonna: annunciations, idylls, pietàs — how becoming that these blazons of God's savage love for humans adorn or darken every main or side altar, street, bedroom, grave and prow! Madonna and Jesus: the two loves collide here as two ships on the North Sea. One doesn't even know what to compare these two wrestling, embracing, and slaughtering loves to: night's tropical blindness, or the candle-spring of a thousand-branched candelabra? The God falling from heaven into a human womb, and Mary shrinking around her child with the sacred limitedness of motherhood: is there a debate more beautiful, dialogue of more heightened sophistry, more Bacchically certain truth? When the Holy Ghost fecundates the Virgin, God definitely betroths itself with the world, with creation: with the purpose, to redeem man, but in its course a lot more happens — although his own being-God is pointed like an arrow to man, this arrow makes huge waves in the air around, in the world, all existence — stars, landscapes, possible histories, originally only of the God fallen to earth because of man's sins, are all rewritten; the celestial furor of love runs through the tree-trunks like transfused blood or an inner whip; even the most simple-minded beetle and the most mendacious Polynesian god-pagliaccio becomes charismatic. God's becoming-human is at the same time (and without one pantheistic touch!) also the world's becoming "love-material": when it became human, God somehow also became flower, sea, it also filled the whole of creation with itself for the second time. This is the broadest materialization of the fact of love: "everything" and "love" overlap.

And this undulating, chaotic boundlessness of love collides with the mother's narrow love for her child: Mary can adore Jesus divinely and in a way worthy of God only if she loves Jesus *only* as a child, in the most animal sense, if she sees nothing else of the world but the body-fragment torn out of her body, if she follows the most primitive selfishness of her instincts — if she forgets Joseph, the workshop, the stable, the star that is nearly putrid with light, the Saracen sultans, the future and the familiar face of landscapes, the angel's resonant, terrible annunciation — and her whole life is "impoverished" to one muscle reflex: the milk-pressing movement of the mamma.

The two loves: one, a few pale veins on the breast, elastically swelling tubes with greenish-wheyed fluid which would make any grown-up vomit; the nipple's small blister resembling skin disease, and a salivating, squelching infant mouth. Nothing more. And the other, of the God flying into the world: the whole scholastic philosophy as eternity's earthly peacock feathers, Parisian cosmetics, the saints' metaphor-degree morality and deeds, the filling up of the whole of nature with forever restless "specters," the lecherous harvest of all kinds of greedy Platonism, the incurable obsession of "spiritualism": there's no point in the world that does not long to leave it for some heavenly home.

(And God, and the "opposition" between Madonna & Jesus, I know very well of course, is not a theological reality but the self-tormenting game of literature, submission to the simple psychological fact that the only satisfying gesture of reality-inebriation is deliberate error.)

12.

Cugnani heard a ringing from afar: he didn't know where it came from, what it was, but his brain swelling with oppositions wanted it to be a procession, for the sake of sacrosanct theatricality. In the afternoon breeze the banners fluttered warmly, with soft plopping — they could barely be distinguished from the wind, being merely colorful warmths. On the narrow little bridges the masts and silks piled up, to scatter on the piazzettas like dandelion tuft in the air. The hymn sounded a shambles: one group prayed in prose, another hummed recitativo-style, and yet another sang longish tunes. Hotchpotch banners, hotchpotch voices and pace of walking: as if the whole procession did unspeakably *not* will itself, although in its grey hesitancy the banners' colliding and, here and there, ascension to heaven there was some eternal necessariness, some splenetic homage to the unavoidability of God. The crowd almost crushed the canopy: its columns bent inwards and its covering tilted, like an umbrella turned inside out on a windy street corner. The clothes were partly stage-motley, and partly unspeakably prosaic and petit-bourgeois.

Every gesture of the procession emanated the impossibility and necessity of God-worship — something of the atmosphere of Euripidean "hoos agnosia sebómen," [11] whose most densely woven petal is the face of those who despair in dying: the soul feels every uncertainty to be as close as an embrace, the void is closer than its shirt, and at the same time this plasticity of uncertainty circling it with its python rings means some divine determinacy, the absolute of secret is nevertheless certainty, and god-like — the forever-inescapability of bodily pain is a precisely drawn hand which it sees, in which it believes, and to which it bows. And the "significance" of the moment! This is the most we, humans, can possess: "significant" moments. Whether these moments are the most useless impressions or the slightly distracted cups of revelation, if what is smuggled in the place of our eyelids is the red petal of mania or if it is the first kick, in our head, of the fetus of realist logic, we cannot know, all we feel is that here, in these moments, *would* be the place for some "great truth," "meaning of life."

The face of the dying (and this blasé-pathetic procession was the precise mimicry of such a gaze) struggles with the horrid disharmony of certainty and ignorance — as awkwardly diminished "tierces alternées," the meanings of knowing and non-knowing follow one another on the skin: these wordplays dance and twitch here with biological punctiliousness, signaling with their bleeding histrionics that knowledge and doubt, "is" and "isn't," are unapproachable alternatives that bloom in zones far removed from reason: every moment of ours was wilted with the thirst for certainty and here, on the threshold of death, the face seems to be unspeakably bored by the oppositions between certainty and uncertainty; its whining mask is looking for something totally different, but far too late and now all in vain. On the face of the dying there is no difference between logic and love: the muscles' desperate convulsions, the obdurate syllogism of blood, the kiss, rather like a gulp gone awry, smeared on the lover: everything is some "enlightened" *conclusion* — and at the same time its every glance, the theme-rapaciousness of the suddenly too elastically rolling eyes (eye-white and pupil get their emphasis in turn, like sunlight flaring up all of a sudden after a leaf's shadow in a summer park's alley, when the wind moves a bough aside) is the threatening arrow of a hunger roused for *eros*. At the height of terror he loves everything: the bed tassels, the medicine phial's bent cork, the bedsheet's fold under him that will from now remain unsmoothed, the known-by-heart contours of the shutter's slats; like some purple, velvety, parasitical, drowning and stifling moss does his last impressionist love cushion those prosaic objects and superficial hallucinations, knowing that love is the only active relation with reality, knowing that none of those objects had ever been worthy of love, that the greatest lie and jest of "carte du tendre" had been the region titled "amour sur *estime*," knowing that this aching "*isn't* worth" begetting now melancholy harmonies, now clamorous tragedies, is yet the sole thing of worth.

"Do we believe in God or not, do we believe in our lover or not, do we believe in our mother or not": these are certainly wrongly put, rather vacuous questions.

13.

The procession crossed a bridge, pouring the crowd between its railings from some narrow tunnel: the banners were still horizontal like the masts of damaged warships from which the scorched-brown sails drop to the water, embellishing destruction with the deathly manuscript initials of smoke — half of the hymn was still growling in the tunnel's narrow pipe, its other half scattered, swooning, in the afternoon air; the priests ambled more higgledy-piggledy than ever: the afternoon's slow, lunch-smelling warmth extirpated piety from the whole group more efficiently than a host of heretic mercenaries — the candles were melting, crooked, in the hands knuckled over with wax drops, and prayer, instead of rising skyward, was circling-curling downwards like the windblown propellers of linden seeds. Under the bridge water rushed with booing stillness: the wonder was that something could *rush* in this whey Venice clotted into its own history and faithlessness, but this rushing consisted of sounds not louder than prolonged, whirling *sh*-s (sssssssh...), and then, quite unexpectedly, perpendicular grooves of *h*-s (hhhhhhhh...).

14.

What is the greatest secret of water: its phonetics, its colorology, or the whorishness of its symbolism? Here water was the picture of all impressionism, all beauty-blossoming neurasthenia, all atheistic naturalness — in contrast, the procession swinging on the bridge was the positivist stage of meaning, worthy love, truth, scissor-and-pasted God. How many times did he despise and mock that dichotomy: water's opalescent natural nihil and the Host's monochrome, dogmatic "there's *only* this," and yet now he saw that, however shameful, this dichotomy must be assumed.

The shadow- and whirlpool-haughtiness of waters, the lethal flirtatiousness of colors squandered on it, the rainbow-masked afternoon steam and vapors above the most distant canals, the secret microscopes of a tiny flower or other, gold-finned fish flashing like lit matches under the bridges' canopy, thousand-tide whim of parasites; the power of the elements, the divine inter-regnum of fire, water, air, and earth in our lives: is it meant only to tickle impressionist composers and painters, to adorn with metaphors the unshapely chambers of our thoughts, for us to defeat them, to treat them like God's cheap cosmetics that He only wears to conquer the rabble? How is it that sentences like "God created nature with its innumerable beauties so as to draw our attention to himself and offer a battleground for defeating certain instincts" — how is it that such, somehow truthful tenets, fail to make an impression? It is obvious that the beauty of nature is mutilated beauty (both logic and neurasthenia feel it to be so), and it is equally obvious that natural instincts can be overcome. And yet the tenet above is not to our taste; we are better off with the nonsense, "the beauty of nature is divine and the last word in existence, and the biological instincts inculcated in us by nature are incontestably powerful."

Nature is unquestionably a great paradox and so is the queen of the elements, Venice's bare feet: *water.* For when it swings at the foot of the bridges with its withering-budding colors, it at once proclaims with frenzied æstheticism the "beauty" of God, but with the irregularity of its movements, the shamelessness of its colors, it flirts with that intoxicating quartet of self-conceit, lack of suffering, irresoluteness and perfect meaninglessness: in-stinct; it instigates against God, instigates to love, to the shun-ning of people, to listlessness, to the stealing of death from God.

Where does this unexplainable credit of shining afternoon waters come from; how is it possible that we can't place it among God's designs on an appropriately low shelf of hierarchy? Why do we feel moved to atheistically worship its satanic nuances & place it above everything?

Is it really that one simply either sees water or not — and whoever sees it will believe it to be God, while whoever doesn't see it imagines not water but merely the dictionary name of "water" to be God's creation?

For the Christian, nature is the book of examples of *beauty* and of *temptation*: half æsthetics & half sin — this duality and paradox is certainly hard to overcome. And love, nature's most natural game, bears this paradox thousandfold: it is at once the source of the most exotic Platonizing and the most nihilistic benumbing-into-nature. For it is precisely the latter that is love's "sinful" trait: *not* the body, *not* sensuality, but the acquiescence in nature's irrational inner sloth, its timeless-spaceless, unconcerned self-servingness, the natural obviousness of life & death, tropical flowering and poisonous annihilation: this is water, this is Angelina, this is sin. "I could be water and then everything would be permitted. I could be water and have neither consciousness, morality, nor God, I would only flow, color, I would be beautiful: I would be the highest degree of existence and non-existence at the same time."

Nature and, above all, the water of Venice, is the awful temptation to exist *not* as human beings: we divinize nature, first and foremost, the so-called primordial elements, with such reckless greed because longing for non-human, non-personal existence belongs to the oldest instincts of our being-human — one could say that this very thirst for the non-human distinguishes and humanizes man. Nature is too great a reality for us to grasp it as a mere theater setting: it is real not for being palpable, material, not for being redolent of positivism — but on the contrary: for being the most mysterious mystery, for being incomprehensible, for rubbing against us and leaving us unsatisfied. Because God is visible, while nature is invisible: that's why we believe water, Angelina, mother.

15.

Under the bridge, near the shadow's dark amoeba-lily undulated a large, strident green, quite light blotch of color; Cugnani had never seen such a marvelous example of smoothness, wave-movement, territorial territorialness, luminosity, ending-on-itself. How does such unexpected smoothness end up in agitated canals patched together from criss-crossing stream-debris: such clearing of velvety tranquility, of provocative wideness, femininely nude expanse? The light green blot was perhaps the slope of one wave which magnified on its transient skin, as on a telescope lens, the slats of distant green shutters: those shutters were far away, small, barely green under their dirt-cake, and yet this water smuggled them here, offering the viewer the superhuman joy of magnifying. And this magnifying was excessively raw, a physical enjoyment of space: one rejoiced over the "bigness" of the quietly hovering green blot as prehistoric hunters rejoiced over the game *bigger* than the usual small felled game — it satisfied their quarry-hunger. And beside being such a "fine sizable piece," how much it lacked the geometric satisfaction of volume: never has spatial expanse been beauty so utterly divorced from space — its "bigness," too, was poetry, color, suggestion of rhythm, dream and flower qualities. Perhaps water and some flowers have that hardly visible quality that intensifies with size, their dreamlikeness, buoyancy, immateriality is heightened: the small flower, daisies or forget-me-nots, for instance, are material, concrete, one might even say, mass; the small froths, abbreviated wave spumes, are plastic, palpable — but huge palm leaves, man-size lilies, wave-

fans rolling for almost the entire width of the horizon, are mystically "empty," ethereal; they deny matter. It was "big": something
rarely managed, that usually bursts when much smaller. And it
was entirely fixed to that place, its margin was surrounded by
the porpoises of small wavelets, black shadow-carps, and glaring red Sun-eels, even inside its body grooves hollowed in like
the shadowless valley between premature girls' March breasts:
and the green surface didn't shift its place, boats glided by, trees
melted like a sleeper's diluted mimicry, now and again even the
bridge's shadow-buckle glitched to the side, but this glaring green
ray-clearing remained there, more watery than water and yet at
the same time as though it had never belonged to water. From
the chatterbox world of canals one always expects mosaics, hues
and combinations — and this green spot was the polar opposite of all that: broad, monochrome, unchanging. That's why, in
spite of all bird-of-paradise mundaneness, there was something
mortuary or at least sickly about it: on the human body, too, a
larger, stiff, smooth expanse shows sometimes, an unexpectedly
smooth skin-court on a wrinkled face, untouched, thin, whitish
skin stretching like upstart without past in the place of a scar: so
did this big, constant light-wave appear on water's age-old zigzag
anatomy, like an artificial eye in the place of the real eye: glass
ornament in place of vision. Under stiff patches of skin we feel
the power of sickness or fragmented death, the magic capable
of changing the body into a statue (for we have always been im-
pressed by the dead, never by the dancers, bacchae, or trapeze
artists): we believe solely in the power of silence, we don't even
consider racket a force — here in the water, too, one felt some
sepulchral tension, death's muscle-less, unwhirling, smooth dynamics; as if the other waves flapped about freely, like bloom
and pollen blown off their stem, but that light green one were
permanently grown into water's invisible, death-wide trunk or
roots — not as a leaf is grown to its bough by one tiny stem,

but adhering to it with all its expanse underneath, invisible to us, like a poster.

16.

What was it, this green? They never settled it. Frivolous aquarelle, or eternal myth? Did some ephemeral twinging of the nerves render it great, or was that blot of color a god? Left and right above him people were standing on the bridge, the candles were sweating with no light in the heat, but the processioners themselves were, with their black silhouettes, like gigantic candles stuck on the bridge — every single figure sublime by being only-shadow: when they were still on the bank at the tunnel's mouth, they could be only tiny chips of reality, prose-fluffs — but the moment they got out from the houses' shadow into the line of the sun's spokes above the canal, they became black shields, long splinters and masks against and before the Sun's insatiable afternoon, with all the terrifying power and nothingness of a specter. Below, the light green blot of color, water, about which no-one could say if it was loud or mute, a vision or a murderous octopus, perfume or Spanish-Madonna mamma; above it, the human shadows with their rationalist blackness, rationalist edges, reason-blindness. "Pane lingua gloriosi" and "sssh… sssh… sssh"! Eternal poles? Will they ever meet?

Angelina, it was you under the water there, you were the water (Ondine!): miracle frothing up from color, night, secret force and laughable uselessness. There can be no difference between eros and water: it fills everything, has no shape, is forever changing and hypocritical, but yet infernally consequent in its murderous faithfulness to gravity (what the free play of waves and shapelessness is to water, to love, is "psychology," the hardly bearable humbug of moods — and what faithfulness to gravity is there, here is the obdurate constant of sensuality). Man (water,

water everywhere) is in the habit of remarking, at the same time, the suicidal contradictions and dilemmas of the emotion of love, and making the eternal bed for lying down.

17.

Once Cugnani sat by the sea: infinite silence and simplicity everywhere — there was not one cloud in the sky, not one shadow or footprint on the vast sandy shore, not one wrinkle on the sea. And on that glass-smooth water all of a sudden a wave appeared, approaching the shore: infinitely long, it stretched from one end of the horizon to the other, had no heralding preparatory protuberances, and towed no train behind; solitary, as though it didn't belong to the sea at all, it drew nearer to the shore, almost above the water, flying like a separate cylinder. It wasn't brought by wind or tide: the whole thing was pure shape, pure movement. If the light green blot of color in Venice was the most exquisite fixedness of water, then this was its most exquisite movement: there was something fateful precisely in its lack of cause or justification, in its feminine physics-lessness — the cross-section of this tube-wave was such a regular circle as only miracles can have. This greyish-blue cylinder flying silkily above the water had no spumes: its imagined wave-crest bent so far in front of it that, having come full circle, it touched the point where the wave started rising from the water surface. And when it reached the shore no next wave followed, there was not a sign of tide — still mirror before, still mirror after.

In the brief little Old Testament of Cugnani's life this wave was the prefiguration of the New Testament woman. Can one separate woman from the sea? A short while ago he had seen at the court of duke R., performed with much pomp, Euripides' *Helen* — he couldn't have said what exactly the play was about, but whenever he could connect something to water he did it with all the daring of dreams. The two Helens: one of them, the real, faithful one lives at the mouth of the Nile, at Proteus' tomb — she is morality incarnate, woman hardening in all the bitterness and rawness of morals, but around her lurks the Nile with all Egypt's pale secrets and sacred malaria, there bounces the Mediterranean, sprinkling the shores of Africa with Crete's masked shadows, there hovers Proteus himself, change, the god who is a thousand times more erotic than Aphrodite, who in his insatiability has now smuggled death's black glass splinter into his kaleidoscope. What musics Cugnani imagined around those mythical facts! How discerningly he chose the instruments, rhythms, and harmonies for the Nile's muddy flooding — how he listened to Proteus' now scintillating, now agonizing chromatics, as the water blows its flute into death, or death plays its organ into the real Helen's acrid puritanism — minute violin-demi-semi-quavers send the sharp green leaves of holiness aquiver, woodwinds legatoed from one beat to the next remind one of the tomb, shadow, death breathing under the mosaic … Honorably Menelaos-faithful Helen, almost iced back into dull virginity: the reed of asceticism (pan flutes, pan flutes!) bends, breaks, blind and ignorant, among death's grove, dream-change, masked god, and hissing Méditerranée.

In Duke R's courtyard moonlight stood in solid shafts and the recently built columns and arcades boomed and fluttered beneath their Bacchic nudity — the moonlight was sharp like humanoid humans, but the bluish stones behind seemed to be of water, fish, electric and laboring sponges that let ink, love, and very big bubbles into the evening: Euripides knew full well that he was cataloguing an acquarium in his tragedies.

And then the other Helen, the one of visions, the pseudo-Helen, the cloud, the "eidolon": the mask for which a country perished, *mask* itself with all its death-innuendoes, vulgarity, fabricated orpheus-eroticism, the burlesque of cosmetics which now swims with returning Menelaos on the tempestuous seas — the ship's passengers don't know themselves if the one they are taking home is a woman, puppet, ghost, brothel-bird, their own hallucination about woman at large, or a flesh-and-blood, sadistic goddess. The storm will break the ship to pieces, waves lash across the deck like bridges, the sails are in tatters, the seamen are all sick, and this unknown Helen is forever strutting up and down on the deck, always dressed in different clothes, with make-up, powder, and mirror. At once she vanishes: the gods take her up into heaven. All the melancholia of beauty, all the irony and cynicism of vulgar celestial coquettishness is voiced by the instruments that immortalize the scene (Monteverdi?). Paris knew that the Helen he abducted was not the real one: while everyone is spreading bawdry anecdotes around his bedroom, he wrestles at night with a ghost, the glaring automaton of "beautiful" which has no body: around their nuptial bed candles burn with licking tongues, almost watery, blabbering-slurping, night-gourmandizing flames, but Helen is untouchable, she remains the rouged-and-perfumed-to-death, bodiless mask of beauty. To compose the nuptial march to that wedding!... This Helen is now concrete like a harlot, now dissolving like mist — Paris sometimes retrieves her from Troy brothels, where she was an advertisement, not object of use, and now spots her among the clouds, hovering-rainbowy, like the divine staffage of sunset.

Menelaos, too, is *at sea* with his broken ship, with vanished Helen: the real Helen *in the sea*, bathing close to Proteus' tomb: when they find her on the cemetery-strand (this, too, is a variation on the birth of Venus!), the Greeks decide to put this real Helen to death. They wrestle in the water, faithfulness bleeds into the water: the ship is all tatters, the crew is a bunch of drunkards, the aged, bathing Helen is all inane virtue. The dead soldiers who ended up in the netherworld because of the mask-Helen see the mask's ascension to heaven: the murderous puppet whizzes up into the skies — there are a thousand orchestral possibilities to represent the puppet's shadow on Acheron's bronze-bushy waters. Because it is water!

And the final melodic conclusion about the two Helens, water's two kinds of whirlpools? One is a wound, the other is a mask: one is *death* itself, the other is eternal *lie*: don't we all feel that, all the time? When we mentioned the fraternity of water and eros, in our simile-impertinence we saw the kin of water's forever gravitating faithfulness and its perpetual change to be sensuality and psychology — and what else is sensuality if not death in love, and what else is "psychology" if not mask in love?

18.

Wound and mask, sensuality and psychology, death and lie: Cugnani remembered well the night which he liked to call his wedding night — dark room with rarefied shutters, and he is lying in bed with a fever. For the moment two colors are playing with one another: moonlight filtered by the slats and the early spring daffodils' yellow on the nightstand. Some time before his illness he got to know a girl, he carried her memory into the night and the fever, like a fish carrying the snatched morsel into Nereid depths. Outside it was spring and night, and can one imagine, desire a more human, fateful, amorous season than those two at the same time: the Moon's budding, ripening, small mimosa beads sprout on the stars' boughs, timid, silky-misty foliage spreads like a fan around the clouds, the wings of one thuggish or pedantic bird stir more excitedly, neurotically, and heroically than before, the boughs bend across night's parapet with after-illness emaciation and sensuously path-seeking optimism, in the air the scent of not-yet-existing flowers calls out with great, procuring arching for the corresponding flowers-to-be-born, there is no grass yet, only muddy, snow-slushy, ugly clots of earth, from among which here and there a big, alien-looking leaf thrusts out, like the strange resurrection of some prehistoric animal; in violet park dawns, between muffled strikings of the clock, a flower scintillates here and there, with translucent Venetian glass petals and with their stamens' tiny, cut-crystal lightnings — and at the same time there is the night, that most expressive metaphor of all utopias, the most-blood-related sibling of all human bodies, black inside of our flesh, our dreams' forever-woven velvet, love's only "in style" vase, our dead parents' last evening dress, ancient posturing and theatricality of all unknown god's, secret's, time's shared, blind Venus.

Early spring and night: what's the need for woman then — aren't these two enough for love *without* woman? At such times woman has no other role but to slightly anthropomorphize, to tailor and trim to us, humans, that primal vitality that fills the whole of existence, and that primal death-likeness that at the same time fills the self-same existence. Many of the Greek tragedies get their titles not from the hero or heroine but from the anthem-singing, lamenting choruses in the background: the supplicants, the women of Trachis, the bacchae, the Phoenician girls. It is the same with love: it is called not after the women, lovers, divas, and brothel-staffage, but after the choruses: the nights, springs, seas, and orphically vibrating stars. The drama's protagonist, goal, essence, is the chorus or the coulisse: why do we then continue to call it coulisse — isn't it mere wordplay?

Moonlight fell on his dead-looking mother who slept by his side with open mouth. What is love? What for? Here are the great rivals: spring and night, like nature's dizzying Janus-hood, and his mother who was but self-sacrifice's thin arrow burring into its bullseye, all love, and yet, in the absoluteness of her ethics, all but death. And between the two great rivals — the mother's eros-less eros, and mysteriously proliferating, human-less nature — here he is, with his famous "love," his maddeningly limitless and shamefully comical love — which consists of what in God's name? Let's see: some impression-debris about a wicked and vacuous girl, and some great, entirely bodily — that is, entirely stuffed-into-the-cottonwool-of-dreams — desire, which was only aggrandized by lying in bed in a crumpled nightshirt. Impression as the feverish patient's obsession, for want of a better word, and some bodily desire that is not directed at possessing the girl and does not even inspire us to onanism, of which we tire, but simply, the pleasure-giving awareness of one's own feverish body, some rudely mystical and practically sensuous general disposition.

Who can decide — what is eros? The death-pale mother, the night and the spring, the shredded little perceptions stolen from girls, or the body's inner solitude? It's all the same: existence was intensively present around his sickbed and Cugnani wanted to enter a personal relation with it. If somebody absorbs with eyes wide open, like the unplugged plugholes of basins, the images of the world, then they can be only amateurs of love: the great lovers have no praxis, just as lunatics are never shrewd salesmen. Cugnani knew well that the girl would never become his lover, not because she didn't want it (she did, what is more, that night Cugnani lived off the words with which she promised to give herself to him), but because love is impossible for human beings: love is solitude's blossoming-stifling utopia, which cannot be trans-"socialized" to women.

How much silence; he was surrounded by versions of enigma and certainty, sculpturally palpable doubt and pious belief, truth and lie, colibri-motley blasphemy and savage self-martyrizing: the whole of life with its "popular" colors and "popular" forms — every object, mood, date known, with its name, goal, past — and yet, what did he know? Nothing.

19.

The yellow daffodils glowed palely; flowers are awake even at night, their timeless day-face is frozen on their petals; they are beautiful, useless, gods, ideas. The yellow cups were richly surrounded with green leaves, partly with small, cypress-like, clear-cut line-grid and partly with large, dark green plates. What is the role of such a yellow flower at night? How does the flower's morphology relate to the morphology of sensuous dreams: are they kindred or opposites? In half-sleep, as it usually happened with him, those flowers grew very big, rustling and dewy like the train of an evening gown as the wearer mounts the stairs: it was like a separate sunrise or birth of Venus within the night: of a sun that doesn't bring dawn, that is no other Moon but the heart of darkness; Venus, who is no æstheticized-apart coitus-preparate but the dance, spring, pleasure-parée of life's most ancient cells.

And the eternal duality of the daffodil-metaphor and daffodil-concreteness: he knew well that this flower inserted into the night is a mythology and knew well that it is a prosaic gift, a produce of gardening. But is it worth making such daytime distinctions in the night? Live, live, love to the fullest as long as it's night, as long as you're alone, free, as the woman is yours: in a matter of seconds you can do everything with her, can equate her with that flower, can lure her to a meeting-place, can perceive her as a momentary jewel in the hair or the companion of twenty years of life — here woman is not a human being, and that's all you need. You needn't decide if love is a lie or a religion, needn't decide whether to adopt the manner of the lyricizing fool or the society racounteur in dealing with her, needn't wait for her, and if she's there, you needn't tire of her, needn't decide if you're faithful or unfaithful to her, you needn't be in any "relation" with her at all — after all, have you ever cleared your relation with the night or the earth? Presences: with the black charme of positivity and enigma — and now woman can be that. This is your wedding night, don't skip it for a woman, a daytime woman, a "woman" woman — don't flee from this night!

It was on this night that Cugnani learnt that love is so unfathomably anarchic that you can't transport it into the morning. The only possibility: at night everybody plays to the end, alone, to the core and bones, their own utopia, making use of whatever reminiscence of whatever woman seen during the day, & letting loose (not in the bodily sense though!) their bodily desire — let that impression-rag dance in the dark (rag! rag!) & let the organs of sense and limbs all go deaf with insatiable desire. This is no orgy. This is the spiritist séance of impossibility: it is then that we feel, in the bed's warmth, in its loose prison, when there is nothing else around us but our own body and sexual organ inflamed-wilted into a problem, that bodily desire points to an impossibility, and that the anarchic breadth of that desire is too much to carry for any woman, mosaic-spliced into society, just as it is too much for any sex-buffoon living solely for their desires on some fairy-tale eros-isle. Love is the momentary or hour-long constellation of the solitary human being caught in a fortuitous milieu: at present, a remembrance, the chance comfortable lying on one another of the two warm legs under the cover, the daffodils' yellow mouths or demon-lips, the birds' beaks in the moon-mist, the slow, slow booming in the earth of spring, like the discernible end of an organ sound, and the misbehaving of the sexual nerves roused by fever.

It is love *in this way*: all that together in this kaleidoscope-pose. And love's most anarchic anarchy: not the kitsch about the unconquerable physical furor of sensuous desire (although perhaps that is not entirely kitsch, que sais-je?), nor the psychologizing jest about spiritual-intellectual understanding and the romantic thirst for such understanding: it is not this that drives lovers wild and renders love impossible, but the fact that the superlative of love is always connected to one sole, momentary place, one ephemeral staging — if I see that daffodil from an angle 10 degrees more tilted from vertical, if I feel the warmth of my legs differently under the cover, if there is more than one fuzzy melodic flight of hair to make woman present, if it is not this spring-leaden silence to sit, like thick snow, on the trees' boughs: then the whole woman, the whole love, is worth nothing. Love is *here*, in this moment, this night time desire cannot be satisfied in the morning, "tomorrow" — if anything exists that isn't directed at a goal, that doesn't drive our body into the future, it is desire: desire is *here* where it is, and when it is it is also its end or, if you will, its satisfaction, although it would be best to drop both the word "desire" and "satisfaction" altogether and put in their place a third one, if we could for one moment still take language seriously.

20.

What was woman for Cugnani? An impression of her body and only her body. But not of the nude body — even if that body happened to be nude on occasion, most of the time it featured not as simple food for instinct but, if one may say so: in its most distant, witty, playful, stylized branchings-out, related to culture: in clothes, picturesque aperçus, in the refined modulations of intonation. Perhaps it is entirely wrong to say that he had impressions of her "body," it was far rather, of her "reality." By "body" one always understands the schematic and inane bait of instinct: woman's material reality, her whole quotidian positivity means something utterly different, and to relish it, even if it is sensuousness and as such, cannot be distanced too far from sexual instinct, is yet very different from the simple kiss-, embrace- etc. inspirations. The essence of these "reality" impressions is, that they are *minimal*: the one-time sticking of one sole thread of hair to the forehead, one wrinkle on the skirt not smoothed down

below the knees, a single nasal *e* in pronouncing a proper name
— never the whole woman, whole body, or whole character.

The unifying concept of the "beautiful woman" was unknown
to Cugnani — he only preserved fragments, scales, and sketches
of a woman for his love. This, too, intensifies anarchy — and
what is meant by anarchy is that the one in love wants to destroy
everything that is not immediately the object of their love. The
one in love (and can they indeed be said to be in love?) who make
the object of their love not one such electrifying minimum of reality, but a whole body or character "en bloc," are not "anarchically"
in love, for the "whole" woman does indeed exist in society in her
preferred "wholeness" — but the isolated thread of hair, wrinkle
of the skirt, or nasal *e* do not — such people in love are sworn
enemies of the "whole" woman, whom they want to kill even in
order to create themselves a world populated, instead of women,
by aquarelle stains and sound-shreds. These have nothing to do
with the *human being*, consequently they have nothing to do with
the body as such on the one hand, as most of the singled-out
reality splinters are not the work of nature but of seamstress-
es, hatters, stocking-makers, and on the other hand the bodily
fragments are so fantastically and obsessively isolated that they
can have no organic connection whatsoever to the "female body."

This was one thing that woman (or what is unwittingly
understood of that), women meant for Cugnani. And the other?
Women were the most ancient movements, the movements
closest to creation, of life, of biological functions — they simply
meant life itself, Ur-plasma, cellular stirrings.

This, then, was his twofold corporeality, sensuality: the fabric
of a stocking and the first, tentative expanding and constricting
in space, of primordial beings.

Together they are the most ephemeral of all the world's
ephemerality: fashion, the eye's fleeting touching on knees,
shoulders, wrists above a "passing show," and then the world's

most ancient constants, living matter's mysterious lifelikeness. So is love most in love. Cugnani thus had precious little to do with faithfulness, but even less to do with Don Juanism: he was far enough from the mere noticing of the woman's character, thoughts, psychic life, but even further away from the body's blind gourmands. He had greater virtues than monogamous faithfulness, and such virtues were indeed so great that they obliterated the fact that perhaps monogamy's ascetic-idyllic passion also lurked in them. These virtues: utter ecstasy before reality's impressionistic sublime (unmediated God, God, closeness to God), and continuous, death-filled awareness of the utter impossibility of love, of impossible-to-exist sexual happiness. On that night, too, Cugnani was at the same time the hallucinating carcass of frenetic happiness and equally frenetic unhappiness — the silent embodiment of his two virtues, madness and death. He was seen now with one woman, now with another: there was talk of flirtation, whereas he was led by the mystical worship of reality, far removed from anthropoid-shaped, well-delineated women — there was talk of spicy cross-betrayals, whereas on those stolen-botched beds he molded death's face. It is far easier to jot down paradoxes and Augustinian dichotomies than simple statements, so it may well seem a superficial rhetorical conceit when Cugnani makes this perfect happiness and unhappiness the essence of his life, although they were in some enigmatic, precise, and real relationship with one another.

When he relished a woman's thread of hair, skirt-hem, or nasal *e*, his experience was first and foremost a feeling of unsayable *gratitude*: gratitude to God, woman, himself, for experiencing the positivity of existence in such divine symptoms. In that grateful glance that he threw on the woman for such an ephemeral trait, there was somehow greater worship of, and respect for, women, a more fanatical and constant faithfulness (although immediately afterward he went to another woman and completely forgot the former) than in the faithfulness of a million "faithful" men. And if this ecstatic gratitude is not enough of a virtue, there is the greatest virtue in store: grief, that is, death as a state of mind. The thread of hair, the crumpling of the skirt, the nasal *e* are: *not* fit for life; for them, with them, nothing can be done, although deed is our essence, after all. There was no end to Cugnani's grieving over this.

V. MESSA DA REQUIEM

Now when, in her black taffeta robe cracking like armor, she took her seat next to the choir on a half-carved stone bench, she realized why those scrawny brats were on her mind: she had had great "loves" & eros-businesses of a historical kernel — but what came to her mind were not the dukes' ice-green, sizzling artesian fountains which swung their barren dew-strings in the wind like flowers grown too tall; nor the bone-white and mud-green ancient castles (in which color is there more noble antiquity: in walls sponge-holed to moss, or in walls stiffened to skeletons?); nor siesta-idling cardinals, pale kings, and "European" bull sigils poured from bedsides. Only the boys. Because there in the cathedral by Monte Solario, which was preparing for the pope's requiem mass and to which probably no more stones would be added, she knew that in love only these two ailments matter: psychology's grotesque crumblings & money's Midas sunflower-positivism. "Balanced men" and women of lyrical passions have precious little to do with that vociferous, misshapen tragedy that goes by the name of "love." Love is this — she said, with fatigued obstinacy, replacing a picture or other between more suitable pages in her prayer-book — love is the scandalous fiasco of analysis and the vulgar triumph of money's near ridiculous power. With allegorizing pedantry, at this requiem she wanted to be nothing else but love's money-nymph: mathematics, not woman, Mercure-formula, not a baccha. And Mercure accepted only the shameful writhing of the enamored "psyche" as his worthy companion: the doomed anxieties of sickly Cugnanis.

The whole town knew that the emperor's army might arrive any moment: death emanated from the summer-steamed grass as lilac scent is unleashed on a room by unexpected winds.

Although armed soldiers surrounded the crowd in the cathedral, everybody knew that at their best they can be etiquette martyrs, but would be obviously unable to defend a single soul. It was early morning — everybody looked like the glassy-flashing specters of dead fish in the depth of the sea, or those *first* steps to Venetian palaces that are just covered by water: the wave above them is so thin that all their cracks show, but as compared to the next step, they are netherworldly, akin to Charon oars which death's bronze fauna has already ensnared in its embrace. Angelina sat in her desk as in a female saddle, stiff and upright, one leg across another, in funnel-necked gloves and with a giant-feathered hat. She was no longer a human being but an organic part of the requiem's text, music, mystical convention: not a woman, not a sinner, not an innocent, not a capitalist condemned to death, not a relative, no mourner, not stone-hearted, not human — but simply a voice, composed with abstract Palestrina rigor, into the Catholic rite of annihilation. It wouldn't have occurred for a moment to the townsfolk or the signors to see in the haughty looks of the courtesan of European fame something scandalous or out of "style": she was part of the world's philosophical structure.

When the choir sounded for the first time (resembling not the brook that surfaces from the depth of the earth but the sea glimpsed beyond the foliage that is gently but definitely blown aside by the wind: not the birth of sound but the unveiling of a permanently-present sound's nakedness, the dropping of an utterly superficial paper mask), the music's Orfeo-wandering re-minded Angelina of her last dream. A half-mad diplomat of the emperor had lately developed the obsession that the pope had innumerable secrets never confessed to anyone, and if they man-aged to find these out, the world could be given a different fate. So the pope had to be captured, threatened with death, a false priest had to be sent in at night to confess him. The neurasthenic diplomat didn't dare volunteer for the role, fearing that St. Peter would strike him dead with his bolt — but he didn't trust anyone on earth, fearing that the mime would use the papal confession for his own ends, like a selfish Prometheus who steals the life-giving spark of Europe entirely for himself, so that the world is cast into eternal shadow. The night before Angelina had dreamt that she herself was that false confessioner: the confession of God's last lieutenant went into a hetaera's hands — prophesies and hidden treasures, world-historical conclusions and royal gossip, everything from boudoir to basilica and from revelation to business which had so far made Europe into Europe, got into her ears, like a ghostly pearl or flower into the most worldly, most sterile shell. The pope was dead and she, mundane extra, would be killed in five minutes' time. She, the classical harlot, is the only one who knows what the papacy had meant, what lurked behind the emperor's empire, who was the real god and what the devil wanted, where the most money and where the greatest value were, where was time's wave-crest and when its slope follows, what is truly valuable and what is perennial humbug: all this she alone knew, for to her it was confessed, and as compared to this knowledge the cathedral's skeptically discontinuous walls, its Gothic columns frozen in their bud, the sickly analysis of adolescent boys in love, the mayor's grandiose Apollo-faced, idol-luxurious nihilism, the emperor's hypochondria of conquest, the soldiers' savage heroism, ships bound to the Holy Land flaunting crusader flags and bankers at their book-keeping in Venetian cellars are all meaningless, hogwash, children's yarns, awful snafus: the leaf is no leaf, music is no music, bird-chirping is no bird-chirping, "that" is not "that," "what" is not "what," everything is *other*, primordially, absurdly other — there is no act, thought, speech, flowering and landscape that is identical to itself: the world of "meanings" which the pope had commended to her ear before his death is radically foreign and distant from all imaginable world-explanations.

On the threshold of certain death there is no difference between reality and dream: when Angelina woke up in the morning, her first thought was that she would humbly offer her secret to the one for whom she came to the town and whom she loved: the mayor. Sharp daylight broke in through the window, and she was still full of dream's Acherontic greenery — the confessional's darkness, the perverse warmth and intimacy-steam of the pope's whispering, dying voice, the limbo-perfume of clap-doctorship and sacrament, the scorching lie-skin of her own disguise, the black-robed emperor's melancholia responding to the code-name, "lake and time," the lecherous mist of loitering intrigue-mongers and spies. It was incredible that Artemis-shouldered dawn and green darkness evaporating from such lethal depths should coexist in one and the same world. But whether this confession was a sickly dream or reality, later she no longer wanted to talk about that with the mayor. The world is so dizzyingly other than it is, that it is impossible to speak about it: if we speak, we only bow to the old world and profane the "ineffabile ultra."

But when, among the tunes of "quidquid latet apparebit," she calmly looked around on the requiem-supplicants, she realized that the now dead pope had confessed the world's secret not to her alone, he didn't drop the transparent keys of nihilism into her nail-varnished hands only ("it is pointless to use these keys for locking or loosing, for it is all the same whether you do the one or the other, and both are Danaidally pointless"), as a November shrub drops its last two leaves: the feverish light of some unsayable knowledge or non-knowledge flickered in everyone's eyes; in every pair of eyes, whether of children, soldiers, musicians, or councilors, one could see that they knew: it was not about this requiem, not about the pope and emperor, not about the half-finished and abandoned cathedral and chucked-off Europe, not love and money, but something else: that plastic, ancient-familiar indeterminacy which everybody carried in themselves, which had never kissed yet when we kissed, which had never prayed yet when we attended mass, which had never been nihilistic yet when we despaired — some eternal inner heresy, negativity's demonically fleshly parasite flower: its color was mirrored in everybody's eyes, its scent clouded every person's lonely gaze. Here everybody betrayed themselves: here only anarchic lonelinesses rested, the little ignoramus-herbs writhing in personality's opium.

The orchestra gradually diminished to a piano, the notes, singled to voices, dropped from the chorus' mouths: a flute splinter or viola tremolo vibrated in the air as the silver of the Moon hidden behind a cloud trembles on nighttime water which stirs its little wings. Everybody was waiting for the *Tuba mirum*. The pope's old brother was perched near Angelina, mixing the festive Latin chanting with village nicknames: like a scared child, he grabbed with both hands Angelina's silk-clad arm. He huddled next to her as if she had trampled his body with her horse. The trumpets sounded, the choir started into its verse, but in the next moment some eerie giddiness crept upon everyone, of which they didn't know the cause: choir and trumpets, violin and horns weren't in unison; some cold, deathly-blue falsity crept, like a snake, among the harmonies, which sounded all the more terrifying, the *smaller* it was — brutal dissonance would have been less frightening than this small slide. This was the first time that the mayor raised his head. It was no longer a head or a face, but only a yellow flame, "torbido e sanguigno," as it was written in an opera that Angelina had heard a month before, and in the midst of that yellow composed of gall and primrose, two black mold-knots: glance and pupil, eyebrows and lachrymal sac were one velvety worm or pussy willow. His entire body and soul was that sole black velvet fruit: in his gaze one perceived not the eyeball's movement, but the fatal and irretrievable sinking of one scale of a balance toward some Plutonic theme. If the mayor now "looked" ahead: then his whole destiny turned there and could never again take a different direction.

At that moment he realized the true cause of the out-of-tune concerting: the trumpets that sounded were not the orchestra's instruments but the battle horns of the imperial army emerging victoriously from the woods (singers step so before the falling curtain) and drawing near the town. The officers riding in front of the troops immediately spotted the town at mass on the steep mountain slope. For a while they galloped up and down, discussed, exchanged messages, then suddenly slowed down the whole forward march, only a small corps separated and cantered to the foot of the mountain, under the cathedral. There they halted and with idol-like stiffness waited, as befits the "religious," for the requiem mass to end. For a while there was deathly silence, but when the mayor signaled to the conductor with his eye (it was the fourteen-year-old boy), the music and choir sounded again. The German and French officers waiting nearby below could see the mayor's eyes: so sway the palm-trees in the netherworld if the sighs of new dead blow among their crowns.

Angelina knew the emperor and was thinking of him: does he indeed want this? That strange, crooked face, as it props its restless, cowardly-feverish rhomb on his white-collared armor neck — does he want this destruction? Angelina could never observe closely how and where that face was crooked: if in its external, geometrical contours or if it was an inwardly, anatomically crumpled fruit. It was always sloping, one straight descending line from the forehead to the beard, as if it were the diagonal of something. He had golden-green, leaf-, and parchment-like complexion, all meek-elegant greenhouse-plant colors, full of tiny wrinkles, Brussels drawings, the delicate mother-of-pearl drops of delicate fevers; both skin and breath-like sweat were thinner than a blade of grass; the nose, the thinning moustache, the short-trimmed hair, the forehead's protuberances were all so meek and microscopically trembling as the flowers of very densely, but very insecurely planted waterside trees: petals, sta-mens, trembling amorous powder. Angelina knew that before the emperor's soldiers launch their cavalry charge into the re-quiem-praying mass, the emperor would summon a confessioner in one of his villas in the woods, probably some inexperienced young boy who had just been anointed that morning, and into the ears of that confession-virgin he would remorse his pope-murdering, town-destroying sin. But for the moment the troops were silent: in his confessional the emperor was fighting more heroically than the soldiers, he was more wounded and worn-out from the remorse over an as of yet uncommitted sin than sin's flashy servants. The long necks, tired manes, and weighty heads of bored horses were swinging-swaying in the wind under their stiff riders as vacillating flowers: they neighed and licked the grass.

By the whitely trickling melody-brook of the Agnus Dei they took leave of everything. How did the 14-year-old child know, what is death and what is music, what is life and inno-cent flower? It seems that scales render "experience" superflu-ous — whoever has sensed to their quick in their childhood den the difference between a C and its half-tone-higher sister (or enemy?) need not descend, like Orfeo, with his lyre into the un-derworld, to look into death's eternal and one-and-only mirror — he knows, without any pilgrimage, the treacherous veins of destiny. Here everybody "has lived"; at this requiem everybody had a past and a history, but it took one inexperienced, score-scribbling child to conjure before them the face of destiny in all its siren-beauty and siren-mendaciousness. In the Agnus Dei the shepherds played their flutes in that embrace of peace of which Angelina daydreamed on her way through the woods with the mercenaries: whether this peace spread its perfume from death's silently closing heretic bud, whether it was divine or amorous, whether it emanated decadence's doubt or Christianity's Giotto trustfulness — who could tell? Sounds have a thousand meanings, but polyphony has ten thousand. The choir swelled, rose, the sharpened lament of the violins soared ever higher on the tide of newer and newer chords: at the end the light-blue sea of harmonies flooded them as the Flood's burying waves did the "it's useless"-foliaged souls of those who don't deserve life.

1934

ENDNOTES

1. "And the gates of hell shall not prevail" (Matthew 16:18).

2. "We believed that your devotion diligently labors for and is in all its dealings concerned with whatever appears to secure esteem for us and the Apostolic See. When, however, we have understood not without displeasure in our heart that recently you have approached the Genoese issues in a way contrary to what would have been our will and intention, we were reasonably and considerably surprised. For we have heard that you not merely fail to endorse the faction of the dear son to the noble man... the duke of Milan, but rather, you are openly adverse to them. If that were true, it would be very grave and highly inconvenient for us, since the duke himself enjoys our well-deserved affection & we are solicitous about his position, as could be observed in many instances" (Tr. Máté Boér).

3. *Empedocles: The Extant Fragments*. Ed., with an introduction, commentary, & concordance by M.R. Wright (New Haven, CT: Yale University Press, 1981) 239.

4. *Ibid.*, 191.

5. "A mild, immortal onrush of perfect love" (Tr. M.R. Wright, 206); Szentkuthy is here quoting Wilhelm Capelle's German translation of Empedocles.

6. "Death comes not tomorrow but today."

7. "It is terrifying, fearful, and strong." *Theophrastus Paracelsus — Volumen Paramirum und Opus Paramirum.*

8. Reference to François Villon's poem, *The Ballad of the Hanged, or Epitaphe Villon*.

9. "A hanged man's last luxury — a pope's first duty."

10. ὡς ἀγνωσίᾳ σέβωμεν: Euripides, *Hecuba*, scene 9, lines 959-960, appr. "thus in ignorance we worship"; cf. "our perplexity may make us worship them [the gods]" (Tr. E.P. Coleridge); "[the gods make us] confused enough to worship them" (Tr. Jay Kardan and Laura-Gray Street). The passage is quoted in David Hume, *The Natural History of Religion* (1757), with the following translation: "The gods toss all life into confusion; mix every thing with its reverse; that all of us, from our ignorance and uncertainty, may pay them the more worship and reverence."

COLOPHON

CHAPTER ON LOVE
was handset in InDesign cc

The text font is *Adobe Jenson*

The display font is *Antikva Margaret*

Book design & typesetting: Alessandro Segalini

Drawing: Mauro Perani, "№ 42" (2016), 33 × 48 cm, ink on paper

Cover illustration: István Orosz

Cover design: CMP

CHAPTER ON LOVE
is published by Contra Mundum Press.

Contra Mundum Press   New York · London · Melbourne

CONTRA MUNDUM PRESS

Dedicated to the value & the indispensable importance of the individual voice, to works that test the boundaries of thought & experience.

The primary aim of Contra Mundum is to publish translations of writers who in their use of form and style are *à rebours*, or who deviate significantly from more programmatic & spurious forms of experimentation. Such writing attests to the volatile nature of modernism. Our preference is for works that have not yet been translated into English, are out of print, or are poorly translated, for writers whose thinking & æsthetics are in opposition to timely or mainstream currents of thought, value systems, or moralities. We also reprint obscure and out-of-print works we consider significant but which have been forgotten, neglected, or overshadowed.

There are many works of fundamental significance to *Weltliteratur* (& *Weltkultur*) that still remain in relative oblivion, works that alter and disrupt standard circuits of thought — these warrant being encountered by the world at large. It is our aim to render them more visible.

For the complete list of forthcoming publications, please visit our website. To be added to our mailing list, send your name and email address to: info@contramundum.net

Contra Mundum Press
P.O. Box 1326
New York, NY 10276
USA

OTHER CONTRA MUNDUM PRESS TITLES

SOME FORTHCOMING TITLES

THE FUTURE OF KULCHUR
A PATRONAGE PROJECT

LEND CONTRA MUNDUM PRESS (CMP) YOUR SUPPORT

With bookstores and presses around the world struggling to survive, and many actually closing, we are forming this patronage project as a means for establishing a continuous & stable foundation to safeguard our longevity. Through this patronage project we would be able to remain free of having to rely upon government support &/or other official funding bodies, not to speak of their timelines & impositions. It would also free CMP from suffering the vagaries of the publishing industry, as well as the risk of submitting to commercial pressures in order to persist, thereby potentially compromising the integrity of our catalog.

CAN YOU SACRIFICE $10 A WEEK FOR KULCHUR?

For the equivalent of merely 2–3 coffees a week, you can help sustain CMP and contribute to the future of kulchur. To participate in our patronage program we are asking individuals to donate $500 per year, which amounts to $42/month, or $10/week. Larger donations are of course welcome and beneficial. All donations are tax-deductible through our fiscal sponsor Fractured Atlas. If preferred, donations can be made in two installments. We are seeking a minimum of 300 patrons per year and would like for them to commit to giving the above amount for a period of three years.

WHAT WE OFFER

Part tax-deductible donation, part exchange, for your contribution you will receive every CMP book published during the patronage period as well as 20 books from our back catalog. When possible, signed or limited editions of books will be offered as well.

WHAT WILL CMP DO WITH YOUR CONTRIBUTIONS?

Your contribution will help with basic general operating expenses, yearly production expenses (book printing, warehouse & catalog fees, etc.), advertising & outreach, and editorial, proofreading, translation, typography, design and copyright fees. Funds may also be used for participating in book fairs and staging events. Additionally, we hope to rebuild the *Hyperion* section of the website in order to modernize it.

From Pericles to Mæcenas & the Renaissance patrons, it is the magnanimity of such individuals that have helped the arts to flourish. Be a part of helping your kulchur flourish; be a part of history.

HOW

To lend your support & become a patron, please visit the subscription page of our website: contramundum.net/subscription

For any questions, write us at: info@contramundum.net

CPSIA information can be obtained
at www.ICGtesting.com
Printed in the USA
BVHW042147230822
645289BV00007B/231